Lady in Ermine

THE STORY OF A WOMAN
WHO PAINTED THE RENAISSANCE

A BIOGRAPHICAL NOVEL BY
DONNA DIGIUSEPPE

Bagwyn Books

Tempe, Arizona
2019

Published by Bagwyn Books, an imprint of the
Arizona Center for Medieval and Renaissance Studies (ACMRS)
Tempe, Arizona

©2019 Donna DiGiuseppe
All Rights Reserved
Print ISBN: 978-0-86698-821-6
eISBN: 978-0-86698-750-9
Printed in the United States of America

To My Parents Ezio & Anne DiGiuseppe

Contents

Foreword

My dear friend Doctor Alfio Nicotra contacted me one day about a woman he met from San Francisco. She had come to Paterno` to see Sofonisba's *Madonna dell'Itria*, but the Church was closed that day. She met Alfio instead, and they traded ideas about the artist for hours. The woman from San Francisco wanted to tell Sofonisba's life story—the entire long, life story—as a history, but also as a novel, a *romanza*.

I invited Ms. DiGiuseppe to join us at the Church of San Giorgio dei Genovesi in Palermo, Sicily in February 2008 to celebrate Sofonisba Anguissola, a member of my family.

With Professor Maria Kusche, Doctor Alfio Nicotra, Professor Vincenzo Abbate, and Ms. DiGiuseppe, we commemorated the extant works of Sofonisba after many hurdles to completing the catalogue because the artist often did not sign her paintings and because her rivals copied those paintings in quantities.

Lady in Ermine captures Sofonisba's 16th century, from lavish court life to its treatment of women. The reader roots for Sofonisba to achieve her dream to paint the king and overcome the challenges of being a Renaissance woman painter.

Count Ferrante Anguissola D'Altoe`

Milan, December 27, 2016

Cast of Characters

Cremona, Northern Italy (1549–1559)
Sofonisba Anguissola, born c. 1535, artist
Amilcare Anguissola, Sofonisba's father, Cremona town Decurion
Bianca Ponzone Anguissola, Sofonisba's mother, daughter of Count Ponzino Ponzone
Sofonisba's talented and educated sisters: Lucia, Elena (nun who once trained at Master Campi's studio with Sofonisba), Minerva, Europa (mother of Bianca), and Anna Maria
Asdrubale Anguissola, Sofonisba's younger brother and family heir, born 1551
Bernardino Campi, master painter, Sofonisba's trainer, cousin of the Campi family of Cremona, master painters Giulio, Antonio, and Vincenzo
Ferrante Anguissola Gonzaga, Sofonisba's cousin
Duchess Margaret of Parma, illegitimate daughter of Charles V, King of Spain and Holy Roman Emperor

Milan (1559)
Duke of Sessa, Spanish Governor of Milan
Broccardo Persico, Cremona noble, Anguissola family friend, Sofonisba's escort

Spanish Court (1560–1573)

Elisabeth de Valois, daughter of Henry II of France and Catherine de Medici, Queen Isabel, wife of King Philip II of Spain

Philip II, King of Spain

Don Carlos, Philip II's son from first marriage to Maria of Portugal

Alessandro Farnese, son of Margaret of Parma, Philip II's sister, and Ottavio Farnese

Don John of Austria, illegitimate son of Charles V; Philip II's half-brother

Duke of Alba, Philip II's counselor and general

Cardinal of Burgos, House of Mendoza, king's confessor

Pedro de Mendoza, cardinal's brother, military officer

Martin Guerre, cardinal's servant

Juana de Aragon, cardinal's distant niece, lady in waiting

Maria de Padilla, lady in waiting, Juana's friend

Isabel de Mendoza, cardinal's niece, daughter of Pedro de Mendoza

Alonso Sanchez Coello, official portraitist of the Spanish Court

Isabella Clara Eugenia (1566) & Catalina Micaela (1567) Infantas of Spain

Anne of Austria, Queen of Spain, Philip II's fourth wife

Paterno` Sicily (1573–1579)

Fabrizio Moncada, second son of the Moncada patrimony, Sofonisba's first husband

Francisco II, minor heir of Moncada patrimony

Aloisa Luna y Vega Moncada, mother of heir Francisco II

Tuscany (January–April 1580)

Francesco de Medici, Grand Duke of Tuscany

Eleonora de Medici, daughter of Francesco, future Duchess of Mantua and patron of Peter Paul Rubens

Genoa (1580–1615)

Captain Orazio Lomellini, illegitimate son of the noble Lomellini, a shipping family of Genoa, Sofonisba's second husband

Giulio Lomellini, Orazio's illegitimate son, Sofonisba's stepson

Catalina Micaela, Infanta of Spain, Duchess of Savoy

Lady of Savoy, daughter of Catalina Micaela

Eleonora de Medici, Duchess of Mantua

Isabella Clara Eugenia, Infanta of Spain, Archduchess of the Spanish Netherlands

Fabrizio Bargagli, Sofonisba's lawyer

Peter Paul Rubens, northern European artist patronized by both Isabella Clara Eugenia and Eleonora de Medici

Palermo, Sicily (1615–1625)

Anthony van Dyck, northern European artist, sketches Sofonisba as an old woman and paints her on her death bed

Ecco la bella e saggia dipintrice
La nobil Sofonisba da Cremona
Che ben oggi si puo chiamar felice
Sendo nell'arte sol perfetta e buona

Behold the beautiful and wise portraitist
The noble Sofonisba of Cremona
Who today may be called contented
To render only perfection and beauty

Giulio Cornelio Graziani (1597)

Part I

Renaissance Girl (1535–1559)

Chapter 1

Prince's Parade: Cremona, Lombardy Italy
September 21, 1549

Sofonisba was alone in cavernous San Sigismondo. As the other parishioners mingled outside after Mass, sweating in their finery, their velvets and satins embroidered with silver and gold, Sofonisba remained in front of the High Altar, transfixed by one tiny face that radiated back at her amid the clusters of angels and patrons that hovered around it. With large pleading eyes, Saint Daria seemed to cry out to Sofonisba.

Sofonisba had studied this painting, Giulio Campi's *Virgin in Glory*, her entire life. Indeed, it was almost as old as she, six years away from twenty. But this morning, the eyes taunted her, beseeching her — no, daring her.

"Sofi, there you are." Her father's deep voice startled her. "I've been looking for you."

"Father, you see her face?" Sofonisba stretched an arm toward the painting, exposing a tiny leather bag. Her father had given her this bag to use as an art kit. He even allowed her to use it during Mass, concealed under her wrap.

Amilcare smiled despite his impatience.

Mass had an effect on Sofonisba. She often lost herself in a world of *invenzione* as she studied the paintings around her, while Father Patrizio mumbled in Latin, his back to the congregation.

"Father, of all these swirling figures, what moves me is one face, there, on the left." She pointed beyond the mountainous Madonna to a small figure. "You see Saint Daria peeking out from the foreground? I feel like she's communicating to me alone." Sofonisba glanced at her father, her enormous brown eyes glistening from her moonlike face. "I don't mean to sound disrespectful." Amilcare had a hand in commissioning most of the church's paintings, one of his duties as a local decurion.

Instead of focusing on Campi's painting, Amilcare's gaze went to his daughter's blackened fingernails, and he recalled an event earlier that week. He and some fellow decurions had gathered at his shop on the town square to discuss arrangements for today's visit from the Spanish Prince. Sofonisba rushed past them on her way home from Master Campi's studio, a rolled-up canvas under her right arm, paintbrushes clutched in her left hand.

"Amilcare, there's your Sofi," one of the decurions said. Amilcare simply nodded. "My friend," the man persisted, "how can you let the girl parade through town like that? Aren't you afraid of discouraging suitors?"

"I only want what any father wants, a better life for my children," Amilcare said quietly.

"And you think the girl will prosper more pretending to be Leonardo da Vinci than through an advantageous marriage?"

Amilcare shrugged off the comment, accustomed to townspeople frowning on his decision to permit his eldest daughter, and her sister, to study in Master Campi's studio, a studio full of men of lower rank — men not related to her — men who might forgo their shirts when the temperature rose. Amilcare had encouraged all his daughters' talents as if trying to prove himself. He might be a member of the nobility now, albeit lower nobility, and a respected decurion, but his past spurred him to promote the family name relentlessly.

"Father," Sofonisba said, drawing Amilcare's attention back to the painting. "How can we see the soul of the Savior when he's overshadowed by the crowd of angels that surround him? That face of St. Daria grips me more than all the rest."

Amilcare smiled affectionately at his earnest daughter. Her ambitions rivaled his own. "Sofi, the prince will arrive shortly. I must meet the decurions. Go home with your mother and sisters and make ready for the parade."

Sofonisba crushed the red geraniums in their terra cotta pots as she leaned over the family's balcony to count the townspeople gathering on the street below. She lost track as they moved about, jostling for a better view of the grand viale leading to the town square. Soldiers began shepherding them aside in anticipation of the prince and his retinue.

"They're coming," cried young Minerva, hearing the clop-clopping of hooves on cobblestone. The Anguissola sisters began angling for a spot on the balcony. Twelve-year-old Lucia elbowed Sofonisba from behind. Elena wedged a hand between the two to make peace. Mamma Bianca and the servant holding baby Europa gathered close. All were smiling, giddy, except for Sofonisba, who felt numb with anticipation.

The parade rounded the corner. The prince's Toledo armor sparkled. Confetti of yellow marigolds engulfed him. Sofonisba stretched across the railing as far as she could to see him. Her pulse raced. She fantasized that he might stop at their balcony to ask her name and then commission her to paint for his collection. She imagined herself curtsying deeply before him, offering him her life's work, "a painting to commemorate Your Majesty's legacy," she would say. "One sees her talent in her eyes," the prince would say for all to hear.

Lucia pushed Sofonisba into the flowerpots, competing for a view the way she competed for attention. A geranium broke off its stem and its innocent red flower fell from the balcony into the flotilla of yellow marigolds and landed right into the prince's lap, nestling between his codpiece and his horse's mane. The stunned prince looked up for the source of the fugitive flower, and Sofonisba felt his steely eyes bore straight into hers. Instantly the prince's eyes softened, from accusation to curiosity. For Sofonisba, the moment felt like an eternity.

As he continued toward the town square, Prince Philip's questioning eyes remained in Sofonisba's imagination, crystallizing her calling. One day she would paint the portrait that showed the king's soul through his eyes — the greatest accomplishment for a, dare she think it? A PORTRAITIST!

Chapter 2

Virgin Portrait with Book, Cremona, 1555

Sofonisba intercepted Marco on his way down the hall to tutor her younger sisters. She whispered to keep her mother from hearing her distract him from his paid duties.

"Master Marco, I have a new concept I would like to discuss."

She thought he suppressed a smile as she tugged his sleeve and led him into the sitting room next to the library where her sisters awaited their tutor. Marco never passed up an opportunity to talk with her. Now twenty, Sofonisba no longer studied under him, but they continued to exchange ideas. The two gravitated toward each other but stifled their mutual attraction. They both knew Amilcare would never consent to a match between his daughter and the tutor. That had been tested two years prior.

She and Marco were discussing her final dissertation, and their fingertips touched when he handed her *The Book of the City of Ladies*. His simple touch shot a spark through her body and an image came to her; the scholar and the artist in their little studio in the back of their little house. She squeezed his hand and smiled up at him. Then, her father's voice came from the hallway. "Master Marco, I think you should leave." Before Sofonisba could object, Marco gathered his books and hurried

off as commanded. She heard the door downstairs close behind
Marco, with her mother's surprised farewell trailing after him.
Sofonisba glowered at her father.

"Was that necessary, Father? Nothing inappropriate
happened."

"Take care with Master Marco, Sofi. You are no longer
a child. Now that you've finished your studies, you can focus
entirely on your art."

Sofonisba straightened. "Father, I would like to speak to you
about Marco. He's kind and gentle, like you, Father." Amilcare
shook his head as if not comprehending. Sofonisba squeezed
her eyes shut, and then opened them wide. "May we consider
him for my future husband?"

Amilcare jolted backward slightly and shook his head. "Out
of the question."

"But why? Why can't I marry him if I see he can make me
happy? You should be happy too — he approves of my art."

"This is an infatuation, Daughter. When a suitable match
arises for you, Sofi, I will consult your opinion, but Marco is
beneath you."

"Beneath me? Look at his accomplishments. Marco is
learned and hardworking, and he has a waiting list for pupils."

Amilcare took a seat and looked down at his hands. He said
nothing at first. He took a deep breath. "We have the Anguissola family crest, Sofonisba, but I didn't always. I didn't have any
name, so to speak. When I was not much younger than you are
now, I had to do service before my father recognized me, two
years filled with plenty of degrading insults." He grimaced and
shook his head. "You see, I was born out of wedlock — a bastard, a natural child if you want to be polite about it. I never
thought I would need to tell you this, but I will never forget what
I endured. I simply cannot let you marry down. Especially after
I've let you train in painting against everyone's advice." Never

before had Sofonisba seen shame in her father's eyes. It pained her to realize that his incessant drive was more than raw ambition; it was a deep need for approval. The episode matured her. It was then that she adopted her father's campaign for legitimacy as her own.

Sofonisba was well over her romantic feelings for Marco now. All that remained between them was friendship and intellectual camaraderie. He was retained as tutor for her sisters and little brother Asdrubale, who was born around the time Sofonisba inquired about marriage to Marco. Her father's birthright confession coincided with the birth of his hoped-for male heir. Amilcare could pass on the name he fought so hard to earn.

"Master Marco," Sofonisba said once inside the sitting room, "I've been pondering how to paint science. I want to do a painting where I can depict the new world of ideas in a way that everyone can understand."

"That's a lot of content for one painting. Will this be a thematic piece, not your usual portraiture?"

"I would like to accomplish the theme within a portrait. I'm thinking of depicting all of science in the portrait of one man. Anyway, I need to find a subject bigger than myself to paint. My self-portraits haven't earned me a commission, despite Father's tireless efforts."

"A depiction of Leonardo, perhaps? A tribute to his tenure under Ludovico Il Moro?"

"Yes. Leonardo could represent all of science. But I don't know what he looks like — I can't misrepresent the likeness of Leonardo da Vinci!"

"Good point. Heresy. How about an astronomer? Not the sailors who navigate the stars for practical transport but a Dominican astronomer, one of those priests coming out of Milan who reads the stars to learn about our world. Ideas are circulating even among churchmen that question our earth's position in the universe."

"An astronomer priest. Science and religion. I could show his craft through his instruments and his pious curiosity in his face."

"And will you sign this piece Sofonisba?" Marco cocked his head.

She generally avoided signing her work in order to appear modest. Her mother often cautioned that it wasn't worth risking unnecessary ire. Sofonisba took a breath. "Very well, I will sign this one. And perhaps . . ." her voice trailed off. "Do you not teach that Leonardo wrote backwards?" she asked.

"It's said he wrote this way so that others could not easily steal his ideas."

"Then, as a tribute to Leonardo, I will sign my Dominican astronomer backwards; I'll shield my modesty the way Leonardo tried to protect his ideas."

"Clever." Marco pointed his forefinger to the ceiling and turned to head for the library where the children awaited him.

By the time Marco emerged from the library after the children's lesson, Sofonisba had progressed in her study. "Ah, Master Marco." She waved a piece of parchment in her hand. "Do you think the Dominican astronomer concept might widen my audience? Perhaps lead to a public commission?"

He smiled at her optimism then sighed. "Your work may never make it into public forums. Have the town decurions yet appointed you to paint for them, even with your father's influence?" He didn't wait for a reply. "And the local courts in Mantua and Parma already have permanent painters, men, Sofonisba. Which court will take a chance on a woman? How could they compensate you? For a woman in your position, accepting payment would demean you."

"Then why do I continue to paint at all if I have no commissions and no place to show my work? I'm twenty years old. My options are narrowing." She looked away from Marco, hoping he did not see her blush, remembering her old crush on him.

"The local lords can only do so much. Submit your work to them as you must, but you will need a higher authority to move the boundaries of decorum and find the acceptance you need as a woman painter."

Sofonisba remembered locking eyes with Prince Philip as he passed under their balcony. "Exquisite advice, Master Marco. But how exactly will I accomplish that? How does someone like me gain access?"

"I travel enough to see the art being produced throughout Lombardy these days. Portraiture has taken deep root in our region since Leonardo's time. You have a natural talent, Sofonisba." Marco pointed at the parchment in her hand. "Perhaps you will be the one to continue what Leonardo started?"

"Please. I can't even manage his script. Look." She held up her scribbled parchment. "At best I can write upside down."

Marco stepped closer to her. "It may require a touch of serendipity, but you must get your work to the king. If he admires it, your sex won't be a detriment. Let your father promote your work to the local lords and don't be hurt when they reject you. It has been two decades since I escaped the life that was expected of me as the son of a butcher, and still I see condescension in the eyes of my patrons." Marco winced. "Be strong and confident until you get an audience with His Majesty. To get beyond the common requires the extraordinary, Sofonisba. You need to produce your true masterpiece."

Goosebumps shot up her arm as he said the word that both encouraged and dismayed her, but more than anything, energized her: *Masterpiece.*

This learned, striving intellectual accepted her and guided her. Marco had been a gift to Sofonisba, even if he could never be more than that.

Chapter 3

Occupation: Milan April 1555

At first, Sofonisba was motivated by the simplicity of Marco's advice: just be at the right place, at the right time, and present a masterpiece to the king. She holed herself up in her studio, determined to produce a piece worthy of her talent, her training, her father, and her tutor. But as days turned into weeks and nothing unfolded, his advice became her burden. The word weighed on her: masterpiece! She no longer had even an idea, much less a masterpiece. Her spirits plummeted. She stood for hours in front of an empty easel in her studio in the rear of the house, formerly the family's gardening shed which they had fitted with windows for natural light so she could mix her colors and air out the smell. She spent days on end beginning new attempts, managing only to waste more materials.

April came, and Sofonisba was still wrestling with her insecurities when Milan announced a new Spanish governor. Fernando Alvarez de Toledo, third Duke of Alba, Captain-General of Italy, acting Governor of Milan, and Viceroy of Naples was set to descend upon Lombardy with an army and the full confidence of the aging Spanish King, Prince Philip's father Charles V, otherwise known as the Holy Roman Emperor.

Alba's first act was to put his son in charge of the Spanish troops in Lombardy. Rumors spread. Occupation was not new to Lombardy. France had ruled Lombardy during the first quarter of the century until the Battle of Pavia in 1525, when the Spanish defeated them and took control. Elsewhere on the Italian peninsula, battles for Italian territory and artistic treasures continued. The Italian regions welcomed or resisted the French or the Spanish as best they could. Until now, the Spanish governed Lombardy loosely, mostly in name. The locals feared that was about to change under Alba and his extended family.

Shortly after Alba's people were installed in Milan, a scandal erupted. Sofonisba heard about it from Marco before he gave morning lessons to the children. He found her in her studio, staring at a blank canvas perched on its easel. "Big news, signorina. It's not taken long for our new overlords to shed blood in our region, not due to Lombard resistance, mind you, but from Spanish corruption."

Sofonisba rolled her eyes slightly at his interruption, feigning irritation even though she was happy for the distraction.

"Alba's enormous entourage in Milan is being housed with Spanish lords, the Prince and Princess of Ascoli," Marco said. "The unit is guarded by a Spanish captain named Pedro de Mendoza—said to be the brother of a powerful Spanish cardinal, the Cardinal of Burgos."

"I've seen this captain in the piazza," Sofonisba said, smiling.

"Sorry to disappoint, but an Ascoli lady-in-waiting has already caught his eye."

"I thought attendants were guarded like nuns."

"Customarily. This cunning lady let down her veil just enough to encourage the captain who must have found opportunities for romance. What he did not know was that an Ascoli retainer caught wind of the affair. The retainer knew he had to prevent Captain Mendoza from bringing disgrace upon the house, so he lay in wait hoping to catch the man sneaking into the ladies' quarters, intending to shame him into ending the affair. The simple plan was botched. Mendoza reacted violently. A fight ensued. Others joined the fray. A man was killed. In the chaos, Mendoza escaped."

Sofonisba was wide-eyed. "Desertion from the king's army?"

"As brother of the Cardinal of Burgos, he must be confident his family ties will protect him. There's more. Reports are that the Duke of Alba flew into a rage and summarily imprisoned the Prince and Princess of Ascoli for failure to control their staff."

"Spanish princes imprisoned?"

"Imagine. Naturally they were released within the hour. I can only assume that Alba wished to impress upon us that he is decisive and impartial. He's already benefitted from the whole sordid affair — earning begrudging respect in town. You know how the merchants value order above all else."

After the scandal, Pedro de Mendoza's reputation grew each time his story was told. Sofonisba could not have admitted to Marco, but she understood what tempted the lady-in-waiting. She had spotted Mendoza in the city center, not exactly a handsome man, but commanding. One day she would paint the swagger of Pedro de Mendoza and title it *Portrait of a Soldier.*

Not long after the Ascoli-Mendoza scandal, Amilcare announced at family dinner that he would leave for Milan at week's end. "The Duke of Alba is convening a council to discuss reforms for the region. He's calling for a foreign Podestà. Naturally, the decurions are curious about the implications — this outsider will be charged to judge legal disputes here in Cremona. I have been nominated to appear at the regional council in Milan."

"Then let's kill two birds with one stone," his wife said. "What if the decurions present Alba with a painting by Sofonisba? If he is as fair-minded as his handling of the Ascoli-Mendoza scandal suggests, perhaps he would be willing to consider a piece from a girl. And he certainly has the king's ear." Amilcare and Bianca both looked at Sofonisba.

"But which piece?" Sofonisba asked.

"I daresay your *Dominican Astronomer* seems too risky to offer," Bianca said. "Especially from a girl."

"One of your self-portraits will do nicely," Amilcare said.

"*Virgin with Book? Girl at the Clavichord?*" Sofonisba sighed. "My little girl self-portraits will be dismissed as dilettante painting, or worse, my ploy to attract a husband. I wish I were ready with the perfect . . ." Her voice trailed off before she could repeat the word she was beginning to despise. *Masterpiece.*

A week later, Amilcare was in Milan surrounded by dozens of representatives from all over Lombardy sent to gather information about Alba's intended reforms. Amilcare was disappointed to realize he would not have a private meeting with the duke as he had imagined. He would have to be assertive if he wanted to get Sofi's portrait to the duke. He saw his chance when he was given a seat on the center aisle in the meeting hall. As Alba proceeded down the aisle toward the front riser, Amilcare stepped onto the processional rug in front of him. Alba instinctively put his hand on his sword, then leaned back and smiled when Amilcare held out a package wrapped in red velvet.

"Your Grace, may I present a gift from the Council of Decurions of Cremona." Amilcare proffered the package to the duke, who took it with a polite nod before continuing to the end of the hall to address the assembly.

Toward the end of the Governor's banquet later that evening, the Duke of Alba sent a servant to invite Amilcare to approach the head table. Amilcare was happy to spot Sofonisba's portrait displayed next to the duke's chair. In addition to being a general and statesman, Alba was known to be an art collector.

Alba gestured to the piece. "Thank you for the gift. The portrait is moving. I see it is inscribed 'Sofonisba Anguissola, *Virgo.*' You give me a portrait of your daughter, sir?"

"It is a portrait of my daughter, Your Grace. She is also the painter. This is her self-portrait."

Alba cocked his head to the side without speaking, a polite smile frozen on his face. Amilcare straightened. "We are blessed with many masters in our region, Your Grace. I admit I made a selection close to my heart. My virtuous daughter Sofonisba has trained with master painters and looks to serve the king with her work."

The Duke of Alba sucked in a quick breath. "The king, sir? You are serious?" He paused and scrutinized the portrait with his expert eye. "Not many fathers would venture such an unnatural role for his daughter. Yet one can see she has talent." The duke looked from Amilcare to the portrait and back again as if judging the character of the man from the quality of the painting. "Dare I say her work reminds me of the portraitist Anthony Mor. Is such occupation common for women in Lombardy?"

"All my daughters are exceptional. However, critics say my eldest paints as if called by God, Your Grace."

The duke closed his eyes and nodded, as if he were considering why God might call a girl to such a craft, then motioned to his servant who touched Amilcare's elbow to escort him back to his seat. His audience with the Duke of Alba, Captain-General of Italy, was finished.

When Amilcare returned home to Cremona, the family greeted him at the door. Bianca asked straightaway, "How did the duke like it?"

"He loved it, truly. He likened it to the work of Anthony Mor."

Reading her father's pat response, Sofonisba said, "So nothing came of it, then?"

Amilcare didn't have the heart to deny it.

Bianca said, "Remember, this duke is one step removed from the king. We don't know where this might lead."

"Nowhere, Mother. It's not a *masterpiece.*" She spat out the word. "I've squandered this opportunity on a little girl portrait that makes me look like I'm angling for a husband." Sofonisba stormed off and disappeared into her bedroom.

Chapter 4

Chess Game: Cremona 1555

As the months passed, Sofonisba tortured herself trying to create something exceptional. Her creativity froze. "Take comfort, signorina," Marco encouraged her. "A masterpiece deserves creative torment. See how I toil," he said, sweeping a hand across the books and notes that covered the library table. Sofonisba was too kind to express her conclusion out loud: Marco toiled in anonymity. Would the same come of her?

She went about the routines of life in her father's house, starting and restarting new pieces, hoping each one to be her masterpiece, only to be continually dissatisfied with the result and then distracted by family responsibilities.

Bianca called to her daughter. "Sofi, check on your sisters. See that they are minding their lessons with Master Marco and that he's not reading to himself in the library again."

Sofonisba knew she had to do her part with chores, but she was frustrated having to interrupt her work to mind her siblings. Wasn't she eschewing marriage and a family of her own for her art? Why waste her time taking care of the little ones? Send Costanza or Gilletta. She went to find her sisters as her mother ordered, stopping first at the library where she saw Marco preparing lessons.

From the sitting room, she heard a familiar laugh. Elena? Sofonisba shook her head, knowing her imagination was playing tricks on her. Elena was at convent, many years now, sent when she was just fourteen. Their mother's explanation that Elena was the best candidate for taking the veil, and that the family couldn't afford six full dowries, had been of no help at all. Her sister's departure was the saddest day of Sofonisba's life, ending their shared ambitions at Campi's studio. All she had left of Elena was a portrait of her in her nun's habit — with graceful hands to represent her abandoned training as a painter.

Sofonisba opened the carved oak door to the sitting room. The laughter she heard was not Elena's but Europa's, taunting her older sister Minerva for losing her queen to Lucia in a game of chess.

"You sacrificed your strongest piece, Minerva." Lucia laughed as she swept up Minerva's queen. "Haven't you been listening to Master Marco?" Marco taught them how to play both old and new chess. In the former, a council of advisors protects the king. In the new game, a bishop and queen replace the council of advisors. The queen has all the power of the bishop but also has the power to move horizontally.

"Bless you sisters — stay there — don't move!" Sofonisba ran to collect her art kit and rushed back to the sitting room to sketch the scene before it vanished. "Don't move, don't move," she begged her sisters, walking backwards to a divan along the wall behind her. Sofonisba took a seat, drawing all the while, racing to capture the image. "Just a moment more, please . . . and there!" As soon as Sofonisba finished sketching, she sought Marco in the library.

"The king sits defenseless as the opponent's queen moves to take him," Sofonisba said, breathless with adrenaline.

"I'm sorry Signorina Sofonisba. To what are you referring?" Marco asked, mindlessly rolling up a scroll.

"The subject for my masterpiece. A chess game — the new chess. The players, my sisters, have layers of meaning on their faces but in the game they play, the king is defenseless; the queen overtakes him. The man waits while the woman acts."

"Reversing the natural order of things, you mean?"

"Exactly," she said, heartened Marco understood.

"A theme for you to remember, signorina." Marco puffed out his chest and tucked the scroll under his arm, looking like a Ciceronian orator. "Now act on your talent. Don't wait to be rescued."

Chapter 5

Michelangelo: 1555–1556 Cremona & Roma

Sofonisba struggled over her *Chess Game* for months. She took great care with the technical execution, no detail too small, only to grind to a halt as she deliberated the propriety of her message. By reversing the natural order of things, as Marco said, was she pushing impropriety too far? Would the decurions ridicule her father? She had invested so much time on the piece, giving up would have defeated her. She fought constant fear of reprisal. She tried to convince herself that her symbolism would be safe among the educated population of Lombardy. She remained blocked.

One evening, when she joined the family for soup, she sat slumped over her bowl.

"Sit up, Sofi," her mother said.

"Progress is slow on your *Chess Game*?" Amilcare guessed. Sofonisba shrugged. "Remember Alba's encouraging words," her father said. "He compared your work to Anthony Mor's. He said you have obvious talent, Daughter. And the Duke of Alba has seen all the greatest masters."

"But no commission from him. No invitation."

"Perhaps it's time we take the next step," Bianca said.

"I agree. We need a strategy to get Sofi's work before the right people," Amilcare said. "Shore up her reputation as a respectable painter, especially before risking offending anyone with the *Chess Game*." He glanced apologetically at his daughter.

"Should we take Sofi to the courts — to Parma, Mantua, Ferrara?" Bianca said.

"A tour of the ducal courts is needed," Amilcare said, "but the travel and wardrobe expenses will cost us plenty. Is there a way to secure her reputation with free promotion?"

"You suggest we show her work publicly? I'm not sure everyone is ready for that," Bianca said, "even with your contacts in the art world."

"Who is the greatest painter we can think of?" Amilcare asked, tapping his chin. "Whose approval would elevate Sofi's reputation beyond our local circles?"

"Why not just offer my services to Michelangelo in Rome!" Sofonisba mocked.

A smile spread across Amilcare's face. "Daughter, you're right. Michelangelo Buonarroti. If we impress the greatest master of all time, your reputation will shine. Then we can proceed to the courts that might patronize you. I'll write him immediately."

Amilcare went directly to his library and closed the door behind him. He sat down at his walnut writing table and took out a sheet of parchment to begin a letter of introduction to the legendary, aging artist. He tapped his stylus to his inkwell. He adjusted his parchment, then tapped the stylus to the sheet, wasting the sheet as blotches of ink ruined it.

An hour later, Sofonisba peered into her father's library, anxious to hear what he had drafted. "Father," she whispered as she approached, peeking over his shoulder to spy an empty page. "You've written nothing?" Her father squinted up at her, not looking like the tenacious man she knew, but more like the man who admitted his birth-status to her.

"I confess. I'm stumped. How exactly does one address such a great man? I do not believe he has a formal title. 'Master' does not seem adequate. I feel humbled by the task. This letter must be perfect."

"How about: *To the Most Excellent, the Most Magnificent, and the Most Honored Soul?*"

Amilcare smiled at his daughter's certainty and nodded his approval, dipping his stylus into the inkwell. That one short exercise — overcoming Michelangelo's salutation — seemed to encapsulate a lifetime of battling his marginal status in a world that recognized title over all else.

Unbeknownst to the Anguissola family, the great Michelangelo needed to be needed at that time for his own reasons, devastated as he was by grief over the death of his partner Urbino. Many months after Urbino passed, Michelangelo was still deep in mourning, as he shared with his friend, the artist and critic Giorgio Vasari,

My Dear Giorgio,

I can barely write, but I will say something to respond to your letter. You know that Urbino is dead. He who was my blessing from God is now my infinite pain. His favor taught me to live, and his dying has taught me to desire my own death.

For twenty-six years, I found him completely trustworthy and loyal, and now that I had made him rich and expected him to be with me as I relax into my golden years, he is gone, and nothing remains for me except the hope to see him again in paradise. At least God has given me a sign that he died happy even though he didn't want to leave me alone in this treacherous world, so full of worries. Such a huge part of me has gone with him that nothing remains here for me but infinite pain.

Your Michelangelo Buonarroti,
Rome, 23 February 1556

Michelangelo had devoted his life to representing the deepest piety and faith, and now, after all his sacrifices for the sake of his art, Michelangelo felt abandoned, alone, and without purpose. He was buried in grief when he received Amilcare's letter on behalf of Sofonisba.

"A messenger from Rome." Lucia burst into the library to find her father to accept the special delivery. "It must be from *him*!" The others appeared from every corner of the house to hear the Master's reply.

"I can hardly believe we have a response so soon." Sofonisba's hands shook as she tore open the letter her father handed her. Bianca tapped her tented fingers together in a sort of impatient prayer as they waited for Sofonisba to read it to them.

"He's requesting that I send him a drawing of a crying child." Sofonisba summarized aloud as she read the note. "He wants a model of sadness. He charges me to represent sorrow in the facial expression." Sofonisba looked wide-eyed at the others in her family, searching for confirmation that they understood the importance of her mission as earnestly as she did.

"I will need a live model," she said looking around for her little brother. "I'll need to make Asdrubale cry." Nobody flinched at the notion.

"He'll soon wake from his nap," Bianca said. "We'll hand him his bread, then take it away. He will cry all right. You must sketch quickly — I can't stand to hear him cry for very long."

They decided Lucia would hold him firmly on her lap in case he had a tantrum. The boy was demanding, and his sisters usually indulged him. Sofonisba had only moments to capture his expression. She would rework the drawing afterward and refine the composition. "Ecco, fratellino, finito," she cooed to her little brother, tossing him a piece of crust before dashing off to her studio to revise her drawing.

For three days, she did nothing but refine her initial sketch. She decided to pose him holding a crayfish with sharp claws to represent stinging pain. Late morning on the third day, she placed her drawing on a mantle and stepped back from it. She took a deep breath. There. She hoped Master Michelangelo would like it. She mulled over what to call it. *Boy after Nap* just did not have a ring to it. Lost in thought, Sofonisba went for a stroll and meandered out beyond the city center, out along the road to Cremona's vineyards, not coming home until after the midday meal was finished and cleared.

She sought out Lucia and found her sister alone in a corner of the music room painting her own self-portrait. Sofonisba's knock startled Lucia out of her concentration, and a small drop of white oil fell to Lucia's shoe.

"Tse, thanks, Sofi. Look at that."

"Sorry," Sofonisba said. She was usually the one chastising another's interruption. Lucia was particularly irritated lately, and Sofonisba suspected that the attention around the correspondence with Michelangelo provoked her sister's jealousy. But she needed Lucia's straightforward opinion. "I'm not sure what to call it."

"Call what?" Lucia was still grimacing at the mark on her shoe.

"My drawing for Michelangelo." Sofonisba's voice went up an octave as she handed the charcoal drawing to Lucia. "The crying child he requested."

Lucia took the drawing in hand and scrunched her nose as she scrutinized it. "Panderer," she said, waving her white tinted brush in circles in front of the drawing.

"What?"

"These over-sized arms? Where are the big eyes, Sofi? Where is the direct gaze to the viewer? You're not even using your own style."

"He asked for a child's tears."

"You could have positioned my figure facing outward looking at the viewer like you usually would. Instead you have me looking at Asdrubale."

Sofonisba recoiled.

"Take heart, Sister." Lucia said more softly. "You do show pain. You're giving the master what he asked for."

Sofonisba left, her sister's words eating at her because Lucia was right. Sofonisba intentionally put more action and movement into the piece, and puffed up the figures more than she usually did, hoping to appeal to the great master's sense of physical grandeur. She fretted over Lucia's criticism, not sleeping the entire night before the courier was set to depart with the drawing for Rome.

By morning, she realized she could not halt delivery of the drawing; delay now would dispirit her — she had to know what he thought, even if the sketch employed his style more than her own. But she finally had a title: *Boy Bitten by a Crayfish*, to remind herself of her sister's biting criticism for not staying true to her own style.

When the courier arrived to transport the drawing to Rome, Sofonisba was as protective as a mother with a perfect newborn. She looked nervously at her father. She had pleaded all week to go to Rome along with the piece to present it personally to the master, but Amilcare refused. "These are war-torn times, Sofi.

Battles can erupt anywhere. Travel over half the length of Italy is out of the question."

"It's irreplaceable, one-of-a-kind. Do you understand?" Sofonisba took a deep breath and handed her wrapped drawing to the courier. "Take care, caro disegno. Make us proud."

Her artwork survived its journey, reaching Master Michelangelo, still deep in mourning for his partner. "I can't sculpt. Stone is nothing but dead to me," he told his friend Giorgio Vasari. "I cannot draw. Charcoal is the ash we return to. All I see is death now, Giorgio. I am dry."

"Damn you, man. Get control of yourself. You have more to do." Vasari scolded his friend.

Michelangelo gazed out the window while he opened the package with Sofonisba's drawing of her crying brother. He let the wrapping fall to the ground, skimmed the drawing, and tossed it to the table as he stared blankly back out the window. Then the master jerked around, picked up the drawing again and scrutinized it more closely, cracking a smile, his first in months. "I understand, Carino," he said to the little boy crying in the drawing, handing the piece to Vasari.

Surprised to see his friend light up, Vasari took the drawing, holding it at arm's length in front of him to scrutinize it. "He certainly has succeeded in capturing the precise moment of a small boy's pain. The piece is inherently intimate," Vasari said.

"She." Michelangelo corrected.

"She?" Vasari asked. "The model rather looks like a little boy."

"The artist is a she. A young woman from Cremona."

"A woman artist? They permit women to practice art in Lombardy? Obviously, it is far away from His Holiness."

"Her father, a lesser nobleman, is a decurion from there. Tenacious fellow. He's been writing me asking that I mentor his daughter. I assumed he was all puff. I didn't expect the girl's work to be this good."

"If you will permit me, I'll circulate this," Vasari said, "See what people think. I'm truly curious to meet the father who permits his daughter to paint."

The day after receiving Sofi's *Boy Bitten*, Michelangelo returned to his work with vigor and began planning his *Rondanini Pieta*.

"Success!" Amilcare exclaimed many weeks later when he returned home waving a letter in the air. "Your *Boy Bitten* is receiving critical acclaim in the Master's circles in Rome. He has written a gracious letter thanking us. He says we can never know how it inspired him. Brava, Sofi."

Sofonisba looked at her beaming father. The joy that flashed in his eyes was something nobody could take from him, acknowledgment fully earned. She had never felt more rewarded than she did seeing this validation on her father's face.

She completed *Chess Game*, confident in her message. Amilcare hung it discreetly in the family library.

Chapter 6

Courtier: 1556

Amilcare left the house for his shop on the town's main piazza and felt smiles on him as he walked, sensing the whole town was talking about the letter from Michelangelo praising *Boy Bitten*. He was startled when his shop door opened only minutes after he took his coat off.

"Good day, Uncle. What a long time it's been," said Stefano Pallavicini, Amilcare's "nephew." Amilcare served Stefano's family a generation ago to prove he was worthy of a noble name.

"Still selling paints, I see. I'm here to pay your daughters' dowries worth on blue paint! One never knows who the next Michelangelo will be. Right?"

"Actually, Stefano," Amilcare said, straightening his shoulders, "did you know the master trained my Sofi?" A small exaggeration, he told himself. "They exchanged work this past year. Master Michelangelo praises Sofi's work."

"I know, Uncle. That's why I'm here. Why not send her over to teach my Maria?"

Amilcare's smile faded at his nephew's suggestion that Sofonisba tutor, but he otherwise hid his irritation. "Please, Stefano, she has no time for that. She'll be off to the courts soon to paint dukes and duchesses."

"Well then, you will be happy for my gold today, won't you, Uncle? You should get her a new dress for her effort."

Amilcare squeezed the countertop in front of him to busy the hands he wanted to clench into a fist. Somehow, he always felt slighted by the Pallavicini, even when it was his turn to boast.

But at home that evening with Bianca, his ambition was ignited. "Business tripled today. Artists all over Lombardy appear to have broken their mental blocks. Families were buying paints for their children's instruction. Just this morning my nephew Stefano ordered a hearty supply of lapis lazuli for his young daughter."

"Pallavicini?" Bianca clarified.

"The same. People are talking about Michelangelo's letter, Bianca. It's an ideal time to show off Sofi. We ought to present her to the courts now," Amilcare said. "Mantua is closest."

"The Gonzaga of Mantua have been art patrons for generations," Bianca said, "but Marco reports that the current duke is reserved. He won't allow madrigals to be sung at court. He says they're too suggestive — he only permits sacred vocals. What would he think of a woman painter?"

"He's on good terms with King Philip. And Philip's father gave him his title."

"True, but the Farnese are linked to the king by blood. Margaret of Parma is Charles V's natural child." Bianca's cheeks reddened slightly at the reference to illegitimacy.

"Then, we'll begin with the Farnese." Amilcare sent a request to call upon the court along with a small painting and a note from Sofonisba. "It would be my tremendous honor if Your Graces would accept this quadretto by my own hand."

A fortnight later, a messenger arrived wearing the yellow and blue regalia of the house of Farnese. Amilcare handed the departing messenger a coin and called to the family from the entry hall. Bianca, Sofonisba, and her sisters all gathered, her brother Asdrubale nowhere to be found.

"That was an elegant messenger," Sofonisba said.

Her father winked at her as he broke the seal. "Dear Signore Anguissola," Amilcare read half aloud, "having received . . . wanting to inquire . . . the duke's permission . . . painted with Michelangelo . . ." He beamed. "Yes, they are inviting us to come to court in Parma!"

"But, Father, you told them I painted with Master Michelangelo? Did you not say, 'corresponded with'?"

"I stretched the truth only a little." His smile showed no regret.

Europa and Minerva both begged to come along. Lucia just shook her head. "This trip will be very expensive for us," Bianca said. "Travel expenses, the livery, a wardrobe. Your father will go solely with Sofi." Europa and Minerva pouted. Lucia shrugged.

The next day, Sofonisba waited for Marco in the library at the hour he was expected to tutor the younger siblings.

"Signorina, I see on your face, you have some news."

"Yes, I do, Master Marco. My parents are preparing to formally present me to the Farnese Court. I'm nervous."

"Of course, signorina, one would be. But do not fear the Farnese. They are dedicated patrons. They have even honored me with a commission translating documents from old Latin-very dense language. And," he lowered his voice, "you might find the unhappy marriage of the Duke and Duchess of Parma plays to your advantage. The duke believes himself demeaned being put to marry a bastard. The duchess, meanwhile, flaunts her bloodline as the daughter, illegitimate or not, of the Emperor. And how do you think she keeps her husband in line and shows off her status, signorina?"

"She patronizes the arts."

"Exactly. Poets to praise her and painters to make her world beautiful. She has retained the Poet Annibale Caro as well as master painter Giulio Clovio."

"The miniaturist whom Master Campi praised?"

"The very same. Work to impress the Farnese and learn what you can from Master Clovio. Take heart, signorina. Greatness does not come easily." His words of reassurance hung like a blessing and a curse.

Amilcare and Sofonisba were presented to the Duchess of Parma in a receiving parlor covered by a frescoed ceiling of flying angels surrounding the Madonna. A young boy sat next to the duchess wearing a jewel-studded, blue velvet doublet.

"Signore Anguissola," the duchess began, "on behalf of myself and the duke, who was unable to be here," she gestured to his empty chair on the riser, "We are delighted to receive you and your talented daughter. It is an honor to be in the presence of one who trained with Master Michelangelo."

Sofonisba felt compelled to clarify, "We are honored to be received by this gracious court." She curtsied low in front of the duchess and the duke's empty chair. "Your Grace, I cannot accept the compliment you give me. I only corresponded, never trained, with Master Michelangelo." Sofonisba glanced at her father as she rose from her curtsy.

"My daughter is too modest, Your Grace." Amilcare bowed deeply before the duchess. "She corresponded with the Master in the sense of the master-pupil relationship and the exchange of ideas. I might add that Sofonisba's *Boy Bitten by a Crayfish* has received critical acclaim in the Master's circles in Rome."

"You mentioned as much in your letter," the duchess said. Sofonisba shifted her weight. "Your pride in your daughter is deserved, sir. In fact, we already knew that Master Michelangelo took interest in her work. Our resident poet Signore Caro told us as much. We were intrigued to meet this young lady in person." She tilted her head toward Sofonisba then gestured to a balding older man wearing a smock. "May we present to you Master Giulio Clovio, our resident painter."

"I am honored to meet you, Master Clovio." Sofonisba curtsied. "I've heard of your exquisite miniatures from my trainer Master Campi."

"I am most honored to make the acquaintance of a virtuosa whose renown precedes her," the elderly Clovio said, lifting Sofonisba's hand for a courtier's kiss, his lips never touching her hand.

The duchess smiled at Sofonisba. "With your father's permission, we shall have Master Clovio introduce you to our collection and perhaps you can show Master Clovio all that you learned apprenticing with the Master Michelangelo. First, please settle into your suites and be our guests tonight at table."

Sofonisba and her father were escorted to chambers that smelled of fresh roses and lavender. Sofonisba breathed in the sweet air and debated what to wear for supper with the duchess. She could wear her black dress with white ruffled collar and sleeves to suggest her seriousness and dedication to hard work, but instead she chose her most elegant dress, made of vibrant orange damask accented with gold thread.

In the grand dining room, they awaited Duchess Margaret. Sofonisba applauded herself; she would have been completely underdressed in that black robe. The duchess arrived with her son behind her, the duke still absent. Sofonisba noticed that the boy seemed to mimic his mother's every move. He glanced where she glanced. He nodded a greeting to Sofonisba as soon as his mother did. Then they went to the head of the elegant table and signaled for opening courses to begin. A team of servants swarmed the table, one stationed for each diner.

"We hope you are finding your rooms comfortable?" The duchess asked Amilcare.

"We are most comfortable, Your Grace."

"We are curious, sir, is it common in Cremona for a nobleman to direct his daughter into the practice of art?"

"Your Grace, we had no choice as my daughter had none. She was called to paint. I hesitated to let her pursue her calling, knowing how it may appear for a female to entertain such things." Amilcare turned up his palms, shrugging slightly. "And yet, in our town, art is highly regarded. We are presently decorating our churches with works by our local masters, and they show glory to God in each piece. Sofonisba seeks only to do her part to glorify her Lord through the humble work of her hands."

Humility has not been my best quality, Sofonisba countered silently to herself. She painted to fulfill her own ambitions — and those of her father.

"May we assume she limits her work to religious themes?" the duchess asked.

"If I may, Your Grace," Sofonisba interrupted. "I have been called to paint portraiture so that the glory of God within each of us may be illuminated. I aim to portray the souls of my sitters." The duchess tilted her head toward Sofonisba, encouraging her to go on. "My goal is not only to show my sitter's status and title but to show her inner qualities." She realized she was exploiting a religious justification, just as her father had. She was Amilcare's daughter, after all. "Yet, I do also wish to inspire by painting beauty. And what is more beautiful than a soul devoted to God?"

The duchess smiled. "Would Master Clovio's miniatures rise to such a lofty goal?"

Sofonisba blushed. "I would be honored and profoundly grateful to learn anything Master Clovio might deign to teach me."

Giulio Clovio's impassive face broke into a smile. "It would be my sincere pleasure to instruct the signorina, if her father would so permit."

"I place my trust in your hands," Amilcare said, bowing with a hand on his chest.

"Then our two Virtuosi shall instruct each other, the one in miniature, the other in showing the face of God." Duchess Margaret signaled the servants, who brought in the next course of the banquet.

Over the next two weeks, Sofonisba and the aged master Giulio Clovio worked together doing exactly as the duchess advised, collaborating in a respectful exchange of ideas and techniques. But the duchess also spent time with Sofonisba individually, taking an interest in her personally, as if making up for having no daughter of her own.

"You are as gifted as any court painter today, that is plain for the eye to see. Will you offer your talents for the courts of Europe, if someone were bold enough to accept you?"

Sofonisba's heart pounded at the thought of being offered a position at the Farnese court.

"You must learn a thing or two about court culture, Sofonisba, so that you can protect yourself and your reputation. First, never contradict your betters. Avoid possessing any unflattering information about them unless you can utilize it. And don't explain yourself to your inferiors. When your image is secure, your freedom will be too."

In addition to the hospitality and the duchess' advice on court behavior, Sofonisba devoured the court's spectacular art collection. With Master Clovio she toured the palace collection, which contained works by the best artists of the era. She stopped in front of a portrait of a voluptuous woman gazing into the distance.

"The Master Titian," Master Clovio said.

She's lifeless, Sofonisba thought, pasting a smile on her face so that Master Clovio did not read the blasphemy on her mind. So — removed. Her gaze should be directed outward to connect with the viewer. But Sofonisba dared not criticize the Master Titian.

Even though the Farnese collection rivaled anything she had seen in her lifetime, Sofonisba could envision her work complementing it.

When Sofonisba woke on the day before their scheduled return to Cremona, she decided to act. She put on her black dress with the white lace collar and pinned her hair back into a tight bun. Then she added a tiny touch of color to her cheekbones. She went to Master Clovio's studio. No one was there. The piece she had just completed stood lonely on its easel. Sofonisba checked the paint. Not fully dry but dry enough not to run. She wrapped it gently in red velvet and drew a deep breath as she lifted it off the easel.

She went in search of the duchess and found her seated next to her son Alessandro in the receiving hall, each of them reading as if passing time before an audience. The circumstances could not have been better. The duchess put her book down on her lap when Sofonisba approached. Sofonisba saw the title, *The Book of the City of Ladies*. It seemed like a sign.

"I would be most honored if you would accept this gift," Sofonisba said, extending the wrapped painting to the duchess who carefully pulled back the red velvet cover as Sofonisba held the frame, revealing a portrait of Master Clovio holding a miniature of Sofonisba.

The duchess smiled warmly with a nod of gratitude as she began to study the piece. Her son smiled and nodded his approval too. "By your hand, Signorina Sofonisba?" she asked.

"Yes, Your Grace," Sofonisba said. Master Clovio entered the receiving hall, catching his breath ever so slightly.

"And now we have our model," Duchess Margaret said. Master Clovio stood next to the portrait of himself. "You have rendered Master Clovio's eyes serious, almost to the point of stern." She nodded at Sofonisba. "His clothing and the dark background together seem to encircle his illuminated face. And the miniature he holds — your face echoes Master Clovio's."

Young Alessandro glanced back and forth between the portrait and his mother.

"The likeness is impeccable, Signorina Sofonisba," the duchess said. "He holds your work dear — the miniature you have achieved under his direction. Is that the basic theory? It's most delightful. Thank you, signorina. We are honored by this gift and will happily add it to our collection."

Sofonisba's pulse raced. The duchess interpreted her symbolism correctly. She barely felt the weight of the painting she continued to hold up. "If I might be so bold, I would be honored above all else to serve as your personal court portraitist." Sofonisba bobbed a curtsy awkwardly as she held the frame in front of the duchess.

The duchess did not respond. The question hung in the air. Sofonisba's pounding heart became a lump in her throat.

"Dear Lady, how," the duchess paused, "interesting."

Sofonisba held her breath. She began to feel the weight of the load in her arms.

"Your Grace," Master Clovio stepped forward a pace. "With a sincere heart I recommend this virtuous painter to you. Just as you see fit to grace me with the opportunity to practice my art at your court, I beg you to consider accepting Signorina Sofonisba in the same way as my collaborator, and dare I say, successor."

The duchess continued scrutinizing the painting, glancing at Sofonisba, back and forth, without saying a word. The pause was torture for Sofonisba, awaiting a single word that had the power to crush or elate her.

"If I may, Your Grace—"

Trumpets sounded. Sofonisba nearly dropped the canvas. A man who could only have been Ottavio Farnese, the Duke of Parma, strode into the receiving hall, still wearing a riding cape and smelling of horse.

"Dear Husband, your safe return is a relief to us all." Duchess Margaret turned to Sofonisba with her hand out, palm up, as if offering her as a prize to the duke. "May I present to you Signorina Sofonisba Anguissola, who has trained with Master Michelangelo Buonarroti. The signorina has graciously offered this court her services as a portraitist. Master Clovio recommends her, and the two of them have begun to collaborate."

The duke nodded to the duchess and young Alessandro, glanced briefly at Sofonisba, then turned back to his wife and frowned. "My dear lady, do not tell me you are actually entertaining such a preposterous idea. A female painter at our court? You will make us the laughing stocks of all Europe!"

Sofonisba lowered the now weighty painting to her side and the red velvet fell with it, covering the painting over. She had moved her queen too soon.

Duchess Margaret showed no emotion. She spoke directly to Sofonisba as if the duke were not there, as if she reached her decision independently. "We do most admire your work, signorina. Equally, we admire your courage in coming here and exposing yourself to criticism. However, we cannot offer to patronize your work at this time. We cannot risk the disrepute of employing a woman at our court in anything other than respectable positions such as ladies-in-waiting, attendants, and the usual service." She lowered her voice as if only Sofonisba would hear and spread her palms up toward the frescoed ceiling. "We, too, are in an unusual position, you see."

"We trust your stay has been most comfortable, signorina," the duke said to Sofonisba, then exited the room without further courtesies. Young Alessandro followed his father with his eyes and then glanced back again at his mother who remained impassive.

The next day, Sofonisba waited alone inside a covered carriage in the courtyard while her father attended to final arrangements for their return travel to Cremona. She felt grateful for her time with Master Clovio, but the duke's fatal condemnation rang in her ears, drowning out the duchess' advice and encouragement. As she continued to torture herself, the massive doors leading to the street opened, and four careening horsemen entered the courtyard.

"Whoa! Groom." One of the horsemen called to the livery attendant as he dismounted. "Water. Now. And alert the duke of our arrival."

Sofonisba heard one of the palace courtiers greet the lead horseman. She could make out most of what they said — something about recruiting men to fight in the North.

"The crown is rallying troops from all sources — the Italian peninsula, Spain, Habsburg Germany."

"You seek knights, horsemen?"

"Some. Mostly we need infantry. We will descend upon our enemy with every available body."

Sofonisba sat motionless in her carriage as the voices receded into the palace. She felt ashamed for lamenting lack of commissions when others risked their lives in battle. How selfish and vain — perhaps it was time to leave all this foolish art behind and lead a normal life. Get married. Have babies. Her worthiness, her work — useless.

Amilcare climbed into the carriage. "We are departing just in time, Sofi. A war delegation has arrived concerning the king's business in the North. This is not the place for a young lady. Let us return home to Cremona."

Sofonisba said nothing the entire ride home.

Chapter 7

The Friar: Cremona 1556–1557

Bianca held outstretched arms to Sofonisba and Amilcare when they returned home from Parma and asked how things had gone. Sofonisba hung up her cape. "The duchess accepted the quadretto we brought and a new piece, a double portrait of myself and Master Clovio."

"That's wonderful, Sofi. And?" Bianca asked.

"And I'm tired from the journey. I'm going to lie down." Avoiding her mother's eyes, she went to her bedroom, missed supper, and slept until the morning. When she woke, the first thing she thought were the duke's words, *laughing stocks*. At the breakfast table Sofonisba slouched into her chair. She sipped a bit of morning broth.

Lucia entered the dining room. "What's wrong with her?" Lucia pointed her thumb at Sofonisba.

Bianca ignored the question. "Lucia, take this package to your father at the square. He forgot it this morning."

"I'll take it," Sofonisba said.

"Not like you to be so helpful, Sofi," Lucia said. Bianca frowned at her.

"I just want to get out," Sofonisba said.

She meandered to her father's fine art supply shop on the town's main square, noticing the red geraniums that lined the windowsills and the potted rosemary plants outside people's doors. She was usually too lost in the world of her *invenzione* to notice the scenery around her. Today, her imagination was blank. She didn't expect to find a customer at the shop so early.

"Sofi, what a surprise, you are just the person we wanted to see!" Her father's smiling eyes told her to wake up and pay attention. "May I present my first born, my daughter Sofonisba, our virtuosa painter. Sofi, my fellow decurion, Signore Chizzola, would like to commission you for a portrait."

Signore Chizzola bowed to Sofonisba. "I would be honored to commemorate my pious brother with a painting by the hand of one who trained with Master Michelangelo."

"I'm sorry, signore. I would like to accept, but I don't know that I can," Sofonisba said, dropping the package she brought on a desk.

Amilcare shuddered. "Sofi—" He glanced apologetically at the decurion. "Signore Chizzola wants a portrait. By your hand. A commission, Daughter."

The door to the shop opened, and Sofonisba recognized a former apprentice from her days at Master Campi's studio. She straightened her posture and turned back around to her father. "Send him to my studio in the morning. Good day." She nodded, exited the shop, and shielded her blush as she left.

Her father made all the arrangements. A date was set.

Sofonisba felt a creeping dread as the day of the sitting approached. The duke's words still filled her head. Brother Chizzola came to the Anguissola home dressed in a simple white habit and black mantle. He had baby fine hair and gentle green eyes. "How do you do?" He bowed to Sofonisba while looking directly into her eyes.

Sofonisba curtsied in response, reading sincerity on his face. "I believe you will be most comfortable sitting here," she said to the friar, indicating a chair in front of the fire, "and Costanza can sit there." She pointed to a chair against the wall near the door for her chaperone.

Sofonisba began sketching the friar. She did dozens of quick studies without committing to anything, wishing she'd prepared more thoroughly for this commission. The duke's words made her question every decision. "Let's break for a meal," she said, well before the kitchen had it ready. She and the friar ate simple bread and cheese and spoke little. When they returned to the studio after, Sofonisba began organizing her materials. The friar slipped away to the garden.

Sofonisba went to tell the friar she was ready to recommence and found him kneeling in prayer in front of a garden statue of the Virgin Mary. She glanced up to the sky and saw a flock of birds heading north for the summer. She inspected her hands, picked at the paint that stained her nails, and still the friar continued to pray. Sofonisba returned to her studio.

"Forgive me, signorina," he said, rejoining her a half-hour later. "I lost track of time." The friar showed no signs of being frazzled. To the contrary, he was the picture of serenity.

"Not at all, Brother Chizzola." Sofonisba tried to concentrate wholly on the friar, find his defining attributes, his inner most qualities. As her sketches evolved, Sofonisba began to assume the friar's calm, the way she had with only one other person, her first collaborator, her sister Elena, the nun.

By the end of the day, Sofonisba felt compelled to talk to the friar to help purge the burden from her mind, to paint more clearly, if nothing else. "Brother Chizzola, I hope I do not overstep my bounds when I say that I find your demeanor infectious. Your presence helps me to catch my breath. I've been very troubled." She glanced at him to see if he looked perturbed by her admission. He cocked his head, urging her to continue. "You must see all sorts of desperate people, and my troubles must be so trivial compared to the work you do. But I feel lost and don't know where to turn."

"Please, speak. What better use for a priest than to relieve a troubled mind?"

"I hope to do your portrait justice," she said. "I want nothing more than to accurately portray your serenity. And I hope to please you and your brother, of course. But I confess that I must do more: I need to catch the attention of a permanent patron. I've already been shut out of one court — my prospect vanished almost as soon as it was within reach. Now I remain here at my father's house." Sofonisba flopped to her stool and her brush fell, splattering paint on the floor. She sniffed back tears.

Friar Chizzola understood the predicament of the Anguissola household and knew it went beyond Sofonisba's artistic concerns. He had helped many parish families negotiate dowries for their daughters. Even with the comfortable trappings of the lower nobility, the Anguissolas faced financial ruin with six girls in the family. Holy Orders were the only options for many girls from families in this situation — and the Anguissolas had already sent one daughter to convent.

Feeling the friar's openness, an avalanche of insecurities rushed from Sofonisba's lips. "I have trained for years with master painters. I corresponded with Master Michelangelo. I've presented myself at court in Parma — the duchess seriously considered me but the duke outright rejected me. He said I would make them the 'laughing stocks' of Europe. Who will take the chance on offering me a position? Where does it leave me? I've been groomed to paint but have no place to do so."

The friar waited for her to calm herself before speaking. "We Dominicans are sent all over the world and witness injustices large and small. There will be those who demean you, but you will find your strength by respecting yourself. We are all closest to God when we respect our human dignity. In the Americas, we are recruiting vast new flocks of Christians to our faith. Many argue that we should enslave these new souls, force them into the church. But there is another voice — a priest who defends the Indians against those who would treat them as savages. At times, he is a lone voice, yet he perseveres with his message of dignity. If you want to express your individual dignity, advocate for it, even if you are that lone voice. Isn't that what you strive to do with portraiture?"

Sofonisba blushed.

"I'm not telling you these things to make your troubles seem less significant," the friar said. "I want to help you find your answer. When others see you as inferior, you must look to your own goodness to find your worth, your dignity as an individual."

Sofonisba dedicated herself to the friar's portrait and finished it in a matter of weeks. The simple coloring of his black mantle over his white habit with the olive-green background lent his face serenity, with eyes that pierce the viewer. As much as she loved her *Chess Game*, she knew this was her best piece yet.

When she showed it to her parents, Amilcare beamed. "You honor us, Sofi. My fellow decurion will be thrilled by your portrayal of his brother. The eyes you have rendered are penetrating. I believe, cara, you have perfected your style."

"I feel change ahead." Bianca nodded approvingly at the friar's portrait. "I'm not sure what exactly, but big changes are before us, of that I feel certain."

Friar Chizzola receded from Sofonisba's life, but his impact on her endured, a voice reminding her to ignore the opinions of others and have faith in herself and in her work. With every rejection, she would have to struggle to rebuild her confidence. With every effort, she would strive to make her father proud.

Chapter 8

Peace of Cateau-Cambresis: Paris April 3, 1559

Hundreds of miles away from Sofonisba's wavering insecurities and ambitions, a different type of priest was pressed to assist a vastly different mission. "How many of my servants must I spare?" The Cardinal of Burgos fumed at his brother, who demanded that even Martin, the cardinal's personal attendant, be drafted into military service.

"I've pledged every last man from our family estates," Captain Mendoza said, "including your church lands, Brother."

"But why my attendant too?"

"We have to impress the new king with our loyalty — that means providing men, now. This is his big chance for victory over France."

"Impress him with *your* loyalty. He's aware of mine. I'm already cardinal, and as such, I need Martin."

"I'll return your man safely once we've won the king's war." The captain shot his devout brother a pointed look. "Don't panic. You'll survive without him."

Captain Pedro de Mendoza was risking no chances. He lost favor with the crown after his tawdry incident in Milan in 1555. The current muster for infantry was the perfect opportunity for him to reestablish his standing — the young new king was

pining for a victory to cement his own reputation and was keeping score of every man's contribution.

On August 10th, 1557 in the small town of Saint Quentin near
the northern French border, Captain de Mendoza rallied his
Spanish infantry to decisively defeat France, turning the tides
in the decades-long Hapsburg-Valois war for territory in Italy
and the Netherlands.

While the captain led his recruits to victory, the battlefield
casualties included the cardinal's beloved servant, Martin, who
lay near death in a pool of blood. The field surgeon ministered to
him as he faded in and out of consciousness. The life of this man
who was a servant, not a soldier, was about to be forever altered.
Without a leg, Martin would be lucky to keep his position as the
cardinal's favorite.

Two years later, France sued for peace. The French Queen Catherine de Medici saw an opportunity. While seated beneath
her wedding portrait, painted years ago in Florence by Giorgio Vasari, she instructed her ambassador, "Harmonious marriages between the realms are the most effective way to preserve a lasting peace." Queen Catherine reserved her influence
for the times it counted most, when it was necessary to guide
the thoughts of some and temper those of others. She knew the
limits of her power as queen, especially as long as the king kept
his official mistress Diane Poitiers. Yet, she never relented when
it came to decisions about her children. Catherine used all of
her influence to see them honored, beginning with her daughter Elisabeth de Valois, the first of her ten children. She would
not think of bestowing Elisabeth's hand on a mere duke. "Mon-
sieur Ambassador, only royalty will do for our Princess Elisabeth. Prince Don Carlos or King Philip."

Elisabeth de Valois' attendants would be handpicked from the elite of France and Spain. "We must ensure a cultured influence on Elisabeth as well. Do not fail to include an Italian in my daughter's court. Spain may have prevailed against us on the battlefield, but we know that the only successful treaty is a durable one. By all means, sir, get us what we need, but let them think it was their idea."

After decades of war, the two reigning Catholic monarchies of Europe began negotiations for peace, and royal blood would seal their pact.

To His Majesty Philip II, King of Spain, from his most humble servant, Fernando Alvarez de Toledo, Third Duke of Alba,

Truly, these peace talks have been directed by God himself. Although we have settled things so much to our own advantage, the French are delighted with it. With these talks we have settled the Italian wars entirely to our benefit. Your Majesty's rightful inheritance is now fully acknowledged.

Most importantly, Your Majesty's posterity is secured with the blessed promise of marriage to Her Excellency, the Princess Elisabeth de Valois, who displays the truly royal graces of an august princess. The Princess Elisabeth will be delivered to Your Majesty with the greatest of honors and pageantry, as this royal union requires. I am at this instant securing the best possible arrangements for her royal court, and I will ensure that her court is utterly to Your Majesty's specifications, complete with the finest of European virtues.

May I kiss your hand and pray God that he might bless me with the honor of standing in Your Majesty's presence once again.

The Duke of Alba, 15 April 1559,
Cateau-Cambresis, Northern France

Chapter 9

The Summons: Cremona, August 1559

Sofonisba heard church bells ringing for what seemed like hours. Bianca ushered the family to the piazza to hear the news. Town criers announced peace throughout the entire Italian peninsula. There had not been universal peace in Italy during Sofonisba's lifetime. Her first thought was to wonder whether she could now travel to Milan or maybe Rome.

Amilcare reported the details he heard from the decurions — a treaty was reached in 15 days that settled all disputes between Spain and France, now allies. France ceded its remaining Italian territories to Spain, and Princess Elisabeth was arranged in marriage to the King of Spain, Philip II, who was already a widower twice over.

Sofonisba remembered locking eyes with Philip II, then Prince Philip, from her balcony so long ago — and how it inspired her to pursue portraiture. Now he was marrying for the third time, and she was still in her father's house. Was she officially a spinster?

While many in France decried the Treaty of Cateau-Cambresis and Spain's lopsided spoils, all were excited for the marriage of a princess. From the moment of her engagement, a princess is the most beloved royal of all, young, and beautiful, and full of the promise of life. Princess Elisabeth de Valois

was certainly that. She was Elisabeth de la Paix, Isabella de la
Paz, and Isabella della Pace. She embodied peace for Catholic Europe. She would need an international court to serve her
every desire.

Once negotiations with the French concluded, the Duke of
Alba set out to assemble a court for the next Queen of Spain and
reflect the new European peace.

Sofonisba slipped away from the family dining table after their
midday meal, leaving others to clear the dishes. She was barely
in her studio when she heard commotion in the courtyard from
an arriving horseman. She ignored the muffled voices, figuring
her mother was offering the horse and rider a drink for their
thirst. Her youngest sister Anna Maria threw open the door to
her studio without knocking.

"Come Sofonisba." Anna Maria pulled at her sleeve. "A messenger has arrived with a summons for you."

"A summons? A summons to what?" Sofonisba followed her
sister downstairs and found her father hovering over a scroll,
his head rolling left to right as he studied each line. He looked
up as she entered the room.

His hands were shaking but his face was smiling. "Child,
it appears our prayers have been answered." Amilcare raised
the parchment emblazoned with the golden seal of Spain's new-
est Governor of Lombardy, the Duke of Sessa, Gonzalo Fernandez de Cordoba. "He requests permission for you to serve at the
royal court of Spain as a lady-in-waiting to the future queen,
Elisabeth de Valois."

Sofonisba and Amilcare stared at each other, stunned.

Bianca, flushed, nearly whispered. "A lady-in-waiting? A
permanent position, then? Not a commission?"

Sofonisba held out her hand for the letter and read it, rolling
her head from side to side, just as her father had, with the same

dumbfounded expression. "It does not say *painter*." She looked from one parent to the other. "Yet I must be invited there as an artist—I can see no other reason for them to want me at the royal court."

"The Duke of Alba must have recommended you based on our gift," Amilcare said.

"Yes, because he certainly did not ask her for her looks, right?" Asdrubale chimed in unexpectedly from the doorway. Ignoring Amilcare's stern glare, the boy pressed on. "Can I have Sofonisba's studio now? I should like to keep my little goat there so he doesn't get rained on in the courtyard when he needs to poop."

"Return to your lessons, Asdrubale," Bianca rebuffed him.

Sofonisba sniffed, dismissing her brother's rudeness, but she was hurt nonetheless, as he intended. She was doing her best to convince herself that she was summoned for her talent.

"We will accept the appointment, of course. We have no other viable option," Bianca said. "The girls' dowry situation remains dire, and I don't think Sofi wants the convent or spinsterhood." Bianca and Amilcare looked to Sofonisba, who squeezed her eyes shut.

"Thank you, yes! Of course I will accept. How can I not?" She bit her lower lip to maintain her composure. "Spain?" She shook her head at her sudden reversal of fortune.

"Spain," Amilcare said waving the parchment. "But we will not accept without assurances for Sofi's safety and security." He tugged his vest. "We shall enlist Broccardo to negotiate the terms of Sofi's service on our behalf."

Their distant relation Broccardo Persico was the leading citizen of Cremona and a member of the Council of Milan. As such, he had a direct line of influence to the Spanish administration. "I will write Broccardo immediately," Amilcare said, going to his walnut desk, thinking aloud as he began to dab his quill into the ink well. "Expenses, sleeping quarters, guardian-ship." He gathered his thoughts as he settled into his chair.

Sofonisba heard the tapping of his quill against the marble inkwell and drifted into her inventive mind. The tapping became the chime of church bells ringing as she proceeded down the center aisle of the grandest cathedral in Toledo, the King and Queen of Spain waiting near the altar to receive her. She imagined offering the monarchs a painting, a scene of the holy family. Mary would be around Sofonisba's own age, with large eyes and a high forehead, offering berries to her child. She would be swathed in a cloak of the virgin's blue, accented with a shimmering pink chemise. *My* Holy Family, she told herself. *My* Mary, a young woman full of promise, ready for her next adventure. *My* Mary, central to the narrative rather than background to the Christ Child.

Three weeks later, the family raced into the courtyard to greet the arrival of a coach escorted by four horsemen, three who carried banners of the King of Spain, the Governorship of Lombardy, and the Duchy of Milan, respectively. A fourth rider withdrew a chest from the closed cabin, buckling slightly as he pulled it from the coach.

"Signore Anguissola," the coachman said.

"I am." Amilcare stepped forward.

"From His Majesty the King," the coachman said, placing the chest at Amilcare's feet as the Milan banner guard held out a parchment enclosed with a golden seal.

The family encircled Amilcare. He read the letter to himself first, then aloud. "Provision for Sofi's passage and security, it says." He paused to glance at his wife. "1,500 silver scudi." He looked wide-eyed at Bianca then back at the chest. Minerva slipped the document from his hand and ran her fingers over the elaborate raised seal. "Milano, August 26, 1559," she read.

Hearing the date spoken aloud seemed to make it official.

"Now we are assured financially," Bianca said.

"That we are." Amilcare turned his back to the chest as if to deny its allure. "But we have not yet formally consented to the summons. We are not yet assured of how and where Sofi will be housed so far from our protection." His voice cracked slightly.

"If we accept this chest," Bianca said, "we accept the appointment. There will be no going back. Is there any doubt that this is what we want? What we have hoped for?" Amilcare did not respond. "Are you prepared to return the chest with those fine guardsmen?" Bianca gestured to the four guards sweating under the weight of their regalia in the fierce summer heat.

The royal horsemen accepted only water before returning to Milan or Toledo or wherever the king might next send them. The chest filled with silver remained with the Anguissolas.

Amilcare agonized for another ten days. Sofonisba read the anguish on his face. She saw he was torn about sending her away — alone. She knew he must be fretting, whether to request leave to join her to protect her, or whether to let her go at all. This was the culmination of all their efforts and ambitions. Her summons to court was his validation as a distinguished nobleman. How could he possibly hesitate longer? She prayed he would come to the correct decision.

After Sunday's midday meal, when the house grew still and somnolent, Amilcare took a deep breath and slipped off to his study.

To His Holy Catholic Royal Majesty,

As Your Majesty's devoted and obedient servant, I oblige your wish, although it gives me great sorrow and deep unhappiness that my dearest daughter will be so far away, she whom we all love like life itself and whom we value above all else for her gifts and manners.

We seek only that our virtuous daughter be housed as if she were in a monastery and with this hope we humbly accept Your Majesty's appointment.

Amilcare Anguissola, Cremona, Lombardy
September 6, 1559

Amilcare forwarded his consent to the crown, knowing that he could not dictate his daughter's conditions at court any more than he could have refused permission to send her away.

Preparations for her departure began to consume Sofonisba and the rest of the family, and seemingly everyone else in Cremona, all curious about the imminent influence of their own local girl.

"Let's tell Amilcare to have more of those New World delicacies sent here from Spain," a fellow decurion said.

"Never mind such trifles," another said. "Have him send us more contracts from the royal court. Our whole region will profit from this connection to the crown."

"Amilcare should trust Asdrubale to maintain the house and go himself to Spain to press for his own appointment."

"He would never entrust the girls to Asdrubale. The boy has yet to prove himself reliable. Sofonisba will have to go alone." He laughed. "Perhaps I should offer to escort the signorina!"

"Ah, Broccardo Persico beat you to that," the first said.

Sofonisba asked her father how long she would be away, as the summons didn't specify. "I served the Pallavicini for two years at their court," Amilcare said. "I should think something along those lines." As much as they both wanted this, two years seemed like a long time to be away from the home she had barely left since birth.

But Sofi redirected her anxiety about leaving to what she knew best. "I want to show my gratitude before I go," she said, "to you and the rest of the family, for everything you have done for me, and to my teachers, all of them, Campi, Gatti, Michelangelo, all the local influences." As she rose to go to her studio to begin executing her fledgling visions, Amilcare felt his first jabs of missing her.

Sofonisba decided on a family portrait that focused on her greatest influence, Amilcare. A landscape in the background would represent the motherland she was soon to leave and also represent her mother who would not be pictured. Amilcare would sit embracing Asdrubale, his heir, his patrimony, and the future of his name. His embrace of Asdrubale would represent his love and protection for all his children, while also acknowledging Amilcare's heir. With them she would pose Minerva — the most literary sister of them all. While the three figures in the painting would document the whole family, the central focus would remain her father. None of the difficulties he experienced in life as a bastard child or financially struggling minor aristocrat would detract from representing his primary truth, his kindness.

Sofonisba positioned Amilcare between the two children, wearing the respectable black garb of a Lombard nobleman and the gentle gaze of a protective father, directed outward to the viewer. Minerva's blue dress and the flowers she held would represent the purity of all his daughters. His arm around Asdrubale dressed in red long pants would represent a bright future for the only male heir. Finally, a little white dog would attest to the familial loyalty of the Anguissola house.

After their final session posing for the piece, Amilcare hung back as Asdrubale and Minerva headed toward the kitchen. "A word, Sofi," he said, pointing to the most comfortable chair in his study, where he had insisted the family portrait be painted. It was here where he first noticed his precocious first-born writing her name at the age of two, drawing extensive designs at the age of three, constantly drawing everything around her, and all that she envisioned in her vivid imagination.

"Your appointment has already improved our situation, Sofi. As of last month, the crown assigned to our family proceeds from a local wine tax, the d'azio dell' vino. The revenue is to be awarded to us monthly."

"We are being paid for my services in addition to the 1,500 silver scudi?"

"In recognition of your new station." Amilcare nodded.

She smiled, happy to see his pride. "When do you think I should offer my services as an artist?"

"First, establish relations with the queen you are called to serve. Think about how you could be useful to her. Maybe she would like drawing instruction."

"Are you suggesting I won't paint at court?"

"You will eventually, but first establish yourself personally and let her see your refinement. Then you can disclose your full aspirations, which are?"

"To paint, of course."

"And?"

"To perfect my art of portraiture. To portray one's soul on canvas."

"Just any soul at court? Whose soul? What is your greatest aspiration, Sofi?"

"I want to paint the king's portrait. I want to portray the king's soul."

"Then promise me, Sofi, you will strive to make it come true."

"Thank you, Father. I promise."

For a tribute to all the art masters in her life, she settled on a portrait within a portrait, a scene of Bernardino Campi painting her. Bernardino trained her, and now she was on her way to the court of the world's most powerful monarch, hopefully, to show off that training. She decided to also execute a *Holy Family*, the one she first envisioned hearing the tapping of her father's quill as he wrote to negotiate terms of her service. With landscape representing home in the background, Mary is youthful, glowing, illuminated, sensual, ready for what awaits. Sofonisba's Mary would be in her middle twenties, right around Sofi's age.

That summer in Cremona was one of the hottest in memory. There were none of the usual cool morning breezes before the midday heat. The long muggy days trudged by slowly. Sofonisba found the time she needed to complete her final projects but often not the energy. The weather made the Anguissola household lethargic, and increasingly sentimental.

"It's too bad we couldn't have Elena at home this summer so we could all be together again," Minerva said.

"At least this farewell won't be as hard as when she left. We were all so young then, and the convent seemed so foreboding," Lucia said.

"May I take over Sofonisba's studio when she's gone, instead of Asdrubale?" asked Anna Maria. Sofonisba winced. She knew her siblings envied the special attention paid her, but they could be callous towards her feelings.

The heat did not deter the stream of townspeople who came to introduce themselves to Sofonisba and request some favor from the king's court. In fact, the Anguissolas felt a new obsequiousness towards them everywhere they went, from the elite and the humble, from the merchants, the notaries, and even the priests. Sofonisba had become an object of curiosity and a target of others' ambitions. "The same people who criticized us for letting Sofi paint now covet our connection to the crown," Bianca said.

One day a horseman came speeding around the corner demanding entry into their courtyard more urgently than most. He was perhaps twenty years Sofonisba's senior. He carried a pack on his back from which rolled canvases protruded. His horse was panting, exhausted.

"I am the artist Giovanni Battista Moroni," he bellowed to Costanza who opened the door to the courtyard below. His voice rang throughout the house. "I am here to speak with the artist Signorina Sofonisba Anguissola."

Sofonisba and Bianca arrived in the courtyard just as he spoke her name. "I am Sofonisba Anguissola," she said, smiling seeing his canvases, but not recognizing the man.

"And I am her mother, Signora Anguissola," Bianca said.

"The honor is mine, signora." The man bowed to Bianca before turning to Sofonisba. "I have come from Bergamo where I paint, specializing in portraiture. May I ask, signorina, have you ever seen my work?"

"Signore, I cannot say that I have."

The painter pounded a fist into his palm, nodding emphatically. "Exactly! That supports my logic: we have a kinship, you and I, an artistic kinship. Please, may I enter, to show you my work?"

Bianca Anguissola gestured for the painter to come inside. He wasted no time unrolling a canvas inside the foyer. "Look, here," he said, slowly revealing his own Dominican friar, "My *Portrait of Gian Grisostomo Zanchi.*" He held it up to Sofonisba so closely she had to step back to examine it.

She gulped. "Signore, if you could see my *Portrait of Ippolito—*"

"Yes, Chizzola! I have seen your *Portrait of Ippolito Chizzola* in Brescia. I saw the connection between us instantly. The similarities are remarkable." Moroni's Dominican friar had little of the gentleness that Sofonisba infused into her rendition, but Moroni showed deep pensive eyes on an illuminated face over green background, squarely echoing Sofonisba's own version.

"Signore, the similarities between your Dominican friar and my own are striking: the coloring, the positioning, the lighting, the depth, and the stark individuality of the pose."

"And here," he said, unrolling another canvas from his worn leather bag. "I use the figure's clothing and instruments to create a narrative of the person but emphasize the face and eyes to depict his soul. When I saw your *Portrait of a Dominican* at the house of Signore Chizzola, I was stunned. I had not before seen your work, nor, I apologize to say, was I aware of your reputation as I make it a habit of not listening to local gossip about other artists — too much jealousy going around to take any of it seriously. I realized that you and I share a common mission. I inquired and discovered that you reside right here in Cremona," he pointed to the ground, "not far from my native Bergamo." He cupped his hands upward, shaking his head in amazement. "Our art is part of a movement, a movement to reveal the individual through portraiture!" The artist wagged his forefinger dramatically to the ceiling.

The two artists talked about portraiture for the remainder of the afternoon.

"I aim to show the range of human experience, using the portrait to honor the individual — the craftsman, the soldier, the mother." He waved a hand across her studio. "I see we both strive to show human complexity through individuals." Sofonisba blushed.

"I see it here." He pointed to her *Holy Family.* "And here." He pointed to her family portrait of Amilcare, Minerva, and

Asdrubale. "And most certainly here," he said, raising his voice as he stood before her *Chess Game*. He walked back to stand before her family portrait and scratched his chin. "I admire the spatial effects that you achieve with the thickness of the paint — an effect many masters achieve only through glazes. And the positioning of your sitters . . ." His voice trailed off as he scribbled notes. "I'm planning a family rendition of my own," he said, "a commission of a gentleman with his two children. Would you object if I were to use your family portrait as a model for the one I am presently attempting? The pose, the manner, the expressions. You manage to convey the essence. I think you have shown kindness in your father, simply by the look in his eyes and the way he embraces his son. I would like to borrow from your pose, if I may, Master Anguissola."

Sofonisba blinked. "No one has ever called me *master* before."

"Then I am privileged to be the first."

Sofonisba felt invigorated by Master Moroni's insights. His visit acted as a summons of a different sort, charging her to remember her roots, and her style, and be true to them as she went forth to depict the truth in others, *al vero*, at the seat of an empire.

Chapter 10

Milan Farewell: November 1559

As they sat down to a meal of pasta al tartufo one day in early October of that year, 1559, Amilcare announced that the family was invited to the governor's residence in Milan. "The Duke of Sessa wrote to say that he has been charged with preparing Sofonisba for her court tenure, and we are to accompany her during her stay."

"Milan?" asked Lucia.

"Me too?" added Anna Maria.

"Milan. All of us," Amilcare said.

"He must be curious about a family of girl painters," Asdrubale said, taunting.

"I'll remind you that your sister is on her way to the king's court," Bianca said sternly. "We should be grateful for the privilege of joining her in Milan."

Broccardo Persico arrived with his horsemen on the appointed day to escort the Anguissola family. Peace was now official throughout Italy, but without wars to fight, many a former soldier resorted to highway robbery to provide for himself. "Ferrante and his men will ride with the carriage," Broccardo said, putting his arm around a young man whose enormous eyes were much like Sofonisba's, her favorite cousin Ferrante Anguissola Gonzaga.

"A beautiful day, Uncle." Ferrante embraced Amilcare before turning back to Broccardo.

"We are in your good hands, my friend." Amilcare clapped a hand on Broccardo's back. He had known Broccardo for thirty years, since the days at the Pallavicini palace when Amilcare worked to earn his own father's recognition. Secure in his privileged birth, Broccardo never hazed Amilcare as some of the other retainers had.

"I would not miss the honor for the world. It is I who now must pay court to you," Broccardo said with an exaggerated bow. Broccardo was a Knight of Jerusalem, a member of the King's Council, and a Commissioner General of Lombardy. He earned several annual stipends from the crown already and a royal pension, in perpetuity, inheritable by his family as long as their bloodline endured. When Broccardo facilitated the Anguissola's negotiations with the king, he did so as a natural part of his duties as Cremona's leading citizen — not seeking influence but expending it.

Broccardo advised they depart without delay, as the heavy carriage would add days to the travel. "We shall be much more comfortable once we reach the governor's residence in Milan, I assure you." The governor was reportedly a lavish entertainer. His guests never left dissatisfied.

The party rode for days without sleeping at an inn. "No need to delay our arrival in Milan nor waste funds unnecessarily," Bianca said. They rotated drivers instead.

Sofonisba was awakened during a dream when they stopped at the city walls of Milan. Broccardo gave the governor's letter of introduction to a guard. The guard's eyes bulged when he saw the governor's seal. He directed the carriage around the people waiting in line and waved them through the city gates.

As soon as they were inside city walls, Bianca exhaled. "Before we present ourselves to the governor, I think we should thank God for our safe travel." They stumbled out of the carriage, shook out their legs, stiff from days of riding, and turned in unison toward the Cathedral across the square from the ducal palace. They entered the church, each of them following Bianca's example as she fell to her knees. Sofonisba was the first to break from prayer, unable to resist inspecting the enormous space within the Cathedral's Gothic walls that seemed to reach for heaven. She rose and walked past her kneeling mother, spellbound by the church. It was at once weighty and airy, enormous but intimate. The dark Cathedral was cool, but Sofonisba was sweating from excitement and nerves. She felt her father's hand on her shoulder. "It's time," he said.

To their surprise, the governor was waiting when they arrived in the courtyard of the ducal palace. The Duke of Sessa, Gonzalo Fernandez de Cordoba, personally greeted the traveling family. "Conte Persico, Signore Anguissola, my distinguished guests, welcome." He saluted the arrivals through his heavy accent. "And this must be the signorina," he said, taking the hand of Bianca and landing a courtier's kiss upon it — his lips never touching her skin.

"You are too kind, Your Grace," Bianca said.

Sofonisba noticed her mother bat her eyes when she held out her hand to the Spaniard.

Amilcare broke in with a low bow. "May I present to Your Grace my most precious daughter, Sofonisba, whom Your Grace and His Majesty the King have summoned." He turned toward the rest of the family. "And my other children: my son Asdrubale" — Asdrubale stepped forward to take the duke's hand, but was stopped short by Broccardo — "And my daughters Lucia, Minerva, Europa, and Anna Maria. My nephew Ferrante Anguissola Gonzaga."

The governor responded this time in his native language, similar enough for them to understand, "You have been blessed. Please, be my guests." And he motioned the travelers inside the palace.

Just as Broccardo promised, the Duke of Sessa did not scrimp on lavish entertainments for the Anguissolas. Dozens of courtiers were gathered, having heard the curious news that a Lombard girl was en route to serve the King in Spain. After the meal, the governor nodded, and a commotion began in the back of the hall. Then a procession approached, and Sofonisba saw the jeweled costumes intended to represent the cardinal virtues: strength, justice, prudence, and temperance, followed by faith, hope, and charity. As the actors moved about the banquet hall, Sofonisba realized that many eyes were fixed upon her instead of the virtues personified. Amilcare was positively beaming.

Then news raced across the dining hall, courtier to courtier, reaching Broccardo who was seated with the Anguissola family. "The Pope is dead."

"We shall celebrate the next vicar and be done with the Carafa pope," the Duke of Sessa announced. Bianca bristled noticeably. Amilcare touched her wrist. "Paul IV was no friend of the king," the duke said, nodding in apology to Bianca.

"And no friend to artists," a courtier said, holding out his hand toward Sofonisba. "They say he ordered Michelangelo to repaint the Sistine Chapel to cover the nudes."

"Then refused to pay him," another courtier interjected.

"Then banished him from Rome," a third said.

Speculation about the next pope dominated conversation. Broccardo said, "A Medici Pope will reign. They say that Cardinal Giovanni Angelo de Medici is in line to be next."

"At least a Medici pope is no longer the threat to Milan that he would have been before the peace."

Sofonisba's ears perked up. She knew the queen she was sent to serve was the daughter of Catherine de Medici. She might be serving a relation to the Vicar of Christ! Her eyes grew wide. Amilcare must have been pondering the same thing, nodding silently as he studied his daughter. Sofonisba felt a sinful dose of pride, happy she made her father feel important.

Unlike their time with the Duchess of Parma, the Duke of Sessa rarely left Sofonisba's side during her sojourn. He accompanied the family on outings around the city center even though he could easily have left them to be entertained by staff and courtiers as Margaret of Parma had. "We shall see the first public clock, installed in 1353," he said, seeming genuinely enthusiastic.

With the duke accompanying them, the family visited the Sforza Castle at the periphery of the city center. The Castle was an old Visconti fortress, updated by Galeazzo Maria Sforza when he succeeded as Duke of Milan. It had been renovated in the generations since, reaching a pinnacle under Ludovico Sforza, Il Moro, who patronized Leonardo da Vinci for almost twenty years. Leonardo was Sforza's court painter, engineer, and architect, and he left behind a treasure of drawings when he fled Milan for Paris to serve the King of France.

Sofonisba and her family devoured the collection of Leonardo da Vinci's abandoned drawings, surprised to learn how much of his work focused on the mechanical rather than the aesthetic. "Look, shoes designed to float," Lucia said, pointing to one display of oddly shaped shoes strapped to flat boards.

They saw his designs for movable bridges and various devices for lifting, pulling, and digging. Leonardo envisioned flying machines and water propulsion devices. He improved on the ancient technology of shipping, designing the first double-hulled ship.

As they continued down the gallery of Leonardo's inventions, they came upon one of his few paintings from his time with the Sforza court, a portrait titled *The Musician*. Sofonisba gasped. And then she recalled Moroni's visit not long ago. "It's like my *Portrait of a Dominican, Friar Ippolito Chizzola*," she said, standing motionless before it "even though I've never seen his work before." She blushed, a combination of pride and humility, realizing her work overlapped with Master da Vinci's. "My friar has a straight-on facial view while Leonardo's *Musician* has a slight sideward pose, but the lighting upon the central triangular faces in both paintings, and the simple inverted triangular vestments on both figures, make my friar the exact mirror opposite of Leonardo's musician. In a sense, an echo of Leonardo's backward cursive!" Sofonisba felt with every creative impulse of her body that these two portraits were connected to each other in the world of *invenzione* the same way she and Moroni were connected. "I follow his legacy," she blurted. Bianca shot her daughter a sharp look.

Broccardo smiled at Sofonisba's bravado. "The musician was Franchino Gaffurio. He was one of Leonardo's closest friends. Together with Josquin des Prez, the three formed the core of Il Moro's court."

"I know that name." Sofonisba tapped her chin. "Marco taught us Gaffurio's music theory, and now we stand before Master Leonardo's portrait of him."

"Yes," the Duke of Sessa said. "You do indeed echo Master Leonardo."

Sofonisba put a hand to her chest and bowed her head modestly, but inside she was ecstatic that Sessa noticed a connection. The duke's observation was more than a compliment — it kindled her hope that the Spanish would accept and welcome her as an artist.

The night before she was scheduled to depart for Spain, the governor asked Sofonisba and her father to his library for a private audience. "I would like to show you how I commend Sofonisba to the king," he said. "I have drafted this." He handed Sofonisba a parchment. Sofonisba took the draft, glanced at her father, and read aloud:

To His Majesty, Philip II, King of Spain,

I commend to Your Majesty this virtuosa of Lombardy, whose great talents speak for themselves far better than any words I could use, as Your Majesty will see once she is before you. I should like to repeat that Sofonisba's parents, who love her very much, and with good reason, have only agreed to send her away to obey Your Majesty, and she has come here with the same goodwill, going so far away and leaving her parents, her siblings, her relatives, her home and her country. I recommend her parents and Sofonisba to Your Majesty, that Your Majesty might show them a proof of your favor.

Gonzalo Fernandez de Cordoba, Duke of Sessa,
Governor of Milan, 1559

It occurred to Sofonisba that this Spanish lord was more accepting of her than the Duke of Parma. She thought of Marco's advice: it required a higher authority — the royal summons — to move the boundaries of propriety.

She looked up from the parchment and saw tears welling in her father's eyes. It didn't matter to her whether Sessa's words were sincere or pandering to the king. The family honor was vindicated.

In the middle of the night when the palace was still, Amilcare sat up in bed with a jolt. "We don't know them, not a thing about them, truly. We don't know where they will put her. I'm sending my daughter alone to another country for my own pride's sake not knowing how she will be treated. I'm putting my honor before her protection. We cannot let her go. We cannot."

"There, there, Amil." Bianca soothed her husband. "This is what we have wanted. This is why she has trained."

In the morning, Amilcare was the first to rise. He put on his finest doublet and his sweetest smile and seemed to have forgotten his dark-of-night qualms.

It was late November 1559, time for Sofonisba's family to return to Cremona, leave her for the indefinite future. She found her mother early. "Mamma, I wish you could come with me to Genoa. How can I pass my last days in Italy without you?"

"Try not to think of them as 'last days.' Look toward your bright future. Oh Sofi! This is just the beginning."

"I fear I won't have anyone to guide me at court."

"You are no longer a young girl. Most women your age have already been married a decade with several children." Sofonisba winced. "What you are embarking on is something very different, and very individual. Only you can navigate it all. Learn to trust yourself."

Sofonisba swallowed hard.

"And, be prudent, understand?" Bianca gazed into her daughter's eyes. "We'll be helpless to protect you from afar. Use your judgment. You have no way to control the conduct of others at court, and there may be those who would take advantage of your unusual status as an artist, or, even, your maidenhood." Bianca was a pragmatist. She knew Sofonisba had only one reputation to earn and protect. If that were broken, one way or the other, there would be no way for Bianca to mend it. "There may be many at the Spanish court who do not accept your calling. They may be quick to judge a woman painter. Stay above scandal, Sofi, or your art might be used against you."

Bianca paused and dabbed the corner of her eye with a knuckle. "I am reminded of the day I gave up Elena to the convent so young."

"Mamma, you will be in my heart every day as I know you are in Elena's. You are a model for all your children." The two women hugged again — Sofonisba's eyes shut tight to push back the tears — until they heard the porters in the courtyard below announce that the horses and carriage were prepared.

Bianca released her embrace first and held out her hand to her daughter. They descended hand-in-hand to the courtyard below where the Duke of Sessa and the rest of the Anguissolas were assembled for a final farewell. Broccardo Persico signaled his readiness with a wave of his gloved hand from the front of the caravan where he and her cousin Ferrante waited ahead of Broccardo's and the governor's retainers.

Sofonisba went first to Lucia. "This could have been you, Sister," she said to her closest rival. "You are as good as I am at portraiture, as you know."

"You're older not better, Sofi. Remember that." Lucia teased.

"Don't stop writing, Minerva. You write so beautifully. Remember, one subject at a time and persevere. You have stories within you to tell. And Europa, promise to write to me all about your progress." They both nodded, and Europa swore she would get her art work shown publicly.

"I don't doubt you, Europa," Sofonisba said.

"Keep up your lessons." She tickled Anna Maria under her chin. "Enjoy Marco's instruction while you can." Sofonisba felt a twinge of pain; Marco had been away from Cremona all summer, and she had no opportunity to say farewell to him before she left for Milan.

"And you best work on your Spanish, Sofi." Anna Maria wagged her finger at her big sister.

Sofonisba went to her brother Asdrubale. With a face devoid of emotion, he reached forward and planted a perfunctory kiss on each of her cheeks and then bowed to her with an exaggerated flourish of his hand, like a stage performer playing to an audience rather than a brother saying good-bye to his sister. She knew she received more than her fair share of their father's attention, but she could not understand why her brother was so cold. Had she not paid him the biggest tribute of all in the family portrait, the boy receiving his father's blessing? She mustered a trite admonition. "Be good to Father, Brother. He needs your help."

"Mother." The two women hugged. Sofonisba took a deep breath, and this time, she was the first to let go.

When she reached her father, they both shrugged knowing no words would suffice. "Cara mia," was all Amilcare could manage, embracing his daughter for the final time. Sofonisba nodded and gulped hard, not able to respond to her father for fear of crying.

The governor cleared his throat. "We celebrate this day with joy and trepidation as a daughter of Lombardy goes forth to represent this worthy region to the crown and to the world. We give thanks to God and pray for her safe journey."

As the governor's groom stepped forward to help Sofonisba into the carriage, a horseman came galloping around the corner into the courtyard of the palazzo careening to a halt in front of the departing travelers. "Signorina!" He panted, waving. "Signori." He called to Amilcare and Bianca, disheveled but smiling.

Marco! The family tutor had practically run a horse into the ground, racing to find Sofonisba before she left for Spain. "I am so glad — I made it just in time." He huffed to catch his breath.

"If I may" — he unrolled a parchment — "I composed a little something in your honor, signorina." Marco cleared his throat and puffed out his chest.

> Behold the beautiful and wise portraitist
> The noble Sofonisba of Cremona
> Who today may be called contented
> To render only perfection and beauty

He lowered his parchment and acknowledged their polite applause. Then he turned to Sofonisba and took her hand into his sweaty palm. "Please do me the honor, signorina, of showing off your refined education at every turn. Remember your *invenzione* and be proud of your work, cara." He glanced at Amilcare, whose proud grin forgave the scholar's forwardness.

Everyone knew that Marco deserved some credit for Sofonisba's success. He inspired her with ideas for her *invenzione*. He reinforced her devotion to portraiture with his theories rooted in the conduct of individuals. In return, she was his muse, inspiring his intellect. The mood lightened with Marco's touching tribute, and Sofonisba set off for the coast behind Broccardo Persico's vanguard.

Part II

Lady-in-Waiting (1560–1572)

Chapter 11

The Spanish Road: November 1559–January 1560

Sofonisba's itinerary left plenty of time to arrive in Spain in advance of Princess Elisabeth for the royal wedding: more than six weeks for a carriage to Genoa, a ship to Barcelona, and a carriage to Guadalajara where the ceremony would take place. Sofonisba traveled with two Spanish attendants provided by the governor. Broccardo's men flanked their carriage. Broccardo and her cousin Ferrante led.

Outside Milan's city walls, she noticed the fallen leaves. The ones still clinging were dark red — like the geranium that caught Philip II's attention a decade earlier. She could not have imagined then what chain of events would lead her to his court, and now she fantasized about her ultimate goal, painting him. She drifted into her world of *invenzione*.

Sofonisba fell asleep and woke feeling hungry. Still groggy, she rubbed her eyes. "Where are we?" she asked her maids in Italian. They continued their embroidery without answering the simple question. "Scusate, dov'e siamo?" she repeated with no more success. "Ahh. Donde estamos?" she said in halting Spanish.

"Barona, señorita," said the maid seated across from her smiling sweetly.

They were barely out of Milan.

They traveled for days with little diversion except short stays and quick meals at residences along the way that Broccardo had arranged. Sofonisba knew she should be working on her Spanish accent, and her French, but she returned again and again to her art kit, sketching as best she could on the bumpy road. She looked forward to Genoa. Broccardo arranged for them to stay at the palace of Admiral Andrea Doria, called "Padre della Patria" for his naval victories on behalf of the Habsburg Emperor.

The carriage jolted to a halt. Sofonisba got out, took a deep breath of sea air, and stared out at the horizon. "The first time you've seen the sea?" Ferrante said, sidling up to his cousin. She nodded, transfixed.

"Wait until you see inside the palace," Broccardo said, joining them.

Servants appeared to escort Sofonisba, Broccardo, and Ferrante up the marble stairs that ringed the courtyard. Retainers watered the horses and tended the carriage. Sofonisba's maids oversaw her bags. They were taken to a sitting room where the aging hero was seated before a fire, a book face down on his lap. He was snoring. The servant cleared his throat, "The lady painter who journeys to the King of Spain."

The admiral sat up. "What?" He rubbed his eyes, struggling to comprehend. Sofonisba devoured the wrinkles in his face, the crevices that time had carved, and his squinty, watery eyes. She reached up and touched her own smooth skin and cringed, imagining her own self-portrait as an old woman.

Even with the Admiral's infirmity, the Doria house functioned impeccably. The staff attended Sofonisba and her entourage graciously. After the days of rough riding, she was grateful for three days in one place — a luxurious palace no less — to rest and enjoy the company of Broccardo and Ferrante that she had missed confined to the carriage.

Broccardo brought news from town. "The French King Henry is dead—lanced at the tournament commemorating his daughter's wedding. They say he was killed wearing her favor—a tribute to her elevation to Queen of Spain."

Sofonisba's face went white. "My queen? The queen I am to serve just lost her father?"

"I am afraid so, cara," Broccardo said in a near-whisper. Sofonisba closed her eyes. "Poor girl." She and her new patroness would miss their fathers together. Empathizing for the young queen, Sofonisba began to feel love for her. In an odd way, it took her mind off the family she missed already.

After several days of rest, it was time to depart for Spain.

"Honored guests, welcome." A captain waved toward the gangplank, inviting the travelers to board the galley. On deck, the captain introduced them to two smartly dressed men. "My brothers and partners in Lomellini shipping, welcome our guests."

Sofonisba curtsied. The men bowed. "Please advise us if we have overlooked any detail for your comfort," the tallest brother said. A deckhand lingered nearby, appearing to be eavesdropping. He had a striking resemblance to the Lomellini brothers. He was a few years younger than Sofonisba, twenty or so, stocky and brutish, but tanned and handsome with a jagged scar by his right eye. Extreme play as a youth or something more criminal? The captain tipped his head toward the deckhand and smirked. The deckhand slipped away.

Sofonisba was escorted to her stateroom where her maids were putting away her things for the voyage.

The sea was calm the first few days. Sofonisba had time to adjust to the seasickness but found it difficult to study her Spanish and French, and almost impossible to sketch. She passed her time strolling the deck as much as the captain allowed. One afternoon she spied the deck hand. Oblivious to her presence on deck, he took his shirt off to wipe the sweat off his brow. She pretended to look out at the sea but caught him in her peripheral vision.

Sofonisba fantasized about the deck hand at night in her bunk. She couldn't put his flesh out of her mind. She imagined clinging to his shoulders as he pulled her from the sea, waves crashing around them.

The next evening, she went for a stroll on deck. He was nowhere to be seen, until suddenly there he was. "My apologies, signorina," he said, bumping into her as he rounded the corner.

"Mine. That was my fault. I walked straight into you," she said.

"You were looking at the clouds, perhaps?" He pointed to the sky.

"I saw a cherub. There," Sofonisba said, peeking to study his face as he regarded the clouds. She inspected his scar. What event nearly cost him his eye?

"That looks more like an animal to me. A dog—the ears." He wagged fingers on either side of his head.

She laughed. "Those are the wings!"

"I see only ears, but maybe now it's more of a pig," he said, palms up. A gust of wind whooshed. "Looks like we're going to have a change in weather."

The captain came on deck with Broccardo. "We're in for a storm," he said to Broccardo, then nodding toward Sofonisba and the deckhand, "You should get your charge below." The captain mock-whispered. "My father's bastard has work to do," then shouting, "Orazio, to your station."

Broccardo strode over to Sofonisba. "Don't mingle with the crew, cara. It's not proper."

Commotion mounted as the crew prepared for the storm. In her cabin below, Sofonisba tried to keep her eyes on the ceiling, which seemed to help her endure the motion of the ship. As her stomach did somersaults, all she could think about was the deckhand. Orazio. She repeated his name in her mind. She envisioned him coming home damp from sailing, finding her at her easel before the hearth — their contented little abode, the sailor and his wife the artist. She shook the image from her mind. She was on her way to the royal court of Spain, provided she didn't die tonight. Why was she fantasizing about this Orazio? Nor had the captain's sotto voce escaped her ears. "Bastard." Had her father suffered such slights when he served the Pallavicini early in life to earn his name? And, of course, if Amilcare wouldn't approve of a match with Marco, what would he think of her deckhand? She felt a pang. Homesick. Anxious. Excited.

She tried to draw to steady her nerves but found it impossible. The harder she tried to take her mind off the storm, the more her thoughts returned to Orazio. Her mind rocked back and forth with the waves, fearing the storm and fantasizing about the young man with the beautiful torso and the mysterious scar by his right eye.

After days of being mercilessly thrown about, their galley had made little forward progress. Sofonisba was confined below deck for the duration of the rough voyage and did not see Orazio again until the day they disembarked, and then, only for a brief glimpse.

The party finally arrived at port in Barcelona, woefully behind schedule. Sofonisba thanked God for their safe arrival, but worried. They still had half of Spain to travel, through Catalonia, Aragon, and deep into Castile in order to reach Guadalajara. The royal wedding was by far the biggest event of Sofonisba's life, and she had counted on having plenty of time to settle in at court before presenting herself to the King of Spain and a Princess of France. The last thing she wanted was to arrive tired, frazzled, and out of sorts.

Upon arrival in Guadalajara, Sofonisba and her entourage awaited admission to the House of Mendoza. "Hail Mary, full of grace," read the yellow, red, and green coat of arms hanging above the iron-reinforced doors to the palace of the 4th Duke of Infantado. "Holy Mother, thank you." Sofonisba echoed the seal, relieved to have reached their destination safely, barely in time for her duties. She scanned the imposing palace front as they waited, cupping her hand to her forehead to shade her eyes against the noon winter sun. They continued to wait as the guards inspected papers for the party in front of them, an elegantly dressed gentleman speaking French to a guard who ignored his explanation.

Broccardo came back to her carriage. "Any time now, signorina."

Then Ferrante stuck his head into the carriage from the opposite side. "Excited, Cousin? I can count two dozen banners out here." He pointed to the horsemen congregating. "They've come from all over Europe."

"Of course I'm excited. Now if they'll just let us inside." She patted sweat off her forehead even though the air was cool.

"No need to be nervous. I'll be right alongside you. Ah, here we go."

A guard waved them inside the castle. In the courtyard, yellow, green, and red attired stall hands greeted them, leading away their horses and carriage. A groom ushered them to a stone stairway leading into the castle through a rainbow of flying banners representing the many houses present to witness the royal union. Her two Spanish maids disappeared with her bags.

Inside, on a red-veined marble floor, stood guards in shining armor. The chaos escalated. Sofonisba felt as if she were inside an ant colony, with hundreds of worker ants scurrying about. The castle's owner, the Duke of Infantado, was a long-time Habsburg defender and a loyalist to the Holy Roman Emperor Charles V. Servants crossed in all directions carrying everything from gold reinforced suitcases, to trays of food, to silver threaded linens and bedding.

"Your Grace Persico." A captain saluted Broccardo with a sweep of his hat.

"Gaspary, man!" Broccardo said, embracing him. "May I present to you the Lady Sofonisba." The captain eyed Sofonisba. "Under my protection to attend the new queen as a lady-in-waiting." The captain stepped back and bowed. "My lady," he said and turned to Broccardo.

"Persico, present your charge to the maids, there. They will settle her into the ladies' quarters, not a place you are permitted, I am sorry to inform you, my friend." Gaspary signaled, and a female attendant in a red cap curtsied to Sofonisba to escort her to the ladies' quarters. Sofonisba glanced around and did not see her cousin.

"I will catch up to you as soon as I am able, Lady Sofonisba," Broccardo called out to her as she was being led away by the maid.

"Thank you, Broccardo," Sofonisba called back over the attendant's head, oblivious to using his given name, mindful only of their hasty goodbye, an inadequate expression of gratitude after the long journey. She reproached herself, but Broccardo was beaming. She followed the red-capped Spanish maid weaving through hundreds of guests decked out in velvets, furs, and jewels. They turned corner after corner in the medieval stone castle before Sofonisba realized the red cap she followed belonged to the wrong maid. Sofonisba had lost sight of her escort.

"Scusi," she called to a servant approaching from the right who continued past. "Er, con permesso," she said to another. "Señora . . . señorita . . . perdon." She tried to grab the attention of anyone who might direct her but every last person was preoccupied with royal duties. Sofonisba had no idea where she should be, and her heavy accent wasn't helping her get the servants' attention. She berated herself for not practicing her Spanish more on the journey. Most importantly, where was her art kit? She had forgotten to put it aside and could only hope it was safe with her bags.

With no one attending to her, she strolled unfettered through the cold stone corridors. Courtiers and churchmen from all corners of Europe filled the halls with a cacophony of languages and dialects. She stopped beside a displayed suit of armor that reminded her of King Philip the day he paraded through Cremona as a young prince. What was she supposed to do? Not one of these thousands of servants seemed able to help her. Only the empty suit of armor attended her as she stood alone in the mass of scurrying servants at the court her father praised as "like a monastery." She might enjoy this freedom, if she weren't so tired and nervous. But the practical reality of this independence baffled her.

She took to snooping, hoping for a place to freshen up. Most rooms she came upon were occupied or locked. She noted silver and golden crucifixes placed above the beds, and headboards, heavily carved but less intricately inlaid with contrasting woods than she was accustomed to. In one room, there was no proper bed, just a large filled pad with no frame. Next to the mattress was a side table on top of which she saw a piece of charcoal suitable for drawing. She smiled and stepped into the room, ready to snatch the crude charcoal to use until she found her art kit, when a harried maid harrumphed behind her.

"Señorita Anguissola." The maid exhaled before launching into a barrage of Castilian too fast for Sofonisba to understand. Clearly the maid wanted Sofonisba to follow her. The maid led her to large room with many beds among which stood a pale lady with ropes of pearls in her hair that contrasted with her elegant black mourning attire. The lady threw a hand up in the air and tossed her head back when Sofonisba entered the room.

"Mademoiselle Sofonisba," the lady sighed, continuing in slow, labored Spanish. "At last we have found you. I am Madame de Vineux, lead chaperone for the ladies-in-waiting and privileged to say an intimate of the French Queen mother, Catherine de Medici." She touched the ruby necklace at her throat. "At this moment I am responsible to see that each of you is ready for tonight's banquet where you will be presented to the royal majesties."

"A banquet, madam? Will the princess not need her ladies-in-waiting to attend to her at the royal wedding ceremony?" Sofonisba asked in her most careful Spanish.

Madame de Vineux pursed her lips. "Mademoiselle, the ceremony will be attended by only those of royal blood. The princess will have other princesses attending her. The ladies-in-waiting will be presented for their service afterward, and you shall be quite honored."

"Yes, truly honored, madam. I apologize for my presumption."

Madame de Vineux signaled for attendants who stepped forward to dress Sofonisba, fitting her into an elegant gown of Florentine silk embroidered from neck to toe with silver thread and pearls. Madame de Vineux left briefly then returned and presented Sofonisba with a small box. "A gift for you from the Queen of France in appreciation of your service to her most precious daughter, the beloved first-born French Princess, soon no longer to be called Elisabeth, but rather Her Majesty Queen Isabel."

Sofonisba's eyes popped at the ruby and diamond necklace facing her. "Madam, I am—

Madame de Vineux cut her off. "You may thank Queen Catherine by post. Now, finish dressing, rapidement!" A maid took out the necklace and put it on Sofonisba. Sofonisba touched her neck and felt the weight of the stones as she fingered their contours.

Madame de Vineux left. The attendants finished dressing Sofonisba, and they left too. After all the hurrying, Sofonisba was again waiting, completely unoccupied, rather like she was back on the Spanish road, alone with her mute attendants. She remembered the abandoned charcoal and scolded herself for not snatching it when she had the opportunity. She fretted about locating her personal bags, in particular her art kit, none of which she had seen since alighting from the carriage.

She decided to try to get back to the room where she spied the charcoal, thinking to pass the time drawing. As Sofonisba retraced her steps to the courtyard, she turned a blind corner and nearly bumped into a servant of the cardinal's retinue, a one-legged man hopping in pain next to a large trunk that must have fallen upon his good foot.

She laughed—then quickly bit her lower lip. She blushed and covered her mouth, but a chortle escaped from behind her hand, born of her sheer exhaustion. Sofonisba was mortified.

The one-legged man looked to the ground and bowed. "My lady."

"Please . . . sir . . . forgive . . ." Sofonisba tried to apologize but could only cup her mouth to stifle her involuntary rudeness. He nodded, his face stone. Sofonisba handed the servant a coin and then removed herself without speaking to him further. She knew her apology sounded insincere through her laughter. She remembered the advice of the Duchess of Parma, not to explain herself to her inferiors. Still, she felt brutish. She crept away from the humiliated one-legged man and tried to find her way back to the ladies' quarters where the attendants had dressed her. She let out a sigh of relief as she approached the outer salon. As she got closer, she heard laughter.

Eight ladies in gowns like hers surrounded three young men in bejeweled velvet doublets. They all turned to look at Sofonisba when she entered the room. Sofonisba curtsied. One of the three men approached, smiling.

He slowly circled her as if inspecting a new piece of art. "Señorita," he nodded, "who have we here addressing her prince?"

Startled, she curtsied again. "Your Majesty, I am Sofonisba Anguissola, from Lombardy. I am here to serve as the queen's lady-in-waiting."

"Lady Sofonisba, from the Italian territories. Please rise. Welcome to my father's court. I am Prince Carlos, and these are your new sisters." He motioned to the Spanish ladies, who curtsied in response. The prince's two comrades stepped forward. "My brothers, Don John of Austria and Prince Alessandro Farnese — also of the Italian territories."

The two young men looked Sofonisba up and down. She curtsied again. "Your Graces."

"You must be the painter who studied with Michelangelo. We were acquainted some years back at my family's court in Parma," Alessandro Farnese said. She remembered Alessandro as the young boy at the side of the Duchess of Parma three years prior, when he seemed to copy his mother's every move. Now taller and less baby-faced, Alessandro Farnese was a dashing young man budding with confidence.

"I must admit that I only corresponded with Master Michelangelo, I did not actually—"

"A woman painter, how unusual." The third young man lifted her hand near to his mouth for an air kiss. "I am Don John, and I will look forward to knowing you better, my lady."

"Ladies," Don Carlos announced, "we will rejoin you lovely beauties after the ceremony."

As the three exited, Madame de Vineux appeared with eight other ladies in tow, all speaking French. With the Spanish ladies in the rear of the room and the French ladies entering, Sofonisba stood between the two groups like a knot in the center of a bow.

"Ready yourselves, ladies" Madame de Vineux clapped her hands. "We must prepare for our formal introductions."

They were taken to a receiving hall to be presented to their new queen. The French and Spanish ladies-in-waiting chatted in their native tongues. Sofonisba roughly interpreted their gossip. "Don Carlos is attractive in a way, but his physique is wanting and they say his personality is, too. His tantrums are the talk of court."

"I thought Don John was quite dashing."

"They say he is only half-brother to the king. He is a natural child — born of a peasant woman."

"The Italian prince is only a half too. His mother was a natural-born of the Emperor."

"Half-brother, bastard — no matter when you have the blood of the Holy Roman Emperor. Farnese's mother Margaret may have been born out of wedlock, but she is one of the most powerful women in all of Europe."

"Then why is she not here?"

"She's serving as the Governor of the Netherlands."

Sofonisba thought back to her time with the Duchess of Parma who was too insecure to lend Sofonisba her patronage.

"They say that Prince Farnese is one of the king's favorites."

"Someone to make peace with, then."

"I hope to make more than peace with him. I can't wait to celebrate after the banquet."

Court did not sound much like the convent her father expected.

Chapter 12

Nuptials: Guadalajara, Spain January 29, 1560

The balls of Sofonisba's feet screamed from pain after two hours of standing in wait for the ceremony procession. It didn't help matters any that her bejeweled shoes had high-heels, the new fashion introduced by the bride's mother, and were stiff from recently being dyed, pinching her toes together. Her hipbones became sore holding up the weight of the heavy pearled gown. The air seemed to evaporate in the crowded room making Sofonisba nauseous. She swayed a bit, but caught herself, praying she would not pass out. Then a breeze swept in as the main doors opened, and Sofonisba gulped for breath, her gasp muted by trumpets.

Velvet and damask rustled. The procession entered the receiving hall, led by the king's son. Courtiers kneeled. As Prince Carlos passed, Sofonisba peeked up and saw that his eyes were fixed on the throne ahead of him. There seemed to be a complex soul in that body, if only one day she could render it.

Next came the king's widowed sister, the Princess Juana of Portugal, then Don John of Austria, and finally Prince Alessandro Farnese.

Sofonisba followed the lead of Madame de Vineux and stood up after this first group. She lifted her gaze, and she thought she saw Don John wink at her. Then she heard the lady two down whisper, "Maria, he winked at you."

"I saw that, Juana. Tonight we will enjoy the banquet."

"Here comes my relation," the one called Juana said. "As the Cardinal of Burgos, my uncle takes precedence over the rest."

"Uncle, Juana?"

"A distant uncle. Still, he's the most influential Spaniard after the royals — ahead of Alba, you see." She waved a pinky finger toward her relation.

"I heard he had to pay for the precedence," Maria said.

"Shhhh," Madame de Vineux interrupted.

After the Cardinal of Burgos, the Dukes of Alba, Infantado, and Veragua strutted toward the royal dais. The cardinal's ornate golden vestments were almost overshadowed by the dukes' diamond and pearl trimmed damasks, but not quite. The Duke of Alba and the Cardinal of Burgos each seemed to be jealously guarding his proximity to the king. Only they had been privy to the king's negotiations for determining precedence at the wedding celebration. There had been gossip aplenty. Alba had argued based on the stature of his ancient house and his record. The cardinal had argued for the stature of the equally old house of Mendoza and his holy role officiating the royal union. The king alone made the final decision, to the benefit of the house of Mendoza and the Cardinal of Burgos. Some around the king whispered, wondering why the cardinal continued to retain his disfigured lackey whose unsightliness offended their sensibilities. They gossiped that the cardinal flaunted his servant as graphic proof of his personal sacrifices in battle on behalf of the crown. Why else would he keep the invalid?

When the procession reached the front of the receiving hall, the room went silent. The courtiers froze in their places. The ache in Sofonisba's feet and back returned. Her queasiness returned too. She felt again as if she might faint. The trumpets sounded, longer this time, until the veins of the trumpeters' necks looked to burst. The king and his fourteen-year-old bride appeared at the entrance. Sofonisba held her breath. She forgot the pain in her feet.

The courtiers kneeled. The royal couple proceeded slowly down the center aisle hand in hand. As the monarchs neared Sofonisba, she could finally see the emaciated new queen, a child wed in a foreign land, her father killed at tournament honoring her — the poor thing was wasting away. The royal couple settled onto their thrones on the riser.

The master of ceremony stepped forward. "His Royal Majesty Philip II, the King of Spain, and Her Royal Majesty Isabel, Queen of Spain." The assembly broke into spontaneous applause for the newlyweds. Sofonisba found herself choking back a lump in her throat. She felt a closeness to Isabel already, even though the two had not yet met.

The master of ceremony motioned to the ladies-in-waiting who stood to the right of the queen, indicating first the Spanish ladies. "For service to Your Royal Majesties, we present Doña Isabel de Castilla, Guarda mayor."

Madame de Vineux winced at the announcement that Isabel de Castilla would be the new Guarda mayor. Doña Isabel was escorted before the queen and curtsied to the floor.

The new queen greeted her, "With pleasure I receive you, Doña Isabel."

Next the master of ceremony presented the young lady who boasted that the Cardinal of Burgos was her uncle. "For service to Your Royal Majesties, we present Doña Juana de Aragon." Sofonisba noticed the Cardinal of Burgos pursing his lips to contain his obvious pride in his relation.

Doña Juana was followed by her friend Maria. "For service to Your Royal Majesties, we present Doña Maria de Padilla." The friends cast a quick look at each other, giddy to be starting their new positions together. The master of ceremony announced each of the eight Spanish ladies-in-waiting by name and title and then turned to the French ladies.

"For service to Your Royal Majesties, we present Madame de Vineux," and on he went down the line of eight French ladies-in-waiting.

After introducing the Spanish and French ladies, he looked up at Sofonisba, then down at the card in his hand, and then up again at Sofonisba, furrowed his brow, and said simply, "Sofonisba Anguissola, Cremonese." Blushing, she approached the royals and curtsied. No title; her official introduction was that of a peasant from Cremona. She was glad her father didn't join for the trip after all.

"Rise," the queen commanded Sofonisba with a smile. "My mother told me about you. You are a painter, yes? You studied under masters — with Master Michelangelo, no?"

"Yes, Your Majesty," Sofonisba said, relieved the queen did not seem offended by her lack of title. She did not correct the queen's reference to Master Michelangelo.

"I studied the technique of drawing, under Master Clouet in Paris," the queen said, nodding. "I look forward to your company, Doña Sofonisba."

Sofonisba blinked when the queen afforded her a proper title of respect. That simple correction to her name cemented her love for the queen.

Then the king turned toward Alba standing to his left, one step down on the riser.

"Don Alba, this is the young prodigy you discovered in Cremona — the one with the bold father," the king said, nodding toward Sofonisba.

"Yes, Your Majesty, I am honored to confirm it."

Sofonisba let out an imperceptible sigh of relief. Her temples pulsed. She curtsied once more, but inside she screamed in gratitude: Grazie, Dio. They approve!

Sofonisba was presented to the widowed Princess Juana of Portugal, King Philip's half-sister, who looked to be exactly Sofonisba's age. She was brought to the three gallants, Don Carlos, Don John of Austria, and Alessandro Farnese who abandoned their earlier flirtations. Dignified and composed, the three princes nodded respectfully to her.

She came before the Cardinal of Burgos who took his cue from the royals' evident acceptance of the Italian lady painter. "Señorita, the pleasure is mine." He nodded respectfully.

When she was brought to the Duke of Alba, he beamed. "As your father welcomed me to your region, let me welcome you to ours." He lifted her hand for a courtier's kiss and guided her to the man on his right, the Duke of Infantado, castle owner and official host. Sofonisba read no disapproval on any of them. They each took their lead from the king and queen and welcomed her. She maintained her prim smile, but inside she was ecstatic.

After the primary introductions were concluded, the assembly was directed into a large dining hall where the ladies-in-waiting were interspersed among the guests at banquet tables while the king and queen sat separately on the dais. Sofonisba was seated between a Spanish nobleman on her left side and her cousin Ferrante on the right. She relaxed in the presence of her cousin and the luxury of speaking in Italian for the first time at court. "Ferrante, I have to tell you what happened after you left me. I feel like a brute. I laughed at an invalid."

"What are you talking about?"

"I got lost in the palace and came upon this one-legged man. He was fuming from dropping a chest on his good foot. I laughed at him, Ferrante! I feel like such a strega."

"So what, Cousin? He's just a servant. You are a grand dame at court. You get to laugh at inferiors now."

"Hardly a grand dame, Ferrante. Did you see all the dukes and cardinals? Anyway, my parents didn't raise me to be a person who laughs at the less fortunate."

"You are in the queen's circle now. Courtiers have been sidling up to me all day. You look lovely tonight, Cousin. Relax. Try to enjoy your debut into the most powerful royal court in Europe."

Sofonisba sat up straighter and took in a huge breath, turning toward aromas beginning to waft into the enormous hall. The service doors opened, and a fleet of servants appeared with trays of food. Sofonisba hadn't eaten all day, a first in her lifetime. She could not recall a time in Italy, unless she was sick, when she ever missed a meal. Even at Campi's studio they found time to break for the midday meal. Seeing the avalanche of food descending upon the dining hall was another first for Sofonisba. The peace treaty must have arranged the kitchen as well, so international were the foods. The banquet began with tasty varieties of spiced and pickled olives and Iberico, similar to Italian prosciutto.

"Mm. Nutty," Ferrante said.

"De bellota," the Spanish nobleman sitting on Sofonisba's left interjected, pointing to the meat poised in Ferrante's hand.

Bowls of steaming pasta were brought in. She took a big whiff and touched Ferrante's wrist. "Marubini in brodo, I'm quite certain it is." She waved her nose back and forth, taking in a scent of home from their Cremonese delicacy. "I wonder if we can credit Don Alba for bringing our dish to court?"

"You may be right," Ferrante said, nodding to Don Alba who was holding a glass in the air toward Sofonisba, toasting her silently from his chair.

After the pasta course, Sofonisba saw so many culinary firsts in quantity and character of food that she began to lose track of what they were eating.

A seafood course was served. They had fried anchovies, clams in white wine and garlic, eel roasted with lemon and thyme, fresh and fried oysters, crayfish, shrimp, muscles, lobster, and an immeasurable amount of cod in every preparation possible.

A variety of meats was passed next. There were sirloins of beef and veal, blood sausages in twenty varieties, roasted pork shoulder and pork loins with herbs, ribs of beef and pork roasted with apples, breaded pork slabs, pork stuffed with liver and fennel, venisons with garlic and peppers, venision ribs with onion, lamb chops roasted with garlic and rosemary, lamb chops roasted with thyme and pepper, mutton casserole, lamb stew with white beans and sausages, roast wild boar with garlic, clove, and fennel, and wild boar sausages. For fowl, they sampled a bird from the New World called a turkey, plus chickens, partridges, quails, geese, and guinea hens with all manner of sauces and sides, including colorful roots from the New World called potatoes, which the courtiers politely avoided.

Because it was King Philip's favorite, the most plentiful dish of the banquet was a simple baked pimento from his New World stuffed with cod and dripping with olive oil. Sofonisba had been so hungry from not eating all day that she had too much Marubini in brodo and then couldn't maintain the pace of the courtiers who seemed to have bottomless stomachs.

Servants poured more wines that night than Sofonisba had seen in her lifetime. She tried to be disciplined, but it was impossible not to imbibe, so very many toasts were offered for the new couple. While the court dined, singers entertained.

Oh, be content that I lament.
I cannot be silent for long.
My castaway desires are crushed by torrential waves.
Oh, be content that I lament.
I believed I would serve a ready joy.
But only a lunatic believes it!
Oh be content that I lament.
I cannot be silent for long.
Even the floods of storms speak for us.
Other clouds roar for them and teach us to beg for help,
And the lips of the wound, while silent,
resonate with pity.

"You know what our singer means with his oh, oh, oh and his castaway desires?" Ferrante paused and rolled his hand. "The torrential waves and the service of ready joy." Ferrante batted his eyes and fanned his fingers. "The lips of the wound, silent but resonating." He made a fist and pumped it up and down. "The symbolism of the piece does not escape you, does it? Even the fourteen-year-old bride understands." They looked in unison at the queen on the dais who fidgeted on her throne.

Sofonisba blushed. Then the Spanish nobleman next to them interjected in flawless Italian, "Of course, the union still needs to be consummated. There is no marriage without it. We should all be happy that our king is blessed with a beautiful bride." Sofonisba's blush turned to mortification.

Consummation of this marriage was hard for her to contemplate. Isabel was so young and wispy. Philip was more than twice her age, but at thirty-three, it was not his age that made him so much older than she, but circumstances. He had already buried two wives. The first he loved, the mother of his son Don Carlos. The second, Queen Mary of England, he barely knew, but her death burdened his soul nonetheless. While the king was not unhandsome, he had aged much since the day he toured Cremona, as if each passing year were a decade. The deep worry lines on his face seemed to contrast as starkly to the young queen's as Andrea Doria's face contrasted with Sofonisba's. In her heart, Sofonisba wished the waifish young princess could have a prince like the Philip who had paraded Cremona years back. Poor young queen. Just lost her father, too. Sofonisba's sympathies made her miss Cremona, and her own father. And Sofonisba was moved with devotion for her new queen.

The music changed from soft ballads to La Gagliarda. It was time for dancing. Heads turned as the guests looked at each other wondering who would be the first to venture onto the floor. Not a soul stepped up. Every last over-stuffed, drunken guest sat paralyzed, intimidated to be the first. The awkwardness was palpable. Heads stopped turning as if courtiers cowered from the honor of being selected. The music continued while the guests hesitated.

"Let's go, Cousin," Ferrante commanded, pulling Sofonisba up by the hand.

"Ferrante, wait, no—"

Pretending not to hear, Ferrante led Sofonisba onto the dance floor before all the courtiers. "This isn't my place," she whispered as he pulled her to the center.

"It is, Cousin. Understand?" He held his hand in position. She had no choice but to match his motion. She tried to sweep a loose curl off her face. She wanted to laugh and cringe both. She saw the courtiers in her peripheral vision smiling primly. Enjoying or mocking? Ferrante was a good dancer and Sofonisba followed his steps gracefully. She remembered her tutor's lessons in formal dance and his admonition that it was a necessary part of a proper education.

As one song blended into the next, other courtiers came to the floor. Sofonisba curtsied to Ferrante and motioned for them to go back to their table. "Ferrante, could you have given me some warning? A curl of my hair was falling in my face!" She half-laughed, half-scolded, feeling thrilled by the dance and exhilarated by its unexpected success.

"You looked beautiful, Sofi. It's pretty, that one curl coming down."

Still breathing hard, Sofonisba tried to regain her composure. "I want to be taken seriously here, Ferrante. Appearances are crucial." As she spoke these words, she thought she heard Doña Juana at the end of the table, " . . . the Cremonese who paints." Her words were spit out more like an insult than a description. Sofonisba turned and saw Juana talking to her friend Maria. They both looked at Sofonisba. She recognized the look on their faces. It was not unlike her sister Lucia's when Sofonisba was summoned to Spain, or to Campi's studio, or to one of the regal courts: jealousy. She turned back to Ferrante, but he had disappeared. She glanced around and spotted him already across the hall, addressing a pretty young Spanish woman.

As Sofonisba tried to compose herself, a middle-aged gentleman and a much younger woman approached. Sofonisba did not know him, but she recognized the squint of his eyes. He looked as jealous of her as the Spanish ladies did after she danced. Had he wanted to be the first to dance?

"Permit us to make your acquaintance," he said, bowing only slightly. "I am Alonso Sanchez Coello, King Philip's *official* court painter, and this is my wife Louisa Reyates Coello." The women nodded to each other. Coello interrupted their greeting. "You must be proud of your grand spectacle at court, dancing before them all." He waved his hand vaguely about the room. "I understand you dabble in paint. How interesting for a woman. Perhaps you can entertain the queen while you ladies have your little outings — paint some pretty flowers?"

Sofonisba forced a smile, ignoring his condescension. She had no desire to start on the wrong foot with the court painter, and she was all too familiar with artists' competitiveness. At Campi's studio, the artists who condescended most ardently were usually the ones who copied what she was doing. "I am most honored to make your acquaintance."

Without any further conversation, Alonso Sanchez Coello turned on his heel, bringing his wife around with him, and headed for the exit.

That one would be a thorn in her side, she told herself. It would be a long time before she and Coello traded ideas the way she had with Moroni, Giulio Clovio, or Bernardino. Would he ever realize their shared connection in the world of *invenzione*?

It was not until well into the night that she found her first opportunity to exit the festivities and make her way to the communal room where she and the other ladies-in-waiting resided. She still hadn't found her drawing kit. Drawing had always helped her fall asleep after a long day, and this had certainly been a long day. But a simple sketch was impossible without her kit. Sofonisba remembered the charcoal she had seen earlier in the other wing of the castle. She took a candle off the wall and retraced her steps as best she could remember to find the room with the charcoal. She heard whispering along the way as drunken courtiers trickled back to their rooms together.

She came to the room with the charcoal and tried the handle. It gave way to her pressure. As quietly as the old hinges permitted, she pushed open the door, recalling that the charcoal was on the small table across the room next to the mattress. At the sound of rustling, she lifted her candle. As her vision adjusted, she saw two men, naked, one on the edge of the mattress facing her, the other on his knees, his back to the door. He had one knee, not two.

"Forgive me," she blurted, turning on her heel, slamming the door behind her. In the brightness of the candle's light, they were unmistakable: the Cardinal of Burgos and the one-legged servant she had insulted earlier. She had seen them clearly, and the cardinal, perched on the edge of the mattress, must have seen her as well. The fury on his face left no doubt.

Damned charcoal! She rushed back to the ladies' quarters, ignoring the painful squeeze of her high-heeled shoes as she sprinted across the cold stone floors. How she wished she had not seen that. What to do now? If only her father were here!

It wasn't just what she had seen. Relationships between men were not new to her. Her favorite fellow apprentices at Campi's studio were Giacomo and Paolo. Sofonisba had seen the way they touched each other when they thought nobody was looking and figured they were more than friends.

But what she came upon here was entirely different. She now possessed information she decidedly did not want. What did the Duchess of Parma say? Avoid possessing unflattering information about her betters.

The expression on the cardinal's face when their eyes met haunted her, how his countenance contorted from surprise to outrage, his eyes, nostrils, and mouth simultaneously widening and narrowing in that short second. There was no mistaking it: Sofonisba had discovered a forbidden relationship, heretofore kept secret, implicating the man who was perhaps the highest ranking individual outside of the royal family.

All excitement from the evening melted into dread. She prayed it would be one illusion she could gloss over in green background and cover up with a heavily cloaked noble sitting conventionally in his library. She vowed to make her next pieces as conformist as possible. But tomorrow she would have to face the Cardinal of Burgos, of the house of Mendoza, who just hours before performed the marriage of the King of Spain to his new queen as dictated by international treaty.

Having lain awake until dawn, Sofonisba woke up late to find the suite empty. There were over a dozen ladies sharing her room and thousands of servants at the castle, and apparently not a soul realized that she had overslept. As she batted her eyes to force herself awake, Sofonisba recalled last night's intrusion. It was not a dream and was not imagined. This situation with the cardinal was real. She would just have to pretend she had seen nothing. The church bells began to sound and Sofonisba realized she was expected at the cathedral for the Mass to celebrate the new couple. She was failing miserably at court. Could she still go home?

She dressed quickly, a difficult feat with her new damask dress, laden with silver and jewels. She looked in the glass to examine her reflection and was frightened by the bags under her eyes. She steeled her nerves and rushed to the cathedral. She was too late. The queen's ladies had already proceeded up the aisle to their appointed positions. The royal procession was organized according to social precedence, and she had no chance of inserting herself into the line without causing a stir. All she could do was to join the end of the procession, take an available seat, and hope for a discreet opportunity to reconvene with the other ladies-in-waiting.

Presiding over the Mass celebrating the new couple was the Cardinal of Burgos — his back to the congregation, oblivious to Sofonisba's tardy entrance. When the time came to go to the altar to receive communion from the cardinal, Sofonisba could no longer hide her out-of-rank position; she was clearly not among the ladies-in-waiting as she was supposed to be. The last thing she wanted was to be conspicuous. She prayed fervently as she proceeded up the aisle to the cardinal. She gazed at his vestments, not simple red velvet like the cardinals wore in Italy, but rather a cape embroidered in gold telling whole narratives in the stitching: the Annunciation of the Immaculate Conception, the Nativity, the Crucifixion, the power of the house of Mendoza.

When it was her turn for communion, Sofonisba looked up to receive the host and glimpsed into the cardinal's eyes as he delivered the holy bread to her lips. His scowl accused her. Scorn was evident in the twitch of his lips and the narrow slit of his eyes. Her mouth was parched. The Eucharistic bread stuck to her tongue like sawdust.

She returned to her position in the rear of the church, where she remained for the duration of the Mass contemplating her transgressions. She had indiscreetly roamed the castle. She was wrong to venture beyond the ladies' quarters. Wrong to trespass on the cardinal's autonomy and thus his authority. The expression on his face when he offered the host told her she violated his honor.

She found the opportunity to slip into her place among the ladies-in-waiting during the recessional. Sofonisba snuck in between the eight French ladies-in-waiting and the eight Spanish ladies-in-waiting, happy now to be the knot in the center of the bow. She vowed to stick close to them.

Later in the day, her cousin sought her out. "Ferrante, it's so good to see a familiar face. Much has happened."

"You know the servant you laughed at?" Ferrante asked, "You must have truly hurt his feelings, Cousin. I saw him riding away from court with a few bundles." Sofonisba blanched, fearing the servant was sent from court because she discovered him with the cardinal. Ferrante misinterpreted her reaction.

"You are too humble, Sofi. People at court relish the opportunity to humiliate their inferiors; it proves one's importance. Don't be so severe with yourself. All you did was laugh."

But that had not been all. She felt responsible for the servant's dismissal but wasn't sure she should confess what she had seen to Ferrante. "How will he manage without his post with the cardinal — and with his infirmity such as it is? He won't again secure such a coveted post. What trials will the deformed man face out in the world?"

"Why such concern over a servant, Sofi? He's not your problem. He must have a family somewhere that will take him back. He probably has some little peasant plot to return to. He is of no importance and will be forgotten now that he's gone from the grandeur of court. Don't fret over him."

Sofonisba wished it were she who was returning home. Could she go back with Broccardo and Ferrante on their return voyage? She knew they would remain at court for the rest of the month. That would give her enough time to come up with an explanation for why she needed to return. She would simply say, "Thank you. I kiss your hand" and go home to focus on her work and leave this complicated life to the courtiers who seemed to relish every bit of it.

Chapter 13

Toledo Santo

As soon as she thought it, Sofonisba knew that going home was not an option. Her pride would not let her prove correct the many who scoffed that a girl wouldn't last. Her goal of painting the king tore at her. And she couldn't shake an image of her father leaving the house to go inform the decurions that his prodigy came home empty-handed.

She was spared any contact with the cardinal in the days following the wedding festivities. Her path did not intersect with the cardinal's, and he came nowhere near the women's quarters. Still, she imagined him lurking in every corner. She knew she had not done anything wrong, exactly, but she should not have been so driven for that charcoal.

Was my obsession the sin of pride?

She tried to occupy herself with her duties. The other ladies-in-waiting seemed to have been groomed for court life since birth. They interjected a perfect twist of phrase, or gestured at the right moment, and Sofonisba did not. Nor did she have any natural allies, unlike the competing camps of Spanish and French ladies who bonded together, vying for the queen's favor. Queen Isabel seemed buoyed by the rivalry — even encouraged it — posing a topic first to the French ladies, then to the Spanish ladies, seeming to judge her favorite responses, like a game.

The tension between the two camps exacerbated Sofonisba's loneliness, making her feel like an oddity in the quest for
the queen's attention. She wrote home as often as she could,
correspondence being her best companion. If only she had her
art kit.

The king was no replacement for her father. He hadn't given
her so much as a nod since her formal introduction. She saw
him only at a distance, either attended by the cardinal or the
Duke of Alba, one or the other always at his heel. It was doubt-
ful that the king, now her official guardian, knew or cared about
her transition at court.

Alba sent Sofonisba a short note promising his undying loyalty, but she rarely saw him. No word from her escorts. Broccardo was busy making deals at the king's court. Ferrante was
chasing deals — and chasing maidens.

Two weeks passed before Sofonisba heard from her cousin
again. He tracked her down after morning prayers, a roll of documents under his left arm that poked her side as he kissed her.
His right arm was behind his back.

"Where have you been? I haven't seen you since the wedding." Her tone was more annoyed than she intended.

"Dear Cousin, I'm so happy to find you." He pulled his hand
from behind his back and held out to Sofonisba her art kit, missing since their last stop on the road.

"Ferrante! Bless you! Where?"

"It was shoved into one of my bags when we arrived in Guadalajara. I'm sorry. I've been too busy to get it to you. I've been
making some important connections here." He patted the roll
of parchment under his arm. "Why are you not busy preparing
to depart?"

"Are we going on an outing?"

"You don't know? Sofi, you are not maximizing your court
potential. You should be at the center of information — the

entire court is transferring to Toledo. Broccardo and I are returning to Lombardy."

"I knew you were set to return to Lombardy. I didn't know I was moving."

"The court can't lean on the Duke of Infantado indefinitely. Toledo is the king's own. I'm sure you will love it, Cousin. He has palaces throughout Castile. Expect to tour them often. The royal court moves around a lot to outpace the plague." She winced. "Don't worry, Sofi. You are in the prime of your life in the jewel of Europe. What's the matter? You do not seem happy."

"Ferrante, I have no friends here. I miss my family. And I'm living with this secret—"

"What about those beautiful ladies with whom you spend your waking hours?"

"They huddle with their own, Ferrante. I feel alone."

"You're here to attend to the queen, Sofi, so why don't you? She is far from her home, too, and a young girl—and the circumstances of her father's death, jousting in honor of her wedding, wearing her favor—I heard she was in the front row when he was lanced to death."

Sofonisba inhaled. "The poor girl."

"And you miss your father. Maybe you should try to engage Her Majesty as a friend, Sofi. We all saw how sweetly she smiled at you during your court introduction."

"Ferrante, there is something I have to talk with you about and it has to be totally confidential. I came upon something—"

"Ah, Your Grace," Ferrante interrupted her as the Duke of Alba appeared around the corner.

"Dear charge!" The duke smiled at Sofonisba. "I regret that the time has come for you to say farewell to your entourage." Turning to Ferrante, the duke gestured outward, inviting him to stroll. "Shall we discuss some details before your departure, noble sir?"

Ferrante shot Sofonisba an apologetic look over his shoulder as the duke ushered him away, leaving Sofonisba still burdened with her transgression, not knowing where to confess it.

At least she now had her art kit. She squeezed its supple leather and imagined holding her sister Elena's hand on the way home from Campi's studio.

As Queen Isabel and her ladies were leaving morning Mass at Infantado's chapel the next day, the cardinal approached them. "Your Majesty, I am your humble servant." He bowed low as her ladies followed and greeted each one with a polite nod. "Madame de Vineux, lovely to see you. Doña de la Cueba, may I kiss your hand." He addressed the French ladies, "mademoiselle," a nod here, "madame," and the Spanish ladies, "señorita," a nod there, "dama."

Sofonisba fell to the back of the line, lingering in the chapel in the hope of evading the cardinal, but he did not budge from his post. All she could do was follow in line and try to appear to be praying, which, in fact, she was. The cardinal's steely gaze shot straight through her. He did not address her at all, not as mademoiselle, madame, signora, or dama, not as "painter" or "the Cremonese," but his eyes spoke revenge.

The day after, as the ladies-in-waiting were strolling the garden, the cardinal passed by and greeted each lady by her title then spat "painter" at Sofonisba. She winced and cast her eyes to the ground, his spittle warm on her cheek. The cardinal had been calling her "painter" all around court, not as in "brava, miracola, virtuosa, like Leonardo," but rather like "lowly, untitled, Cremonese who paints." He was shaping her reputation in very few words. The insults felt doubly cruel: he belittled her as a craftsman while she had no chance to paint at all.

She feared his manipulations were beginning to take root. As the ladies-in-waiting were rolling the queen's hair ribbons in preparation for the move, the cardinal's relation Juana de Aragon held out a red ribbon to Sofonisba. "Here, painter," she ordered. Soon others began to address her simply by her given name or "painter" rather than "señorita" or "doña."

The day before the court was set to depart, Sofonisba received a note from Broccardo asking her to meet him in the garden after the midday meal so that he could say his farewell. She wasted no time getting there, anxious not to miss the chance to connect with her family friend before he departed. She ran up to him and gave him a tight embrace, clinging to him until she sensed his discomfort.

"I apologize for being so forward, Broccardo. I am so sad to lose you and Ferrante." Tears welled in her eyes.

"Sofi," he said tenderly, putting his fingers to her cheek.

She put her hands on top of his, feeling the reassurance of a trusted friend. How could she tell Broccardo about the cardinal? "Who will I turn to when you and Ferrante leave me?"

"I'm sorry I must go," he said, touching a finger to her chin. "I have business in Lombardy now that I've secured the king's backing on certain issues. I will sing your praises at home, cara. And," he hesitated, "if you need me to, Lady Sofonisba, I will return in a moment's notice." A tiny rim of water filled his eyes now. "If you just say the word, all that is mine, is yours." He gave her hand a light kiss.

She was touched by his sweetness. "Broccardo, I'll miss you. Please return soon. I will welcome your news from home." She embraced him affectionately, comforted by his familiarity. He was the first to pull away. He picked a pomegranate blossom dangling from the garden and handed it to Sofonisba.

"And I you." He touched his chest, bowed, and then turned from her and disappeared around the corner.

Sofonisba did not dwell long on Broccardo. She wanted a private moment with Ferrante to share the burden of her secret, but courtiers were everywhere, readying for the move. Her only chance to speak with him was very public, leaving no opportunity for confidences. "Please tell Mother and Father how well adjusted I am here." She lied. She could not bring herself to say anything that would worry her parents more than they undoubtedly already suffered.

With Broccardo and Ferrante gone, Alba would be her only champion. And in the constant tug of war between the Duke of Alba and the Cardinal of Burgos to win the king's attention, Alba seemed to be losing.

A city of servants prepared for the court's transfer from Guadalajara to Toledo, the seat of the most Holy Order of the Inquisition. From the moment the move was announced, the cardinal flaunted his authority, ordering servants about and taking over duties normally reserved for the Duke of Alba's staff. The cardinal seemed to be preparing for more than a move.

Relocating the court was a massive affair. Packing the kitchen, the sleeping quarters, the stable, the chapel, each with its own royal specifications, and the sheer number of people to be transported, made the move no less than the march of an army.

The king and queen were to be preceded and followed by the royal guard. The cardinal's carriage would follow the king and queen, and the Duke of Alba was to go out third in the line of power. The duke greeted Sofonisba as courtiers arrived for the lineup.

"Congratulations, Lady Sofonisba! You are to ride in the royal carriage."

Sofonisba blushed at the unexpected honor. "Thank you, sir." She curtsied.

"No need to thank me — it was the queen's doing. She asked for you specifically to learn more about your training."

Sofonisba squeezed her art kit tightly.

"Until we meet again in Toledo," the Duke of Alba said bowing to her.

Sofonisba went to rejoin the ladies-in-waiting who were called next to be arranged into carriages. Her palms sweated as she contemplated reminding the king of that long ago day when their eyes locked as he paraded past her Cremona balcony.

The grooms called the ladies forward one by one, addressing each as "Mademoiselle" or "Dama" while they loaded them into their proper carriages.

"The Cremonese who paints," the groom announced as he motioned Sofonisba forward. She looked to the right and then to the left, confused to not see the royal carriage. The groom waved to her impatiently and gestured to a carriage further down the line.

"There must have been some mistake," she said. "I am to ride with the king and queen."

The groom's upper lip twitched. He cleared his throat. "That carriage has already departed," he said, pointing her again to the rear.

Sofonisba went back to the carriage indicated and took a deep breath as she settled herself inside the empty compartment. At least she would have plenty of space as she consoled herself. What had happened to her big honor? She held her loyal art kit tighter.

Then the carriage door was opened, and two couples were ushered in, scooting Sofonisba into the corner. The men wore black capes marking them as merchants. The older of the two greeted her first, "Good day," he said, nodding to Sofonisba. "Good day," echoed the woman next to him wearing an expensive but unadorned silk dress — the merchant's wife. The second couple nodded at her politely.

Sofonisba realized she had been assigned to a carriage with the merchants who supplied the court. She thought of her father's shop on Cremona's main piazza. She felt a cold sweat in the February chill.

As the carriage bumped along the road, she attempted to draw. She only managed rough lines but was happy for an excuse to avoid conversation. She kept her head down and focused on her work, all the better to eavesdrop on her fellow travelers. The merchants seemed to know more than she did about what lay in store for Toledo.

"I heard the king intends to host an Inquisition to celebrate his new marriage." The merchant nodded sternly. Sofonisba took a sharp breath. They didn't seem to notice.

"I heard that the Cardinal of Burgos is to serve as Grand Inquisitor," the second merchant said tugging on his ill-fitted doublet.

Sofonisba sat up with a jolt but managed to hide her horror. She prayed. She prayed, and she drew. She prayed for peace from the cardinal. She prayed to paint. She prayed that she could make her father proud. But sitting in the merchants' carriage, her dream of painting the king felt ludicrous. If the cardinal could contrive the insult of placing her with the merchants, what would happen in Toledo when his influence grew? And worse, was this the king she had dreamed of painting ever since she was little? Would he be a vengeful king instead of the dreamy prince she adored so many years ago on her balcony?

She remained silent, and her traveling companions let her be. If anyone recognized her as one of the queen's ladies-in-waiting, no one risked the impropriety of asking. With this complete lack of interaction between them, Sofonisba escaped having to explain her situation. With that, at least, the Duchess of Parma might have been proud. She knew she could not remain invisible for long. Upon arrival in Toledo, she would have to begin the humiliation of catching up with her proper circle, forcing her to acknowledge that she was made to ride near the back of the procession.

After three days on the bumpy road, the caravan reached the city walls of Toledo. The merchant next to the window pulled back its curtain, and a cloud of dust wafted into the compartment. Sofonisba coughed at the dust, then opened her eyes to a kaleidoscope of pedestrians outside, people from all walks of life, seemingly from every nation, province, craft, and language known.

The caravan stopped for fresh horses necessary to pull the carriages to the top of the steep hill in the center of town where the castle and cathedral were located. Protocol required starting with the royal carriage at the front, followed by the highest-ranking carriages, each one lumbering up the hill in proper order. After two or three hours, Sofonisba and her fellow passengers were still waiting to advance.

"Won't be much longer, gentlemen," a groom informed the passengers.

The merchant's wife rolled her eyes. "Excuse me, sir, do you not see the lady here? Can't you get us to the front of the line?"

"We will have you in before dark, madam," the groom said.

After an hour more, they were up the hill and inside the castle courtyard. The village of servants assigned to attend the caravan did not make its way back to the end of the procession where Sofonisba and her companions rode. She felt like she was experiencing her arrival in Guadalajara all over again, finding her inquiries met with deferrals. Fortunately, her bags were taken for her so she did not have to lug them around the ancient palace while she sought out her proper place. Just as in Guadalajara, Sofonisba worked her way down the halls, around the scurrying servants, snooping everywhere, praying she would not intrude upon someone's private moment.

She found her way to the upper level rooms where balconies overlooked the plaza below and received the coolest wind. Thinking this a likely setting for the ladies' quarters, Sofonisba opened the door to let herself in. The windows were shuttered closed. She heard a young girl crying quietly but could not identify who she was in the dark. Sofonisba's curiosity propelled her forward. She went to the window and opened the shutters to let in light, risking what she might find. Perhaps it was her need for personal contact that encouraged her to reach out to this solitary girl.

She turned from the window and was stunned to see young Queen Isabel. Of all the people at court, the queen was the one person who never managed to be alone, yet somehow she had evaded Madame de Vineux, the ladies-in-waiting, the servants, and all the ambassadors eager for her influence. Sofonisba approached the queen slowly and put a hand on her shoulder. This crying girl looked so young, not much older than Sofonisba's sister Europa.

The breach of etiquette startled the queen who looked up as if annoyed, but then softened into a smile seeing Sofonisba though her tears. "Dominus Illuminatio Mea." The queen broke the silence in Latin: The Lord is my light. Half prayer for guidance, half plea for attention, Isabel seemed to be inviting Sofonisba into her prayer. Thanks to Marco's tutelage, Sofonisba was proficient in Latin.

"I do not know how you were made to ride in the rear. That was not my intention at all. In fact, I requested that you ride in the royal carriage. Please forgive me that I was too preoccupied to see my request obeyed. I was hoping we could pass the journey together to discuss your work. I am tired of all the squabbling among the ladies." The queen took a quick breath, and her lower lip quivered. "I miss my mother. And I am broken-hearted for my father." She looked directly into Sofonisba's eyes. "Are you aware of what he is preparing here in Toledo?"

Sofonisba could not very well repeat the gossip of the merchants. "I heard the king plans to celebrate the royal marriage somehow."

"Celebrate? He plans an Inquisition! The king bragged of proceedings he oversaw last October in Valladolid. When a young nobleman pleaded for his life, our king responded that if his son were as wicked, he would carry the wood to the pyre himself. How can I love such a man as my lord and husband? And if, as he professes, he could willingly commit his own son to death, what protection will my children have if—" Queen Isabel abruptly stood up. "I ramble. Pay no heed. Your room is at the end of this corridor, Lady Sofonisba."

They both realized that the queen had said too much. She lost control of the restraint that governed her every word and movement; letting her guard down to Sofonisba for a brief moment, she betrayed her husband the king. Treason.

Sofonisba retreated obediently to the ladies' chamber, reminding herself of the Duchess of Parma's advice: avoid negative information of one's betters.

Now two secrets to forget.

Inquisition preparations began soon after they settled into Toledo. A tense atmosphere pervaded court. The ladies of the queen's circle did their best to appear proper, not permitting a stray lock of hair. Sofonisba heard only whispered snippets about what actually transpired: hundreds tortured. Teeth, eyes, fingers, and toes pulled from them. Skin put to fire, or torn from their bodies. Limbs stretched until they were pulled from their sockets. Organs removed while the suspect was still conscious. All prompted by anonymous tips and coerced confessions.

Afterward, the Cardinal of Burgos strode into the court's dining hall and confidently sidled up to the king. Before the entire court, the cardinal and his king were unified in their mutual dedication to total religious conformity throughout the land, a mission to purge from Spain every Protestant, Muslim, and Jew, every fornicator and sodomite. They proved their dedication with an ocean of blood.

Only Sofonisba threatened the cardinal's façade. He discredited her because she knew his secret. If only she could convince him that she was ready to forget about the whole unfortunate intrusion. Instead, feeling impervious from the Inquisition, the cardinal taunted his imagined nemesis.

"Painter," he bellowed across two tables so that everyone could hear, "I hear that you paint portraits. That must be a simple enough task for a woman — no need to trouble yourself with ideas behind the painting, as the masters must. Certainly, a full theme is best left to the rational minds of men."

On one level, this challenge was too much for Sofonisba to ignore. She could tick off dozens of women writers to prove the rational minds of women: Vittoria Colonna, Laura Cereta, Tullia d'Aragona. Marco had encouraged her to read them all. She could engage the cardinal on her own symbolism or the concetto and *invenzione* in every portrait. She could recite her conversations with Master Clovio, Master Moroni, and Master Campi to educate the cardinal on the full body of debate behind the discipline of portraiture, certainly among northern Italians.

But why? What if he trapped her into some statement about female reason, especially in the current court atmosphere?

Sofonisba lowered her eyes. "Of course, Your Excellency. I dabble in pretty pictures others might enjoy."

"I beg to differ." A melodious voice came up from behind her. "Lady Sofonisba, virtuous, ingenious, graceful Lady Sofonisba." Alessandro Farnese came to the defense of his countrywoman bowing low to Sofonisba. "My mother, the emperor's daughter, always regretted that she did not invite the Lady Sofonisba to reside in a permanent position at her court when she had the chance. As verses sing the praise of Lady Sofonisba throughout Lombardy, my mother realized she had squandered a valuable opportunity." Then he gave another exaggerated bow to the artist, as if to say, "At your service."

To a prince like Alessandro Farnese, a scuffle with the Cardinal of Burgos was like a duel of wits, one that he could enjoy simply for sport.

Sofonisba, on the other hand, knew that any repercussions for lack of decorum would fall on her. "Sir, you are too kind. I only aspire to do the queen's bidding."

Queen Isabel caught the whole exchange from her seat near the cardinal. She gave Sofonisba an almost indiscernible nod and distracted the cardinal with a change of topic.

Alessandro returned to Don Carlos and Don John to flirt with the other ladies-in-waiting.

In bed that night, the queen's private treason and the cardinal's hypocrisy spun around in Sofonisba's mind. She only wanted to paint. The duchess' advice could not have been more appropriate. She drifted off to sleep thinking of Campi's studio, wishing she could be there now discussing theory with her pals Giacomo and Paolo.

Chapter 14

Lady Painters: Madrid and Mantua 1560

Sofonisba had barely fallen asleep when Madame de Vineux clapped her hands before dawn. "Rise ladies. We attend Her Majesty shortly in the cathedral for Mass." Servant girls laid gowns on their beds as Sofonisba and the others sat up. "A gift from the Duke of Infantado," Madame de Vineux said, and a quiet aside to Madame de Rembere, "Happy to have us gone from his estate."

The gowns had high, square necklines, Spanish style. Their silks were overlaid with intricate laces. "No jewels," Madame de Vineux instructed the servant girls.

The queen emerged from her suites. "To the cathedral," she said, the same accent as Madame de Vineux. Her ladies-in-waiting followed her. Sofonisba dreaded Mass with the cardinal, but the radiant gold cathedral never failed to seduce her with its beauty. The craftsmen in Lombardy used gold to accent frames and doorways, or to highlight portals and pediments decorating buildings, but here the walls and statuary seemed to be entirely encased in it; gold climbing up to God. Sofonisba craned her neck, scanning the five stories of statuary stacked like golden cliffs. She followed the queen's lead and knelt before the altar.

Soon she was lost in her thoughts. The Gothic church stirred her imagination just like San Sigismondo did when she was a little girl. The cardinal forgotten, she was back in the world of *invenzione* from which all her paintings originated.

Sofonisba was happy to see a priest arrive in a simple linen frock, the queen's personal chaplain.

Queen Isabel waited for Sofonisba after Mass. "Lady Sofonisba," always *Lady* with Queen Isabel, "I have a favor to ask." The queen leaned close to Sofonisba and whispered in Latin—breaking her strict public regimen of speaking only Spanish since the day of the Inquisition.

"At your disposal, Your Majesty," Sofonisba responded in decent Latin. Once again, she offered up a Grazie, Marco.

"It seems that all this court can do is pray and gossip about the families scandalized by the Inquisition. We abound in news about the families ruined and those enriched off the confiscated property of the condemned—the cardinal in particular."

Sofonisba shuddered at his mention. Queen Isabel didn't notice.

"Sooner or later, one must occupy one's mind with knowledge, don't you agree, Lady Sofonisba? As your countryman Castiglione advises, the full life requires engagement in the arts, does it not?"

Relieved for the change of topic, "I agree with Your Majesty wholeheartedly. My tutor recited him often."

"Your tutor? Can you instruct as well as paint?"

"Yes, Your Majesty. I have five younger sisters and a brother in my family."

"Teach me." The queen's eyes sparkled. "Master Clouet was never my dear friend like you are, Lady Sofonisba."

Sofonisba crossed herself. "I will be most honored, Your Majesty."

Queen Isabel stifled a giggle with a finger to her lips. "You will be a vast improvement over Clouet — the bore."

"We will paint together *al vero*," Sofonisba said. The queen's excitement was infectious.

"I'll see to whatever you require, Lady Sofonisba. No one will dare to stop me."

When the queen and her train of ladies returned to the Alcazar, turning right to their quarters, Queen Isabel pointed Sofonisba to a corridor on the left. Sofonisba heard Madame de Vineux, the Camarera Mayor, and Doña Isabel de Castilla, the Guarda Mayor, revising bedding assignments for the ladies-in-waiting. In the continuous territory squabbles over precedence and vicinity to the queen, Doña Isabel sided with the Spanish ladies while Madame de Vineux typically sided with the French ladies. The Spanish ladies felt their familial connections and shared nationality with King Philip gave them precedence. The French ladies felt their kinship with the queen gave them the right to greater intimacy with her.

Sofonisba trailed Queen Isabel past the main floor suites. They found a quiet wing of the castle and stopped before a heavy door. Sofonisba pushed it open. They both looked left and right. Sofonisba gestured for the queen to enter. The room was spacious and had a southern exposure. "Your Majesty, I'll ready this marvelous space immediately."

Queen Isabel smiled. "Yes. Let's begin right away!"

They returned to the ladies' quarters, and Queen Isabel went directly to her private suites. Bedding negotiations were silent, for the moment. Sofonisba felt all eyes upon her — a blend of curiosity and envy. Juana de Aragon crossed her arms. Sofonisba took a chair in the communal parlor.

The title "lady-in-waiting" perfectly suited what they did much of their days: wait. They waited for the queen's command or any hint from her of what she might next want. They waited for the king's approaching footsteps to know when to disappear into the background. They waited for outside news. They waited for something, anything, to occupy their long hours waiting. Mostly, they filled their hours gossiping and feigning needle-point. Sofonisba could not wait to paint, if nothing else, to break up the monotony.

"Do you think the queen should be monopolized by *the painter*?" Juana asked the room. "Is it really quite proper for the Queen of Spain to be attended by the painter, *solely*?" Juana spat out the word solely. The others raised their eyebrows, but no one responded. "And we wait for her bidding." Juana pressed.

Queen Isabel returned to the parlor. "Lady Sofonisba, please join me in my private chamber." Sofonisba could not resist smiling at Juana de Aragon. The other ladies stared down at their needlepoint as Sofonisba followed the queen into her suites.

"I've been thinking of our new project," the queen said, patting a spot on the divan next to her for Sofonisba to sit. The queen's parlor overflowed with treasures. Portraits covered her walls — of her parents, Henry II of France and Catherine de Medici, of her sister Marguerite de Valois, and her brothers Charles and Fran-cis — along with masterpieces from her dowry that Sofonisba didn't recognize. Among them was a Botticelli, if her lessons from Marco were accurate. Then her jaw dropped.

Sofonisba walked up to a drawing — a pudgy-armed crying angel.

"My mother gave me this drawing to place in my future chil-dren's nursery, when I am so blessed. I love its innocence. It's a true work of Master Michelangelo — one of several renditions, I was told. My mother's agents acquired it in Rome not long ago."

Sofonisba turned around to the queen wide-eyed. "Your Majesty, I promise you — I can show you how to do that." Sofonisba simply could not break the dictates of modesty on such an incredible scale — the ultimate compliment: Master Michelangelo had copied Sofonisba's *Boy Bitten*!

"Let us return to our studio now, Lady Sofonisba," Queen Isabel said. "We will plan our décor right away." Isabel and her new favorite exited the queen's suite. The other ladies silently rose as the queen and Sofonisba crossed the parlor to the ladies' quarters.

They sat down after the queen and Sofonisba exited the room, but Sofonisba could still hear Doña Juana de Aragon break the silence. "My family *collects* art. We have Flemish and Italian pieces. We keep them in the family chapel. But we don't *paint* it ourselves."

Perhaps it was the nervous tension of the moment, but Maria de Padilla stormed past Sofonisba to spill her breakfast into the latrine. She had been nauseous lately.

Sofonisba did her best to get the new studio readied promptly. One afternoon when she was organizing materials, she thought she heard footsteps outside the door to the studio, but nobody knocked. When she heard footsteps again later that day, she hurried to open the door and saw Coello scurrying away, recognizable by his smock. It was the first time she'd seen the court painter since he introduced himself at the royal wedding banquet.

For much of the next two weeks, Queen Isabel spent most daylight hours with Sofonisba in their studio. One morning, the queen handed her a small package wrapped in red velvet. "Lady Sofonisba" — the queen clapped in anticipation, a huge smile on her face — "Open it!"

Sofonisba unwrapped the supple cloth to find two small glass vials, one with red liquid, the other with black. She held them up to the light.

"Colors from the new world!" Queen Isabel bounced with excitement. "I asked His Majesty to impose on that surly court painter of his. Master Coello has a storeroom in which my maid discovered great supplies of red and black colors. The king explained to me that the one is derived from a prickly pear found in his New World territories, the other from a special wood they find there. I thought we could enjoy them."

"Yes, Your Majesty, we shall. This is a precious gift. I thank you." Sofonisba smiled. A simple explanation for Coello's spying.

When Sofonisba and Isabel returned to the ladies' quarters, their fingers dirty with flecks of color, the queen announced, "My ladies, you shall all learn to paint. I wish for you to join me in lessons from the Lady Sofonisba."

Juana de Aragon's face became hard as stone. She said nothing until the queen went into her private suites. "It is one thing for the queen to indulge her interests with this painter. The queen reigns. Furthermore, she is married. How proper is it for an unmarried Spanish princess to do such — such — *work*? What right does this painter have to impose these indecorous expectations on a proper Spanish princess?" Then she turned toward Doña Isabel de Castilla, the Guarda Mayor. "Is it not your role to protect the ladies from such diversions from propriety?"

"It is not our place to criticize the queen," Doña Isabel said firmly. "Perhaps you should try to appreciate the queen's suggestion."

"I, for one, look forward to the lessons," Madame de Vineux said. Her conviction settled the matter. Madame de la Rembere y Viemes and Mademoiselle Ana de Riberac nodded in agreement.

The next morning, after the queen's toilet and wardrobe, a process that lasted the better part of two hours, she gathered her ladies. "This will be a good education for you and a happy way to pass your time, I am certain. Let us proceed to the studio." She motioned to Sofonisba to stand next to her and then smiled at them all, setting the tone. Each lady smiled back in unison, like sunflowers smiling up to the sun. The proud queen led the way to the studio, looking satisfied and invigorated.

She stopped before the door, gesturing for the others to enter as she remained in the corridor. "You are in my Lady Sofonisba's good hands, dears. I will return to inspect your progress later in the morning." With that, the queen left Sofonisba in charge of her court.

"Do any of you have experience drawing?"

They shook their heads. "Tsst," Juana of Aragon scoffed.

"Any requests for what you would like to learn?"

They shook their heads again. Juana held one palm out and looked at the ceiling.

Sofonisba decided to start the ladies with basic instruction for drawing a face. "Now then, please, ladies, if you could pair off and face one another, we will study how to divide the face into proportions from the top of the head to the eyes, the eyes to the nose, and the nose to the chin." She handed each a pencil and blank parchment. "Begin with an oval in the center of your page and divide it with a horizontal line and a vertical line like so. You will see that the bottom of the nose generally lies halfway between the brow line and the bottom of the chin."

The French ladies promptly began to experiment. "Voila," Ana de Riberac said, standing back to inspect her lines. Madame de la Rembere nodded approval at her neighbor's fledgling success.

"En Espanol," Madame de Vineux chided.

"May I please have a cloth with which to hold this disgusting charcoal?" Juana asked, scrunching up her nose.

"Of course," Sofonisba said, knowing as she handed Juana a piece of cloth from her side bench that it would smudge any line Juana drew.

Juana pretended to grasp her charcoal with the cloth but let it slip from her grip. It broke into a hundred useless pieces on the tile floor.

"Oops," Juana said, putting two fingers to her lips.

"Please, have another." Sofonisba maintained a prim smile as she handed Juana a new piece of charcoal.

"Did you say to draw a square, painter?" Juana asked.

"An oval, señorita."

At first, the Spanish ladies followed Juana of Aragon's lead. They were coy with their questions, fumbling with their materials, and impossibly slow. As the morning progressed, most of the other Spanish ladies forgot themselves and began to enjoy the diversion, even joking some with the French ladies. Juana maintained her resistance, sighing much of the time. Her friend Maria de Padilla copied her.

When they rested for their midday meal, Juana raced out of the studio, trampling the broken bits of charcoal around her on her way out, smudging a trail out the door that seemed to illustrate her feelings about the lesson. She went directly to her great-uncle, by marriage, twice removed, the Cardinal of Burgos.

"Tell the cardinal that his niece Juana of Aragon is here to see him," she demanded of the cardinal's secretary, who immediately stood to comply with her commanding stature.

Still, the secretary clarified. "Niece, señorita?"

"Close enough, just get him," Juana ordered.

She wasted no time on pleasantries. "Dear Uncle, it is my honor to serve our family name here at the court of our great king. Am I not expected, after all, to promote our family's interests? How can I possibly accomplish the family's objectives when I am subjected to these distasteful drawing lessons?" She nodded at the cardinal's confusion. "Yes. The queen has decided we must all take drawing lessons with the *painter.*"

"The painter?" The cardinal tapped a forefinger to his lips.

"Yes, the lady painter. And worse, shall I have to defer my natural precedence to the painter who occupies all the queen's time and attention? How can I possibly get close enough to the queen to be of any service to our family if the painter, of all people, is occupying the queen's time?"

"Drawing lessons." He repeated the words more to himself than his niece.

"Look at my fingers." She held up her right hand — a faint dusting of black from the charcoal.

The cardinal broke into a smile.

"I hardly see the humor, Uncle."

"Dear Niece, I am pained to see you disgraced like this, you, a princess of Aragon. The painter has not so lofty a rank, now has she?"

"Her family has some rank, not high, minor nobility at best, nothing like our family's pedigree."

"Then you should prove your superiority at all times and ensure that the lady painter is viewed in the proper light to accurately reflect her status. I, for one, do not see that she warrants a title. She is, as you say, a *painter*. I say that makes her more a servant than a proper lady-in-waiting, would you not agree?"

Believing she had the cardinal's support to take down the queen's new favorite, Juana rejoined the other ladies at the banquet hall for the midday meal. The French ambassador, the Bishop of Limoges, was speaking to Queen Isabel.

"With permission, Your Majesty, I shall write to the queen mother in Paris and have the supplies sent immediately. And if I may personally add without offending Your Majesty's modesty, Your Majesty paints as well as any master."

"You do me an honor by your compliments, sir. This pastime does make me happy."

Sofonisba sensed the redoubled efforts of Juana of Aragon and Maria de Padilla to sabotage the classes. A favorite trick was to drop brushes and things near Sofonisba's feet, apologize for the imposition, but then wait for her to pick up the item that fell. They continually addressed her by her first name or by spitting "painter." Once or twice, they forgot to include her in outings they arranged for the queen.

"Oh dear, she spends so much time in her studio, I did not think about her," Juana explained.

The queen did not seem to notice the slights, either because she was happily immersed in painting and did not listen to their banter, or because she was focused on her own mission to be the perfect Queen of Spain and Daughter of France at all times.

Sofonisba was grateful to be painting, and even enjoyed teaching, but could not deny the belittling effect of the insults.

The cardinal was more sophisticated in his methods. Like his niece, he persisted in denying Sofonisba a title when he addressed her and marginalized her at every opportunity. But more often, he asked questions that forced her to choose between her modesty as a lady-in-waiting and her competence as a painter. "How can a female possibly paint accurately, like a man, when she does not participate in the world as men must?"

"I paint what I see reflected in my sitters, Excellency."

As the winter months turned to spring, the experiment of teaching the ladies-in-waiting began to fade. One morning the queen announced, "Ladies, while I appreciate your progress in the art studio, I do not believe it warrants the distractions you make to Lady Sofonisba in her work, nor to me in mine. I have decided to locate a separate studio for you, permitting Lady Sofonisba and myself to work quietly in the primary studio."

Sofonisba looked around at her sister ladies-in-waiting seeing both relief and irritation on their faces. At least now she would not have to babysit them.

But the cardinal was unrelenting. "A female cannot reason like a man, therefore she does not have the capacity to create intelligently, never mind a masterpiece." Or, "God's calling for women is to reproduce. It is sin to stray from that calling. Thus, there is no place for women outside of the home, especially dabbling in vain arts — slovenly."

Sofonisba learned that he was to remain at court all spring long, after most courtiers departed to inspect their properties; his estates were smoothly run off the labor of his tenants and the administration of his local Bishop.

They fell into routines of Masses and meals and outings, and then hours and hours where she and the queen painted while the other ladies dallied in their makeshift studio or fiddled at needlework. Their formal art lessons were over, and Queen Isabel did not seem to care what they were doing, so happy was she to be painting individually with Sofonisba.

Sofonisba rose before dawn one spring morning to finish details on a piece she was preparing to send to Cremona as an Easter present for her family: a self-portrait — to reassure her family that she was fine. The portrait required one last touch of color. Timing was tight — she reminded herself that she had only a short time to work, dress, and present herself for Mass. Sofonisba was calculating how long it would need to dry before being handed over to the messenger. She raised her candle up to illuminate the studio. At first, she was concerned that the candle lighting was not right, and she would have to return midday for natural light. But her motivation to send something home propelled her. She became engaged in her work.

Sofonisba was so absorbed in placing just the right accent on the eyes — wanting to convince her family that things were going well for her — that the sound of church bells startled her. Mass. She was late again. She raced out of her studio and back to the ladies' quarters where her dress was laid out for her. Attendants were scurrying around, paying little attention to Sofonisba. She hurried to dress and managed to catch up with the others. She caught her breath and settled into the procession.

The Cardinal of Burgos was presiding, his back to the congregation as usual. His eyes never met Sofonisba's during the Mass. When it was time for communion, Sofonisba went to the altar with her hands in prayer, pointed devotedly up to heaven. She closed her eyes and opened her mouth holding out her tongue for the bread. She expected to feel the thin host. She waited for what seemed like eternity. Finally, she opened her eyes. She could not avoid the cardinal's accusatory stare as his eyes bulged at the sight of her tented fingers, darkened with paint. She had forgotten to scrub her hands.

Sofonisba instinctively looked down at her sullied hands, an admission of her guilt. She knew how it appeared: Lacking decorum! Imprudent! Disrespectful of the church! "A lady should keep her hands pure for prayer." Was this the sword on which her tenure at court would die? She prayed to be protected from the cardinal's wrath. He put the host on Sofonisba's tongue but did not make the sign of the cross over her. He moved on to the next person. No Blessing? Did it count as communion without the blessing?

Sofonisba left Mass in a state of anxiety. She remembered the road to Toledo and the expressions on her fellow passengers' faces as they discussed the Inquisition.

Her father's face flashed into her mind. She bit her lip to stifle her fears.

The cardinal had her where he wanted her. If she talked now, he could claim she was his enemy at court, an impious painter, falsely accusing him. She was petrified of the cardinal, but how could he know she would never tell on him, never gossip about what she saw? If only he understood how ready she was to forget all about her intrusion upon him and his servant!

The cardinal decided to plant a spy in anticipation of having to return to his territories for the summer. He needed an earpiece at court, but he had confided too much in his distant relation Juana of Aragon. After all, Sofonisba was a lady-in-waiting to the queen he was bound to serve, and Juana was too aware of his animosity toward Sofonisba — and too indiscreet — just like a woman — gossiping at every move. What if she suspected the cardinal's ulterior motive and chattered about her suspicions?

The cardinal had an immediate niece, Isabel de Mendoza, the daughter of his brother Pedro, commander of the battle in which the cardinal's dear attendant Martin lost his leg. Pedro de Mendoza was a hero. Surely his daughter would be awarded a vacant position in Isabel's court if one became available. The cardinal just had to find the right pretense to replace his distant relation, Juana of Aragon, with his niece, Isabel de Mendoza.

Sofonisba was painting in the studio when she was startled by a knock at the door. A messenger handed her a thin parchment. She gave the man a coin. He tested the metal between his teeth as she opened the letter and began to read. It was not from Cremona but from her sister at convent in Mantua.

My Dear Sofi,

I apologize for the long silence between us. I speak to you daily in my heart as if we were still little girls walking home from Campi's studio together. How often I wish I had your opinion.

I have corresponded inconsistently with the family over the years by necessity. At first, I was prohibited from writing by the rules of my novitiate. As soon as I was permitted the privilege of correspondence, I wrote like a mad woman to Mother solely, leaving myself no time or energy to write to you sisters.

However, for the past several years, it has been nearly impossible to write. The reason is not, as you might hope, that I have found peace with my position in life and enjoy the spiritual serenity I've always needed. Rather, Sofi, I have been far too busy to write, even while I think of you constantly.

Every night when I lay my exhausted body down, I wish to confide in you, Sister. Remember at Campi's studio when the others shushed us, called us whispering women? Remember how we vied for Campi's attention? In my mind, Sofi, we talk into the night, every night, but I am too tired to write when my numb body feels like stone. It is all I can do to discard my habit, change into a nightgown, braid my hair, and rinse in the basin of my tiny cell with water that I barely have the strength to bring up from the well.

Yet, it is also so exciting, Sofi. We work from dawn to well past sunset. In addition, I serve as administrator and teacher. When the local patrons come, I act as the primary tour guide and representative in the financial transactions. Our work is pious and also very profitable, Sofi, producing religious art for personal chapels. We have a ready market of families from all over northern Italy who want a religious piece from a sister's hands. The number of families desiring devotional art for their private chapels appears boundless. Our convent is becoming financially independent. Now we are always supplied with meat and cheese. We can eat well and still pay our exorbitant rents to the diocese.

Sofi, do you know how this all began? Father heard from his friend in Florence, remember the poet Annibale Caro, about a nun called Suor Nelli, an abbess of the Convent of Santa Caterina. Signore Caro owns a religious piece of hers and so do many of the elite of Florence.

Father heard the stories of Suor Nelli's success, and of course he thought of his poor daughter, torn from her education and her promising life as a painter to be sent off to the convent. I know with my full heart that Father feels undiminished guilt for sending me to the convent, especially so young. He expresses regret over the decision in every letter he writes. He badgered our abbess to permit such work in our convent. Once Abbess agreed, Father spread the word to his friends. Now we have an avalanche of commissions to fill.

Still, Sofi, is it heresy for me to wish I had the type of freedom you do? I can only imagine how wonderful it must be to have the court beckoning for your talent. Lucia wrote that you were the first to dance at the royal ball. You must be a bit overwhelmed by all the attention, but the excitement must keep you from feeling homesick.

And, Sofi, after all this time I must apologize. I know I often neglected you to dote on Minerva. Sometimes, the competition between the two of us riled me, and I needed distance from you. You were just that much better than I! But now I see you as my lifelong inspiration. I call out to you in my thoughts, and sometimes you appear in my dreams, always the same, I see you painting your self-portrait. I believe God is telling me to keep painting. Do you think so? Will ever we meet again?

Your loyal sister Elena, called Suor Minerva
Mantua, 1560

Sofonisba wiped a tear. If only Elena knew.

Dear Elena,

The fault for our long silence is mine as well, but I too speak to you in my heart daily. How I wish I were working alongside you. As hard as you labor, you are honored, and your passions are rewarded. I cannot say the same.

At court, I toil not so much with my paints and brushes as I do with whispers and even outright insults, yet I remain in the warm embrace of Her Majesty the Queen whom I serve with all my loyalty and conviction. Otherwise, I paint or draw every moment possible, so I should try to not complain to you who work so hard for your daily maintenance.

My prize here remains the opportunity to paint the portrait of His Majesty the King, even though I rarely see him and never talk to him. I fear my goal will be subverted by the conceits of this court, but I am determined to persevere as I promised Father that I would. My sisters here are no substitute for you in the least. I dream of you often too, always the same way: we are walking home from Campi's studio. You and I are always talking about our pieces. You are my muse.

Fondly recalling our shared childhood,
Sofi, Toledo, Spain

P.S. Please do not write Mother and Father that I am anything but happy here!

She walked her letter to the court courier, imagining holding Elena's hand as they walked home from Campi's studio. She could almost hear her young sister's voice telling her not to listen to the insults, to simply focus on the joy of her work.

Sofonisba handed her letter to the clerk along with a coin. She took a deep breath, swept a stray lock of hair into her cap, and stood tall before returning to the ladies' chamber to dress for that evening's banquet.

Chapter 15

The Prince, the Cardinal, and the Painter:
Spanish Court 1560

While the Lenten season had been a somber time at court, with spring came new stories about the three young princes. The sagas of their love affairs were becoming regular fodder for gossip. Even Sofonisba couldn't resist listening — and contrasting Don Carlos to his father as a young man touring Cremona. The king seemed so much more valiant and majestic at that age. Don Carlos was not like his father. He was a rascal.

Maria de Padilla returned to the ladies' quarters breathless with news. "Prince Carlos is injured." She panted to catch her breath. "I heard he was chasing a servant girl down some steps off the latrine. She must never have imagined the Prince of Spain would follow her there." Maria patted her forehead with a lace handkerchief. "Well, he did follow her, and they say he lost his footing in the process, slipped down the stairs, and hit his head on the edge of a trough. He is laid up in bed, and they cannot revive him. The king is in a rage! They say he is blaming Don John of Austria and Alessandro Farnese for not protecting the prince."

The court was in a state of suspense during the prince's illness. Sofonisba noticed a new restraint at court, like the days after the Inquisition in Toledo. Doctors administered leeches for ten full days, but Don Carlos' condition continued to deteriorate. When his fever and coma persisted, they called a Morisco doctor from Valencia. As an added precaution, the Duke of Alba arranged to have the embalmed body of San Diego de Alcala taken to the prince's bedside. The local saint was known for his healing powers.

Don Carlos recovered in the Morisco doctor's care. Spain officially celebrated, crediting the intervention of San Diego for the prince's blessed recovery. The king expressed his profound gratitude. "We shall beseech Rome to canonize our holy San Diego de Alcala, a heavenly reward for saving the life of the prince."

Sofonisba heard Maria's sobs early one morning. She heard Juana of Aragon's tirade later that afternoon. Four months after the royal wedding banquet, the signs of Maria de Padilla's shame were becoming clear, and Maria had to go. She would be removed from the queen's entourage and hidden away into a quickly arranged marriage to a local lord before her offspring arrived. Because the two were so closely associated, Juana of Aragon was removed alongside Maria de Padilla. The cardinal simply had to drop the innuendo to the king.

"It pains me, Your Majesty, to denigrate the honor of my own family, even if, in my defense, she is only a distant relation to my line. The shame that found Señorita de Padilla—" he paused. "I daresay my distant relation was complicit. I believe young Don John and Alessandro Farnese may have been corrupted by Juana's behavior as well. It is said around court that her influence precipitated the prince's injury." The king jolted almost imperceptibly. "Someone must have encouraged the damsel's hide and go seek games that led the prince astray," the cardinal said, "certainly not the princes Don John and Farnese."

King Philip cocked his head and waited for the cardinal to continue.

"We must be sure to protect the queen from any appearance of impropriety by her ladies. I will replace my compromised relation at once. May I suggest in her stead, the daughter of my brother, the commander Pedro de Mendoza, whose bravery at the battle of Saint Quentin, Your Majesty will recall, helped to bring such overwhelming defeat to our enemies?"

By the middle of May, the cardinal's niece, Isabel de Mendoza, the daughter of commander Pedro de Mendoza, replaced Juana de Aragon. An unassuming noblewoman, Estefania Manrique, supplanted the disgraced Maria de Padilla.

In time, the three princes resumed their sport. As soon as Don Carlos was fully back on his feet, he was bedding servant girls and seducing officers' wives, only more surreptitiously, until the court swung fully back to its vivacious self.

Sofonisba took note of how quickly the mores at court shifted, by month and by rank. She promised herself that when the time was right to return to her work, she would take no risks — no voluptuous Mary for a *Holy Family*, no *Chess Game* messages, state portraiture solely — perhaps with just a touch of symbolism. She stayed as close as she could to Queen Isabel.

The cardinal held a small reception to present his niece at court, announcing that he would remain with her until summer, plenty of time to acquaint her with court life. "And that I may attend to His Majesty," he added, bowing to King Philip. The cardinal's duties included a baptism for the infant daughter of the king's portraitist.

At midmorning, the cardinal found the painter Alonso Sanchez Coello at his easel, the artist's head tilted to the side, contemplating his current execution, a portrait of the king's sister, the Princess Juana. "Master Coello, sir," the cardinal interrupted the painter's reverie. "Forgive my intrusion."

Coello looked up from his canvas, startled to hear the cardinal — especially his civility. "Painter" was his usual. Coello tried to think of anything the cardinal might be investigating. Adultery? Sodomy? Who could charge him? He was faithful to his wife. He attended Mass. No heretical ideas. His portraits were conventional in the school of masters Mor and Titian. The king was about to stand as godfather to the painter's new daughter. What could the cardinal want from him?

"I need but a moment of your time, and then I will distract you no further from your worthy occupation. I admire your work, Master Coello. The court of a great king must have the finest court portraitist, one, I might add, who reflects the decorum of this court properly. One who will only glorify the court and not scandalize it with impropriety."

Master Coello soaked up the cardinal's new interest.

"I have a little concern, Master Coello, sir." The cardinal paused as he regarded the incomplete portrait of the king's sister. "If I may be so bold as to suggest that we share a mutual, shall we say, distraction, to our missions. One that threatens your domain and which may well tarnish the reputation of this great dominion."

Coello couldn't imagine anything he and the cardinal shared. The cardinal had vast wealth, while the painter scrimped to furnish a nursery for his child; the cardinal had no children to provide for, at least none recognized at court.

"I refer to your rival, and in certain ways mine, the lady painter." The cardinal's face remained expressionless.

Coello resented the new girl, but tarnish the reputation of mighty Spain? "I find the girl a nuisance, that is true, but I do not see how she rivals Your Excellency."

"I do not find it appropriate at this most Catholic court that a woman should practice her dilettante painting in such a public manner, traipsing about court, insisting noble Spanish ladies paint like cottage women, distracting them from their prayers, their service commitments, their duties — attracting them to vainglorious pleasantries while true Christian women carry on the duties of their sex."

Coello had rather liked Sofonisba holed up with the ladies-in-waiting or the queen. At least she was not poaching on his commissions for the king. Still, he feared Philip's eye falling on the girl's Lombard style. The idea grew on Coello that the cardinal's disapproval of Sofonisba could be useful to him. "How may I serve Your Excellency?"

"We need to prevent the girl from getting to the king. We must see that she is put in her place. Do you understand, Master Coello?"

Coello began to nod, then shook his head.

"I am to preside at your daughter's baptism. Because the king is standing as godfather, it is expected that you will host a banquet afterward. You control the guest list for your innocent daughter's party."

"Does not propriety dictate the list?"

"The queen has eight noble Spanish ladies and an equal number of French ladies who hail from the high nobility. If you, sir, feel it appropriate to exclude the painter from your daughter's holy baptism, I will not protest." The cardinal tipped his head to Coello. "Good day, sir."

Coello considered the dynamics — exclude the girl due to her insufficiently high rank and disreputable occupation? Hypocrite. And yet, was it not different for a man? The girl insults the natural order. And the king was his territory, the king's portrait his prize.

Coello informed his wife, late that night after supper. "We will spend handsomely on our daughter's baptism to honor our name."

"I am doing everything possible on a frugal budget," Señora Coello said. "I am content to wear a gown I already own, and we will use the family baptismal gown for our daughter. I have trimmed back the banquet to manageable courses."

"Don't go too far, Wife. Be sure to keep the table generous. We cannot risk appearing miserly. On the contrary, we must limit the guest list to only the most important people. Show it to me now so that I may inspect it." She handed him the list she had prepared and waited patiently for him to read and strike names.

"I'm sorry, husband, did you mean to strike the queen's lady-in-waiting?"

"Only the most important will be invited."

"Sir, she is usually in the queen's company."

"Would you like to question my decisions further?" Coello rose from the table, stretched his arms, and retired for the night. The baptism reflected Coello's hard-earned status. Guests would be treated to the finest culinary delights the Spanish empire offered.

At the banquet, the cardinal bellowed to Coello. "A fine day, nothing but the best. I appreciate your selective audience. Nobody disreputable from the queen's court."

Seated nearby, Madame de Vineux bristled. "Disreputable, Your Excellency?"

The cardinal glanced about, "No one here taints the name of our sovereigns, my lady."

"Correct, Your Excellency, the ladies of the queen's court are of finest distinction."

The cardinal said nothing, an insinuation hanging in the air. The effect was insidious. Courtiers spent the remainder of the occasion inspecting the room to discern who was not present, guessing whom the cardinal found disreputable.

"Of course, my uncle refers to the painter who spends her days at her dirty easel. Shameful!" Looking much like her predecessor Juana, Isabel de Mendoza twitched her nose indignantly. "And shameful of us for allowing it!"

It was not lost upon Sofonisba that she had been excluded from the baptism. The other ladies-in-waiting spoke of the Coello banquet for days. She tried to rationalize that it was Coello's competitiveness that kept him from inviting her. He showed none of Campi's, Moroni's, or Clovio's spirit of collaboration, nor even Michelangelo's.

But Isabel de Mendoza made it seem like something more when she echoed the cardinal over and over. "The Coellos are to be commended for their refined taste. How refreshing it was that they did not invite the entire court — solely people of distinction." The other Spanish ladies nodded in agreement.

The full weight of the insult dawned on her. Sofonisba realized it was a calculated slight, and the cardinal's mark was all over it. She exited the ladies' quarters to take refuge in her studio.

Chapter 16

The First Anniversary: January 1561

As the first anniversary of the king and queen's marriage approached, the court prepared to fete the couple. People wanted a royal baby to seal their expectations. Don Carlos had recovered from his accident but seemed more petulant than ever. The consensus at court was that a second in line was essential: Carlos was vulnerable physically, mentally, and personally. The stability of the realm required an alternate heir. But with no sign of the queen being with child, and no royal announcement, fetes were scaled down to modest affairs. The royal couple celebrated their anniversary privately.

Queen Isabel came less often to the studio, rarely to paint, but occasionally to sit for Sofonisba to paint her portrait. Sofonisba had taken to keeping her sister Elena's letter tucked in her wrap to read for support. It gave her companionship of sorts as the other ladies-in-waiting avoided her. She had not seen the queen at all this week. She was startled when Madame de Vineux burst into her studio one afternoon.

"Come quickly." Madame de Vineux caught her breath. "We are needed in the chapel, every one of us. The queen has been struck by fever. Come, pray with us." Sofonisba threw on her wrap, touching her sister's letter like a rosary, and followed Madame de Vineux.

Normal life stopped as the court was gripped by the queen's illness, more intensely than even it had been for the prince. Sofonisba remained with the other ladies-in-waiting, and they all prayed incessantly in the chapel. On the third morning, a maid interrupted the ladies' prayers. "Her Majesty the Queen wishes to see Madame," the maid whispered to Madame de Vineux as Sofonisba and the other ladies searched each other's faces for understanding. At least the queen lived.

"God bless her," Madame de Rembere whispered, squeezing Madame de Vineux's hand as she passed her. The ladies-in-waiting prayed more fervently. Sofonisba felt like they were unified for the first time.

Madame de Vineux soon returned, her eyes red from tears. "The queen is preparing to die." Their hopes dashed. "She asks for you, Lady Sofonisba."

Sofonisba glanced at Isabel de Mendoza, whose cheek twitched. The unity of their shared sympathy for the queen was threatened. She left the chapel for the queen's chamber, passing through the ladies' quarters on the way and spotting her neglected art kit on the marbled bedside table. She would make a gift of it to the queen, to inspire recovery, to say, 'This is what we will do as soon as you are well.' What else did she have to offer?

She was immediately admitted to the queen's chamber. The tiny queen's white face stood out in the dark like a Lombard portrait. Queen Isabel motioned for her to approach and looked down at the art kit in Sofonisba's hand, then at Sofonisba kneeling at her bedside. Sofonisba's tear fell onto the leather cover of her art kit as she offered it to the queen. "Your Majesty, please accept my humble gift. I look forward to watching you use it at our next lesson."

Queen Isabel smiled lightly, then closed her eyes and fell asleep. Horrified that she had taxed the queen, Sofonisba looked up at the attending physician, whose nod confirmed that it was time for her to leave. She set the art kit on the queen's bedside table, a marbled one similar to her own but with a golden monogrammed façade that gleamed like a halo in contrast to the queen's sickliness.

As she closed the door to the queen's chamber behind her, Sofonisba saw King Philip hurrying down the corridor toward her. She instantly knelt to one knee. "Your Majesty," she said.

The king mumbled under his breath, "Italian," and shook his head like he was reviving himself from a dream. "You write, dear Lady, correct?" and without waiting for a reply, "Dispatch a letter to our beloved's mother in Paris. Tell her in your shared language how we fear for her daughter's life. Write it as a daughter would, affectionately. Tell her what a mother needs to hear. My messenger will dispatch it at once."

"Yes, Your Majesty," Sofonisba replied, already beginning a mental draft.

Dearest Royal Mother,

My heart grieves with every beat to inform you that your treasure, your daughter Isabel, the most sinless, royal angel to walk this earth, fights with each breath to remain in our presence. We, her ladies, pray for her every waking moment, as we will pray for you, dear lady, the saintly mother who gave the world this precious being.

Your ever-loyal servant and attendant to
Her Royal Majesty Isabel, Queen of Spain,
Lady Sofonisba Anguissola,
Toledo, Spain, The Year of our Lord 1561

She handed her note over to the royal messenger hoping she had found the right tone to accomplish the king's task, a personal letter to the queen mother in France whom Sofonisba had never met — her first meaningful encounter with the king, under the saddest of circumstances.

At the end of the third week, Queen Isabel was still bed-ridden with fever. Sofonisba spied King Philip one day leaving chapel looking like he wore his mourning gown. He had already buried two wives. His first wife, the mother of Don Carlos, died before her 18th birthday, just after the prince's birth. The death of his second wife Mary Tudor was relatively recent. King Philip looked like he would not survive losing Isabel; especially not without producing even one spare heir.

King Philip managed every aspect of Queen Isabel's care. He instructed the staff personally on the details and directly scrutinized their work. He ordered daily Masses sung to the newly canonized San Diego de Alcala whose intercession had helped to save Don Carlos' life.

Then, on the first day of the fourth week of the queen's illness, Madame de Vineux came breathlessly into the ladies' quarters. "Queen Isabel's fever broke! She will live! God bless her!"

Each one of them crossed herself with true joy at the news of the recovered young queen, who now assumed a touch of saintliness, having conquered such a long-raging fever. For another brief moment, any petty differences among her ladies vanished.

King Philip, however, appeared around court looking defeated rather than relieved. He did the appropriate things. He gave all thanks to God at an elaborately celebrated Mass. He showered Queen Isabel with gifts. But he did not look happy. He did not sweep Isabel off for romantic private time. He did not ask Sofonisba for a personal letter to the Queen of France. Instead, he wrote a terse note to Queen Isabel's mother, in Spanish, stating that the fever had broken, her daughter continued to get better, and they were giving thanks to God.

Then he escaped. The most powerful monarch in Europe eluded his court under cover of darkness and left with the companionship of a lone squire. He rode all night and all day and all the next week, literally abandoning his court, his responsibilities, and his entire royal life. He must have been confident that Alba would run things in his stead, and he was correct. Rumors spread, and Queen Isabel was becoming frantic. Nobody knew where the king was.

When he returned, he explained himself and his absence to nobody. Instead, King Philip announced that it was time for change and renewal — time to stake his claim. He decided to construct his new capital, "in the very heart of Spain," he said, "the one woman that nothing can take from me." As if a building could protect him from more loss, he was determined. "It will be so immense, so weighty, so solid, my capital will endure at all costs." King Philip immediately commenced plans for his Escorial, his personal fortress, house of worship, and mausoleum that was to represent the strength of his life. Or his fear of death. Some said that the two-time widower realized that he was powerless to protect himself from the potential hurt of another lost spouse. All he could do was pad himself from any further pain.

He withdrew from Isabel and retreated to a loyal noblewoman, Doña Eufrasia de Guzman, a lady-in-waiting to his sister Princess Juana who served as their liaison. In no time, the entire court knew that the king had taken a mistress. Sofonisba could see that her queen was devastated. She hardly ate for days on end and seemed to sleep more during the day than at night, when she took to pacing and praying. Her still open, fifteen-year-old heart was broken. No matter that the queen had been conditioned to infidelity, brought up to be worldly about it by a mother who tolerated infidelity for years between her husband King Henry II and his mistress Diane Poitiers. Nevertheless, young Isabel's heart was in pieces. Her husband's betrayal was written all over her wasting body and hollow eyes.

Madame de Vineux confided in Sofonisba. "I'm concerned about the queen, Lady Sofonisba. The king's behavior is destroying her as he quests for immortality. The infidelity itself is his need to be young and vigorous after the queen's illness, no?"

Sofonisba looked down at her hands to avoid responding — such harsh words against the king — close to treasonous. She remembered Isabel's own laments against the king before the Inquisition. She reasoned that Madame de Vineux's words only proved how much she loved Queen Isabel, even above the king of the land.

Madame de Vineux's was the only criticism Sofonisba heard spoken against the king's affair with Doña Eufrasia. The rest of the court saw the king's behavior and were complicit, behaving more frivolously and flirty as if to make his betrayal more acceptable.

Meanwhile, all sorts of contracts were being negotiated for the construction of Philip's new capital. Money was flowing and courtiers were vying for every ducado to be earned. Wine and entertainment were used to promote and seal deals. Ambitious courtiers showered Don Carlos and his brother gallants with gifts and bribes that the three cycled back into gambling and other entertainment.

The economy of Toledo erupted with inflation.

Finally, it was time for the entire city-court to be moved en masse from the grandeur of Toledo to Madrid, still an undeveloped and unrefined wasteland.

Unlike the insulting journey to Toledo, Sofonisba rode in the queen's carriage to Madrid along with Madame de Vineux and Madame de Rembere. The queen insisted on Sofonisba being with her, and this time her message was not ignored. The king rode separately with his mistress Doña Eufrasia and his sister the Princess Juana, who acted as a type of human shield to keep the queen from witnessing her husband's betrayal.

While the king's grand Escorial was under construction, the court was to be housed outside Madrid at El Pardo, formerly a royal hunting lodge for the king's father, the emperor Charles V.

"They say that this is the place where Don John of Austria's commoner mother conceived him," Isabel de Mendoza gossiped. While called a "lodge," it actually had dozens of bedrooms and corridors with secret interconnecting passageways. The king appointed Isabel and her ladies to the most elaborate suites, detailed with the richest tapestries and the finest silks and linens, all overlooking the beautiful garden at the opposite side of the palace from the king's own suites — with Doña Eufrasia's room nearby.

Philip distanced himself from the queen, staying busy with his usual duties running the empire and immersing himself in architectural plans with his architect Juan Bautista de Toledo, recently arrived from working in Italy. While the king's devotion to his project sheltered him from his commitment to his wife, Doña Eufrasia occupied his leisure time.

In response, Queen Isabel retreated to Sofonisba's recomposed studio to escape the gossips. She dredged up the strength to reengage her talents. Where her mother had been a patron, Isabel would be an artist. Whether for sheer pleasure or to save face over the king's neglect, she vigorously renewed her sessions with Sofonisba. She ordered extra furniture to decorate the new studio, divans to relax on and tables to sit at. They painted and talked together, and Sofonisba worked on the queen's portrait every day. She was relieved to have started it before Isabel's illness, when her face still radiated a happy new bride. It captured a truly light-hearted Isabel, not the serious wife she had become in such a short period, worry registering on her teenaged forehead as she fretted how she could achieve her most important official function when the king's energy was directed elsewhere.

When rumors of Philip's infidelity reached Catherine de Medici in Paris, the queen mother's loyal friend Madame de Vineux wrote to soften the news. "Queen Isabel ignores Doña Eufrasia. She spends her days praying or painting. Your Majesty's daughter is the best in the world and will soon surpass her teacher at painting."

Catherine de Medici had experienced her own difficulties conceiving at first, before she bore ten children. The French Queen must have understood Isabel's predicament better than anyone and knew it would all get better after the birth of a son. She began inundating her daughter with the same tips she had received a generation prior, all manner of concoctions to stimulate fertility.

For her part, Isabel concealed her thoughts from court and even with Sofonisba — never criticizing the king or mentioning his new mistress. Sofonisba couldn't help admiring the queen's resilience in the face of having to bury so much inside. But the artist was more adept at reading faces than the queen was in hiding her thoughts. Sofonisba saw the hurt beneath the queen's façade. Might she help to console her? Was not one of her functions here encouraging the queen to open up?

"Your Majesty?"

"Mmm?" Isabel dabbed white highlights to the cheeks of the self-portrait she was attempting.

"If Your Majesty would like to share anything with me, I will be your most loyal servant."

"I will let you know." The queen smiled. "Maybe I will need you to find me some admiring courtiers, hm? Handsome *young* ones?"

"I could, uh, perhaps . . ." Sofonisba stammered.

The queen chuckled. "I jest, Lady Sofonisba. When I'm ready, I doubt you will be my liaison of choice. But you are sweet. Let's distract our minds with our art, shall we, yes?" She seemed to be an experienced sophisticate and a needy teenager at the same time.

Meanwhile, time alone with the queen was time tucked safely away from the cardinal, who had eased his campaign against Sofonisba ever since the queen's illness. His niece Isabel de Mendoza was less bossy as well, even though she continued to be disingenuously sweet or dismissively cold toward Sofonisba. The other ladies-in-waiting seemed to appreciate how Sofonisba helped lift the queen's spirits. They brought little treats to the studio during the day and offered assistance for errands to make the queen and Sofonisba comfortable. And Queen Isabel was thriving at her lessons.

But Sofonisba could see the cardinal's influence at court was undiminished. He stood next to the king at every juncture. She sensed he was lying in wait for the right time to pounce. Whether or not he intended to do anything, he succeeded at keeping Sofonisba always on edge.

Chapter 17

Al Vero

The extra time the queen spent in the studio allowed Sofonisba to complete her first official court portrait, *Portrait of Isabel de Valois, Queen of Spain*. As an artist, she was pleased. As a servant of the court, she was anxious — for the queen to approve of it and love it, for it to remind the king of the queen's loveliness and distract him from Doña Eufrasia. Most of all, she selfishly wanted him to love it as a work of art. As much as she wanted him to adore his wife, she wanted the king to pine for Sofonisba to paint him the way a lover pines for his beloved, the way she felt as a fourteen-year-old when her infatuation for her prince melted into her desire to capture him on canvas.

"Sofi," Queen Isabel unwittingly used Sofonisba's childhood nickname. "The king has informed me that your portrait of me will be unveiled when he announces a new diplomatic mission to His Holiness in Rome."

"An honor, indeed, Your Majesty!"

Sofonisba couldn't sleep the night before the unveiling. She rose early to go to her studio and sketch. An unexpected knock at the door startled her. She looked up to see a familiar face — her happy childhood personified.

"Ferrante! What are you doing here?"

"Didn't they tell you?" He kissed her cheeks. "I've come with Broccardo. He's serving as the king's emissary to the Pope. You didn't know? How is court treating you?"

"My work, I think, is good. I'm showing my first official portrait tonight, and I'm feeling queasy, but dare I say, the portrait is good!"

"Of course, Sofi. I would expect nothing less. How is court *life*?"

Finally, she could unload her burden. "Ferrante, I have to tell you something. But you cannot share this information with anyone. Promise? Absolutely?"

Ferrante nodded. "You can trust me. Sofi, what is it?"

"After the royal wedding, I didn't find you. So I left earlier than most, but still very late in the evening."

"Yes, I was enjoying the lovely women of court — very welcoming. Go on."

"I saw something I should not have."

"And?" He curled his fingers toward himself. "Come out with it. What did you see?"

"Lovers." She paused. "Men. Two men."

"Ooh."

"Not just any men, Ferrante. Remember the invalid I insulted?"

"The cardinal's servant?"

"Yes. And—"

Ferrante snapped his fingers

"The cardinal and his lackey! Of course! What nobleman keeps an invalid servant at court unless he has another use for him? It made no sense to me that such a ranking cardinal would have a disfigured attendant, especially at a royal event. Now it makes sense. The attendant was an easy mark for the priest. He kept the priest's secret in exchange for the perks of the position. Who knows? Maybe the lackey was happy to oblige. Believe me, Sofi, your information is good as gold. Why don't you take advantage of it?"

"It's not my business, Ferrante. It's plaguing me. The cardinal has daggers in his eyes for me."

"Sofi, you mean to tell me that you hold the possibility of the most exquisitely juicy blackmail and *you* fear *him*?"

"Don't tease."

"Oh, I'm not teasing, Cousin. You're naive. Cara, you know I love you and that is why I am glad to see you. But I went home last time with four contracts. I've come along with Broccardo this time expecting to return home with more. He's been reaping in the profits from your fame back home. His appointment to represent King Philip to the Pope in Rome? Think that was from being Cremona's first citizen? Your father is coming out of debt. Your parents could not afford to arrange your marriage but your sister Europa is being contracted to a wealthy nobleman who is willing to take a cut-rate dowry to attach himself to the Anguissola name, now that you are at the king's court. They are talking about Bianca Pallavicini as your brother Asdrubale's bride. She is well out of his league. Sofi, you may be the only one *not* taking advantage of your status here."

Sofonisba looked at her fingers and flicked a speck of paint from her nail. She felt ashamed, whether from her naiveté or the injustice of her situation.

"Why don't you confront him head on with your information?"

"Let's see, the king's right-hand man, a cardinal of the church, is charged to stamp out heresy through the Inquisition in Toledo. Even the queen heard the numbers — hundreds, thousands maybe."

"Word reached us in Lombardy," Ferrante said. "You'll find no more debates these days about what to think of the Council of Trent. None at all. Now it's all, 'I'm more pious than you.' And

have you heard about the business your sister is doing in devotional pieces? Everyone wants an altarpiece made by the hands
of sacred nuns. I hear the bishop stops by her convent, so polite
with Elena, so deferential. These nuns have influence now. How
about you follow your pious sister's lead, Sofi, and take advantage of opportunity?"

"And if the cardinal retaliates?"

"If you don't want to profit from this information, as certainly you could, you at least must be confident that you are
in the dominant position. You have the cardinal in check, don't
you see?"

"Ferrante, I fear he is always one move away from a
checkmate."

"That is in your head, Cousin. Be realistic. Tonight you have
a portrait being unveiled, yes? That is the test of your security
here. Impress the royals with your talent and your service. As
long as the queen wants you, what can the cardinal do?"

"But he has the ear of the king."

"Just like in chess, Sofi. Guard your queen; don't put her out
too early. Save her for when she can do you some good. Until
then, bide your time. And be assured, Cousin. You are at the
center of power; you are in the middle of the chess game."

"Dear Ferrante, it's good to have you here, but I prefer to skip
the games."

Sofonisba didn't see Broccardo until later that evening when
courtiers began arriving at the grand banquet hall. "Carissima,"
he said as he approached her with open arms and a kiss on each
cheek. "What a lovely court lady you have become. May I say
how beautiful you are tonight?"

"Signore Persico," she said, feeling her father's protective-
ness in Broccardo's kisses.

"You loom large now in our hometown, cara mia." He put his hand to his chest. "Verses proclaiming your talent are circulating in Lombardy, and the masters are applauding the self-portrait you delivered home last Easter."

"How are Father and Mother and my sisters and brother?"

"We are all so very proud of you, cara," he said. Was he flirting? "It is my honor to be here, not only for my mission to Rome, but for the pleasure of seeing your lovely face." They were interrupted by the king and queen, arriving together at the banquet hall for the first time since the king's great escape from Toledo. Behind them came the Cardinal of Burgos in his golden robe.

Sofonisba was given a place of honor at the front banquet table, near the royals, close to the painting that was to be unveiled. A drape was placed over the portrait to conceal it until the proper moment. Broccardo and Ferrante were seated next to her. The king and queen were seated together, with Doña Eufrasia nowhere in sight. The queen's nemesis was replaced by Sofonisba's portrait of the queen, positioned on its easel to the king's left.

When it was time to unveil the painting, the king rose from his seat and, waving aside his attendant, began to lift the corner of the drape himself. It occurred to Sofonisba that this simple act was the most servile task she had seen the king perform. The king removed the drape and stood blocking the painting from the court's view as he took time to scrutinize it. The room was silent.

For Sofonisba, the suspense was palpable. She gripped the edge of the banquet table. When the king turned, he caught Sofonisba's eye but did not linger. Sofonisba felt no urgency in his gaze, nothing like that moment on her balcony in Cremona during his parade so many years ago. She squeezed harder.

The king faced the courtiers. "We thank our lovely lady-in-waiting for her beautiful picture of our queen." The queen batted her eyes and nodded. The assembly applauded.

Sofonisba forced a smile, but inside she felt like her lungs were strangling her heart. Beautiful picture? Nothing about her talent, her vision? No reference to importing her Lombard style? Nothing close to showing the queen's soul? The king gutted her portrait with a few words of meaningless flattery. Why would he ever choose her for his own portrait?

The cardinal's smirk seemed to echo her conclusion.

The Duke of Alba raised a glass. "To our most radiant queen and her lady-in-waiting, the lovely Lady Sofonisba."

Sofonisba blushed, mortified to be toasted when her verdict was death.

Queen Isabel walked slowly over to the easel as if inspecting the piece from each pace, squinting to examine a highlight on her double's cheek when she stood before it.

"No portrait ever executed by Master Clouet has shown me truly as you do here, Lady Sofonisba. For your eye, and your talent, you have my heartfelt gratitude." The hall applauded again, and the queen smiled at Sofonisba nodding sympathetically. "Shown me truly." Sofonisba was touched that Isabel knew the right words to soothe her.

When the applause subsided, the king announced, "The portrait of our queen shall be delivered to His Holiness in Rome with the upcoming mission."

Sofonisba sat back in her chair. Rome! Perhaps the king admired the painting after all? Or maybe he feels no attachment to it whatsoever and has no regret giving it away? Sofonisba was confused. She longed for approval of her work and a sign that she was not at court for parties and card games.

In the ladies' quarters after the banquet, Sofonisba drafted a note to send to the pope along with the painting. Her hands trembled. She may have died with the king's trite response, but the honor of this bequest to the pope was undeniable.

Holy Father,

It is my singular grace and favor to present this likeness of Her Majesty the Queen, which I am happy to offer freely, recognizing the fatherly affection that your Holiness demonstrates for my Lady.

If it were possible to demonstrate before the eyes of your Holiness with the brush the beauty of the soul of this illustrious queen, your Holiness could not see anything more wonderful. But in those aspects that art is able to render I have not neglected to the best of my ability to show Your Holiness the truth.

I remain your very humble servant,
Sofonisba Anguissola, 16 September 1561.

As she lay down for sleep that night, the king's perfunctory response spun round and round in her head, and the dark of night intensified her doubts. Maybe the king did not truly approve of a female painter at court. Perhaps the cardinal has influenced him.

Six weeks later, Broccardo went searching for Sofonisba as soon as the royal grooms took his horse and bags. "There you are. I was told I'd find you here," he said scanning her increasingly cluttered studio. "I know what anticipation you must be feeling. I too am gripped by suspense for what I would like to know." He handed her the weighty parchment with the holy papal seal on it. She tore through the wax with a fingernail jagged from stretching a canvas and read to herself.

Esteemed Lady Sofonisba,

We have received the portrait by your hand of our most Serene Queen of Spain, our very dear daughter whom we love as a father loves his daughter. You have beautifully and diligently represented her goodness and the beauty of her soul. We thank you and promise you that we will treasure the piece among the things we value most in this world. We commend you your virtu,' your marvelous talent, and we send to you our continual blessings.

May Our Lord God protect you.
His Holiness, Pius IV, 15 October, 1561

Beautifully . . . represents the beauty of her soul . . . treasures it. The affirmation she so longed to hear! If only the king had responded as enthusiastically.

"Well? What does he say?" Broccardo asked.

"Oh, Broccardo. Look." She handed him the letter and nodded, encouraging him to read. After he finished, he took her hands into his.

"Success! Your father will be so proud." She let the Pope's praise erase the king's lukewarm reaction at the unveiling.

At night, she wondered whether to share the Pope's letter with the court. After all, the public nature of the unveiling and the king's decision to give it to the Pope made the letter a court issue, did it not? She rationalized away her modesty. She showed her letter to the queen.

"Mmm," Queen Isabel murmured as she read. "He refers to the beauty of the queen's soul but not her likeness. Shall I take this as an affront to my beauty?"

"I should think it only a compliment to the beauty of your inner self, Your Majesty."

Isabel smiled. "I tease you, Lady Sofonisba. It's obvious His Holiness is most pleased with your work. Rest assured. His Majesty will be, too. You will see."

The next week Sofonisba received a note from the Duke of Alba. Her stipend was to be increased, and she was now to be paid "extraordinary" pay, to supplement a budget for entertainment and servants. Sofonisba sent Alba her gracious thanks.

The Princess Juana came to her studio. She now wanted her portrait done. So did Don John of Austria. The Duke of Parma, who once said Sofonisba's presence at his court would make him the laughing stock of Europe, wrote to the Spanish court requesting a portrait of Alessandro Farnese by Sofonisba's hand. She did not forget the duke five years prior and the depression his words had provoked in her — and how the Friar's words of encouragement helped her through it.

Broccardo asked her for a private walk in the gardens. No one seemed surprised to see her walking alone with her fellow countryman and one-time chaperone. "Sofi, I have known you your entire life. I was already making my mark in the world when you were starting at Master Campi's studio. Now, look at you. Your father could not be more proud. Your mother is waiting for my full report on your conditions here. They both worry about you so far from home. They want nothing more than your happiness. As do I." He cleared his throat. "Other than my natural daughter Ippolita, I have no family of my own, and I am now in my fortieth year." He straightened his back and stood taller. "While in Rome I earned my release from the vow of celibacy I once took to become a Knight in the Order of Saint John of Jerusalem. My recent status as envoy between the king and the pope facilitated my petition. I can think of no better match for me than you, dear Sofi, Cremona's virtuosa and her leading citizen." He touched his chest. "It is time for me to take a wife, and

I have chosen you, my dear, dear, Sofi." He went down on one knee. "Sofonisba, will you marry me?"

Only with those last words did Count Broccardo Persico's voice crack, however slightly.

Sofonisba closed her eyes and caught her breath. Images flashed before her—her bedroom in Cremona, little birds painted onto the rafters, the lines on her mother's face as she instructed the kitchen girl, her sisters and brother in the library, her father in his study. Would she end up a spinster if she said no now?

Broccardo must have read her confusion as elation. He stood up and swooped her into his arms. She pushed him back.

"Broccardo, I am sorry. Please, forgive me. I don't mean to hurt you, but I cannot. I just cannot. My place is here right now." She could see his bewilderment—he never anticipated rejection. How could he? Defeat was not part of his life story. Broccardo Persico was successful at everything he touched.

"I don't understand," he stammered. "Do you realize the life I am offering you? Sofi, do you know how many women would beg for the opportunity to be my wife?" His eyes darted back and forth, pleading and incredulous.

Sofonisba adjusted her hair and Broccardo straightened his doublet as they both regained their composure. Sofonisba could still feel the warmth of his embrace. She touched her cheek. She knew she might regret her decision. And how tempting to escape the cardinal's evil eye for good. "I, I, I am truly flattered. If things were otherwise, Broccardo, if I were a different person, if father didn't expect that I, that I would. . . ." At a loss for the right words, she tipped her head to the side as if to beg his understanding.

"Well, then, Lady Sofonisba. I will leave you to your rest." Broccardo bowed to her and backed away, disbelief painted on his face and self-reproach on hers.

Why could she not accept Broccardo? He boldly requested papal dispensation from his holy order to marry her, showing how devoted he was to her. He was kind and handsome. Their ten-plus-year age difference did not bother her at all. He was active and robust. She enjoyed his company, and he loved her family, and the feeling was mutual. Plus, he was truly the first citizen of Cremona, a diplomat, connected to the king. Broccardo was everything she could want in a husband, and dowry was no longer the issue it once was for her family.

Was she using her promise to her father to rationalize her own ambition? The pope's praise lifted her spirits after the king's tepid response. The challenge gnawed at her — to paint the king's portrait. She wasn't ready to leave court without a chance at that prize. And what about her duty to her father to honor the family name? How could she stop now?

Broccardo remained at court for several weeks more. While he seemingly avoided Sofonisba, his eyes followed her every move when she entered the banquet hall. He wore his hurt on his sleeve as if this were his very first experience with rejection. The entire court surmised she had refused a marriage proposal from one of Lombardy's leading nobles. What woman ever gets such freedom of choice in how to live her life?

Sofonisba made sure to seek out Broccardo to say a proper goodbye before he departed Madrid for his return to Lombardy. She wanted to thank him for everything. She brought him two gifts. One was a self-portrait. She hoped he would accept it in the spirit in which she gave it, her devoted friendship. The second was a smaller rendition of her *Portrait of Princess Juana*, which she had executed while working on the princess' official portrait. She wanted to reciprocate his generous offer of marriage with a generous gift of her own.

"Signore Persico, it would do me great honor if you would accept these two portraits by my hand." She held them out to him.

Broccardo took the canvases from her and studied each of them slowly and carefully. "These are beautiful, Lady Sofonisba. Please, you do not need to give me such extravagant gifts."

"They are all I have to give to show my appreciation."

He took a sharp breath as if the word "appreciation" stabbed him in the heart. He tugged on his doublet and cleared his throat. "Then I will never part with them," he said, bowing to her. She, too, knew, as soon as "appreciation" came out of her mouth instead of "love," that she had made the correct decision in refusing his offer of marriage.

Sofonisba had seen very little of her cousin Ferrante. He had accompanied Broccardo on his mission to Rome and back again to Madrid. Then he spent most of his stay wielding his influence among the courtiers.

Ferrante found his cousin in her studio on the morning he and Broccardo were set to return to Lombardy. "Before I go, I want to make certain you feel secure with the Pope's praise. The fact that you broke a certain someone's heart gives you an added allure, Cousin."

"Please don't remind me. I feel like a scoundrel."

"You only enhanced your prestige. And what of your imaginary nemesis?"

"No word from the cardinal. No insults lately. Either he has forgiven me or ..."

"No 'or.' Know that you are fine. Aim to paint your king. I am returning home a richer man than I expected. Now I can move out of my father's house prior to receiving my inheritance. What fun I shall have as an independent man. All thanks to you, Cousin."

Amid all the attention that swirled around Sofonisba after she received the pope's letter, the person most tortured by it was Master Coello. "She really shouldn't have it both ways, now should she?" He lamented to his wife. "She is here to attend the queen. I am here to execute the official court portraits. How can I protect my influence at court if that woman can use her position with the queen to take my commissions from me? And yet *I* do not take the queen away from the court for days, weeks even, at a time. How am I supposed to portray the royal family when I don't have full *access*?"

"Dear," Señora Coello said, "the king and queen require so many portraits. Could you not possibly—"

"But then she pretends, 'Oh, sir, I'm so dainty,' does she not? I bet you anything she wants to paint the king. She has the ambition of a man under those pretty little fingers. No doubt she aims to step on my toes there, too. Well, I won't let her. If the reign of Philip II is going to be portrayed at this court, I will be the painter to do so! I will follow Master Titian, not she!" Coello clutched his chest as his bitterness squeezed the breath out of him.

Sofonisba was alone in her studio the next day working on the concept for a painting when Master Coello rapped on her door. She had virtually no contact with him on a daily basis. He had a large, active studio in the king's wing of the palace and was usually busy supervising his assistants.

"Master Coello, what a surprise. Would you like to come in?" Sofonisba had buried the insult of the baptism so well that by now she had forgotten it. Her surprise to see him overrode any lingering hostility. In response to her invitation, he poked his head into the studio and gave a suspicious look around.

"Hmm," was all he said, then curtly, "Good day." He turned around and left, not waiting for her reply. Even though her studio remained inferior to his in size, he was obviously disgruntled to see her well-appointed and light-filled space. It reminded her of her days at Campi's studio. If it weren't for the friendship of Giacomo and Paolo, Sofonisba would have suffocated from similar cattiness among the apprentices. She had plenty of social obstacles to navigate without having to placate Coello.

What did he have to complain about? Coello had a permanent official appointment. He had his wife and children with him and seemed to sacrifice nothing for his art. In contrast, she was admitted as a lady-in-waiting and had to guard her image as both a lady and as a painter. And Coello had access to the king. His antipathy toward her felt utterly undeserved, almost as if he were provoked into it.

Sofonisba's anxiety seemed to reflect the atmosphere at court. She noticed that Don Carlos recovered physically from his fall the year prior, but his mental state appeared to have deteriorated. His charm turned to sarcasm. His dashing demeanor became snide. Yet, Don Carlos still had the ear of the king, who appeared not to notice his son's decline. Courtiers gossiped that Don Carlos feared a rival to the throne, the baby the entire country had prayed to receive. They whispered that his accident unleashed his temper, worsened his madness. He lost more and more control over his emotions. In contrast to the cultured, noble king he was expected to become, Don Carlos appeared defensive, angry, and self-absorbed, and the court looked toward a replacement heir ever more desperately.

But Don Carlos still had his loyal comrades, his aides de camp. He and Don John of Austria, the king's illegitimate half-brother, and Alessandro Farnese, the Italian prince, ran around court testing its limits. They never suffered a word of recrimination, no matter how indecorous their behavior. It was known that they paid generously to silence servants and marry off servant girls. Don Carlos was the instigator and mastermind while Don John and Alessandro were his lieutenants. The leader had a reputation for adventure, and the time and money to play.

Sofonisba could tell from the queen's laments that Don Carlos and Isabel were growing closer. "Only I can understand how it feels to be neglected by the sovereign you love and left to present a happy face of family unity and loyalty." Or "The prince and I are natural companions. Our royal blood binds us." They each were equally free from actual responsibility. It was only a matter of time before they became confidants.

Toward the end of the year, the Farnese ambassador returned to Spain and made a public request to King Philip. "Your Majesty, the Duke of Parma sends his compliments for the exquisite portrait of his son by the hand of the virtuosa Lady Sofonisba of Lombardy." The ambassador held out his palm toward Sofonisba standing to the right of the queen. "The duke requests your leave for a dozen copies to be made of it," he said, bowing first to the king and then to Sofonisba.

"A dozen?" King Philip said. "Farnese does like to see his house glorified. Tell your lord that he will have his copies, but we will put Coello on it. We have a special assignment set aside for Lady Sofonisba."

He nodded to Queen Isabel seated next to him, who beamed her smile to Sofonisba, who kept her lady-in-waiting quarter-smile in place as best she could as she screamed inside with joy: The queen had secured her the king's portrait — sooner than she hoped! Sofonisba glanced at Coello, whose angry eyes darted from the king to the cardinal to Queen Isabel to Sofonisba.

"We are confident Farnese will reward Coello handsomely for his efforts," the king said. "We expect separate compensation for each of the dozen pieces." Coello's face softened. In a sentence, the king had secured a sizable commission for Coello to copy Sofonisba's work a dozen times.

Sofonisba looked down at the pretty ruby ring on her finger, her compensation for the original portrait. It did not pay for the paints, but her reward was not a material one. She would paint the king! She kept her eye on her goal, happy to think it was just around the corner now.

The next day Queen Isabel approached her in the studio. "Lady Sofonisba, are you curious about the king's special assignment?"

"Of course, Your Majesty." Sofonisba set down her brush.

"You are to paint the most tender person in my life, the one who most touches my heart. While we are not physically intimate, I feel for his troubles," the queen continued. "A tender soul who is trapped under a world of responsibility, with so very few rewards and so often misunderstood. Dear Sofonisba, I want you to find his sweet spot deep down. He can be so tender."

How devoted she was to the king, even while he betrayed her. Sofonisba waited eagerly for the words that seemed frozen in the queen's mouth. "You will paint the portrait of my dear friend Don Carlos."

Sofonisba's heart sank as the queen continued.

"We know the power of art and how important a portrait can make one feel. People talk like the prince is mad, but I know he is a beautiful person weighed down by his royal role in life. In many ways, Lady Sofonisba, the prince is I and I am the prince. Can you possibly understand, dear lady? Don Carlos needs to feel valuable."

The queen's histrionics only made Sofonisba's assignment feel more like an obligation than an opportunity. Yet, how could she refuse Queen Isabel? "Yes, Your Majesty. I understand, but . . ." Sofonisba had trepidations about the fitful prince. "Your Majesty, will I be alone with the prince as I paint him?"

"Just attend to his tender moods," Queen Isabel said sharply. Then her voice softened. "You will be perfect for him, Sofi. It's surely better for the prince to spend his days with you than with Coello. You will help bring out the prince's positive attributes. We will have a lady chaperone."

Sofonisba knew she had to handle the prince gingerly given his notorious mood swings. The first day he arrived at her studio jovial. "If I didn't know him better, I might think Alessandro was smitten with you, Lady Sofonisba," the prince said.

"You are too kind, Your Highness."

"Let us begin. Paint my image that the realm might adore its next king."

As Sofonisba began her study, a scowl spread across the prince's face for no obvious reason.

"Your Highness, how would you like to continue? May I do anything to make you more comfortable in any way?" He seemed to have a strong need to be heard, like a child.

Don Carlos' moods vacillated repeatedly during their hours together. He went from agitated, to slouchy, to fidgety, and then seemed comforted by the calm of the near-empty studio. She thought of her younger brother Asdrubale, so different from the prince and yet similarly situated — young men whose larger-than-life fathers left them little room to shine. Sofonisba's apprehension about the prince turned to sympathy. She regretted not being closer to her only brother.

She finished her portrait of Don Carlos without depicting the prince's troubles. She fought the recollection of sitting in church as a young girl imagining she would show only truth in each portrait, *al vero*. She gave Don Carlos a sensitive, almost pensive face, peeking out of a bejeweled, ermine-lined doublet, the vestiges of his power hiding his tender soul and his neediness. Sofonisba couldn't deny she compromised her work for the sake of a flattering portrayal to protect the prince.

Chapter 18

Francesco de Medici and Bartolome de las Casas: Spanish Court 1562–1565

As her second anniversary in Spain approached, news of a woman painter at Philip's court reached Tuscany. An agent for Cosimo de Medici, Duke of Tuscany, acquired Sofonisba's drawing *Little Boy Bitten*. The agent sent it to de Medici with a drawing by Michelangelo, *Cleopatra*. They were intended for the duke's newly constructed Accademia del Disegno.

> To His Excellency Duke of Tuscany,
>
> Permit me the honor of sending Your Excellency a drawing most dear to me. This beautiful drawing is by the hand of a woman, can you believe, among all the many excellent painters, a noblewoman from Cremona, now a lady-in-waiting to the Queen of Spain. One may compare it to the master Michelangelo's and see it is equal in beauty and *invenzione*.
>
> Your humble servant
> Tommaso Cavalieri, January 20, 1562

A woman artist at the Spanish court hardly fit Cosimo's vision. He decided he needed someone in Madrid to be his eyes and ears. He didn't want events passing him by, lest anything affect the title he wanted the Spanish King to bestow upon him: Grand Duke of Tuscany. He selected his son Francesco to go observe the king's court and report what he found.

In May 1562, Francesco de Medici arrived at the Spanish court to fanfare befitting a royal, as his father had pre-arranged. Twenty-one years old, Francesco quickly befriended Don Carlos, Don John, and Alessandro Farnese. The young gallants discovered the courts of Madrid and Florence had much in common.

By autumn, Madrid began receiving reports from the Medici court of fever racing through Italy. Despite doctors applying leeches and taking pounds of blood, Francesco's brother Giovanni had passed from this life.

Another letter soon followed: We cannot know why the Lord has taken our beloved son Garzia so soon after his brother Giovanni. Then, just before Christmas, a third: Francesco's mother died of heartbreak, making certain that no more of her babies would predecease her.

Word raced through court that not one, but three, Medici died, all within weeks of each other. "Of course, the plague," courtiers surmised. "Or foul play, perhaps?" a few speculated. Francesco dedicated a Mass to his family and ordered the chapel shrouded with banners of Florentine silk. Innuendo lingered over the timing of the Medici deaths.

Francesco approached Sofonisba in her studio. "Lady Sofonisba, I have been remiss in finding you even though you are the reason I am at court."

"Your Excellency," she curtsied, brush in hand. "Please accept my deepest condolences, sir. I am truly sorry for all your loss."

He gave a quick nod in reply, then inspected the canvas she was working on. "I believe it is an appropriate time to commemorate my family line — the living line. I should like my portrait by your hand." He fingered the edge of the canvas.

"I would be most honored."

"Do you know I was painted by Agnolo Bronzino as a child? In spite of recent family tragedies, and perhaps because of them, we must project the resilience and fortitude of the Medici house, lest others feel it is vulnerable." He paused. "Therefore, let us present my own image as healthy and robust — to reassure the people." He cupped a hand under his chin and turned, offering his profile. "Let us begin tomorrow."

But Francesco did not call upon Sofonisba. She heard rumors he was preparing to return to Tuscany. She chanced upon him at banquet the following week.

"Ah, signorina, alas, I will not have time to sit for my portrait before my departure. Yet, I should like a piece by your hand. Do you have one to spare for me, that I might bring back home for our collection?"

He'd forgotten her, and now he wanted a gift? "I would be most honored," she said with a curtsy.

The next day, she found him surrounded by attendants, preparing for his journey. "Your Excellency?" She knocked on the door.

"Yes. What is it?"

"The piece you requested." She raised up the painting to show him one of her early self-portraits that she brought from home as part of her portfolio.

"Ah yes. Come in." He took the painting from her and inspected it. "A sweet rendering. I will add it to my family's collection. You must come view it there someday." Francesco de Medici turned his back to her, his casual invitation the only compensation she would receive.

Sofonisba later heard from Madame de Vineux why he abruptly changed his plans. His younger brother Ferdinand was awarded a cardinalship that became vacant at his brother Giovanni's death. Francesco feared his inheritance was being handed out while he remained in Spain — he had to get home before anything else was redistributed.

Court life continued: power and politics, boredom and games, personal alliances and petty squabbles. The cardinal was occupied with Escorial negotiations. Sofonisba tried to be a ready friend to the queen but avoided the gaming at court for time in her studio. Isabel sought out Sofonisba's company when she needed a break from court gossip or the erratic Don Carlos.

The monotony of routine was broken by a visit from her cousin Ferrante. "Sofi, I'm becoming quite a success at home, and I have you to thank. My business deals have afforded me freedom. I'm a new man. We sing your praises in Lombardy, don't you know? I hope you feel your status here is more solid than when last we spoke?"

"So it seems. I only suffer the occasional condescension of one Spanish lady in particular. The cardinal spends most of his time on plans for the new capital. I see him rarely. I hope he trusts that I am no threat to him."

"Well, if he threatens you in any way, you just come to Cousin Ferrante. I'll protect you!" He grinned and wagged his finger melodramatically in the air.

1564. Sofonisba was in her fifth year at the Spanish Court. In spite of the cardinal's sporadic shows of animosity, her reputation as an artist and as a woman was intact. Her parents were proud, and happy with the stipends, increasing every year. Sofonisba was honored to help her family. She wrote home frequently and always received timely replies. More and more, the details about court felt normal while the details of life in

Cremona sounded foreign. Still, with every letter, she became homesick.

One item she could not report: she was nowhere near her goal of painting the king. Her only interaction with him had been that personal moment when she composed the letter about the queen's illness for the French queen mother years ago. Sofonisba still didn't have court painter status like Coello. Even though she had painted Queen Isabel, Princess Juana, Alessandro Farnese, and Don Carlos, Coello remained the official court portraitist. When Hapsburg Archdukes Rodolfo and Ernesto came to Madrid for their court education, they were sent directly to Coello for portraits.

Coello's wife gave birth to their second child, a girl.

Meanwhile, the court relentlessly scrutinized Isabel's fertility. Her mother in Paris kept track of her courses through ambassadors, and courtiers took note of her girth. They reasonably worried that her wispy body could barely carry a child. The kitchen offered the best jamon Iberico de bellota, the creamiest of Manchegos, but the more they plied her with meats and cheeses, the less she seemed to eat and the thinner she grew.

Then the worst news possible: Philip's mistress Doña Eufrasia was with child.

Queen Isabel confessed her jealousy to Sofonisba in the garden the morning she heard the news.

"It's brutally unfair! The whole world is watching for me to be with child, and now it's that woman who's pregnant with Philip's child! How can I do my duty if the king neglects me?" Isabel pounded her palms on the stone bench where they sat.

Sofonisba had to say something to soothe the queen's mounting frustration. "Your Majesty, if I may, I have some information you might enjoy."

Sofonisba was never the one with gossip, being sheltered as she was in her studio, but she was privy to this news because the

Duke of Alba had approached her only days before. "Your Majesty, you might be interested in a conversation I had recently with Don Alba. He asked me if I recalled a scandalous incident in Milan in 1555 when he was first assigned there — a notorious love affair turned into bloodshed at the Ascoli palace. Alba imprisoned Prince Ascoli briefly for failing to control his household. I remembered it well. It was quite a scandal and my father praised Alba's decisiveness and impartiality. Alba came to see me the other day to ask whether Prince Ascoli's reputation suffered any from the scandal. He was delighted when I reported that it had."

Queen Isabel shook her head. "I hardly see how this relates, Lady Sofonisba."

Sofonisba tilted her head closer to the queen, practically whispering even though they were alone in the garden. "Don Alba has learned that Ascoli is now a widower. He believes the disgraced man to be a good match for Doña Eufrasia. She is being married off and sent away to reside at Ascoli's country estate."

"Alba. God bless him." Queen Isabel went to her knees before a Madonna statue in the garden.

Later that month, the queen arranged for Sofonisba to be awarded two special lifetime pensions and an increase in her stipend. And then, even though Sofonisba's rank truly did not warrant the honor, Isabel shared her precious news with her confidante first. "I am so happy I can barely find the words to express my blessed state. Dear Sofi, I am with child," Isabel said, making a sign of the cross over herself. Sofonisba crossed herself as well.

News of the queen's pregnancy spread throughout Europe as fast as a courier could ride. Isabel was radiant. A week later, she miscarried. Her wispy body shrank to no more than a skeleton.

"You are young. There will be more," the ladies tried to console her. "Now we know you can conceive." The queen dismissed them from her chamber.

"Not you, Sofonisba. Stay. Advice and more advice. I hear their judgment in all of it. I am a failure. I have not succeeded at my singular duty. You don't console me with false words, do you, Sofi? Surely, you know what it is like to be judged and to feel jealous of women with children."

"Yes, my queen," Sofonisba whispered. Certainly, she was accustomed to feeling judged and, increasingly, she felt a tinge of wanting to start a family of her own. She returned to her studio, and to a waiting letter from Cremona. How she needed the reassurances of home now.

My Dear Sofonisba,

The Lord has seen fit to take our dear Minerva from us. She was in good health and as lively as ever. She simply cut her hand. The next day she was dead. It was all so sudden. We cannot know the Lord's ways. We know that we must trust in Him.

We pray you are well and in good health.
Your Devoted Father, Amilcare, Cremona 1564

Sofonisba dropped her arm to her side, clinging to the parchment, and stared out the window. She felt helpless — the queen's miscarriage and now this. She was gripped with the feeling that she should return home to comfort her parents.

Dearest Father and Mother,

> I cannot imagine how it must be on one day to have
> a house full of children and the next to realize that
> not only were two of them away indefinitely, but now
> one was lost forever. I wish I were there with you — to
> console you and have you to comfort me. If you wish me
> to make the journey home, I shall do so gladly...

She crumbled her parchment and began again:

> I wish I could be there with you. I would return this
> instant if the queen did not rely on me as she does.

Isabel's miscarriage provoked a new barrage of advice letters
from her mother in France. The queen was expected to produce
an heir to bind the two countries with blood. France needed
peace with her neighbors more than ever as internal religious
divisions between Catholics and Huguenots grew steadily
worse. Letters were always of two themes: fertility and family
marriages.

Daughter,

> You must put your mind to conception above all
> things. My apothecary suggests ... my alchemist predicts
> ... my astronomer has foretold that your time is near.
> There remains the heir Don Carlos, who was
> originally intended for you. Therefore, can you not
> secure his union to one of your sisters ...

Sofonisba saw the queen wince every time she read her mother's
letters. Queen Isabel returned to hiding in the safety of Sofonisba's studio where she could be free to lose her royal composure
and vent her fears. "My mother advises me in every letter about

my courses, my meals, my relations with the king. I am a complete failure no matter what I do if I am not pregnant!"

Regardless of protocol, Sofonisba was a big sister now if she ever were. "Your Majesty, I don't see you as a failure. I know how it feels to want to be a mother and to feel inadequate, incomplete without it." This time, as she comforted Isabel, Sofonisba felt her belly cramping, her womb's own plea.

In time, teenaged Isabel put the miscarriage behind her and returned to the world of her royal peer Don Carlos, trading Sofonisba and the art studio for life as a young, privileged queen. Don Carlos was the last person to judge the queen adversely for failing to produce an heir. His succession remained unchallenged as long as she was barren. He embraced the revived queen. Plus, Don Carlos had more disposable time for the queen as he slowly lost his retinue. Don John of Austria was leaving to join the Spanish armada. Like King Philip, Don John was the son of the Emperor Charles V. Unlike Philip, he was illegitimate. Don John had to prove himself in battle. Perhaps he also wanted a break from court. Don Carlos was becoming increasing unstable, caught up in the tension over Isabel's duty to produce an heir and his own anxiety about her succeeding. Gossips whispered about inappropriate relations between Queen Isabel and Don Carlos. Don John must have discerned that this was a sensible time to escape court, at least for the time being.

And Alessandro Farnese was leaving for the Spanish Netherlands to be married to Princess Maria of Portugal in the presence of his mother, the Duchess of Parma, Regent of the Low Countries.

As 1564 became 1565, the court remained preoccupied with the state of the royal marriage and the queen's womb. Sofonisba tried to be a sensitive and loyal companion to the queen. Whenever pangs of homesickness or grief over Minerva's death struck, Sofonisba worked to conceal her sad feelings from the queen.

Isabel may have been Sofonisba's best friend at court and confidante, but Sofonisba relegated her personal longings to private
moments so as to not upset the queen and distract from the
royal mission to produce an heir.

The cardinal seemed consumed by plans for the new capital project. Sofonisba heard talk of him now and again but was
spared any interaction. She hoped he was assured by now that
she had no plan to disclose his private information.

One afternoon when she was painting in her studio, a
groom brought her a parcel that had arrived by special courier
from Cremona. She began to open it, sensing a framed painting beneath the velvet wrapper. She quickly tore past the letter,
going straight for the piece.

It was a painting signed by her sister Lucia. Sofonisba held
the portrait up and walked over to the window to examine it
in the light. The letter fell to the floor, and she left it there as
she continued to admire the portrait. The portrait had beautiful details and symbolism, but what struck Sofonisba most was
Lucia's emphasis on the kind eyes of the sitter. Her sister was
thriving! Sofonisba imagined all her sisters painting together,
discussing their progress. How she wished she could be in their
midst, for just a short time. An image of Minerva came to mind.
Sofonisba's heart constricted. She set the painting down gently
and picked the letter up off the floor. It was not written by Lucia
as Sofonisba expected, but by their father.

Dear Sofi,

We are at a loss for words. Only the Lord knows why
we have been allotted this overwhelming share of grief.
It hasn't been a year yet since Minerva died and now,
your sister Lucia has passed too. Enclosed is Lucia's
most recent piece, her portrait of Dr. Pietro. Remember

our dear friend? We send it to you as a memento of your sister, may she rest in peace.

Your Grieving Father, Amilcare,
Cremona, 1565

Sofonisba let the letter fall from her fingers. A chill shot up her spine when the paper struck the stone floor. This time, her helplessness was complete. How could she be of comfort to her parents — only one year after Minerva? How would they manage? She knew she needed to go home. She could not permit her ambitions to get in the way. Just a short visit, now when they most needed her support. The weight of her family pain was greater than her need to paint the king or attend the queen. She decided to request leave.

"Your Majesty," she said to the queen the next morning, "it has been near five years since I have been home. My parents have just suffered the death of a second child in the space of one year." Isabel cocked her head to the side but did not ask for details. Sofonisba continued. "I believe it is an appropriate time for a visit home to comfort my grieving parents. A short visit."

The queen's look of concern turned to shock. "But my dear Sofi, whatever would I do without your kind companionship with all my troubles? To you, of all people, I have shown my intimate love."

Sofonisba was stunned by the girl's selfishness. How could Isabel be so heartless? Sofonisba could feel her face grow beet red. Could the queen not see Sofonisba's pain? But what could she do? "Of course, Your Majesty."

Sofonisba cried herself to sleep that night, and many nights after, praying for the souls of her two dear departed sisters. Her poor parents. Dear Mother. Father. She ached for them.

Royals could not see other people's needs. Why had she expected anything else? Sofonisba knew she had to rely on her own inner resolve. She fixed her mind not to dwell on her grief for Lucia, Minerva, her parents. She tried to be consumed by Isabel's need to give life. She couldn't deny that a wedge of bitterness snuck into her loyalty for Isabel.

Sofonisba managed a self-portrait to repress her grief: close, solemn, three-quarter view-one eye connecting, one eye obscured-Mother, Father, I'm with you, yet so far away. She signed it and back-dated it, "Sofonisba Angosciola P. 1564." Spanish pronunciation. P for *pittrice*. One year when tragedy struck twice, and she was too encumbered at court to go home.

The court's fixation on the state of Isabel's womb and its gossip about her relationship to her stepson was broken by the return to court of the very old, and highly respected, Fray Bartolome' de las Casas, King Philip's boyhood tutor. "The friar is going to argue the case he put forward in his *Los Tesoros del Peru*," one courtier observed incredulously. "He says Spain has no moral claim to the Inca's New World land and its silver. Good luck convincing King Philip."

The old priest's argument seemed far-fetched, but because of his age and stature, the king granted him the privilege of a royal disputation. Casas would have full opportunity to present his arguments, as unpopular as they might be.

Everyone was fascinated by the New World — and curious how anyone could dispute Spain's moral claim to its treasures. Casas was to preach to a full house. Even the ladies-in-waiting were welcome to attend the debate. The king quoted the scholar Juan Luis Vivres, who advised that women must be educated to make correct moral decisions. Sofonisba was thrilled that actual *ideas* would be discussed. She missed her sessions with Marco.

The procession entered the grand hall. The Cardinal of Burgos preceded the friar, his golden vestments clashing with the friar's woolen robe. Sofonisba snuck a glance at the cardinal as he settled into his high-backed chair. He seemed to search for her, too; he stared back, his old hostility undiminished.

Friar de las Casas wore a simple scapular. One personal attendant followed him. He bowed to the king and queen on the risers, then to the cardinal, then to the general assembly. Then he turned and bowed to his attendant before picking up his notes. He bowed to a servant. Sofonisba remembered the Duchess of Parma's advice years earlier to never defer to an inferior. How different this humble friar was — everything about him exuded humility and kindness.

"Most honored sovereigns." The friar bowed again to them. "Honorable lords and ladies." He bowed to the audience. "Let us begin with a moment of prayer." The aged priest bowed his head in silence, and the assembly followed his lead. Then his demeanor changed entirely. He became animated and dramatic, and his voice projected as if he were preaching over the roar of a raging river. "Even though the Indians may be heathens, it is immoral to deprive them of their freedom and possessions. Nor are they to be enslaved. Rather, they should be able freely and lawfully to use, possess, and enjoy freedom and ownership of what belongs to them. The only moral claim we have is to draw the Indians themselves to the faith of Christ by preaching the word of God and the example of the good life." He continued passionately for over an hour.

When he finished, the room was quiet. The equality Casas preached stunned the courtiers. Their worldview could not conceive of it. How could Indians deserve equal standing with pure Spanish blood? But Sofonisba was drawn to the friar and found him persuasive. His studied intellectualism and perfect Latin lent credibility to his arguments. His conviction spoke for itself. She was moved by his compassion.

On his throne King Philip patiently waited, expertly reading the room. When he rose, he held his arm outward to Casas, inviting the priest to him. The king embraced him and kissed him on each cheek. The courtiers whispered in awe of his rare display of affection. "Our beloved Friar Casas shows us the way of love," the king said. "How we must love. How we must guide our Indians with love. We will use only love as we raise them up as our own."

The courtiers applauded the king's sentimentalism.

Love? Was that all he heard in Casas' disputation? Sofonisba heard the demand that Spain leave the Inca's land and silver alone. We will use only love as we raise our Indians? Like children? She realized the king was recasting Casas' argument, appearing to embrace the ideas while, in reality, rejecting them.

Sofonisba wanted her king to accept the noble priest's thesis. She wanted to see her king as a captain of righteousness. Casas was so convincing to her that she felt the king had to agree with Casas' demand for protection of the Indians' land and traditions.

Master Coello must have read the consternation on her face. He clinked his spoon to the side of his goblet. The courtiers went silent. "Does the painter from Cremona believe the Indians should be treated the same as Christians?" He practically shouted the question from his table across the room even though he had everyone's full attention already. No one could escape the awkwardness. How rude it was to query a woman openly about what she *thinks*.

Sofonisba instinctively looked at the cardinal. He smirked. The conundrum was plain to her: if she answered dimly that she was just a woman, she risked losing credibility for her ideas, her *invenzione* so important for her work, as Coello well knew, as well as her identity. Whereas a political response would be unbecoming for a lady-in-waiting, her role, her duty.

Coello sat back and crossed his arms over his chest knowingly.

Sofonisba tried to collect her thoughts, pausing long enough that a few courtiers began to snicker. The cardinal's eyes were as wide as those of a child who'd been given a present to unwrap. For Sofonisba, there was only one way to proceed. Fortunately, the Ascoli scandal was fresh in her mind.

She cleared her throat. "I can only speak to my own experience, sir. When Don Alba came to oversee the Milan Territory, my homeland, he handled a notorious scandal with fairness and impartiality. The respect he showed the locals gave my father confidence that the duke would govern our land fairly. I observe only that Friar de las Casas' disputation on fairness toward the Indians is compatible with the way the duke judiciously governed Milan."

She inclined her head toward the Duke of Alba who raised his glass to her. Then, she glanced at the king to measure his reaction — his disapproval of her candor. King Philip smiled, almost skeptically, but familiar in a way, somewhat like her tutor Marco. She couldn't put her finger on that expression. Then she knew: the prince parading on his horse, her first spark for portraiture, and the spark in Philip's eyes. She had passed a public test of wit, and the king approved.

Queen Isabel raised her right hand and a parade of servants arrived with the first course of the evening. The distraction saved Sofonisba from further questions. Across the room, the cardinal and Coello seemed to be arguing, throwing animated hands about, shaking heads. As she looked up in between bites, Sofonisba saw their eyes on her, dark with hatred and envy.

A month later Sofonisba received a letter from her father in Cremona, a note really, scribbled in haste.

Daughter, use your connections in any way possible. Your cousin Ferrante was taken for investigation by the office of the Holy Inquisition on suspicion of heresy. Father Patrizio cannot get any more information except that the order did not appear to come from Rome but from the Spanish Inquisition in Toledo. We have no more information than that. We don't know what prompted it. We do not know where he is being held. We are frantic.

Your Desperate Father

Chapter 19

The Queen's Image: Spring 1565

Sofonisba shuddered. What had Ferrante ever done to warrant an Inquisition? He was not a Protestant sympathizer; he didn't think very deeply about religion at all. She tried to recapture the king's smile in her mind. She felt she had his support. She could only conclude the cardinal was responsible. He was trying to intimidate her, knowing she was close to Ferrante.

Her instinct was to go to the queen. But what if her troubles worried the queen and affected the queen's fertility? She considered the Duke of Alba. He once pledged to be her protector. Would he intercede into a church investigation? Surely the duke would help. She would not trouble the queen with this. Not yet.

Before she could approach the duke, she received another letter from her father.

Dearest Daughter,

I hope with my whole heart that you are well. We have no news of your cousin.

But your sister Elena! If only we had the funds back then to keep her home. Sofi, the convent has become a prison for Elena. I haven't seen with my own eyes as I'm no longer permitted entry, nor is anyone. I only have reports from Father Patrizio. They are enforcing the clausura. The convent has been sealed, entirely bricked up. Only a one by ten-inch hole is left for passing notes inside the convent, and those must be routed through one designated porter. No man may pass into the convent but the porter, who only goes as far as the inner door. The nuns' art studio has been dismantled. It was called 'a sin against nature' for the nuns to be earning such money with their hands. Then the paints, the brushes, and every last piece of art work was confiscated, 'for back rents.' It all happened so quickly. One day everyone in Lombardy was happy that the nuns were producing religious pieces, the next day, gone. What could have provoked such a sudden reversal? We have no more information.

I regret more than ever that I sent your sister there. Now I feel I have been forced to abandon her. I will never abandon her in my heart,

> Heavy with grief, Your Father,
> Amilcare

First Ferrante and now this. Sofonisba could no longer wait. She went to the office of the Mayordomo Major to find the duke and presented herself to the guards. "Lady Sofonisba to see the Duke of Alba," she said.

The guard studied her, surprised to see a woman. "You will need to wait, señorita. The duke is in conference. Would you care to sit?" He motioned her to a chair.

After a half hour, the door opened and the duke came striding out. She jumped to catch up with him. "Your Grace," she called. He was already heading down the corridor.

"Lady Sofonisba." He glanced back at her without slowing his pace. "Walk with me. I'm on my way to present an idea to the king that concerns the queen."

"Your Grace, if I may, I don't want to disturb you—" She caught her breath to keep up with his galloping pace. "But a very serious situation has developed back home, and I don't know where to turn for help."

"Ah, dear lady, problems at home. Yes. I am all ears. But first I must attend to a problem on this home front. Come to find me this afternoon, and you will have my full attention." With that, the duke strode ahead even faster, letting Sofonisba know she should not follow him.

She had to defer her personal life to that of the royals.

Now that the king was returning his affections to the queen, Alba put himself to healing Queen Isabel's damaged reputation. "Your Majesty," Alba bowed low as he entered the king's study. He had been the king's confidant and advisor since Philip was a boy, but remained steadfastly deferential to his monarch. "I should advise Your Majesty that there are political ramifications to the queen's childlessness. There is a certain agitation roiling at court — rumors that the queen is more loyal to France than to Spain — and that she refuses to be with child. Even that she refuses to be with her husband, preferring the company of her stepson. In fact, some gossips blame the queen's affections for Don Carlos as the cause of her empty womb."

"Preposterous!" the king responded.

Nevertheless, it was clear to both the king and the duke that the queen's reputation had to be protected before consequences affected the realm. If sentiments began to turn against Isabel because she had not yet produced an alternate heir, those sentiments could turn ugly toward the crown in other ways. Court

gossip was the first sign of discontent. Left to fester uncon-
trolled, gossip could turn into conflict.

The king knew some of the ridiculous suspicions whispered
about Isabel and Carlos. Alba didn't add what else the gossips
charged: that the king's affair with Doña Eufrasia was retaliation for his wife's affair with his son. The king had no problem
dismissing the stories. He knew first hand of Isabel's efforts to
get pregnant by him and did not doubt her loyalty to him. He
saw and approved of the rapport between his wife and son. The
queen had a happy effect on Don Carlos, who was at his best
around her.

"If I may," Alba said, "it has been reported that the French
queen mother is currently touring the French provinces with
the boy King Charles IX. You might consider sending Queen Isabel to the border to reunite with her mother who might proffer
some maternal advice on the" — Alba paused — "succession situation," his preferred euphemism for her inability to conceive.
"Meanwhile, a regal state visit with Queen Isabel as your representative would serve to boost the queen's image with the people." He waved his arm across an imaginary crowd. "Her status will be rehabilitated when the people see how Your Majesty
entrusts this mission to her. In addition, we mollify the queen
mother who has been requesting a reunion with her daughter
ever since the wedding."

The king nodded, seeing the appeal of Alba's advice, but
hesitated. "We are loath to acknowledge the protestant sympathizer," the king began. "She keeps the Huguenots as close as
she keeps her dwarfs. But we do recall how our own state visit
to the Italian territories boosted our reputation when nobody
thought we could ever succeed Father the Emperor. That was
a lifetime ago," he reminisced. "There's nothing like being given
some authority. We suppose it won't hurt for Isabel to get some
maternal advice, too, on our" — he rolled his hand — "succession

issue, as you say. Yes. We will send the queen to meet her mother at the border."

"Very good, Your Majesty. I shall see that every effort is made to honor the queen's appointment. Of course, a state portrait will be essential. May I suggest, Your Majesty, that given the queen's spirits, she might find it comforting to be in the presence of her ladies as her state portrait is painted? May I suggest that the Lady Sofonisba be utilized during this sensitive time rather than your official portraitist?"

"Coello won't like that. He's still put out by her assignment to paint Don Carlos."

"No doubt, Your Majesty. Yet surely he prefers to put the queen's comfort before his own pride. The Lady Sofonisba has been a most trusted and sisterly companion to the queen. We do aspire to have the queen happy in spirit so as to be painted in the best light."

King Philip chuckled to himself thinking of the look on Coello's face when he was ordered to copy Sofonisba's Farnese portrait. Perhaps the Italian girl was the right choice.

"It does require considerable time together. We have often regretted the hours spent posing. It is a tediously prolonged process and the queen is fragile now. Yes. Have the girl paint the queen. Meanwhile we must prepare the queen on policy. She must insist that France enforce religious conformity. France must expel or contain the Huguenot rebels. We will not contemplate another royal marriage between the countries unless France agrees to this basic principle of non-toleration. Queen Isabel must not deviate from this policy. She will attend this conference as our representative, as if she were the person of the king himself, and she will not waiver from our message."

"Understood, Your Majesty," Alba responded.

"And where is this conference to be held?" the king asked.

"The nearest opportunity would present itself next June at the town of Bayonne, on the French Atlantic coast."

"Then have the cardinal host the entourage in his territory — Burgos is on the way to the coast." With that edict, the meeting was adjourned. Duke Alba bowed low and exited the room backwards, never turning his back on his monarch. With Alba's low bow, the king did not see the irritation on Alba's face.

Alba was happy to have wrestled the portrait from the cardinal's man Coello, only to have the king nominate the cardinal to entertain the entourage. Alba knew that his rival would use his position as host for self-aggrandizement, possibly at the expense of the duke himself. Alba had scored a victory, only to have the battle lines redrawn.

Still, Alba and King Philip were mutually dedicated to preserving Isabel's image and supportive of a mother-daughter reunion if some maternal advice could help Isabel to conceive.

That afternoon, the duke found Sofonisba in the garden. "Lady Sofonisba. I have some fine news for you."

She breathed a heavy sigh, relieved to see the duke as he approached. She had been on pins and needles all day, unable to do anything but pace as she waited to solicit Alba's help. She doubted she could free the nuns of San Vincenzo from their clausura, but maybe she could influence Ferrante's situation.

"The king has bestowed upon you a tremendous honor, to paint an official state portrait," Alba said.

Sofonisba couldn't believe it — the king's portrait, *now* of all times?

"You are requested to paint Queen Isabel." Don Alba beamed. Sofonisba winced. Fortunately, Alba didn't seem to notice. "You must present the image of a serene queen who is happy to represent her lord the king before all the world." He outstretched his arm and made little circles in the air. "The portrait will be unveiled at a diplomatic conference with the French when our queen has her longed-for reunion with her mother. For the king to assign this to you rather than to Coello bodes well for you, Lady Sofonisba. Now what was it you wanted to discuss?"

She handed the duke the frantic note she had received from her father about Ferrante.

Alba squinted slightly to read. "Your cousin? The one who escorted you here with Count Persico? What put him at odds with the Inquisition?"

"Nothing, sir. He's not a Protestant. Can you help us get information? I don't know where else to turn and certainly can't disturb the queen with this."

"No! Don't bother her with this. She must focus on her mission. I will make some inquiries. Have patience."

"Thank you, sir. My family is in your debt."

"Don't fret. Get to work on the queen's portrait. I'll see what I can do."

Sofonisba returned to her studio not entirely convinced the duke saw the urgency of her request. His response was too casual. But if she couldn't disturb the queen with this, then all she could do was wait for Alba's response.

She followed his advice and got to work on Isabel's state portrait. Immersing herself in artistic reverie helped her calm her shattered nerves. She would show a fully regal Isabel, a royal partner to the king, invested with all of his authority. In Isabel's hand, she would place a miniature portrait of the king to proclaim to the world that the queen stands for her husband and that nobody should question this authority. And if she were sent home in shame tomorrow, the miniature of King Philip would survive as Sofonisba's meager opportunity to paint him.

Now if only Alba could get Ferrante out of harm's way.

The cardinal rushed to Coello's studio as soon as he heard the news. "You have failed miserably, Painter. The girl has been assigned to paint a state portrait of the queen." The cardinal's nostrils flared. "The *official* state portrait, for a royal audience with France!"

Coello leaned back and regarded the cardinal curiously, as if the artist began to reconsider his alliance with the churchman. Coello was not a political man full of scheming and intrigue; he was just an artist looking to protect his commissions from competition. Once upon a time, he would have quivered under the cardinal's gaze. He did not cringe now. It dawned on him that perhaps the cardinal was compromised in some way that had to do with the girl.

"I know why I dislike the girl, Your Excellency. She's usurping my privileged position — but why you, sir? If the king approves of her, if the pope approves even, why are you so bent on crushing her? Whatever has she done to you, an esteemed cardinal of the church? She is nobody compared to you."

Coello's simple scrutiny exposed the cardinal.

"I wish only to protect the name of our great sovereign as he risks the condemnation of all of Europe." The cardinal gestured vaguely in the air as he exited the studio, slamming the door behind him.

Coello scratched his head. He was beginning to understand the cardinal.

The Cardinal of Burgos saw as much himself. Coello questioned his motives and proved less than competent at handling intrigue. The official court painter's performance at the Friar Casas banquet seemed to earn the girl greater respect rather than take her down. The cardinal couldn't rely on Coello. It was up to the cardinal alone to keep the girl rattled, to make sure she didn't think too much of herself and her position and was never comfortable enough to check him — to reveal him. Apart from Martin, she was the only person who knew his secret. It was crucial that Sofonisba remain marginalized enough to keep quiet. He had to act before the conference, lest her state portrait of Queen Isabel make her truly influential at court.

The ladies-in-waiting were attending the queen to change her undergarments. The queen had received her courses again and the ladies were offering every consolation they could imagine. "Your Majesty," Isabel de Mendoza said, "my dear uncle the cardinal tells me that soon we will be traveling through the beautiful Spanish countryside which can only cheer Your Majesty. And he will host us at his estate with every elegance and refinement at his disposal. You are sure to have the most delightful stay in Burgos, Your Majesty. We will see to it."

The other ladies continued their swooning and comforting. Sofonisba withdrew to the rear of the room and absorbed this new information. Burgos. As host, the cardinal would be responsible for the entire convoy. If he could maneuver to insult her on the caravan to Toledo, what could he do in his own territory, with Sofonisba in his care?

She did her best to conceal her anxiety from the others. In her mind, she ticked off a list of her supporters: Could she be confident of Isabel's affection, even love? And there was King Philip's smile at the Casas disputation. And of the Duke of Alba's support? She squeezed her eyes shut thinking of Ferrante incarcerated. The state portrait was as important to her own security as it was to the queen's. She would immerse herself in executing it before their journey, as much to perfect her rendition as to forget about the cardinal.

She saw him only one more time at court before their departure. He appeared to be counting his trunks as footmen carried them through the corridors and loaded them onto carriages. Sofonisba crossed his path on her way to studio.

"Family well, painter?" He did not wait for an answer before following his servants into the courtyard.

The party was scheduled to depart Madrid early on the morning of April 9, 1565, to arrive in time for supper in the town of Pozuelo, just outside Madrid. Before the caravan set out, Sofonisba went to look for the Duke of Alba, who would not be attending the conference.

"Your Grace," she said, knocking lightly at the door to his office where she found him preparing final documents for the entourage. The Duke of Alba looked up, irritated, until he recognized her.

"Ah, Lady Sofonisba, how excited you must be for the presentation of your state portrait."

"I wish I could be, Your Grace. But I'm rather concerned for news of my cousin."

"Ah, yes," he responded as if remembering.

"Have you had any information about his whereabouts? My family is desperate," she pleaded.

"Dear Lady, attend to your duties with the queen at this conference. I will continue my efforts."

"I thank you, sir, with my full heart. You will have my family's eternal gratitude if you can help us protect my cousin." She tried to keep the distress out of her voice. But would he do anything? As she climbed into the carriage in which she would ride with the queen, Madame de Vineux, Madame de Rembere, and the queen's portrait, her excitement was tempered by her concern for Ferrante.

The reality of the journey was quickly upon them. The cardinal had prearranged every detail. They dined at Pozuelo and departed in time to settle for the night in Galapagar, where they remained through the midday meal. That night they slept at Guadarrama. They departed in the morning, on to Espinar where they slept. And so began the routine of riding, dining, sleeping.

After weeks on the road, the caravan arrived for an extended respite at the Monastery of Mejorada. The entourage was received reverently and each traveler was assigned an individual monk's cell in which to sleep and pray. The privacy was profound after the close conditions of traveling. For the first time in Spain, Sofonisba spent a night alone. The solitude exacerbated her fears and then gave her time to pray over them with every ounce of her pious heart.

She prayed that the cardinal would simply let bygones be bygones. She prayed for peace and forgiveness for anything she might have done. When her thoughts returned to Ferrante and the reach of the cardinal's power, fear threatened her faith. "Dear God," she whispered again and again, "please just make him leave me alone; make him go away!" She prayed like a small child afraid of the bogeyman. His threat was a phantom: intangible but real. Only her prayers and wishes lulled her to sleep each night at the monastery. She prayed the entire eight days of their stay.

When the entourage departed the monastery on June 25, the other ladies-in-waiting chatted excitedly, happy to end their monastic vigil. For Sofonisba, leaving the monastery meant being one stop closer to Burgos and her tormentor. The party passed through the enclave of Tordesillas, and the stories told gave Sofonisba a chill.

Two generations prior, the people of Tordesillas opposed King Philip's father, Charles, supporting instead Philip's grandmother Juana, daughter of the most Catholic monarchs, Ferdinand and Isabella. Charles declared his mother insane, "Juana the Mad," and imprisoned her so he could rule in her stead.

Some saw Don Carlos' imbalanced disposition as proof of the grandmother's infirmity, but rumors never died that Charles V fabricated his mother's insanity to take the crown off her head.

Sofonisba touched her forehead, dizzy to hear of a Spanish princess, a daughter of the Catholic Kings no less, usurped by a fabricated reputation.

The royal procession continued to slog its way through central Spain, the physical inconveniences foremost on the minds of the travelers, except for Sofonisba, who was consumed with anxiety about the cardinal's power over Ferrante. The party was soon to arrive in Burgos. Sofonisba felt sick.

As the ladies gathered around a drinking well at their last stop before Burgos, Isabel de Mendoza boasted loudly. "I am thrilled! We will luxuriate in my family's estate. I'm sure my uncle the cardinal will say Mass at the cathedral. It's so beautiful. I prefer it to Toledo's — all the gold — and the stained glass and the tomb of El Cid. Of course, the Mendoza family is the most prominent house, and my uncle the cardinal will treat us to only fine elegance, not all this squalor!" She fanned herself with her fingers.

Nobody noticed Sofonisba's anxiety.

Within the hour, a horseman called to the front of the procession, detaining the captain. The captain brought news to the queen's carriage. He bowed deeply, and a bead of his sweat dripped onto the dirt in front of him. "Your Majesty, we are advised that it is not safe in Burgos. The town has been swept by plague." At the mention of plague, the queen and the ladies in her carriage all leaned back, as if the word carried the contagion with it.

"The city is decimated." He shook his head. "More than half the population has perished. It would not be safe there for Your Majesty. We will circumvent the city center and stay outside

its city limits, at another Mendoza estate in Tardajos. We have
been assured that Your Majesty will be made most comfortable
there."

The royal procession rerouted to Tardajos, just outside the
confines of Burgos. Servants greeted the party. "We expect the
cardinal this hour, Your Majesty. With your permission, a High
Mass is planned for this evening to pray for God's blessing and
protection."

The evening hours passed and the cardinal never arrived.
The queen and her entourage retired to bed after a short Mass
said by the queen's chaplain. In the morning, there was still no
word from the cardinal. The captain was eager to get the entourage out of the infested region. "With your permission, Your
Majesty, we will resume our journey immediately. It's possible
that the cardinal is consumed by his duties. It does not seem
prudent to await him further."

"Yes, captain. You are wise to suggest it. Let us proceed to
the coast."

Sofonisba let out a heavy sigh. After all her fretting, all the
long hours praying in the monastery, she wouldn't even have to
spend a night under the cardinal's watch. The entourage continued its journey to Bayonne, bypassing Burgos and the cardinal entirely.

Three mornings later, the captain requested leave to speak privately with the queen. The ladies stepped aside, tempted to
eavesdrop — until they read the consternation on the captain's
face. Sofonisba could see the queen's reaction. Her eyes were
large when he began, then grew even wider. She put her hand
to her chest, then nodded, seeming to absorb the news. When
the queen returned to her hive of ladies, she earnestly regarded
each one in the eye before speaking. She paused at Sofonisba

ever so briefly and tilted her chin down. Sofonisba knew the news had special meaning for her.

The queen approached Isabel de Mendoza and took her hand. "My dear, you have my condolences. We cannot know the ways of the Lord. We can only trust in his guidance. I'm sorry. Your uncle the Cardinal of Burgos is dead. Dead from the plague like so many of Burgos."

The cardinal's niece put a hand to her mouth to stifle a cry. The ladies crowded around her offering their support. Only Sofonisba held back. She could barely breathe. Her prayers in the monastery — how she prayed for the cardinal to be gone from her. She prayed so hard, so piously, as piously as she had prayed for anything, even for painting the king's portrait. How could she give condolences for a death she caused by the force of her own prayers?

The cardinal had planned to catch up with the entourage, but he began to have the lethal swellings. In no time, his armpits, neck, and groin oozed, and his fever reached a deadly peak. With death upon him, the cardinal feared for his eternal soul more than his worldly reputation. He reviewed the span of his life and prayed to be forgiven. He could never reverse putting thousands to death during the Inquisition in Toledo, but he hoped to find forgiveness for some of the personal wrongs he had committed.

Lady Sofonisba,

I write to you in the most desperate of personal circumstances, God having seen fit to punish me for my sins by afflicting my territory, my family, and my person with this sickness from the eternal fires of Hell.

I am too weak to detail the many slights I made against you at court for which I now seek your forgiveness

before I reach my judgment day. I so feared you for the
information you possessed and the threat of disclosure.
I beg you to understand the constraints of my position.
But as I lie dying, it is only you who can help me correct
the ill I have done to one man, for only you know he had
a special relationship to me. Out of fear, I cast this man
out of my employ, and out of my personal protection,
when he had done nothing but serve me loyally, even in
war. I enclose here to your personal oversight a sack of
gold, to be sent to the village of Artigat . . .

The cardinal had undermined Sofonisba's credibility because
she knew the secret that would ruin him. With his deathbed
apologies, he hoped to make amends.

Then, he managed a second letter.

Dear Martin,

I write from my deathbed to seek your forgiveness
for casting you off without warning or provisions for
your journey home, nor any of the rewards I promised
you for your years of loyal service, especially after your
singular sacrifice serving my brother at the battle of
Saint Quentin. I sent you away summarily, caring only
for my own reputation and position, never inquiring
about you since.

Please accept this bequest to help you live out your
days in comfort, to atone for my sinful self-preservation.
I send you this gold in a humble and inadequate attempt
for forgiveness and pray it finds you contentedly
reunited with your family.

Repentantly,
Francisco de Mendoza, Cardinal of Burgos, 1565

The cardinal sent for a special messenger. "Give the package to the Lady Sofonisba who attends the queen. She will be among the queen's ladies in the royal" — the cardinal paused and coughed — "the royal delegation. Make certain that only she gets this package and that no other eyes see it." The cardinal pointed to the package on the table and offered a coin to the messenger.

The messenger pocketed the coin and lifted the package, lurching forward slightly, as if not anticipating the weight. He looked at the cardinal and then shook the package, cocking his ears at the coins' heavy jingle. He glanced at the nobleman dying before him and whispered, "Forgive me, Father. Times are hard."

The package and the letters of repentance never reached Sofonisba.

All she knew for certain was that she prayed passionately at the monastery for the cardinal to be gone, and now he was dead.

Chapter 20

Catherine de Medici and the French Court: Bayonne, France June and July 1565

As the entourage headed for the coast, Sofonisba remained as white as a ghost, mulling over the litany of sins she felt she had caused by the force of her prayers to escape the power of the cardinal. She had prayed to God to send the cardinal away, and he disappeared, and an entire town was taken down with him. God answered her prayers. The monotony of the travel exacerbated her guilty conscience and fed her active imagination. She was a monster. She envisioned Dante's circles of hell. She would be placed in the seventh circle, for the violent. She thought of her tutor Marco and his vivid dramatizations of each ring. Maybe she would be put in the lowest circle, for the treacherous, because her prayers had betrayed an entire town.

The cardinal's grip on the artist in life grew even tighter in death. Excited to finish the journey, the others did not seem to notice Sofonisba's disquiet.

Queen Isabel put aside her mourning for the dead of Burgos as her family reunion neared. The closer to the coast they got, the giddier the queen became. In addition to her mother, the queen would be seeing her younger brother, the minor King Charles IX, and sister, Princess Marguerite, whom their mother desperately wanted to see married into Philip's house.

Even with her excitement, Queen Isabel decided that the food in the coastal town of San Sebastian was so exceptional that they remained there a day longer than planned. They feasted on endless fresh seafood paired with the local wine that was poured high above the glass to bring out its effervescence. Isabel drank to calm her nerves.

They intended to meet the French royal party on the fifteenth of July in the town of Bayonne. Then, as Queen Isabel and Madame de Vineux were discussing the upcoming reunion, the rotund Queen Mother of France pranced into camp astride a white horse, only accompanied by a contingent of ten soldiers. Sofonisba was surprised to see Queen Isabel break into a near run to greet her mother.

"I could not wait another day to see you, Daughter," Catherine de Medici said from horseback. "Let us thank God for this reunion and celebrate together!" Guards rushed to the queen mother's side to help her down. Servants rearranged seating. Soon, Queen Isabel and her mother Queen Regent Catherine withdrew for a private conversation on makeshift risers. Sofonisba was relieved to have time to compose herself before meeting Catherine de Medici. She slapped her cheeks trying to put some color into them — she looked pale the last time she spied a looking glass.

No further introductions that night.

The royal confidentiality continued the next day. Not even Madame de Vineux, the queen mother's trusted friend, was invited to join the two queens who rode together in one carriage to the town of Bayonne, on the Adour River, where winding, narrow alleys were squeezed between town walls and the riverbanks, three centuries of English Plantagenet rule crammed into them.

The entourage stopped at the bank of the Adour where decorated barges greeted them. From there, they floated past waving townspeople. The barges stopped at a dock draped in the banners of Spain and France, Hapsburg and Valois. Queen Isabel was presented to her brother, the boy King Charles IX. Sofonisba saw an awkward moment of shuffling after the queens were lifted from the barges.

Madame de Rembere correctly answered the question on Sofonisba's and the other ladies' minds. "There's some confusion about precedence. Who goes first: the boy king, the reigning older sister queen, or the regent queen mother."

There was no confusion about the last place position of Isabel's unmarried sister Princess Marguerite. The boy king took precedence. After almost an hour of formalities among the royal family, they approached the tent of ladies-in-waiting. The ladies rose and lined up, curtsying to the floor until each was presented to the boy king, his mother, and the royal princess.

When Sofonisba stood before Catherine de Medici, the queen mother spoke in her native Florentine Italian, Dante's Italian, which Sofonisba learned from Marco.

"Dear Sofonisba, I have heard many lovely things about you, dear things from Madame de Vineux about how well you treat my daughter and exciting things from my artists. You have quite the reputation for portraiture. I am told you studied with Master Michelangelo."

Sofonisba remained in her curtsy. She did not have the fortitude to clarify. "I am most honored to serve Your Highness" — her voice cracked — "and most pleased if I entertain Her Majesty in any way."

"An artist who is modest, no less. Your work is more than mere entertainment, I hear. Later, we will talk."

Sofonisba could feel the other ladies-in-waiting watching her, jealous, just like after the first dance the night of the royal wedding banquet. Their envy seemed so trivial now.

Ferrante's smile flashed in her mind. Could the queen mother have some influence over the Inquisition in Lombardy? Contacts in Rome? Dare Sofonisba describe the ordeal to her when they spoke again? Did not courtiers ask favors of Queen Isabel at each stop along the route to Bayonne? Didn't the queen mother thank her for her care of Queen Isabel? Couldn't Sofonisba ask for the protection of her family in return?

Sofonisba convinced herself to act. She had to do what she could. The Duke of Alba had accomplished nothing so far and her cousin remained imprisoned.

The elaborate introductions were concluded, and the parties settled into the various residences arranged to house them for the conference. Isabel and her ladies were invited to stay at Le palais episcopal, located near the Gothic Cathedrale Sainte Marie, along with Catherine de Medici and her ladies.

The entourage rested, and the royals spent more time alone getting reacquainted, away from prying eyes and ears. That evening, the first of a fortnight of fetes and banquets began with the unveiling of Sofonisba's state *Portrait of Isabel, Queen of Spain*. The portrait was covered in purple silk and carried to the royal riser by two servants who placed it upon an easel facing the royals. Queen Isabel gestured for Sofonisba to join on the riser where she, Queen Mother Catherine, and young King Charles sat.

Sofonisba clasped her hands together to hide their shaking, feeling her usual anxiety about showing a piece, compounded by the dogged guilt about Burgos and worry for Ferrante that weighed on her. She had eaten nothing. She felt as faint as the day of the royal wedding, the day her cousin pulled her onto the dance floor.

The boy king watched his mother as if gauging her reaction, much like Alessandro Farnese copying the Duchess of Parma. Catherine de Medici rose and walked close to the painting.

She inspected it for many minutes, long enough that Sofonisba pushed aside her guilt over Burgos, forgot about Ferrante, and fixated on her need for Queen Mother Catherine to love it, to approve of it. The waiting felt endless.

Sofonisba heard courtiers beginning to cough and clear their throats awkwardly.

"The queen holds a miniature of the king's likeness in her hand. She has him in the palm of her hand, no?"

Isabel shot a quick look from Sofonisba to her mother. The joke did not provoke the intended levity. King Philip was not under the thumb of anyone.

Catherine nodded to her daughter, almost in apology, and continued sternly, "What this rendering roundly proclaims is that our beloved daughter comes to this conference with the full authority of her husband the king. She holds his likeness in her hand just as she holds his trust in her royal bearing, dedication, and honor." The queen mother bowed her head toward her daughter who beamed at the public affirmation of her importance. Catherine's maternal instinct achieved the first goal of the conference: with very few words, she recognized her daughter's authority and boosted her reputation.

Sofonisba's rendering helped make it possible — an honor, she knew, that got her one step closer to her goal of painting the king. She tried to bask in the queen mother's approval of her painting. But by night, the glory faded to anxiety and dread, dread that her prayers at the monastery provoked the plague of Burgos and the cardinal's death. Sofonisba was reminded of her guilt every time she glanced at Isabel de Mendoza whose lifeblood appeared to have drained away with the demise of her family — which then reminded Sofonisba of her cousin Ferrante's predicament for which she was certain she was also responsible.

One evening a few days later, a play was to be performed about Queen Sofonisba, the ancient Carthaginian queen after whom Sofonisba was named. Catherine de Medici requested to be seated next to Sofonisba for the performance. She peppered the artist with expert questions about painting: oil on canvas versus tempura on wood, background landscapes versus solid green, the new source of red from the prickly pears of the Americas. "You know Giorgio Vasari painted my wedding portrait." Sofonisba concentrated hard on the conversation to not get distracted by the internal conflicts weighing on her.

The queen mother wanted details about Sofonisba's lessons with her daughter and the ladies-in-waiting. "Has anyone distinguished herself?"

"Your Highness, none were as eager or as talented as Queen Isabel."

"Now how did a girl from Lombardy come to study with Master Michelangelo, may he rest in peace?" The queen mother and Sofonisba made the sign of the cross over themselves at the same time, making Catherine chuckle.

Sofonisba was not going to add dishonesty to her litany of sins. "Your Highness, I cannot claim to have studied with him. My family corresponded with him and he critiqued a drawing of my infant brother crying."

"And did you have the opportunity to meet my Florentine cousin Francesco de Medici? I heard he visited your king's court, no?"

"I did have that honor, Your Highness. In fact, I learned that his father Duke Cosimo of Tuscany acquired the drawing I just mentioned, my *Little Boy Bitten by a Crayfish*."

"Then you can be certain it will be displayed, as Cosimo does like to show off his collection. Did you know Francesco has been betrothed to the Emperor's daughter, Giovanna of Austria? Another peaceful alliance through marriage."

The queen mother leaned closer to Sofonisba. "After the performance, I will have you to my suites." With that, the queen mother turned to Madame de Vineux, seated on her other side, for the duration of the banquet.

Sofonisba sat back in her chair and let out a slow breath, startled by the French queen's private invitation, but also a bit teary — the personal attention and shared language comforted her. It made of her think of her mother Bianca. She took a sip of wine. The Txakoli's effervescence washed down a lump in her throat.

A groom fetched Sofonisba later that evening to escort her to the queen mother's suites.

"Dear Sofonisba, do come in," Catherine de Medici warmly greeted her in Italian, now using the informal "tu." Sofonisba curtsied. "Do rise. Let us be friends. And you must tell me every detail of my daughter's life that I have missed these past five years. Tell me in our mutual language so that we may share as mother and daughter that I might relive some of what I have lost."

"The queen is so lovely," Sofonisba said, and sniffled. "She is most generous with her ladies-in-waiting and" — Sofonisba caught her breath and wiped her nose with the back of her hand mindlessly — "and she always . . ." Sofonisba burst into unexpected tears. "I apologize. Your Highness is so gracious." She was mortified to lose her composure.

"What is disturbing you, child?"

"I hate to bother you . . . with my troubles," Sofonisba stammered.

"I have lost five years of my beloved daughter's life. Let me make up for that loss with some mothering now. What is the matter, Lady Sofonisba?"

Sofonisba took a deep breath and unloaded, "I prayed for the cardinal to leave me alone because he has tormented me so, and probably sent my cousin Ferrante to the Inquisition, and my family is a wreck, and I prayed for him to be gone. I prayed hard. Then he died of the plague along with half of Burgos. God heard my prayers. I am responsible for the death of thousands because I feared one man. I have caused such evil by my selfishness."

The queen mother's eyes grew wide but then she relaxed into a Mona Lisa smile. "Now slow down child. You don't truly believe you caused the plague of Burgos with your prayers, do you?"

Sofonisba dabbed her nose with her pearl-lined sleeve.

"I prayed for eight straight days — in a monastery — reverently, urgently, for him to be *gone from me*." She was pleading with her eyes for the queen to understand.

The queen mother put her hand under Sofonisba's chin. "Cara, forty years ago in Florence I prayed for the emperor's soldiers to be gone from me when they imprisoned me in the Murate convent, shouting obscenities regarding their intentions for me, which I will not repeat. Am I therefore responsible for every plague that has run its course through the emperor's army? Preposterous, child! Your prayer cannot compel the Lord to any conduct. You may only pray for your own fortitude, patience, peace, and forgiveness, only for assistance with the interior of your soul, not the coercion of God's actions. Only the Lord knows his ways." Catherine de Medici smiled broadly. "The most important thing is to forgive. Forgive the cardinal and your heart will be lifted. But, cara, why did you need the cardinal gone from you? Did he disapprove of your talents? Object to a woman painter?"

Sofonisba batted back tears trying to accept Catherine's absolution. She knew she had to confess it all. "I went somewhere I should not have gone. I saw the cardinal — somewhat, ahh — indisposed. I should not have seen it. I was imprudent."

"So you found the cardinal with his hand in the cookie jar? Cara, if every indiscretion were vindicated our world would be in a constant state of war." The queen mother leaned forward. "What did you see, child?"

"It is difficult to express, difficult to find polite words to say—"

"Polite words? Polite words to describe an indisposed cardinal? A buggerer then, of course. Cara mia, how awkward for you to come across such a thing. No doubt late at night, after festivities or some such occasion?"

"How did you know?"

"The world is not a very mysterious place. We all need love, no? A little tolerance can do so much good. I fear your monarch is misled. If he would adopt a tolerant mindset, so much conflict could be averted. We should seek peace through love matches, not conquest and suppression, no? But that is another matter. You had absolutely no influence over the plague of Burgos or the cardinal's death. As the queen mother of the most Christian nation of France, I absolve you. Now think no more that you have done harm. Go in peace and rest. Later, after you have forgiven the cardinal, and yourself, we will have our talk about my Isabel, and you will tell me everything you know. And I will seek information about your cousin. Ferrante Anguissola is his name?"

"Ferrante Anguissola Gonzaga."

"Gonzaga. I will inquire. I promise you."

With the French queen's words ringing in her ears, Sofonisba returned to her accommodations. The color began to return to her cheeks.

In bed that night, she dwelled on Catherine de Medici's assurances and decided to have faith in them, reminding herself over and over that she was not responsible for the plague of Burgos and the cardinal's death. Then she did the harder part.

She searched her heart for any residual fear or insult. She put a coat of forgiveness over them — and painted away the bitterness. She wished for the cardinal only that he might rest in peace. Sofonisba had been so mired in guilt over her prayers in the monastery that she had not considered how life at court would be different without the cardinal and his subtle campaign to keep her on edge. His insults loomed over her the way prejudice against her as a girl dampened her early years: a nagging sense of being degraded without any recourse. No longer wary of the cardinal, might she now be free to develop artistically — and personally — without the threat of retaliation? Her singular goal remained to paint the king. Her mind, and heart, could now be clear for the task.

Now, if only she could help Ferrante.

After weeks of banquets and reminiscing, the queens were compelled to begin the formal negotiations for which the conference had been arranged. They met privately in Catherine's rooms, decorated with royal tapestries and bursting with trays of fresh fruits and local delicacies. King Philip was ever-present in the form of the miniature that Sofonisba had embedded in the queen's state portrait. One look at the painting reminded Isabel that she had no room to deviate from her husband's strict instructions for complete Catholic conformity.

"Dear Mother," Isabel said, "your own Chancellor L'Hopital is an acknowledged Huguenot. My king demands that L'Hopital be replaced by a professed Catholic."

"My dear," Catherine de Medici retorted, "How Spanish you are now. What of tolerance? Did not your father the king, may he rest in peace, retain Chancellor L'Hopital? How can you claim the man a Huguenot? Let us not slander our lords but rather unite our realms further through marriage. Your sister Marguerite would do well for the Prince Don Carlos. Your brother Anjou is a match for the Princess of Portugal, the king's widowed sister."

"Please, Mother, you insist again on the impossible. My king will not agree to these matches until you have banished the Huguenots from France. Office holders must be required to pledge Catholic. Protestant worship must be prohibited. France must accept the terms of the Council of Trent. Orthodoxy is the only righteous path."

"Daughter, my reign has witnessed death and destruction from such orthodoxy. Tolerance brings harmony to France."

"That harmony cannot endure, Mother. My king will not rest until he has purged his neighbors of the infidel in any form. You will compromise your lofty vision when you see it lacks foundation. Your vision cannot contain the Protestants. How will it help when the Turks are at your door?"

"Daughter, my battles at home concern the right to think and pray as each one of us sees fit, not the threat of Turks."

"Then my king's battleground is more extensive than yours. He is obliged to guarantee the safety of the seas. Can you not appreciate that at least from your birthplace?"

"I appreciate from my childhood that your king's father the emperor sent soldiers to kidnap me from the Murate convent and threatened to offer up my twelve-year old maidenhood to his soldiers as their warriors' prize. That kind of protection in the name of religious uniformity does not inspire a sense of security. No. Toleration does."

"Ahh, Mother." Isabel sighed at her mother's relentless obstinacy. "I cannot deviate from my mission. I must hold fast to my king's strict instructions on religious orthodoxy. He will not entertain marriage alliances until that goal is achieved."

In unison, the two queens looked at Sofonisba's state portrait of Isabel and its miniature king. His invisible presence overshadowed the queens' progress. Isabel's reputation and credibility were at stake if the negotiations failed.

"Daughter, I will not let you return to your king empty-handed. Let us begin with that on which we might agree." Catherine de Medici sat down at her writing table and personally began to draft notes. "I will concede this, in the interest of peace: First, France will agree to convene an assembly. Second, Huguenots will be excluded from said assembly. Third, we will examine the findings of the Council of Trent. You may assure your king that we make these promises only at the insistence of his virtuous queen who tenaciously represents him."

Isabel squeezed her eyelids to fight back the quick well of tears. Her mother's simple terms made a success of the conference, at least for Isabel's purposes. However modest, the French queen mother's concessions permitted Queen Isabel to return to Madrid with a signed international accord. The achievement would elevate her profile. A barren queen could not afford to be perceived as weak and useless as Catherine de Medici well knew. She would not let her daughter's image suffer.

"Now my dear, as to your more pressing problem. It is not by prayer that you will produce an heir. Let me tell you some things about men." Catherine de Medici offered her young married daughter some tips she could not have properly disclosed on the eve of the girl's wedding. "Try all of that. And then you pray."

The ladies-in-waiting were left to their own entertainments during the political negotiations. Sofonisba used the time to draw the Basque countryside.

"Lady Sofonisba," Catherine de Medici's maid found her outside. "Her Highness wishes to see you now."

Sofonisba immediately followed and curtsied to the floor when presented to the queen.

"Please rise, Lady Sofonisba and come receive a token of my love." The queen mother held out to her a red velvet box.

"Your Highness, I—" Sofonisba was startled to receive a gift from Catherine de Medici.

"Do open it!"

Sofonisba opened the box to find a diamond ring set in gold, more valuable than any jewelry she had ever owned. "You are too generous, Your Highness."

"Accept this gift as a mother's heart-felt gratitude toward one who loves and protects her daughter."

"I will cherish your gift always, Your Highness, and—"

The French queen raised her hand. "I have something else you will find most valuable." The queen handed her a document stamped with the seal of the Archdiocese of Milan. Sofonisba looked up pleadingly at the queen who nodded for her to open it. Sofonisba broke the seal. Her Latin served her well.

"It's a proclamation"—her voice trailed off as she read until she reached the magic words—"absolving Ferrante Anguissola Gonzaga . . . *a matter of clerical oversight*?" Sofonisba looked up at the queen incredulous that her worry was so abruptly put to bed.

Reading the shock on Sofonisba's face, the queen explained. "There is no love lost between my distant cousin Pope Pius and myself, but we do share a name. And we have traded art. In fact, I tried to get him to give me your first portrait of Isabel, but he declined, saying it was too precious to him. After you told me of the straits your cousin was in, I sent an envoy on your behalf to Rome. My man rode the horses practically to death, but we did what was needed. He reports that Pius was happy to intercede in a case for a relative of yours. It was truly your name, not mine, which saved your cousin. The pope loved your painting of Isabel, Lady Sofonisba. His intercession into Ferrante's matter was his way to reciprocate." The queen mother waved a hand in the air. "The case against Ferrante was apparently baseless, in any event. There was no evidence. If the Cardinal of Burgos did manufacture the case against Ferrante, he certainly did a minimal job of it. You have been a true friend to my daughter. This is *my* reciprocity."

"Thank you, gracious queen, for your intercession on behalf of my family. How can we possibly repay our gratitude for this tremendous deed?"

"Take care of my daughter in my absence, and your gratitude will be spoken in volumes. And now, for that talk we still need to have. I want you to tell me *everything* about my daughter . . ."

On the second of July, the French royal family had their private farewell and then the Spanish entourage set out on its return journey to Madrid, again skirting the decimated town of Burgos.

For five years she had fretted over the cardinal's hold on her. She let the realization sink in. With Ferrante's safety assured and no cardinal to fear, Sofonisba slept peacefully in her carriage for most of the journey as it lumbered along back to Madrid.

Queen Isabel tugged her awake. "Lady Sofonisba, I've been reflecting on our time in Bayonne, my first true diplomatic mission. I feel with all my heart that I did justice to my obligations — to my country *and* to my mother country, for peace between these nations. You helped, Sofonisba, my ambassador. Not just your painting — you served as envoy to an inquiring mother, yes?" The queen smiled. "I believe you have earned your reward, and I believe I know what that is." Isabel put her forefinger over Sofonisba's heart. "I think you would like to paint the king, *non*?"

Isabel's teasing French "no" tore straight into Sofonisba's core. "More than anything, Your Majesty."

"Perhaps we can both find new opportunities to attain our goals. When the time is right, I will approach His Majesty."

Queen Isabel cupped her hands over her mouth, but Sofonisba could see her royal smile by the twinkle in her conspiratorial eyes.

The queen was eager to take advantage of her mother's words of wisdom, *away* from the frenzy and scrutiny of court. She spoke to the king as soon as her entourage was comfortably settled back in the capital. She used Sofonisba as her foil.

"I suggested to His Majesty that we take an intimate sojourn to Arejunez, a small party, to focus on simple time together. And that after the success of my state portrait in Bayonne—" The queen held still a moment as if posing for her portrait, then whispered, "—I reminded His Majesty of your many years of service to the crown and your personal service to me." She curled a loose lock of hair around her forefinger and pouted her lips. Sofonisba dug a finger into her palm, the wait was interminable. "*Oui*, so that you may paint him, Lady Sofonisba." The queen clapped her hands.

"Your Majesty," Sofonisba reached out and took the queen's tented fingers between her own, "God bless you!" Neither woman minded the forward breach of protocol.

Sofonisba was readying supplies for the journey to Arejunez when a rap at the door startled her. She turned to see Master Coello peering inside. "Good day, Lady Sofonisba." He entered and offered a bouquet of gardenias.

She took the bouquet. "Thank you, sir," she said, squinting as if to understand.

"My peace offering, dear lady. I hear you will paint King Philip. Such an honor. I believed that honor was to be exclusively mine." He squeezed his eyes closed momentarily. "But now I see it is not. I accept your appointment, as I must. Imagine, though, did you ever think our crusader of Christianity would submit to a rendering by a woman?"

"Sir, you ask that same question while you say you accept it."

"Forgive me." He nodded. "I am from a small village in Portugal. A woman painting the king's portrait is peculiar to me. Do you know how my villagers would laugh to hear it?"

"You have a young daughter, do you not Master Coello?"

"Yes, she is just five this year."

"The age I began to draw."

"Perhaps I will teach her," he said vaguely, "perhaps I will. Good day, Lady Sofonisba." With that, her former rival exited her studio. Maybe he would become like Moroni yet. She could only hope.

The plan was interrupted by war. Ottomans captured the Island of Malta, a prime Spanish stronghold off the southern tip of Sicily. Don John was put in command of a counterattack. The king was gripped one hundred percent by Malta. It was not the hour for personal missions.

A bloody August. By September 1565, victory at Malta. Don John and the Knights Hospitaller ousted the great Suleiman the Magnificent. Banquets and parades flooded Madrid.

When the euphoria died down, the queen returned to her quest. "A fresh victory seemed the ideal time to remind the king about the possibility of a little sojourn," Queen Isabel reported to Sofonisba. "I suggested that His Majesty might like to see himself painted in your Lombard style to commemorate our victory."

After a lifetime of desire, Sofonisba's opportunity to paint the king was upon her. She felt a sense of awe like never before, not for the queen, nor Don Carlos. Her life's dream. But the Inquisition? His coldness to the queen? Reality butted her ideal. How would she represent him? Ambition propelled her. The decision of how to render the King of Spain weighed on her. Her imagination froze — or rather she willed it to shut down. She fought back her inner conflicts. The king had to be presented conventionally, astride a horse in military regalia in honor of Malta. She could follow Master Titian. But, no, she knew she had to do more. She could not rest on copying another, even Master Titian. She had to be the master. The Master.

But what did she know about the king's soul? She knew he wanted another son more than anything. And he needed for his wife to feel loved. As soon as the royal party settled at Arejunez, the king sent for Sofonisba. Then, it came to her. She would render her king as Isabel's devoted lover.

"If Your Majesty would please be so kind as to place a hand on your chest like so ... Yes. That's it. And the lily — please, Your Majesty, slightly to the left. Yes. Thank you. Your Majesty is quite natural at this."

"Lady Sofonisba, you are most kind." He politely nodded to the blushing painter. The king was a natural. He sat patiently still for as long as Sofonisba asked. In fact, Philip II was the most still sitter she recalled painting. Even so, she did a series of studies of him, drawings from which she could paint patiently afterward so as to not detain His Majesty in her study for the weeks it would take to get the piece right. She would do her family name proud, she mentally told her father. Her rendering of the king would stand with Master Titian's.

The intimate royal party dined and danced and relaxed in Arejunez. She took up the queen's suggestion and gave the king's portrait a dark olive Lombard background, staying true to her roots, highlighting his face and hands. White ruffled collar and cuffs set off his adoring countenance and the hands that offered flowers to his beloved.

She heard her tutor Marco's voice. The word "masterpiece" still haunted her. She tore up the parchment. She rubbed her temples as she consulted her studies. Marco's ringing challenge had the same effect now as it did then — creative paralysis. The piece was too important. She toiled but could not produce something *worthy*.

The only person who seemed to notice her lack of execution was the king himself. "Lady Sofonisba, how is my portrait proceeding?"

"Your Majesty, I spend my every waking hour perfecting it." She dropped to a curtsy.

"I do hope we can unveil it here in the lovely setting of Arejunez. It would make the queen so happy."

"Yes, Your Majesty," Sofonisba said, still kneeling.

While the rest of the small entourage enjoyed the idyllic life at Arejunez for two months more, Sofonisba struggled with the king's portrait every moment. By mid-November, the sojourn was over. The royals were to return to Madrid for the holidays. Sofonisba had not perfected the king's portrait. She couldn't unveil it as it was.

She sheepishly knocked on the king's anteroom door. Her voice cracked. "Permission to see His Majesty." She was admitted straightaway, and the king smiled up from his correspondence as soon as she entered his receiving parlor. Sofonisba curtsied low but steadfastly looked in his eyes rather than at the ground, as much to appear confident as to inspect the elusive features.

"Your Majesty, as your loyal servant, I must apologize. As an artist, I must be certain. Your rendering is not yet perfect. I cannot offer it before we return to Madrid. I promise Your Majesty, it will be finished, and it will be ideal."

The king gently nodded. Sofonisba was relieved. Her relief faded as he continued to nod — slowly — without a word.

"Very well," he said finally, his cheek twitching faintly. He returned to his correspondence. She saw the same patronizing look he gave Friar de las Casas after the disputation. She turned around and quietly exited the king's receiving parlor to prepare for the return trip to Madrid.

Chapter 21

Castilian Summers 1565–1568

The king and queen returned to Madrid and the Escorial negotiations that filled the king's anterooms. Courtiers vying for contracts pledged their undying loyalty to the crown and left lilies for the queen they hoped would soon carry an alternate heir.

The king was too busy to inquire about Sofonisba's progress on his portrait. His renewed preoccupation with the construction project did nothing to help her portrayal of him as lover. The more the Escorial project progressed, the slower her work seemed to go.

The queen, on the other hand, looked radiant. "Lady Sofonisba, I believe Arejunez did the trick! I have just informed His Majesty. We will have our heir."

Sofonisba went down on one knee, half curtsy, half prayer, and the queen raised her up by the elbow. "Stand before me, Lady Sofonisba. I want to thank you for your part. I do believe your portrait sessions helped His Majesty to relax. It helped to distract him from his work. But something more, I believe. Somehow, you softened him."

At least she had earned the queen's gratitude.

Once the news was official, the court focused on preparations for the royal baby. Nothing took precedence over the safe delivery of the alternate heir to the king's erratic son Don Carlos.

And in the process, just in case, the queen drafted her last will and testament.

"Sofonisba, I make no secret of my gratitude to my ladies who will all be amply provided for in my will. However, not each of you will take equally. To you, Lady Sofonisba, I designate 3,000 ducats and a brocade bedspread from my mother, one that I cherish."

"Your Majesty, I don't want any bequest if it means I take it by your death."

"My dear Sofi, do you know you are the only of my ladies to decline a bequest? And so, of course, you must not. Now, take note. The sisters of the Convent of Saint Agatha made this bedcover. Their waters are renowned for aiding conception. Save it for your own marriage bed, which I hope you will one day be blessed to see."

"I want only the safe delivery of your prince, Your Majesty." Sofonisba crossed herself.

"Unfold it." The queen gestured to the bedspread. Sofonisba unfolded the beautiful cloth to find her treasured art kit wrapped in it, the one she gave to Isabel during the queen's serious illness in Toledo.

"Your Majesty, I cannot accept this. It's yours now."

"Please, Lady Sofonisba." The queen smiled. "I know you gave me your art kit when I lay dying to give me hope. It was all you had to give. And it did help me. Even in my delirium, I could see it on the table and envision our time together in the studio. The kit reminded me of life. It helped me to persevere. Let me return it to you to honor our shared passion. And, of course, I should not have the opportunity to use it in my state. Keep it for your sojourns."

Sofonisba took the kit from Isabel, touched by the young queen's optimism.

She was inspired to complete her depiction of Philip II as Isabel's lover. She got immediately back to work, following most of her original ideas from the Arejunez version. Nobody interrupted her.

She was done before she knew it.

"We shall have a festive unveiling of the king's portrait, Lady Sofonisba!" The queen said. "We are so happy these days! The unveiling will be an ideal time for a party! And your rendition celebrates our fertile royal love, no?"

When Sofonisba next entered the banquet hall, all eyes were on her, and courtiers made room for her to pass. She did not yet know it, but she was being touted as "the prestigious lady painter."

Catherine de Medici heard from Madame de Vineux that Isabel was hosting a party for the unveiling. She sent cases of an effervescent wine from a vineyard not far from Paris. Isabel opened a case the night before Sofonisba's unveiling and the ladies-in-waiting tasted the wine before the rest of the court. The queen poured Sofonisba several glasses.

When Sofonisba returned to her bed in the ladies' quarters, there was a beautiful bejeweled gown laid out for her for the unveiling, a gift from the king. She noticed a letter next to the gown. It was from Cremona, sent by special courier. She was hesitant to open it given the bad news in the past, feeling a selfish fear of ruining the unveiling. But she couldn't resist. She took a deep breath and steadied herself for more tragedy.

My Dearest Sofonisba,

We have not been so excited by a visitor since the king himself paraded through town as a young prince. Our home has just been blessed by a visit from the

illustrious painter and writer Giorgio Vasari. He had
seen your *Boy Bitten* at Michelangelo's studio a decade
ago and heard your praises sung by the Pope himself.
Then, when he learned you were serving at the king's
court, his curiosity brought him here to see how we
raised you to become such a talented woman.

My dear Sofi, he has praised your virtu.' He praised
your *Chess Game* and the *Family Portrait* as true
masterpieces. He said they were executed so well the
sitters 'seem to breathe,' his words, Sofi. He said you
make your sitters look truly alive! My child, we are so
very honored and proud of you.

Your Loving and Devoted Father,
Amilcare, 12 June 1566

Sofonisba paced the ladies' quarters as she read, thrilled by Vasari's words: *truly alive*. Tears welled at her father's words — honored and proud — her ultimate reward. Her chest seemed to
tighten. She began to bite her nails, mindlessly tearing at her
flesh. A drop of blood trickled from her index finger and fell to
her shoe. She remembered the drop of paint that fell on Lucia's
shoe the day her sister accused her of pandering to Michelangelo with the way she rendered her brother. Pang. Loss. Mourning. Homesickness.

Her breath became short. Sofonisba knew her portrait of
the king was not right. And the unveiling was tomorrow. She fell
asleep fitfully and woke up in the middle of the night when the
castle was still. She lit a candle and crept out of the ladies' quarters. In the quiet of her studio, she contemplated the portrait.

She carefully took her canvas from its easel and knelt down
on the tapestried floor with the painting facing her on her lap.
She gazed into her king's eyes. They were not right. She scanned

the canvas top to bottom. She held up one hand to frame his face, then quickly cupped her mouth. This was not her masterpiece. She could not deny it: the deep conflict she felt over his ordering the Inquisition at the start of his marriage to Isabel. It infected her imagination. She could not render him as a lover.

Sofonisba stood directly in front of the canvas and gaped. She bit the sharp corner of her jagged fingernail, then she drove it into the white that illuminated the king's royal doublet. She pulled at the dried oil, lifting up a stream of color that ran up to the king's neck. The line of color continued, stretching off the canvas — straight to His Majesty's royal face. The line ripped through the faulty eyes.

Done.

She slapped her forehead. Instant regret.

Fool! What have I done!

She threw the decimated canvas to the floor and stomped out of her studio — the quiet corridor amplifying her sobs.

She did not fall asleep until dawn, waking to the sound of church bells. She had overslept for the Mass celebrating her royal portrait, just as she had the morning after the royal wedding banquet, after stumbling upon the cardinal and his servant.

Sofonisba caught up to Queen Isabel and the other ladies-in-waiting in the church. The queen smiled knowingly at her, as if believing the artist slept late due to the champagne the night before. She could not burden the queen with her impulsiveness. She had to face her failure. After Mass, she went to the king's receiving parlor to ask for an audience and was quickly admitted past waiting courtiers.

"My dear!" The king effused as if greeting a longtime friend.

"Your Majesty." Sofonisba whispered in return, picking at her cuticles.

The king pursed his lips. "Ah, we do not have our portrait, now do we?"

"Your Majesty, my greatest calling is to perfect your portrait and show your truth."

"Alas, perhaps we expect too much from our queen's lady."

"Your Majesty, I will not fail in this. It is only a matter of time."

He tilted his forehead toward her and smiled. "Yes, but for present, let us focus on the queen's blessed state and forget these trifles, shall we?"

In Arejunez he was patronizing about her success. Was he now resigned to her failure?

The unveiling was quietly cancelled. Nobody said a word to Sofonisba. She didn't know if people were being polite or simply didn't notice as they obsessed over the next male child. Surely he would be named Philip III, the courtiers all predicted.

The day of excitement arrived. On the tenth of August, the queen went into labor. Some said it was a sign from God — the anniversary of the king's great victory at St. Quentin. Her ladies-in-waiting divided themselves, alternating between attending her in her chamber and praying in chapel, so that at any given moment the queen would be supported each way. Churches throughout Madrid were full of praying women.

Taverns were full of toasting men, raising glasses to Philips II and III.

After two days in labor, Isabel delivered a healthy girl. She asked that Sofonisba be among the first admitted into the queen's chamber. "What a waste a girl is, Lady Sofonisba." The queen sobbed while the nurses wrapped the infant.

Sofonisba's heart broke for the new mother who was disappointed in her own flesh and blood, the baby she tried so hard to produce.

"Dear Queen, she is your blessing and your health is our greatest happiness. You must rest, Your Majesty. You have a princess. She is beautiful." Sofonisba vowed right there to render the girl beautifully when the day came to paint her.

The collective disappointment at court when the girl was announced was like a communal sigh of regret as if they were all spent from praying so fiercely for a boy.

King Philip would not have it. "We give thanks to God for bestowing this blessed angel of heaven upon us. We can find no greater joy than this blessing of a child and we could not have loved a boy any more than we love this precious princess. We shall love and provide for Isabella Clara Eugenia better than any parent has ever for any child. God protect her always."

He also got right back to trying to produce a male alternate to Don Carlos.

Sofonisba was free to return to the king's portrait. His devotion to the new princess made Sofonisba wonder whether she could reimagine him as a lover. She worked off her studies from Arejunez, resuming a pose with the king's hand on his heart. She tried to render his eyes to reflect his love for Isabel. But it was as if she could not achieve a true gaze from the king to match his pose as lover offering lilies to his beloved. Not that it was technically difficult — a dash of white, reflections in the chandelier, like the spark when he smiled at her after the Casas disputation, like the spark she saw at the prince's parade so many years ago? From where did his spark derive? Where would she locate it?

Dark background, illuminated face and hands. Gaze directed outward, connecting to the viewer. And yet. And yet, she had already disappointed him twice. She had to get something to him.

Sofonisba quietly gifted her portrait of the king as lover with a polite note. In return, he sent her a lovely pearl studded

velvet gown and a note of thanks. No formal unveiling. No public acclaim. Most of all, Sofonisba knew in her heart, no *al vero*
masterpiece. She had finally painted the king's portrait and
achieving her life's goal felt utterly disappointing. *I'm sorry,*
Father.

Just over a year later, on October 10, 1567, the King and Queen
of Spain were blessed with another baby, a girl, and they named
her Catalina Micaela.

Within the month, they were back to trying to produce a
male heir.

"Take them to the nursery," Queen Isabel demanded of the
governess. The little princesses' crying was disturbing the nap
the queen desperately needed to rest up for her duty later that
night.

Her responsibility to get pregnant again was keeping her up
night after night. The continuous scrutiny made her agitated.

She complained openly to Sofonisba on their daily stroll in
the garden, the queen's only time off bed-rest. "You see how the
king adores Isabella then ignores Catalina Micaela? If the next
one is a girl, he might put her to death!"

"Please, Your Majesty." Sofonisba looked over her shoulder.
Such words could be construed as treasonous.

"It's true. Isabella gave him hope for a boy. Catalina Micaela
dashed his hopes for one. Now his spirit for trying is burdened
by this legacy of failure — my failure, Lady Sofonisba."

As if to emphasize the urgent need for an alternate, the
existing heir Don Carlos grew increasingly petulant in a life that
didn't meet his expectations. "I have the blood of an emperor!"
Don Carlos bellowed to anyone present. "I was born to rule. Yet
my life is wasted at this court, while you all hope to replace me!"
No one contradicted him.

"I try to soothe him." Queen Isabel confided to Sofonisba. "I tell him that his blood is precious and pure. I flatter him over and over to help his poor frayed nerves, the dear boy." Isabel swayed slightly as if rocking a baby. "He will reign as a great king, I assure him — even while I pray to replace him with another, the heir I know my king demands of me. I am torn between my loyalty to my friend and my duty to my husband, his very father."

Prince Carlos was determined to rule, even if he had to plot against his father in order to succeed. "My father does not advance me! He entrusts the Netherlands, my own birthright, to mere dukes!" He complained to his old friend Don John of Austria, recently returned to court from military service. The prince must have believed that whatever his mission, he could rely upon his comrade's loyal support. When the court was tipsy from holiday toasts for the New Year, Don Carlos disclosed to Don John his plot to install himself as King of the Spanish Netherlands with Don John at his side.

After all they had been through together, Don John could not commit treason. Instead, he betrayed his friend's trust and repudiated him. "It pains my heart to confess, Your Majesty, that Don Carlos is plotting to exploit religious strife in the Netherlands and install himself as ruler. The prince is raising funds from opportunists at court who hope to misuse the prince for their own gain."

Sofonisba was in the banquet hall on the thirteenth of January when the king's personal guards arrested the prince, taking him to the tower of the Arevalo castle where his allegedly insane great-grandmother Juana mysteriously died thirteen years earlier.

"I wonder why the king took as long as he did," one courtier said.

"I expected this two weeks ago," another said.

"But there's no male heir to replace him," a third said.

"Yet," the first courtier corrected.

By May, Don Carlos was still languishing in the castle when Queen Isabel discovered that she was again pregnant.

"I must tell His Majesty but I don't want word to reach Don Carlos. The prince is fragile now. I wouldn't want to hurt him further," Queen Isabel told Sofonisba. "I will tell the king in private, and we'll keep it a quiet family matter until the baby is born, please God."

The king appeared to have no such reservations. He ordered an all-court banquet to celebrate the blessed news.

The queen approached Sofonisba in her concern for Don Carlos. "I've got to get to the prince to assure him that he is first, that my baby will not replace him but will follow him. I must get to the prince in prison, and you must help me, Lady Sofonisba."

"Dear Queen, I don't think that is wise in your condition!"

"I will bear a monster if he is born from the guilt I feel over the prince's state."

"Your Majesty, you are not responsible for the prince's sensitivities." Sofonisba remembered the reassurances Catherine de Medici gave her in Bayonne absolving her of guilt over the cardinal's death and the plague of Burgos.

But Queen Isabel persisted.

"The poor dear never had a mother. He grew up with the knowledge that she died giving birth to him. His father, the king, abandoned him emotionally. I am the only one who has ever loved him and I cannot betray his friendship any longer. If word of my pregnancy has reached him" — she shuddered — "it will crush his spirits. I must get to the prince to comfort him, and you, Lady Sofonisba, will accompany me."

With a combination of bribery and the simple fact that the queen was hard to refuse, Isabel and Sofonisba managed to persuade the guards to arrange for them a secret meeting with the imprisoned prince. A carriage for the Arevalo castle was arranged.

"Dear queen," Sofonisba pleaded as they descended the slippery wet stairs, "are you quite sure we should go through with this? Think of your child."

"I must see the prince." The queen squeezed Sofonisba's hand hard as she pulled her along to what could only be called a dungeon.

The gaunt prince held out his hands to Isabel as soon as the guards admitted the women to his cell. "Isabel, my friend. You love me. I know you do. You know I am the first-born male. You know this is my birthright. My inheritance."

"How right you are, my dear," the queen said, "nobody is taking anything from you."

The prince frowned and turned suddenly hostile. "Do you think I don't understand the threat of my rival to the throne? I've been trampled by Don John's betrayal, kicked in the stomach by the defeat of my Netherlands option, and now, you too, my friend, with your new pregnancy. I just cannot bear it. You are certain to have a boy this time, or the next." He grimaced. "My rightful inheritance is being stolen from me, and, you, my *dear* friend Isabel have betrayed me! Go!" He turned his back on the women and receded to the rear of his cell.

"Please, Carlos," Queen Isabel begged. "Don't let us part like this. I came here to prove my loyalty to you. I love you. You are like my own son." The queen tried to find the right words. The prince wouldn't look at her. Sofonisba put her hand on Isabel's shoulder.

"Get her out of here!" The prince bellowed at Sofonisba, who took the crying queen's hand and pulled her up the slippery stairway, back the way they came.

The following week, the third week of July, the twenty-two-year-old prince was found dead in his cell. "They say that he starved himself to death," a courtier reported. The news spread through court like wildfire.

Most courtiers were relieved and expressed no remorse. King Philip ordered the customary year of mourning for the death of his son, but returned to his work and his routine. The king's conduct told the world that Don Carlos' death was not to interfere with priorities, the proper functioning of the court and empire.

At first, the king's detachment was interpreted as a sign of his prudence. Then rumors began to spread. The same court-iers who clamored for an alternative heir speculated about the king's involvement in Carlos' death. "He covers his guilt for mur-dering his son," they whispered. "What else could explain his lack of sorrow for Don Carlos' death?" Rumors persisted, but nothing could be proven, and no one cared enough to investi-gate. What would anyone do if it had been murder?

There seemed to be no true grief for Don Carlos except from the queen. As Sofonisba sat at her bedside, the queen confided her worst fears. "I killed the prince, Lady Sofonisba. I fear that I myself have caused his demise, that the child I must bring into this world broke his spirit."

"Please don't think such things, Your Majesty," Sofonisba said. "You did not kill the prince. You were his true friend. You gave him only joy."

"I didn't secure his release from prison. I did not risk rela-tions with my husband for him. I could have intervened, helped the king to understand how siblings compete for their father's attention, and persuaded the king to take pity on his son. I know how it feels to be the child of royalty. One moment you are paraded before all to examine and then invisible the next. You are always on guard to project the correct image. You can never make a mistake. Carlos was so lost. He needed something to be his, to know he mattered. But I only protected myself." The queen put her hand on her belly.

"Please, don't think such things, Your Majesty. You have to rest your mind." Sofonisba tried to find the right words to console the queen without disclosing the family news she received that morning: her recently married sister Europa delivered her first child, a girl, and named her Bianca after their mother. Sofonisba was an aunt for the first time and it gave her a sense of hope that she tried to harness to comfort the queen.

But no words could assuage the queen's guilty conscience. She continued to not eat or sleep. Instead, she paced about, fretting and blaming herself incessantly for the prince's death.

On the morning of October 3, the queen went into early labor. Just as with the birth of the Infantas Isabella and Catalina Micaela, the ladies-in-waiting alternated attending the queen's bedside and praying for her in chapel.

Sofonisba prayed fervently for God to protect Isabel, keep her safe, and protect her child. She lay down that night chilled to the bone from kneeling for so long on the stone floor and was back in the chapel the next dawn when she heard the bells ring out announcing the delivery. She raced to the banquet hall eager for the blessed news.

"The child was stillborn. A girl," she heard a courtier say.

Sofonisba ran to the queen's chamber but couldn't reach the queen's bed through the mob that crowded the hallway.

"Dead! The queen is dead!"

At the age of twenty-two, Isabel de Valois was gone.

Squeezing her eyes shut to fight back her tears, Sofonisba prayed that her queen's soul would find peace. Almost immediately she began to worry over what would become of the two little princesses without their mother.

King Philip hardly left his bedchamber. This man who exercised personal discipline in all things did not dress or wash and stopped eating anything but small servings of bread and broth for almost three weeks. He did not appear publicly until October 21 when he made an announcement.

"We shall withdraw to the Escorial. We shall bring a minimal household and entourage, including only our confessor, the Infantas and their governesses, and the Lady Sofonisba with whatever attendants she requires."

The assembly whispered. Sofonisba was shocked to be included in the exclusive entourage.

The cornerstone of King Philip's Escorial, about 28 miles northwest of Madrid, had been laid in 1563. Five years later, it was still far from completion. The king's apartments and the monastery were not yet ready. Accommodations would need to be arranged for the king's lodging. The only thing settled about the enormous monastery, library, and palace was its dedication to Saint Lawrence, on whose feast day the Battle of Saint Quentin was won in 1557.

Logistical arrangements were quickly made for the small party. Sofonisba rode in the princesses' carriage that followed the king's own. She clutched the art kit Queen Isabel had returned to her so recently, wondering how she would render the motherless girls, the only reason she could imagine for being included in the entourage.

Within days, they were as comfortably ensconced at the Escorial as its incomplete state allowed. It was not long before the king sought out Sofonisba for her task.

"Dear Lady Sofonisba, please take a seat." He indicated a chair. "We hope you are not uncomfortable here with this small party and these unfinished accommodations." They both glanced around the undecorated room.

"My only regret is that the queen is not with us, Your Majesty." She curtsied before taking the heavy wooden chair offered.

"That is why you are here." His chest rose noticeably as he took a deep breath. "We are in despair at the loss of yet another wife, one so young and lovely. She looked destined to live a full life." The king stopped and swallowed hard. "Do you, as an artist, truly believe that art can touch a person? To console in mourning?" He closed his eyes as if contemplating the question, not seeming to expect her to answer, and so she waited for him to continue. "We would like to call upon you, Lady Sofonisba, to help us locate the most optimal position to house a very special piece of art here at our Escorial. This palace is to be our spiritual escape. Here we intend to be surrounded by soothing images, inspirational ideas, even the tombs of our ancestors, whose royal legacy is our burden and our destiny. We have brought you here, Lady Sofonisba, to determine the ideal location for the masterpiece from which we find more comfort than from a cross. Please." The king gestured for Sofonisba to precede him out the parlor and down a corridor where he led her to a lone easel on which a draped painting rested. He lifted the cover, gingerly handling the cloth, reminding her of the unveiling of Queen Isabel's portrait. He raised the drape to reveal van der Weyden's 1435 painting, *Descent from the Cross.*

Sofonisba's eyes grew large at the masterpiece. She noticed the king in her peripheral vision, his eyes devouring the painting too, as if searching for consolation.

"We should like you to determine the perfect placement for this masterpiece within the Escorial so that we may meditate upon it and feel its compassion, its pity. We look to you to determine that optimal location, Lady Sofonisba, because we believe that you have" — he paused and swallowed hard — "the sensitivity that you showed to our beloved Isabel." She blushed realizing he was pushing back tears. "She recommended you highly," he managed to continue. "She could trust you. The problem with courtiers — everything they say becomes suspect. Yet, the queen had no question of your loyalty."

Sofonisba felt a twinge of guilt recalling the bitterness she felt toward Isabel after Lucia's death when the queen refused Sofonisba's request to visit Cremona.

The king let out a long, slow breath. "We are pained and exhausted. We are so burdened by what happens in this world. If it were not for the business of Granada and elsewhere which cannot be abandoned, we do not know what we would do." He rubbed his temples. "Perhaps we do not regret the delays in our negotiations with Germany because certainly we are no good for the world of today. We know very well that we should be in some other station in life, one not as exalted as the one God has given us. We pray to God in heaven to be treated better."

What could she say? She knew words would not stop his pain. Her sisters' deaths were fresh again. She remembered the deep need for comfort she felt then. She reacted by impulse — reached out and touched the lace of the king's sleeve. Then she let the back of her forefinger brush the top of his hand.

The king sucked in a sharp breath and heaved up his shoulders. He seemed to not breathe. Silence. She began to fear she had breached royal protocol with her touch, but the king dropped his shoulders. He sniffed. Sniffed again. Face in his hands, a pitiful sob, the king bellowed, "Carlos, Carlos, Carlos!" His tears fell onto the floor between them.

"Your Majesty," Sofonisba stammered. Any lingering questions surrounding the death of Don Carlos vanished for her. The death of his son pierced the king as it would with any father.

The king sniffed and stood straighter. He put his hand to his heart — Philip II as Lover. "Lady Sofonisba, you have touched our heart. We trust your sense of compassion. Please, help us place the van der Weyden piece."

Together the artist and the monarch looked up at the masterpiece. Sofonisba read its message of empathy in Mary's form, perfectly echoing her son's limp body, as if to say that when the child dies first, the parent dies too. She could see how Philip found commiseration meditating on this sad, moving narrative. She needed no persuading to understand the healing power of art.

She had witnessed the king's vulnerability, and he was more human to her now. She was driven to find the perfect chapel to showcase the masterpiece that comforted him. Sofonisba spent the next many days quietly in each of her prospective sites, looking and listening during different times of the day to test whether the mood and lighting properly accentuated the painting.

The king, meanwhile, spent entire days on his knees in his personal chapel. At times, he ordered the young Infantas to attend while he prayed. Isabella was just two and Catalina was only an infant, so they came with their attendants.

Over the next two months at the Escorial, Sofonisba saw the king do nothing but pray. He prayed without resting. Then he would confess. And then pray. Not Casas, not any of her dear parish priests in Cremona, not her mother, not a soul touched the depth of piety that Sofonisba witnessed in her king during those months of mourning for his son, his wife, and the daughter who was not to be. Witnessing the depths of the king's prayer, she began to feel guilty at not having mourned more for her sisters, even knowing that she sacrificed her mourning for Isabel's sake.

Fortunately for the empire, the king had established a smooth-running government. Little intrigues and minor instances of corruption erupted in his absence from court, but generally, the ministers could weather the daily workings of government while Philip prayed.

On the morning she had designated to reveal her choice of location for *Descent from the Cross*, she went to inspect the painting in its place and to check the morning light. It would be her final sign of whether she had chosen well. She looked up at the epitome of pity and felt a pang for Isabel. She missed the queen who had become her intimate, even if they were never true equals. She stepped back a pace and then another, inspecting the masterpiece at each point, backing up until she abutted the opposing wall, bumping it and destabilizing a crucifix which swayed back and forth along the stone wall like a pendulum.

It struck her that the king was not truly a lover. His heart was full of duty, not amore for Isabel. He didn't really put his queen above himself, did he? She was not his Laura, his Beatrice, his ideal. He looks to the Lord to overcome the tragedies he suffers. He prays.

She roused herself from her reverie, confident the van der Weyden showed blessedly in its new home. She felt ready to master her dream in one more rendering of the king.

When the mourners returned to court, Coello was front and center awaiting the arrival of King Philip and his small entourage. The senior artist bowed respectfully to his king and then turned to Sofonisba. "Welcome, distinguished Lady Sofonisba." Coello lifted her hand near to his lips for a polite courtier's kiss, the art kit she clutched dangling in the air between them.

Sofonisba delicately requested permission to take back the king's portrait. Preoccupied as he was in his grief, he granted her permission without hesitation. This was her final chance to reach her goal, to render the truth of the king. Any excuses now would fall on deaf ears.

She clung to hope.

Definitely a dark Lombard background, for her father. A touch of red, for Catholicism. Simple black vestments, for Friar de las Casas. High hat. Mourning but studious. One simple medallion. Hands praying the Rosary, fingering a bead, palms upward, open to heaven, almost not present. Eyes gazing at the viewer yet through the viewer, lost in prayer. The spark, dim. Shiny armrest. We need every support we can get.

Sofonisba could not render Philip II as a lover, but as a man of prayer. In the depth of the king's sorrow, Sofonisba found her *al vero*.

Chapter 22

Succession: Madrid 1568–1572

The mood at court was somber, but succession was precarious so Alba urged the three-time widowed king to remarry. With two infant daughters, a half-brother, and a couple of nephews as the only candidates for the crown, a fresh start for King Philip might clarify the succession question.

One courtier gossiped, "They say the king is so disinterested in his next bride that Alba held up the Hapsburg family tree in front of him and the king threw a dart at it. The dart landed on his twenty-year old niece Anne, the Emperor's daughter."

"Don't believe it," another rebuked. "This marriage reunites the Habsburgs. The marriage of an emperor's son with an emperor's granddaughter cannot possibly have been arranged by chance — Alba sent delegates to Rome to arrange the dispensation for the king to marry his niece. The match was carefully decided."

The bride's father held the title Holy Roman Emperor that he inherited from his brother Charles V, along with Germany and Austria, when Philip received Spain, the Americas, and the Italian and northern territories.

Elaborate arrangements were made for the arrival of Anne of Austria. Queen Isabel's ladies-in-waiting were invited to remain in the new queen's court or to return to their homelands, having faithfully served the late queen. Each one chose to return home, except Sofonisba.

She explained to her parents as she begged their forgiveness.

Dearest Mother and Father,

We are each released from service here, given the queen's passing. All of the other ladies-in-waiting are returning to their homelands, and I, too, yearn to return to my home, to you, and my sisters. The Campi clan too. How I miss you all.

But I feel compelled to remain here at court for the sake of the late queen's little girls, who don't understand where their mother has gone. They rely on me more than ever since our time at the Escorial. The king has been asking me often to accompany them, to comfort them, and to help them to mourn, but yet accept that their mother is gone. This is not the role that called me to this court. The Lord knows I never expected to still be here at thirty-four years of age. But for the present, it is the role that feels correct for me. It won't be for long. I beg you to accept this decision for the time being and to forgive me for not returning immediately.

I pray for the day of our reunion.

Your devoted daughter,
Sofi, Madrid, 1569

Sofonisba dedicated herself to the little Infantas voluntarily. But the irony was not lost upon her: even though her charges were royal ones, her duties now looked much like they did during her last years in Cremona watching over her own younger sisters.

"The Lady Sofonisba came as an artist but now serves as Governess," one courtier commented loudly as Sofonisba brought the little princesses into the banquet hall.

"An appropriate role for a spinster," another said.

"Oh she still paints, too. 'Lady Sofonisba, can we color?'" He mimicked the royal princess begging the artist's attention.

"Though she is seen with Master Coello on occasion at his studio. Perhaps they mix their paints together?" The two courtiers laughed.

In early autumn, 1569, a gold-and-jewel studded carriage delivered Anne of Austria, the new Queen of Spain. The Austrian Habsburgs spared no expense to impress their Spanish cousins.

Late at night, Queen Anne settled into her apartments to meet her new court of ladies. She requested that Sofonisba be brought to her. Her accent was heavy, but her grammar was flawless. "I understand you served our late Queen Isabel and that you are an artist, Lady Sofonisba." The queen gestured to Sofonisba to sit down next to her.

"You are correct, Your Majesty."

"Then you know the only reason I've been matched with my old uncle is to get fat with an heir. Do you know that no one thought to ask whom I might like to marry?" Not waiting for an answer, the girl queen continued, "No dashing young duke for me. No. Only my old uncle would do. I don't understand why, really, after all the complaining my father does about old Philip. Couldn't Father have found a younger monarch for me? Um? Lady Sofonisba, I would like you to paint me to capture my maiden beauty, before it becomes wrecked by duty."

Sofonisba thought about Isabel and didn't know whether to laugh or cry at the queen's innocent vanity. Her tone of entitlement was unmistakable. "I will be most honored to render my beautiful queen."

Within the year, her *Portrait of Queen Anne of Austria* showed a beautifully bejeweled and regal queen, who in no time at all was pregnant. By Christmas, 1571, Fernando was born and Spain had her male heir.

While the king's home life settled down, events of the empire flared. The Holy League that King Philip had assembled of Christian Europe was preparing an offensive against the Turks. He chose his half-brother Don John to command the offensive.

"They say that the king wants to banish from court the man who reminds him of his son's death," one courtier gossiped. "The king acts grateful to Don John for exposing the prince's Netherlands plot, but it's a two-edged sword, see? In exposing the prince, Don John betrayed him — the illegitimate betrayed the fully royal prince. To the king, Don John has some penance to do. King Philip gave Don John the command to earn his keep, so to speak."

"Don John must be just as happy to remove himself from the damning eyes of the king and assuage his own guilt over Don Carlos."

Don John was ordered to the Mediterranean. Alessandro Farnese was summoned from the Spanish Netherlands to serve as second in command.

"Both men need the redemption. They're each responsible for Don Carlos," another gossip speculated.

"We all saw their recklessness. They induced the prince to vile conduct. They brought him to the taverns and the whorehouses in disguise — led him straight to the syphilis that made him crazy. His father might have offered him a military command post had he acted more responsibly," another said.

In October, after months at sea commanding a fleet of 206 galleys from his vessel, the *Real*, Don John was revered as a national hero. Bells rang out announcing his victory at Lepanto. Te Deums were sung in the churches. Ambassadors wrote their sovereigns throughout Europe: "A tremendous victory at sea in the Mediterranean. A victory for Christianity over the Ottoman infidel!"

Sofonisba cringed at the estimates she heard touted at court.

"The Ottoman commander Ali Pasha had 230 galleys," a courtier explained. "Yet, Don John only lost 13,000 men. Ali Pasha lost 25,000!"

"They were no match for the Holy League," another courtier boasted.

Sofonisba tried to imagine how to render the number: 38,000 people dead. She envisioned a singular commander, Pedro de Mendoza, the model for her *Portrait of a Soldier* in 1555. She tripled the figures and thought of her family portrait, the trio of father, son, and daughter she painted before she departed for Spain. She considered her masterpiece *the Chess Game*, four figures. Had she ever painted a group larger than four? Could a painting ever represent this magnitude of loss of 38,000 individuals? The scale of it shook her to the core. She pictured her *Portrait of Philip II Praying with Rosary* and fell to her knees at the crucifix, torn by her mixed feelings for the tormented man who ordered such loss of life. May God forgive him for the slaughter he had wrought.

She knew her time at court had reached its natural ending. There must be more to life than service to the crown and its objectives. She wanted to make a home life in Lombardy. She turned her thoughts to Broccardo, wondering if she could find the right feelings for him to agree to marry him, if he would still take her. He was so good to her family. He cared for her parents. He mediated Europa's marriage contract not long ago. He was the first citizen of Cremona. They could live there and in Milan. Dare she see if he might still be interested?

Sofonisba's letter gently inquiring about Broccardo Persico's health arrived in Lombardy two weeks later, three days after he was found dead of infection at the age of fifty-one.

Broccardo. Lucia. Minerva. All dead. She had been at court a dozen years. Her goal to paint the king was achieved. She had foregone raising a family of her own. News of Broccardo's death on top of the tremendous devastation at Lepanto took a personal toll on Sofonisba. She sunk into a depression, finding it difficult to get out of bed in the mornings. She felt spent and wasted, as she carelessly confided to one of the new ladies-in-waiting. "I'm thirty-six years old this year, and I suppose I will never have a family of my own. Nor, I imagine, will I paint another portrait of the king, since I now mostly attend the royal princesses."

"Perhaps you should not lament so loudly, Lady Sofonisba," the new girl said. "You may sound ungrateful."

"You're right. I adore my charges. But I long to return home to Lombardy."

"And you know it's not too late for you, Lady Sofonisba. Plenty of women have given birth at your age. Why don't you ask the queen to release you? Go home."

Home. Yes. It was finally time.

"Your Majesty, if I may be so bold," she asked the next afternoon when the ladies surrounded Queen Anne in the gardenia gardens, "I have served at this court faithfully for almost twelve years now and I do pine to return home to Lombardy."

"And perhaps a family of your own, Lady Sofonisba?" the queen teased.

"Perhaps." Sofonisba smiled.

"I will present the idea to His Majesty this evening," the queen promised.

"The lady Sofonisba has served faithfully at court for more than a decade and would like to return to her homeland."

"How long has she served?" King Philip asked.

"Almost twelve years, Your Majesty."

"Then we will find her an Italian to marry." King Philip raised his glass to Queen Anne and they toasted Sofonisba in her absence.

"She must have someone of title. We can bestow her with pensions. It's her family name that needs our support," Queen Anne observed.

Over the course of the next year, the royal household made arranging Sofonisba's marriage a priority. One night, the master of the banquet struck his banner to the ground to command the attention of the diners. King Philip surveyed the assembly and stopped on Sofonisba.

"It is our honor, our pleasure, and may we add, our sadness, to declare the match we have selected for our own Lady Sofonisba." A flurry of whispers went up about the woman who had been dismissed as a permanent nanny.

Sofonisba was paralyzed. He had decided without even consulting her? King Philip noticed her stone face but must have read it as anticipation. He smiled broadly. "And as our lady has requested an Italian, we have secured a most illustrious prince in our Italian territories. His name is Fabrizio Moncada, second son to the Moncada dynasty of Sicily."

Sicily! That was not even Italy. No, no. She had said Cremona. Anywhere in Lombardy. Sicily — no! That was as far as Madrid. Maybe farther!

"And our most noble Señor Moncada," señor not signore? "The son of one of Spain's oldest and most prestigious houses."

A Spanish nobleman? *No! No! No!* Sofonisba's thoughts screamed out the protests she dared not profess to her king.

"And so, we personally pray God to protect the Lady Sofonisba," the king continued, "and to bless her marriage. May she live in peace all the days of her life." And the entire assembly rose and toasted her.

Sofonisba plastered a smile on her face, hoping her pounding temples did not disclose the panic in her heart. She couldn't possibly decline after such a formal, public announcement. She would appear at best ungracious, at worst treasonous. Yes, she wanted marriage, but so far from home? Distance was the last thing she needed after such long service in Spain. And to a Spaniard? In Sicily?

She thought about the Spanish prince and princess Alba had imprisoned in Milan when she was still at home in Cremona. The viceroys and governors were the worst: all the royal privilege but none of the ultimate responsibility. She shuddered. Then, just after thinking of him, the Duke of Alba cornered her in the banquet hall.

"Lady Sofonisba, may I congratulate you on your prospective match. I am pleased to inform you that the king has approved my requests for certain lifetime pensions for you. The funds will be housed securely in Palermo at the royal customs offices there. Seven pension accounts, Lady Sofonisba, from the royal treasury, from which you may draw quarterly support payments for the rest of your life. You will be secure financially. In addition, you will take your inheritance from Isabel's bequest, and, of course, any jewels given to you by those grateful for your renderings. You will leave court a wealthy woman, Lady Sofonisba, and a most impressive match! You must be elated."

"I am most honored by the very dignified match the king has awarded me." She tried to be grateful, but her tone was flat.

The duke was caught up in his own pride, having secured for his charge such generous pensions. He beamed with happiness.

Sofonisba's future was set. She had to resign herself to it. Maybe he would be her prince charming. For a moment, she was a young girl in Cremona awaiting her prince to pass under her balcony.

As the legalities of her marriage were being negotiated, Sofonisba was increasingly eager to leave court, under any circumstances. The ebb and flow of court culture had swung into full conservatism. The sparks of frivolity from the days of the three gallants were long gone, but what replaced it was a more severe tone than she could ever recall. It pained her when she heard the king's tirades over events in France where wars of religion were raging. His demands for more concessions to Catholic orthodoxy seemed to fuel France's wars. She remembered Bayonne, where Catherine de Medici advocated tolerance.

Sofonisba could not say aloud, but another reason she wished to return to Lombardy, in addition to being reunited with her family, was that she thought of it as a place of open-minded thinking. She remembered the debates she and her tutor Marco used to have, never replicated at court, no matter how sophisticated the courtiers professed to be.

As if to highlight the contrast, Alba proclaimed a new policy toward the New World Indians, which he called the Royal Ordinance on Pacification.

"We dedicate ourselves and our mission to making our New World conquests in a more Christian manner. To that end, let us observe as follows —" The duke handed the scroll to the court crier to read to the courtiers:

Discoveries are not to be called conquests. Since we wish them to be carried out peacefully and charitably, we do not want the use of the term 'conquest' to offer any excuse for the employment of force or the causing of injury to the Indians.

We are to seek friendship with them through trade and barter, showing them great love and tenderness and giving them objects to which they will take a liking.

The preachers should ask for their children under the pretext of teaching them and keep them hostages. By these and other means are the Indians to be pacified and indoctrinated, but in no way are they to be harmed, for all we seek is their welfare and their conversion.

When the crier finished, the hall was silent. Then Alba said, "The king authored the final clause — concerned as His Majesty was for the souls of the Indians." The assembly applauded.

The Ordinance on Pacification was implemented immediately. Indian children were taken from their parents, dressed in European clothing, and sent to mission schools built off the unpaid labor of their parents, where they were taught in Spanish to be Christians.

Sofonisba was waiting in the ladies' receiving parlor for an hour or more. She was expecting the king's lawyer to bring the contract for her signature. Her signature was a technicality, as it was the king, in lieu of her father, who was the legally contracting party.

She decided to go herself to the clerk's offices in the king's wing, normally limited to men. Women didn't enter into contracts, negotiate, or own property, and it was considered unseemly for a lady to associate herself with such messy business. But she had better things to do than wait. Mostly, she was eager to see the contract that would seal her fate.

Sofonisba rapped on the door to the clerk's offices. The man who opened the door for her held an open book in one hand.

He wore no jacket, just a white shirt, the sleeves rolled up. He examined the unexpected woman over his spectacles. "May I help you, madam?"

"I am Lady Sofonisba Anguissola. I've been expecting a lawyer to bring me my marriage contract." At the sound of her voice, dozens of heads popped up out of volumes of books to inspect a woman among them. "I didn't know there were so many of you," she said.

"Of course, madam. A great empire needs lawyers. You know what the old adage says, 'the devil is in the details.'"

"Then would you kindly send my lawyer?"

"Of course, my lady, we will send him straightaway."

As she turned to leave, a chill went up her spine. The devil is in the details.

A team of lawyers descended upon Sofonisba's marriage contract. The Moncada were an old, lofty, and powerful family with marriage ties to the crown in Spain and the Aragonese of Naples. Her contract was extensive. The lawyers delineated her wealth right down to the last pearl: her dowry, her pensions, and many, many jewels and gowns.

The groom Fabrizio Moncada pledged the standard language, "to conserve and manage the dowry for his spouse and their heirs" and pledged that the dowry would be returned to Sofonisba in the event of his death. Then, the Moncada lawyers inserted a second clause, in a footnote, that Fabrizio would agree to not spend the dowry unless Sofonisba gave permission and "unless she is assured goods for the amount."

"What does it mean, 'goods for the amount?'" she asked.

"You will take nothing short of what is owing to you, Lady Sofonisba. Your full dowry will be returned to you in the event of your husband's death."

"So this is for my protection?"

"Yes, madam."

The royal lawyers had clearly thought it all through. They impeccably detailed her assets. She felt it was all under control. Her pensions were to be redeemed at the customs office in Palermo. Withdrawals required her personal signature or that of her designee.

"Now, do you write, Lady Sofonisba?"

"Dear sir, in which language?"

"Forgive me. I should not doubt your education."

"And yours, sir? You do not speak with a Castilian accent. Where were you educated?"

"I am from a small village in Andalusia, madam. Educated by priests. They thought I would become one of them but I wanted to see the world. They sponsored me at the university at Salamanca. There I chose to study the law as I saw a path to advancement for a country boy like myself. Otherwise, it would be the monastery for me."

"You have risen through your profession" — a parallel to her own life — "You miss your family?"

"I'm an orphan — no family."

Sofonisba had a family but could not return to them.

With the assistance of lawyers, the marriage of Sofonisba and Fabrizio Moncada was meticulously documented. Her formal marriage arrangements were a sign of how far Sofonisba had risen in Spain. She arrived a minor noble and left a grand dame. Like the lawyer, her profession raised her up. But to have lawyers designing her estate and a royally decreed marriage to a Sicilian prince she had yet to meet: these were the maneuvers not just of nobility, but of the king's world. She had the full backing of His Majesty.

Her prestige was amplified that night when her marriage arrangements were feted with a banquet in her honor, a scrumptious royal feast. She remembered how hard it was to keep up with the diners at the royal wedding a dozen years earlier. Court life had changed that. She consumed the twelve-course meal with ease now.

Toward the end of the evening, King Philip rose. "The Lady Sofonisba came into our charge to attend the late Queen Isabel. She did so with grace and love for Her Majesty. She has cared for our precious daughters as a sister would. She has welcomed our new bride. She has graced our court with her tremendous talents. Let us all rise and make this toast to the illustrious Lady Sofonisba: that the grace, love, and beauty you bring to our court follow you all the days of your life. May your marriage be blessed."

The entire assembly rose, not a snicker, not a note of sarcasm to be heard. From Coello to every last courtier, Sofonisba received an admiring tribute, replicating the king's tone. Any insult ever lobbed at the "the Cremonese who paints," whether for her craft or her status, was now forgotten.

She had painted the king, fulfilling her promise to her father, fulfilling her promise to herself, honoring her family name. Those childhood goals had been achieved. Her former motivation was extinguished. Now it was her own life that needed her care and attention.

Part III

Legacy (1573–1625)

Chapter 23

Dynasty: Paterno ` Sicily 1573-April 27, 1578

Two Spanish ladies accompanied Sofonisba as she was paraded through Madrid, royal guards shooing the farmers, laborers, maids, and merchants for her carriage to pass. As she boarded the galley bound for Sicily, the crew lined up to receive her. "We are at your service, Lady Sofonisba," the ship's captain greeted her. "The stateroom has been appointed for your comfort. We expect a smooth voyage." He waved an arm toward an open door leading below deck.

The cabin had woolen tapestries on the walls and silk pillows on customized divans, like a sort of tomb crossed with a boudoir. She strolled the deck for fresh air. She was embarrassed to realize she did not know their itinerary. She asked the first-mate, "Sir, when do we arrive in Palermo?"

"Palermo, my lady?"

"Our destination."

"Ah, *Paternò* you mean to say. We will disembark at Catania in a fortnight. From Catania, you'll need a carriage to Paternò."

"How far is Palermo from there?" She knew Palermo was where she could withdraw her funds.

"About a two-week ride overland, one by sea, my lady." The first-mate touched his chest, as if he wanted to apologize for disappointing her.

Sofonisba tossed in bed that night and reminded herself that surely she could rely on her husband — they were a family now. She drifted off to sleep thinking of her voyage in 1560, the deck hand with the scar by his eye, and his beautiful torso.

The galley arrived on a sunny day in the bustling city of Catania. Sofonisba's attendants readied her belongings and escorted her off the ship. She scanned the crowd on the dock for her new husband. Her heart raced when she saw an elaborate carriage with the Moncada crest.

A servant approached and bowed to her. "I am called Rico. I serve Signore Fabrizio. He has asked me to send his regards and to inform you that he will be joining you at the palace." Rico took Sofonisba's trunks and began to load them onto the carriage.

"A chance to freshen up before meeting my bridegroom." She pushed back a curl that fell from her velvet hat and thought of the Duchess of Parma. She settled into the carriage, pulled out her art kit, and began to sketch the coastline as the carriage left the harbor. The ships receded from view. For the ten-hour carriage ride to Paterno`, Sofonisba buried herself in her work. As they neared the hilltops of Paterno`, she tried to imagine her new husband. She reread her father's latest letter, so crumpled the writing was beginning to fade.

Of course, I was surprised that the king arranged for your marriage without my prior consent, but I understand he acted in my stead, in your best interests. My heart aches that you do not return to us, but swells with pride as you honor the family with your esteemed marriage to a distinguished ruling house. I never intended for you to remain away from home for so long. But Sofi, I know you have the resilience within you to navigate this next transition as well as you did the last. This is truly a new beginning to your life. I wish for you only love and God's blessings.

Your Devoted Father,
Amilcare Anguissola, June 1573

Resilience. The word returned to her over and over during the journey to Paterno'.

A uniformed guard bowed to Sofonisba when Rico escorted her into the Palazzo Moncada. She was disappointed that no family assembled around the door to greet her. She felt a pang of missing her parents. An older gentleman approached, tall and commanding. "Allow me to make your acquaintance, dear lady," he nodded. "I am Don Pedro, Duke of Vibona, grandfather of the young heir, and head of this household." He swept a hand across the room. "And here she is —" A young woman curtsied. Her square mouth and pointy chin were overshadowed by a rodent-like nose. "Aloisa dear, come meet your new sister-in-law —"

"The new wife of my dear brother-in-law." Aloisa looked left and right, palms upraised, and turned to take Sofonisba's hands into her own. "Welcome to my palace, Lady Sofonisba." She put her hand on the shoulder of the child at her side. He was dressed in a dark blue silk suit, trimmed with lace and studded with gold. "Francisco, I present to you Lady Sofonisba who is now your aunt as she is married to your Uncle Fabrizio."

Sofonisba curtsied to the little boy who looked bored.

"Where is uncle?" the boy asked.

"He will attend presently," Aloisa said. "Your groom does not choose to pass much time at the palace these days, but surely he will soon be here to collect his new bride."

Aloisa de Luna y Vega was just a toddler when Sofonisba was making her reputation as a young artist in Cremona. Aloisa's influential parents, whose wedding was officiated by Ignatius Loyola, arranged for their daughter to be married to Caesar Moncada, heir and prince of the house of Moncada and older brother to Sofonisba's husband Fabrizio. The year after Caesar and Aloisa were married, their baby Francisco II was born. By the time the baby was two years old, his father was dead. Aloisa became a twenty-year-old widow. Caesar died without a will, leaving his minor heir behind. Traditionally, custody of the minor passed to the paternal next of kin — in this case, the boy's uncle Fabrizio, Sofonisba's husband. Knowing that the guardianship of her son was in jeopardy, Aloisa went to her father, Don Pedro. Fabrizio Moncada, the paternal uncle, did not have the experience or the spine to match the don. Against legal precedent, the maternal grandfather Don Pedro de Luna became the legal guardian of his grandson and moved his family into the Moncada palace with his daughter Aloisa and her young child. Not having sufficient personal funds of his own, the snubbed Fabrizio continued to reside in the family palace alongside his sister-in-law's newly ensconced relatives.

Two teenaged girls came to the parlor and curtsied to Sofonisba. Don Pedro introduced them. "May I present my other daughters Aleonora and Bianca — the Lady Sofonisba." Sofonisba curtsied back.

They chatted about Sofonisba's voyage, the sea weather, and other polite topics for most of an hour. They heard boots trudging down the hallway.

He appeared in the doorframe flushed, wearing falconer boots, vest, and cap — and smelling like a horse. A chiseled face. Severe. He looked some years older than Sofonisba, perhaps mid-forties. Handsome in a rugged way. Definitely not soft.

She struggled to recall whom he resembled. *Portrait of a Soldier. Pedro de Mendoza.* Sofonisba shuddered.

Fabrizio walked slowly toward Sofonisba, assessing her head to toe. A forced smile. "Madam," he murmured, lifting her right hand to his mouth, stopping short of kissing it. "I trust your journey was comfortable."

Aloisa, Aleonora, and Bianca glanced at each other.

Fabrizio softened his tone, "Come dear wife, let us show you your new home and attend to your every comfort. We will resume with the others at supper."

He led her down a corridor, peppering her with questions. "Is the king still sound of mind and body?"

"Very much so."

"Does he have firm control of his court?"

"Most definitely."

"Does he continue to ride and hunt?"

"When he is not at work or prayer."

He stopped at the door of what was to be Sofonisba's private suite, gesturing for her to enter. "Please, freshen up and rest." A maid was unpacking Sofonisba's trunks, laying her things into drawers. The two Spanish ladies provided for her voyage had returned to Spain on the next vessel back. As the new maid was putting Sofonisba's things away, she opened up the art kit.

"Attention," Sofonisba blurted, too late. Brushes she had tossed loosely into the kit fell to the floor, splattering specks of dried paint onto the marble.

Fabrizio rolled his eyes. "Well, madam, I will see you at supper. Until then." He bowed slightly and absented himself, leaving Sofonisba to her maid.

After more than two hours, an attendant came for Sofonisba, leading her to a grand dining room where others were already seated. Don Pedro sat at the head of the table and Aloisa at the other. On the third side were the sisters Aleonora and Bianca. On the other were two place settings. A chair was offered to

Sofonisba. Fabrizio's chair was empty. Aloisa delayed the soup course as they waited.

"Tell us, how is the king's health?" Don Pedro asked.

"And how is the new Austrian queen?" Aleonora asked.

"How does she compare to Queen Isabel?" Bianca asked.

After an hour or more, Aloisa whispered to an attendant. The soup was served and the meal began without Fabrizio.

After the meal, Aloisa stood to retire. "Please let us know if you need anything at all," she said, gesturing to the servants.

"Thank you, Sister," Sofonisba smiled. Aloisa nodded in return.

Court banquets were more personal than her first family meal with the Moncada.

Fabrizio returned very late that night and went straight to Sofonisba's suite. She had been in bed for hours but was not yet asleep. The scenes of her cold welcome played over and over in her mind. She heard a light knock on her door before Fabrizio pushed it open, stumbling as he began to unbutton his doublet, which he tossed to the floor before getting into her bed with the rest of his clothing still on.

"There you are," he said as he grabbed up her nightgown and heaved himself on top of her, catching her long hair under his elbow.

"Ow," she said.

"But I have not begun," he replied.

"My hair."

"Uh. There."

As he prodded impatiently, she was haunted by a vision of the errant eyes on her portrait of Philip II as lover, the eyes that were wrong because the king did not love his wife as she needed him to. Within fifteen minutes, Sofonisba and Fabrizio were officially married and he stumbled back to his own suite.

What had she gotten herself into? Sofonisba cried herself to sleep.

In the days that followed, Fabrizio spent most of his time away, hunting or falconing during the day, gambling and carousing most of the night. He dropped in on Sofonisba for casual conversations here and there and occasionally for quick meals. He visited her at night rarely, but always late and drunken.

Sofonisba's main company at the palace was Aloisa, Don Pedro, and the sisters Aleonora and Bianca. Don Pedro filled the role of head of the household naturally with his doting daughters around him. They were polite to Sofonisba, and in time, began to open up to her and inquire about her family and to share about theirs, especially about her new husband.

"Fabrizio was born and raised in this palace, the second son under the shadow of his older brother Caesar," Aleonora explained. "When Caesar died, Fabrizio lorded over the palace like he had finally gotten his due. But my sister Aloisa took over the reins in no time at all. She was not about to lose her son to her indolent brother-in-law. She simply leaned on our father and pressed him to serve as the boy's guardian and, of course, Father was happy to do so. Fabrizio put up no real resistance. He's lazy, yes? But the prince's estate is *substantial*—" her eyes grew wide "—and the guardian controls the estate, so I don't know why he didn't try harder for it. He is the paternal uncle, so he does have that right. In any event, he doesn't spend much time at the palace anymore. He's usually away with his companions. We wondered if married life would change that. Apparently not, hmm, Lady Sofonisba?"

Sofonisba smiled politely.

For the most part, however, the younger women were not much interested in Sofonisba, who was twice their age. Her new married life was dreadfully lonely. It reminded her of the early days at court, before she and Queen Isabel became friends. For the time being, her art kit would have to be her only faithful companion.

She retreated into her artwork to occupy herself. Not wanting to create any problems in her new household, she simply set up an easel in her suite. She used colors she brought from Spain and simple herbs to supplement when she could. The light in her suite was all she needed. After a couple of weeks, however, Aleonora complained of the paint smells, and Sofonisba was provided a little room near the kitchen, much like the one she set up in Cremona as a girl. She had expected to have less time and opportunity to paint in married life. On the contrary, she discovered that she actually had endless freedom to paint.

While life with the Moncada felt nothing like home, at least she had her one constant, her art — and the security of her royal pensions.

Fabrizio came to her studio, a bouquet of red roses in hand. "I have not yet been treated to a tour," he said, glancing around at the colors, brushes, wood, and canvas she had assembled.

"Please come in," she said, happy for his first sign of interest. "Would you like to see my portfolio?" she said.

"I would be delighted, my lady." Fabrizio said, uncharacteristically tender.

As they viewed her work together, Fabrizio inquired about the sitters and the history of each piece, and about Sofonisba's own feelings about her work. It was undoubtedly the most attentive he had been toward her since her arrival. "I look forward to dining with you this evening. We do not spend nearly enough time together." Fabrizio kissed her hand, letting his lips linger on her skin before departing.

She put on her most flattering gown that night. Fabrizio appeared at her bedroom door before supper. "May I have the honor?" He offered his arm to escort her to the grand dining room for the first time.

After the servants laid out the final course and returned to the kitchen, Fabrizio turned to Sofonisba. "Dear lady, our household is obligated to pay a debt at cards I owe to Signore Riccioli. We will need to make an immediate withdrawal from your funds."

She glanced around the table. "My pensions must be claimed in person at the customs office in Palermo."

"Then one of your jewels will do as collateral for now."

She knew she would not refuse. What was hers was his under the law and according to the church. A family debt was a family obligation.

Aloisa had a taunting look in her eyes.

"Of course, Husband," Sofonisba said.

Fabrizio nodded his head ever so slightly in her direction. "Well now, we shall attend to the notary tomorrow." Aloisa smiled, looking both disappointed and amused. The notary arrived at noon the next day with prepared documents, and everything was settled in time for the midday meal.

Days later, a special messenger arrived from Cremona. With a sense of foreboding, Sofonisba trembled as she opened the post.

Dear Sofi,

It is with a sad heavy heart that we must tell you that Father is dead . . .

She dropped the letter, not reading the details. She felt as if a hole opened in her heart and her soul spilled out onto the marble floor. She looked up at the ceiling and swayed, unsteady. The rock of her life was gone. She went to the family chapel and got down on her knees before the golden cross.

"I have not seen Father in over thirteen years," she murmured. "Dear God, I never intended all this time to pass without again seeing the man to whom I owe everything." She prayed for her father's soul. The pain of losing him without one last visit tore at her. Had King Philip not sent her here, had she returned to Lombardy, she could have had one last visit. She had sacrificed a final farewell to her father for a loveless marriage.

The chapel could not assuage her hurt. She crossed herself and stood up, pulling her wrap tight. She needed a priest. Sofonisba went to the town center and entered the Chiesa della Santissima Annunziata. She walked the nave of the empty church and knelt before an altar. "I don't know what you have in store for me, Lord, but Father could not have died at a worse time. Did he know he was dying when he told me to be resilient? Was he trying to tell me I would not have him for long? That I have to take care of myself now?"

She tried to think of her husband as family. She wanted to have faith in her marriage and trust Fabrizio. What was hers was his. Wasn't that marriage? They had a shared future, even if they rarely shared a bed.

She crossed herself when she was done and genuflected. When she stood up, she came face to face with a priest. He furrowed his brow. "Child, would you like a blessing?" he asked.

"Yes, father," she said. Tears welled in her eyes.

"Nel nome del Padre, e del Figlio, e dello Spirito Santo." He made the Sign of the Cross and gave her a knowing smile. "You cannot control the feelings of others. Trust in God. Try to be resilient. Life is difficult at times."

The priest could not have known how perfectly chosen his words were.

A week later, Fabrizio came to her with another gambling debt. "Grimaldi pulled the trump card from his sleeve, but how could

I prove it?" He shrugged. "It would be my word against his, and then we would have to duel it out. I succumbed to his demands. Alas, we owe him a considerable sum."

His debts were her debts. She thought of her father. Resilience. Family.

"Husband, perhaps we could spend evenings together instead of you gambling?" She hesitated. "Perhaps discuss starting a family?"

Fabrizio tilted his head as if confused. "I." Pause. "Well, yes. Certainly. Now, will you excuse me?" A very tight smile and a nod. "Tonight then, my lady." He bowed and left the room. Fabrizio was on his horse to meet his fellows before the evening meal was announced.

A month later Fabrizio approached Sofonisba in her studio.

"I thought I would find you here, dear wife. We have a little matter to discuss regarding obligations to our local militia." He paused. "The militia protects our town and this palace — and has considerable expenses. We shall need to make a withdrawal from your pension."

He smiled. Was he apologetic or condescending? She studied his face.

"Just how did you provide for the militia previously?" Sofonisba surprised herself by her tone, but she was losing faith in him.

"We were woefully in arrears. Best keep the militia happy."

The Moncada lawyers prepared a form for her to sign permitting Fabrizio to make the withdrawal on her behalf. Gambling debts continued. Sofonisba questioned him each time and he always had an excuse. She began to worry and asked the lawyers for an accounting, but Sofonisba had no choice. She was forced to either pawn jewels, one by one, or take more advances on her pensions.

She heard her father: *resilience*.

She took up religious themes as she painted by day and turned to prayer for comfort as she retired to bed alone at night. If only she had seen Amilcare one last time. She had not prayed so hard since nearing the town of Burgos.

Fabrizio suggested that they find a separate residence and set up their own household. Sofonisba was uncomfortable with the idea because of their finances and also because she grew up with a large family, then spent all those years at court, and now had an extended family of sorts, however cold. How would it be to have only Fabrizio and the servants to communicate with? On the other hand, she would be out from under Aloisa's constant scrutiny. Maybe it would be just what she needed, to be in charge of her own domain, run her own household, set down roots in the wake of her father's passing.

They acquired an elegant house that was larger than they needed. They hired a cook, and servants, and footmen, and withdrew from Sofonisba's pensions to support them.

Sofonisba and Fabrizio were at their new domicile when they heard Aloisa's tragic news. Don Pedro was dead. Sofonisba sucked in her breath, thinking of Amilcare. Aloisa was now a twenty-two-year-old widow — with no powerful father to protect her, her young son, and their massive estate.

Fabrizio Moncada saw his opportunity. "I relinquished my family estate once; I will not again!" Access to Sofonisba's estate over the past many months had emboldened Fabrizio's sense of possibility: he would manage the boy's estate as he did his wife's, based on traditional male guardianship. Unlike his cowardly approach after his brother died, Fabrizio was determined to assert his full rights this time. Now he had Sofonisba's pensions and her contacts at the Spanish court to support him.

"Dear Sister," he addressed Aloisa, "I have come to talk to you directly, and sensibly. I am the boy's uncle. It is only proper that I control his education. He needs my guidance and my wisdom in ways of the world."

"Please, dear Brother, know that I honor your concern for my son, and I will make certain his needs are met at all costs."

"Be realistic, Aloisa. Being a mother is no qualification for guardianship. May I remind you that you are a Moncada by marriage only, a mere widow. You have no male protection. You risk your son's education and security for your vanity."

"If you imply, sir, that I cannot manage my own family, my own affairs, because of my sex, then you are wrong."

"As uncle, I am in the best position to protect him. I must insist, dear Sister, for my nephew's sake."

"Gabriella," Aloisa called from her silk divan to her maid, "please see Signore Moncada to the door. Thank you, sir, good day."

It was an unavoidable fact of life, and they both knew it. Aloisa hailed from an old Spanish bloodline — with all the privilege, money, and connections possible, but all that was not enough to secure guardianship of her child. As far as the magistrates of Palermo were concerned, she needed a man to head her household.

She had no choice but to secure a marriage. Aloisa went to Signora Amorella who arranged such things for the leading families.

"He is the Duke of Montalto. His name is Antonio Aragona e Cardona and his house is as great as your own, if I may be so bold. His lands are extensive. His title is secure. He is a widower. He looks to increase his holdings."

"Excellent. I'll take him," Aloisa said.

"There is one condition on which he will not relent: he will remain in Naples with his lover. He will have no regular contact with you. This marriage will be a match in name only."

"That suits me perfectly, madam. I can take care of myself."

Aloisa also shored up her claim by betrothing her son to her new husband's daughter from his first marriage. Aloisa's son Francisco II stood to marry Antonio's daughter Maria, also known as Duchess Maria Aragona Cardona e la Cerda. This marriage would join the feudal estates of the Moncada, Paterno`, Aderno, Centorbi, Biancavilla, Motta Sant'Anastasia, and Caltanissetta to the territories of the Aragona-Cardona including Montalto in Naples and Collesano, Petrailie, Belici, and San Filippo in Sicily. These two influential houses now had a double alliance.

"Let Fabrizio better that one!" Aloisa gloated.

Fabrizio was not deterred. "That woman thinks she can control the Moncada? That she should manage our estates? That her sham marriage to her so-called husband in Naples can protect the boy? My nephew sits defenseless with no real father. As his uncle, I am the sole rightful guardian of this house and my own name. Of course, I have no desire to take the boy from his mother," he reassured Sofonisba daily. "I only want what is best for his sake. The widow of my deceased brother thinks too highly of herself. I've decided to press my claim with the king."

To His Royal Majesty, King Philip II,
Most Gracious Sovereign,

The Principessa Aloisa, by subterfuge, claims herself to be guardian of the boy, gravely prejudicing the boy's interests, and she resents me, Don Fabrizio, the boy being the son of my brother, and prejudices my claim to the guardianship. We seek only traditional justice from our sovereign . . .

Your loyal vassal,
Fabrizio Moncada, Paternò Sicily, 1578

Three weeks went by, and then four. A month became two, and still the king did not respond to Fabrizio's letter. Her husband complained to Sofonisba. "Can I not be assured that the Moncada seal gives my letter priority with the king?"

Sofonisba was becoming more pious than ever. She painted when she could for diversion and stimulation, but she retreated to prayer often in her loneliness. She longed for her sisters, the family she had once believed she would return to after she retired from court. She also thought more and more wistfully of court life itself, especially the bond she had with Queen Isabel. She never anticipated that marriage could be so lonely. She expected a partnership she could share.

She prayed daily for understanding. "Dear God, why, after all my years serving another family, after losing father without a final farewell, why have I been given to this cold, unfeeling man? Is this my punishment for a selfish life of painting? Am I doomed, Lord, to a lifetime of" — she paused — "this unhappy detachment?" Sofonisba knew she was sinful even to ask. "God forgive me for losing faith. I know you have a plan for me. I submit to you, Lord. Help me to understand your path for me."

"In the name of the Father, and the Son, and the Holy Ghost. Amen." Fabrizio's voice had a teasing lilt as he completed her confession standing behind her.

Sofonisba froze. She had not realized she was praying her laments aloud.

Fabrizio knelt beside her before the altarpiece in a new doublet with elephant tusk buttons. "Please forgive my intrusion, wife," he whispered into her ear, keeping his gaze upon the crucifix. He put his hands together, pointed his fingers up to heaven, and closed his eyes as if in prayer.

She waited, mortified, but as the moment grew longer, embarrassment turned to anguish. She reflected on what her husband had heard her say. Wives could be put aside, or worse, for such betrayal. Who knew what would ignite Fabrizio's sense of entitlement.

But he had only one agenda and had seen his opportunity to press the point. "Aloisa is squandering my nephew's inheritance, advancing vast sums to the Aragonas, in detriment to my house, and yours. Tomorrow we will see to the notaries and execute a release of funds from your Palermo pension. We shall fund a voyage to Spain to press our righteous claim in person before the king!"

Fabrizio made the arrangements for his trip, sparing no expense. He engaged the highest-born sea captain he could find to take him to Spain — Don Carlo Aragona, who happened to be a cousin of Aloisa's new husband Antonio Aragona.

The day before Fabrizio's journey was scheduled, Aloisa came to visit Sofonisba. "Sister, your dear husband continues to advance his monstrous claim, seeking to tear mother from child."

Sofonisba lowered her eyes. She felt caught in the middle. "Aloisa, Fabrizio does not look to separate you from your child. He simply wants to act as the boy's guardian."

"Your husband cares only to possess his nephew's estate, the same way that he has acquired control of yours, Lady Sofonisba."

The accusation stung, but Sofonisba bit her lip. She knew there was no stopping Fabrizio from petitioning the king. She was relieved at the sound of her maid Gioseffa bringing in a tray of lemon almond biscuits and sweet wine.

Sofonisba woke the next morning at the break of dawn to say her farewell to her husband, summoning every ounce of personal commitment she could muster for him. He was not her lover, but Fabrizio was her husband. She told herself she was being resilient. She even considered that maybe his claim was righteous. Aloisa was the mother, but not a Moncada. Perhaps the king was the appropriate person to adjudicate this Solomonic choice.

She rode to the dock in the carriage with Fabrizio, remembering her arrival at this same port years earlier when Rico was sent to greet her. She bristled at the memory and took a breath. She mentally counted the years of their marriage and her age. They could have had children by now. They could have become a family if only Fabrizio . . . regret spun around in her mind as the carriage brought them closer to the port. A tinge of bitterness seeped in giving her a sudden resolve, an armor to guard her heart as she said her farewell. "God protect you, Husband." Sincere concern for the risky sea travel ahead, and no more.

"Well then, yes," he said. "Let us depart."

With that, Fabrizio and his eight men boarded a ship captained by Don Carlo Aragona, the named Prince of Castelvetrano and Duke of Terranova, and a relation of Antonio Aragona, Aloisa's Neapolitan husband.

Rico drove Sofonisba back to Paterno` in the carriage alone, the same way she arrived. When she entered their home, it felt strangely barren. Fabrizio's absence seemed eerily permanent.

She painted daily and found herself thinking often of Marco, her tutor from long ago. Sometimes she tried to rekindle the crush she had for him, just to feel something, but more than anything, she wished she had a dose of *invenzione* now, the kind that flowed through her after their long conversations. She felt stuck in the suspense of this family drama, patently at the center of it and yet on the periphery. A sense of foreboding clung to her.

"Are you the Lady Sofonisba, wife of Signore Moncada?" the messenger huffed. She nodded. "Condolences, signora," he paused, panting. "Pirates attacked the signore's ship off the coast of Naples. Signore Moncada and his eight men were killed."

Sofonisba's eyes grew wide and her knees buckled. She thought of the Monastery outside Burgos — her prayers for the cardinal to disappear. Had she prayed for Fabrizio to be gone from her? She tried to remember. She recalled Catherine de Medici's words of assurances in Bayonne.

She motioned for the servants to give the messenger a drink. "What more can you tell me, sir?"

The messenger downed his diluted wine. "They took no money or hostages. Only Signore Fabrizio and his men were found dead. Carlo d'Aragona and his men were escorted to Naples and feted for their miraculous survival." Sofonisba shuddered. "Nothing more is known. I am sorry for your loss, signora."

She looked into the eyes of the humble messenger and saw his sincere compassion. Even if the duchess would have disapproved, she reached out to grasp his hand, squeezing his fingers inside her own, the feel of his rough skin reminding her of the moment she touched the king's hand to console him. "Thank you, sir." She handed him a coin before returning inside to her empty abode.

Sofonisba's marriage was over without ever really taking root.

Chapter 24

Madonna of the Sea: Sicily April 1578–December 1579

Word of Fabrizio Moncada's death spread quickly across the island. Aloisa arrived at Sofonisba's door in a new black satin mourning gown embroidered with pearls. "Dear Sister, my condolences for the loss of your husband."

"Thank you Aloisa. It's all so sudden."

"Piracy is rampant — every voyage is dangerous."

Sofonisba clutched the neckline of the mourning gown she still wore for her father and tried to accept her sister-in-law's sympathy. Guardianship of Francisco II meant control of a fortune. But surely Aloisa would never order the murder of her son's kin. They discussed plans for Fabrizio's funeral procession.

That night Sofonisba tossed for hours, wondering if she should request an official investigation into her husband's death. She awoke the next day smelling the orange blossoms outside her window. Her mind raced with *invenzione* rather than inquiry. She would paint the Madonna who protected the sailors and have faith somehow that this was the will of God.

She became engrossed in her work and neglected an inquiry. She wanted her painting to be a tribute to Sicily whose beauty filled her lonely heart, and to her husband, even if he never did. Perhaps she was mourning the marriage she wished she could have had, a marriage like her parents had.

Weeks later, a messenger arrived from Madrid.

My dear Sofonisba,

Words cannot express the sadness we felt upon
hearing of your loss of the honorable Señor Moncada
whose marriage we well recall arranging. Please know
that you are always welcome back at court, and your
return would most please us, especially the Infantas, as
well as our dear wife Queen Anne. Enclosed please find
the amount of 500 scudos to help assist you in your time
of need.

Your ever-faithful protector,
Philip, September 1578, Madrid, Spain

Sofonisba put a hand to her cheek, touched by the king's use
of his Christian name. Yet it couldn't quell her loneliness. She
needed to return home to Lombardy.

First, she knew she had to extract her dowry from Aloisa
and take control of her pensions in Palermo. She paid a visit to
the Palazzo Moncada. "Sister, I think it is time that I returned
to my family in Lombardy. It's been eighteen years since I left
home, and under the circumstances" — she spread out her
palms — "I see no pressing reason to stay in Sicily."

"Sister, you are welcome here under my protection indefinitely," Aloisa said sweetly.

"You are most kind, but I feel pulled toward Lombardy."

"As you wish. We shall miss you." Aloisa's lips curled into a
tight smile.

Sofonisba steeled her nerves. "Shall I call for a notary in the
morning for the transfer?"

"What transfer, Sister?"

"My dowry, to my family. I believe that was how the lawyer described it," Sofonisba said.

"Well, Sister," Aloisa replied without pause, "according to your marriage contract with your dear deceased husband, the Moncada are only responsible to provide you with the *use* of your present domicile. I am fresh from a meeting with my lawyers. It's delightfully simple. We have no obligation to return your money if we permit you to remain in your domicile." Aloisa batted her eyes, a look of triumph. "While we do enjoy your company, Lady Sofonisba, we truly have no opposition to you leaving Sicily to return to your home of origin. We simply demand that your funds remain under our control. As you recently impressed upon us, a woman is not competent to guard her own accounts. Now let's see, were those your words, Dear, or am I thinking now of my lawyer's counsel? No. I believe your words were 'This has to do with the Moncada patrimony' — isn't that what you told us, Dear?"

"Sister, my position is not the same as a small child's."

"Is it not? If you leave Sicily, Lady Sofonisba, you forfeit your domicile and, thus, relinquish your dowry. And dear Sister, our lawyers advise that your pensions must stay in Palermo according to royal instruction. You will need to apply for withdrawals from Palermo. We have assumed your protection because we are in the best position to do so, as you well know — having made a similar argument?"

"Aloisa, Fabrizio was the boy's uncle. Who was I to tell him he did not deserve custody?"

"My point, dear Sister, is that when my father died, you and your husband asserted that my child must be under his uncle's protection because a mere woman did not possess sufficient strength of will or character to guide and protect him. Was that not the rationale?" Aloisa fanned herself.

"Fabrizio believed that as the boy's uncle — "

"You sent a petition to the king, under your name, Sister, asking that Fabrizio take control of my flesh and blood because I, as a woman, was not competent to do so, did you not? You asserted the necessity of male guardianship — you cannot deny the same for yourself — it's an old Roman law principle."

Sofonisba recalled the Andalusian lawyer who drafted her marriage contract in Madrid. For her own protection, he had assured her.

She would have to fight to get her money back. She needed a representative. She hired a carriage that afternoon and rode to Catania to seek a solicitor.

"Sir, I am embroiled in something of a dispute with my late husband's family for the return of my dowry and the release of certain pension accounts in their control which bear my name and are my sole property, awarded directly from His Majesty King Philip II."

"My profound sympathies for your loss. I will be most happy to assist you. Of what family do you speak?"

"My late husband was Fabrizio Moncada, senior male of the House of Moncada."

The lawyer cleared his throat. "Madam, I certainly know — er, knew — Signore Moncada. I represent his family in many matters. Thus, I am afraid I cannot assist you as I may not advise you contrary to the interests of my client, Contessa Aloisa de Luna y Vega Moncada Aragona."

Aloisa had hired all the best lawyers in the area. They were unavailable to represent Sofonisba.

News raced across the empire: Philip III was born in Madrid. Queen Anne died in childbirth. Sofonisba made a Sign of the Cross, thinking of the young queen she met a decade ago, concerned about pregnancy ruining her figure.

Death and change surrounded Sofonisba. With her father gone, she had only Asdrubale to turn to. The younger brother she hardly knew was now the legal head of the Anguissola family. And regardless of her connections to the king, she needed a man to assert her legal rights.

Asdrubale lost no time joining his sister in Sicily. "Dear Sister, you have hardly changed a bit." He kissed her cheeks in greeting. He was a portly, bearded man of twenty-seven, a squat version of their father.

"You don't know how precious it is to kiss the face of family, Asdrubale. I am so happy to have you with me. What news do you have from home? How are our sisters and our little niece Bianca? How is Mamma?"

He winced. "The girl grows like a weed"—he paused—"but our sister Europa died shortly after I last wrote to you. It was sudden. She did not suffer. Her daughter Bianca is cared for by our mother and Anna Maria."

The news felt like another dagger to her heart. If she had returned home as soon as Fabrizio died, she may have seen her sister one last time.

Asdrubale did not waste any time getting to the topic of her financial quandary. "Let me understand. Aloisa says the house satisfies the dowry return?"

Sofonisba nodded.

"And has a lock on all the lawyers in Catania?"

She nodded more emphatically.

"Surely, I will have better success. Let me handle the matter, Sister. Leave it to me. Now, the more prestigious procurators will cost more money—we'll need to spend funds to protect them."

She was hesitant to acquire any more debt, but she wanted to have faith in her brother's conviction. She also realized that her first priority was to return to Lombardy, even if the distance made it harder to withdrawal her pension money.

She needed to put down roots. Cremona was the place she thought of as "home."

Over the next many months, Asdrubale frequently traveled to Palermo to meet with customs officials on his sister's behalf. He filed notarized fides vitae in all the government offices to identify himself as her guardian. The process stretched out for months and into the following year, 1579.

The morning after returning from one such sojourn, Asdrubale sat down with Sofonisba.

"How did it go in Palermo?" she asked.

"The customs officials continue to refuse to release the pensions to a northern bank."

"Doesn't this sort of transfer happen every day in the empire? How does the king send funds to the Spanish Netherlands?"

"I don't think the king is funding anyone these days. It's more the reverse. Spain needs money badly for her wars against the Protestants in the Netherlands and the Turks in the Mediterranean, not to mention dabbling in France and Italy. It makes sense that the customs officials are possessive of their assets. And they are all in bed with the Moncadas and the Vegas and the Mendoza-Alba-Sessas." Sofonisba laughed as Asdrubale mocked an exaggerated Castilian lisp, miming as if twisting the ends of an elongated mustache. She continued to rely upon her brother in Sicily. For over a year, he met with lawyers, trying to collect her dowry and protect her pensions. The litigation seemed endless.

Her palazzo was full of reminders of Fabrizio and their hollow marriage. She felt rootless, still mourning the marriage that wasn't. Loss overwhelmed her. She dealt with her conflicting emotions the best way she knew how. As Asdrubale carried on with the lawyers, she immersed herself in her work, finishing her tribute to her husband and the island of Sicily whose natural beauty won her over again and again, even when she pined to return to Cremona.

The piece had to be different. She would not honor Fabrizio with a court style portrait. It could not be focused on him as an individual, not *that* man. She decided to employ a completely new style, one she had seen on the island, a tribute to the sea that took Fabrizio — the sea she prayed would eventually take her home.

But still — an illuminated face, the style of the Anguissola circle.

On June 25, 1579, Sofonisba went to the Chiesa della Santissima Annunziata and looked for the priest who had blessed her after her father died. "Pardon my interruption, Father," she whispered, finding him in a side chapel contemplating its ceiling. "I have something for your mission. I would like to donate to your holy church a humble piece, my recent *Madonna dell'Itria*, which I painted in the memory of my deceased husband Fabrizio Moncada. It honors the Madonna who protects seafaring travelers."

"We will be most honored to receive it, my lady," the priest beamed. "I, in particular, will be most delighted. I'm a bit of an art critic myself, if the Lord does not strike me down for saying so. I will see that your piece is well placed and preserved for posterity."

"Thank you. Father, I do not even know your name," she said.

"I am Father Alfonso. They call me Fra Alfio." He winked, for a moment reminding her of her cousin Ferrante.

Sofonisba's litigation lingered. Aloisa's lawyers conceded nothing. "Let's return north no matter what the cost," Sofonisba pleaded with Asdrubale. "Authorize someone locally to handle matters so that we may return home to Lombardy by the New Year."

After months, he found someone. "I've located an agent to submit our fides vitae," Asdrubale said over a midday meal of sardine and octopus salad with oranges, almonds, and greens. "He has his own grudge against Aloisa Moncada. He'll be tenacious for our interests."

By late November 1579, Sofonisba and her brother Asdrubale were ready to depart for Sofonisba's homeland, her pensions, inheritance, and dowry still in limbo.

"A Genoan captain will take us north. He says the autumn was mild and winter has been slow to come. He expects a safe voyage," Asdrubale said. They were to sail to Genoa, the port from which she departed twenty years earlier. Sofonisba had surprisingly few bags but many canvases.

They left for the galley shortly after dawn on a mid-December day. She took one last look at her Sicilian abode before climbing into the carriage. The pale sky framed her house like a still life of her marriage. She held her cloak tight at the neck. A short carriage ride to the port and the sky was in full bloom. The sun warmed her face, crystallizing the moment that seemed to demarcate a new life for her, whatever that might bring. She took a deep breath then exhaled. A gull dropped to the sea, wrestling its prey, the rings of its whirlpool fanning out — a simple moment of wonder, of pure experiential freedom.

Independence.

"My sister, Lady Sofonisba Anguissola Moncada — Captain Orazio Lomellini." She remembered him straight away by the scar near his eye. The conversation they'd had twenty years earlier, aboard the ship bound for Spain, came back to her: "You were looking at the clouds." "I saw a cherub. There." "That looks more like an animal to me. A dog. The ears." "Those are the wings behind the cherub." Her pulse raced now as if she were being reunited with her first love — that singular experience of open-hearted vulnerability. The burly man only hinted at the boy with the beautiful torso she had met back then. The scar had faded very little, but he was no longer a lowly deckhand.

"I've only met one other Sofonisba," the captain said, bowing.

Asdrubale looked from his sister to the captain and back again. "Please, Captain, if we may be escorted to our cabins," he said.

"My pleasure. This way." The captain smiled, escorting his noble guests to their cabins below.

"What was that?" Asdrubale said when they were alone.

"What do you mean," Sofonisba asked.

"That look? At the captain."

"What look?"

"Sister, keep your wits about you. You are a Moncada widow."

Asdrubale tried to keep his sister away from the captain on this modest-sized galley where she had few obvious peers. He interfered on deck when Sofonisba strolled for exercise and the captain was near. When the honored guests dined together in the captain's cabin, Asdrubale sat between them, interrupting anytime one inquired of the other. Still, after a week of glances and nods, Sofonisba was certain her attraction to the captain was mutual.

The captain stole a private moment with Sofonisba. "I've worked my way up in this company. I am part of the family and yet — my father acknowledged me only after years of service." He examined her face to see if she understood his meaning. "I was raised in the family business but I've had to prove myself at every turn, unlike my *legitimate* brothers."

Sofonisba's heart pounded. The captain's life story echoed her father's.

"Now, I own my own vessel," he waved a hand across the deck, "and I've put aside a little nest egg."

"Modest as well?"

"I'm just reassuring you, Lady Sofonisba *Moncada*," the captain bowed before slipping away.

Sofonisba thought she saw him blush.

That evening, after supper, they strolled the deck. Asdrubale was nowhere in sight. Orazio looked over his shoulder and turned again to Sofonisba, taking her hand into his and putting it gently to his lips for a soft kiss. "Goodnight, cara," he said. "I will dream of you tonight and look forward to seeing you tomorrow."

She looked forward to the dawn.

It was midday before they had another private moment together. The captain found Sofonisba at the same spot on deck. "Good day, Lady Sofonisba." She could see the veins at his temples pulsing. "We are alike, you and I. I may not have been at the king's court, but I have made my own mark, as you have yours. I'm certain already — I am in love with you, Lady Sofonisba. Marry me."

He held out to her a small package wrapped in blue silk. Sofonisba began to unwrap it when she heard Asdrubale approach. She tucked the package instinctively under her wrap.

"What does he want with you?" Asdrubale asked his sister, his back to the captain. She had no desire to hide.

"The captain has asked for my hand in marriage."

"Your sister and I would like your blessing," Orazio said.

"That is absolutely out of the question, and you know it, Sister," Asdrubale said through clenched teeth without looking at Orazio. "A working captain? You are the wife of a prince. Do not belittle yourself in this way. Do not demean our family name. What would Father say?"

Sofonisba flinched, then envisioned her father's kind eyes in the family portrait.

"I am a free widow, Asdrubale, and I know my mind." She thought of the gull diving into the sea, the ringlets flowing out into the unknown.

"A union such as this would take the family backward, Sofonisba."

"Yes, and my first marriage was prestigious. Yet Signore Moncada never looked upon me with the love that shines in the captain's eyes, not in the least."

"You are talking like a stupid girl."

"Asdrubale, I may be your charge technically, but I am not a child. I am forty-five years old and I've made up my mind. And by the way, Brother, the captain is a Lomellini — a very respectable family."

"And, I've learned, a bastard." Asdrubale closed his eyes and nodded toward Orazio. "I won't consent, Sister. I am only protecting our family." Asdrubale turned and stormed away, not waiting for a reply.

Sofonisba remembered the package and took it from her wrap.

"Open it," the captain said. She unfolded the silk damask cloth to find a gold chain with a replica of St. Christopher, the patron saint of travelers and storms. "This will have to do at the moment, my love."

"Sir — "

"Please, call me Orazio." He took her hand and kissed her fingers. They looked up together and saw the main sail thrust wayward. "A storm is gathering. Please consider my proposal below deck, Lady Sofonisba."

"Sofi," she said, turning toward her cabin. She took one last look at Orazio as he raised an arm to cup his mouth and bark an order. His doublet pulled up and she spied his torso, thicker than twenty years ago, and more masculine.

She returned to her bunk below where her brother was waiting with one last warning.

"It's him or me, Sister. Think about it." He slammed her cabin door. She heard his own slam shut seconds later. He was right about one thing: she did feel like a stupid girl—a giddy, happy one.

A knock on Sofonisba's door—"Come in," she said, "Asdrubale, I—" She stopped short, surprised to see the captain instead of her brother.

"Lady Sofonisba—Sofi—I will get straight to the point as this storm is building. Have you considered my proposal?"

"My brother refuses to give his blessing."

The ship rocked. The lanterns swung from the ceiling.

"We have the law of the seas." Orazio said, smiling. "I am in command. On my ship, you don't need his approval."

She searched his face. He looked sincere. Dare she? She thought of the ringlets on the sea. She was free. The decision was all hers. "Yes."

Orazio walked determinedly over to her, slipped her dress over one shoulder and kissed her neck. She felt goose bumps spread up her body. She turned to kiss him.

He whispered vows in her ear, "*Cara, vera et legitima sposa,*" and cued her for hers, "*Caro, vero et legitimo sposo.*" They pledged marriage to each other and hastily made love in the disarrayed cabin—more exciting than anything she experienced in years with Fabrizio.

"Don't think I'm being cavalier. I will check on you when I can." He bent over and kissed Sofonisba on the lips before exiting the cabin.

She knew her gamble. He could easily disclaim vows made in secret, but at the moment, she didn't care. Her royally sanctioned marriage to Fabrizio had brought only loneliness; this was her chance for love, foolish or not.

"We are forced to dock on the Tuscan coast," Orazio yelled at Asdrubale, who paced the galley, getting in crew's way. "Oh, and your sister and I have married."

Asdrubale shook his head in the whistling wind. "What?"

"We married."

"WHAT?"

"I SAID, WE MARRIED! I MARRIED YOUR SISTER AS CAPTAIN OF THE SHIP. IT IS DONE." Orazio didn't wait for a response. He turned and continued shouting orders to his men in the December rain as they maneuvered for the port.

Asdrubale went below deck to find his sister. "Could I have heard the captain correctly? Married? How can that be? I did not approve. There has been no negotiation. No dowry. No agreement."

"Asdrubale, I am a grown woman. Orazio married us under his authority as captain."

"You defied me." The chaos outside the cabin drowned out his words but his anger was written on his face. His fists were clenched as he muttered an oath, kicking the door to her cabin. He holed up in his own until the ship was docked at the port of Livorno.

Sofonisba gathered herself and her belongings as best she could. When she came up on deck, her brother was making his way down the gangplank. She ran to the side of the ship, pushing past deck hands to reach him as he disembarked. "Asdrubale!"

Asdrubale's head turned only slightly. He responded without turning around. "Don't expect me to be there for you when you need me next. And after I dropped everything to go down to Sicily to help you." He swatted his hand backward as a farewell.

She watched him disappear into the crowd and raised her chin. It was time to be responsible for herself.

Chapter 25

Tuscan Honeymoon: de Medici Portraits
December 1579–April 1580

Orazio found a carriage to take Sofonisba to a local convent in Livorno, the port town on the coast of Tuscany where their galley docked. "You take refuge, dear. I'll stay at the port to secure the vessel, and I'll join you as soon as possible."

When she arrived at the convent, Sofonisba reached into her purse for a coin to tip the driver and realized Asdrubale had her money. A young sister of the Convent of Santo Mazzeo took Sofonisba by the hand and led her to a seat next to the fire, handing her a cup of broth. Sofonisba shivered feeling its warmth. Lavender hung in large quantities from the ceiling. She forced a smile, still shaken but relieved to be safe among the sisters and the sweet scent of the drying blossoms.

"And your husband, signora?" One sister asked.

"He remained at the port. For the ship. He's the captain. He married us. He had the authority. As captain. The captain has the authority of the sea." She realized she still felt disoriented. She hadn't planned to divulge what could only be called an elopement. The sisters glanced at each other.

"Don't worry signora. We will send for Father Giacomo in the morning."

Sofonisba sucked her breath in when the priest appeared the next day. He looked like Amilcare, in robes. She mentally sketched him, thinking of the family portrait of her father, Asdrubale, and Minerva.

"Father Giacomo, we have a grand lady in our care." The Abbess gestured toward Sofonisba. "This very noble and distinguished lady has been grounded by the storm."

"Ah, that hit the coast yesterday? Everyone is talking about it. There was considerable damage at the port."

"Father," the Abbess lowered her voice, "our situation involves the lady's honor. She and her betrothed — her spouse — were married on that ship, by the captain himself."

Father Giacomo turned to Sofonisba and practically whispered, "Signora, are you at any risk of deception by the captain?"

"None."

The priest studied the artist's face at length. "What God has joined, let man not put asunder. Fetch me when the captain returns and we shall marry you again, in the church."

Sofonisba sketched and prayed as she waited for Orazio. The sisters decorated the church with boughs of lavender. A full day passed, and Orazio did not come. Sofonisba heard the sisters whispering but fought any doubts. She had brashly married against her brother's command. What did she really know about Orazio after all? But this was her first truly independent act — now well into her forties. She could not lose faith. She clung to her decision because it was hers.

Sofonisba did chuckle about the arc of her life. After all her struggles at court to protect her name and reputation from the cardinal's disparagement, she was throwing caution to the wind with an impulsive new marriage to a man she hardly knew.

Orazio arrived later that day. "The ship suffered extensive damage. The cargo, too. We've taken a substantial loss from this. I could not break away. There was never a moment to get a message out. My sincere apologies, my love. I'm sorry I left you alone so long."

"I wasn't alone. I had the sisters."

They had a small church ceremony attended by a dozen local nobles as witnesses, easily enticed once word leaked about Sofonisba's tenure at court. A modest but elegant meal followed. The sisters put little lavender bouquets on the tables, tying them with the lavender's own stems. Sofonisba thought the simple purple on green may have been the most beautiful thing she had ever seen. She felt contented. Lavender cookies with sweet wine after.

The newlyweds retired to a small inn, exhausted. The proprietors offered a simple platter of salami and cheeses for their late supper.

"Care for more wine?" Orazio offered, pouring Sofonisba a glass without waiting for a response. "As soon as you boarded my galley, I saw the girl I met twenty years ago. I fell in love with you then. Now I believe we were meant to be together." Orazio's eyes seemed to bore into hers.

She felt her body temperature rising. She tried to forget her brother's disapproval and the hastiness of their marriage. Sofonisba raised her glass to him. "Meant to be together," she echoed.

Regardless of any problems in store for the newlyweds, their first private night together was their own. She was forty-five. She wondered if it was too late to start a family.

"All the cargo on board — including all our personal effects, has been impounded until we pay taxes required for returning residents."

"Residents? We hardly reside here at will," Sofonisba said. "Do you have any friends here who might assist us?"

"My connections are north in Liguria and south in Sicily." He shrugged. "I don't have any personal contacts in Tuscany."

Sofonisba hesitated. "Many years ago, I made the acquaintance of Francesco de Medici when he came to court. I hear he's now the Grand Duke of Tuscany. When I met him, his father Cosimo ruled. His father sent him to court, in part, to learn about me, the woman painter." She fanned her fingers in the air.

Orazio raised an eyebrow.

"He probably won't remember me," she added. "He requested I paint his portrait but did not find time to sit for it. Before I had the opportunity, he departed. I gave him an early portrait of myself instead. Come to think of it, he did promise me hospitality if ever I were in Tuscany."

"Then write to him. We can use his assistance."

The grand duke's reply arrived on Christmas Eve. Sofonisba read it aloud to Orazio, shaking her head.

The nobleman Asdrubale Anguissola has petitioned to intercede in an urgent matter to avoid the dishonor of his family. He informs us of your love for a sea captain and he disapproves of said union. He beseeches us to prohibit such union, to avoid a marriage disapproved by your family, to a person not as high-ranking as your position should warrant. Lady Sofonisba, as your Lord in this territory, we must caution you not to marry beneath your house and your status.

Francesco De Medici, Grand Duke of Tuscany,
December 24, 1579

She glanced at Orazio. If he felt insulted, he hid it well. "I apologize for my brother," Sofonisba said. "I was hurt when he left, but I never expected anything like this."

"Does your brother think he can block our marriage with a petition? That's preposterous," Orazio said.

"And he's distracting the grand duke from our customs issue after running off with my purse."

Orazio smiled at his wife's prudence.

"I'll write to the grand duke and explain everything. I cannot let Asdrubale dictate our new life together," she said.

To His Excellency, Grand Duke of Tuscany,

With the greatest of respect, I must confess, *mi capito tardi*, you caught me too late. Just as marriage is made first in heaven, then on earth, ours has been sealed . . .

"Surely he cannot mistake my meaning."

"Nor do I. Put that down, love," Orazio whispered, pulling her by the hand to their bedroom.

The couple had an appointment at the Medici palace in mid-January. They left Livorno for lodgings in the center of Florence, several rooms in the palace of a noble family that needed income to pay their taxes to the duchy.

"I wonder what the grand duke will say about rejecting his advice," Orazio said on the carriage ride.

"We did not reject his advice exactly. His letter arrived *after* Father Giacomo married us."

"You know, the rumor at port is that he murdered his first wife."

Sofonisba shook her head in disbelief. "The daughter of an emperor?"

"They say that he and his mistress poisoned her. All of Florence dismisses Cappello as a Venetian *courtesan* and rejects their natural child because the grand duke has four children from his first wife."

As soon as their carriage arrived at the Medici palace, Sofonisba and Orazio were escorted to the grand duke. He was sitting in a receiving parlor with a woman to his right and a pouty but pretty young lady on his left. He nodded knowingly when the footman announced Sofonisba and Orazio, seeming to recognize the artist straightaway.

"Ah, the lady painter so well loved by Philip," Francesco de Medici said smiling.

"It is an honor and a pleasure to see Your Grace again," Sofonisba said curtsying, "and to present my husband, Captain Orazio Lomellini." Orazio bowed.

"Sir," the grand duke nodded to him. "The grand duchess," Francesco de Medici gestured toward his wife next to him.

"You are most welcome at our palace," the grand duchess said.

"And the Lady Eleonora de Medici." The sad-looking girl nodded at the guests, batting her eyes and pursing her lips. She seemed to be fighting hard to keep her composure.

"Please sit." Francesco de Medici gestured to the chairs opposite them. "Refreshments?" He waved a servant forward who offered a tray of liquors and candied fruits.

"Lady Sofonisba, let me first say that I was shocked by your lack of candor. Your first letter refers to a matter of taxes but not to your own contested nuptials. You did not intend to mislead me regarding the captain, did you?"

Sofonisba's eyes widened.

Francesco de Medici waved a hand dismissively. "How can I not forgive you, after your sweet gift to me back in Madrid?"

So, he remembered.

"You will be pleased to know that I display your piece at my new academy. Patrons are astonished that a woman could paint so well. Dare I say that I, too, find consolation in your unconventional profession as my beloved Florence has yet to embrace my new wife, the grand duchess." He gestured toward Bianca Cappello, who was fondling her necklace. "You are both, shall we say, novelties among women."

The sad-looking girl winced.

The grand duke turned to Orazio. "Please, Captain. I invite you and your virtuosa bride to remain my guests during your stay in Tuscany."

Francesco de Medici then insisted on leading his new guests on a personal tour of his collection. "I daresay I am more expert than my agents at spotting an important piece. Knowledge is most important for a prince, don't you agree, Lady Sofonisba? Was not Philip an eager scholar, always in his library?"

"You do take after the king, I would say, Your Grace," Sofonisba smiled.

"What do you think of my Chinese porcelain, Lady Sofonisba?" he asked as they passed a display shelf.

Sofonisba inspected the blue markings on the delicate white porcelain, a fine job, she was certain, but hardly as refined as those in the king's collection. "They are exquisite, Your Grace," she replied.

"Exquisite!" He laughed. "I made this myself in my studiolo."

"I could not have known the difference from the work of a true Chinaman," Sofonisba said, curtsying.

"Ah! There, I've fooled the king's own court portraitist!" Francesco laughed again. "Lady Sofonisba and Captain Lomellini, I will gladly see to your taxation problem and will arrange a duties exemption for you. Your cargo will be salvaged as best as possible. I daresay, however, I have no influence over your relations with your brother. Captain, while you are in Tuscany, you shall be an honorary member of my guard. You may take assurance of my protection. And *Signora Lomellini*" — Francesco de

Medici bowed to Sofonisba — "a portrait perhaps? I've regretted not having time to sit for one while we were acquainted in
Madrid. Perhaps now that you are here at your leisure? And one
of my daughter perhaps?" He gestured to the pretty, sad young
lady.

"I would be most honored." Sofonisba curtsied, already envisioning Francesco's portrait. She would paint her patron with
book in hand to show his desire for learning — while also paying
tribute to her return home, echoing her self-portrait with book.

Sofonisba decided to experiment with a new lighting technique.
Utilizing light from an open door behind her, she illuminated
Francesco's face and hands, making him appear to be emerg-
ing from the shadow of the studio. She imagined the light at the
end of a long dark tunnel. When she came out the other end, she
would be home again.

For the following two months, the newlyweds took comfort in Francesco de Medici's hospitality, enjoying an extended
honeymoon of sorts. The grand duke had his own motives — he
pampered Sofonisba, knowing she had the king's favor.

Sooner or later, the couple had to broach the business of
marriage.

"A match-maker usually arranges these things," Orazio
said. "To me you are priceless, but your dowry must be part of
our marriage agreement, especially as we must leave no doubt
about our legitimacy."

"This is awkward for me too, especially since there seems to
be no way I can fund a dowry at present."

"Then, may we agree on an amount, ahh, say, 5,000, to be
paid whenever Palermo delivers your pension money?"

"And you are entitled to share my pensions as they become
due to me" — she corrected — "to us." She held out her hand for
a handshake.

"Done," Orazio agreed, tucking her fingers into his palms and pulling her to their little bedroom, "but let's not seal this with a handshake."

Once Sofonisba had enough of a lead on Francesco de Medici's portrait, she turned her attention to his young daughter. "Mistress, I will be most pleased to paint your portrait while my husband and I are in residence."

"Yes, as Father says," the girl responded flatly.

"Would you like to begin today?"

"Why not?" The girl shrugged and pulled at her silky brown curl. "After I freshen up, I will see you in your studio."

As Sofonisba waited for almost two hours for the girl to finish freshening up, she contemplated the pose and expression to capture in the portrait. She could not help comparing the little infantas a decade earlier, holding the same sad, pretty expressions. They had lost their mother too. She decided she would not hide the girl's sadness, but rather honor it, with a beautiful, illuminated face — large soulful eyes searching for understanding and love, yet hesitating. Her hand would rest on a table, echoing her father's portrait. Someday, she might no longer be sad, if she could get to a point of forgiveness.

Once the portraits were drying, Sofonisba began to feel useless in Tuscany. She wanted to visit her mother. She needed to go home. She wanted no more regrets. "I was hoping we could make our home in Cremona," she told Orazio.

He looked at her apologetically. "I have to be near the port, my love. The sea is my business." Sofonisba grimaced. He stroked her cheek. "You will find everything you could want in Genoa. Trust me. We will be happy there."

The damage to the galley had been repaired during their months in Tuscany. They set sail for Genoa within the week, blessed with clear April skies and the calmest voyage Sofonisba had ever sailed.

Nobody from Orazio's family was on hand to greet the couple at port when they arrived in Genoa. Had their hasty marriage offended the Lomellini? Orazio hired a carriage to take them to his modest palazzo nearby. It looked humble but elegant, much like the house in which Sofonisba was raised in Cremona, albeit smaller. There were no bursts of the regal gold of the king's court or the Moncada's palaces. Surveying it, she felt hopeful — a fresh start on a new life.

The walls could use some art.

In a matter of days Orazio's family did come to call on the newlyweds. Orazio's brothers Gabriello and Bernardo Lomellini and their families stopped by unannounced one Sunday after attending Mass. Orazio greeted his brothers and kissed their wives before introducing them to Sofonisba. "I am honored to present to you my bride, the illustrious portraitist Sofonisba Moncada Lomellini."

Orazio's oldest brother Gabriello stepped forward. "We welcome the dear wife of our *fratellastro* into our family," he said, bowing.

Orazio called her Moncada, yet his brother responded with "half-brother." The family dynamics were becoming clear to Sofonisba — Orazio was still marginalized in this family, just as he had been on board twenty years prior.

Orazio's sisters-in-law Antonia and Beatrice peppered Sofonisba with questions about royalty. Did the court provide her with gowns for the fetes? Was the king as pious as people said? Was Queen Isabel more French or Spanish? What was Catherine de Medici like?

Sofonisba fielded their questions for most of an hour before she put a hand to her mouth for an exaggerated yawn.

"We look forward to entertaining you again under less spontaneous circumstances." Orazio walked to his brother, extending an arm toward the door.

"Well, that was — nice," Sofonisba said after her in-laws departed.

"I apologize that relations with my family are somewhat stiff."

"Their visit made me crave my family more than ever. When can we get to Cremona? It's been twenty years, Orazio. I'm eager. And truly, I won't feel our marriage is legitimate until I have my mother's blessing."

"Yes, write your family. I want to meet Mamma Bianca." Orazio lifted Sofonisba's hand for a kiss.

Dear Mother,

My beloved husband Orazio and I are settled in Genoa and are awaiting the chance to see you and receive your blessing for our marriage. We are prepared to depart as soon as you wish us. I want nothing more than to see your dear face and to know you are well. Your new son-in-law, who is very kind and dear to me, longs to meet you. I also have a painting to give to you and twenty years to recount.

Your Loving Daughter,
Sofi, Genoa, 1580

Sofonisba dabbed her quill on the side of the inkwell when she finished, the tink-tinking transporting her back to her childhood and her father's first letter to Michelangelo.

Chapter 26

A Family Reunion: Genoa to Cremona 1580

Word spread that Sofonisba had settled into Orazio's house.
Local artists began to call upon her to pay their respects. She
was flattered to be asked to stand as godmother for the newborn son of a local painter. "I hardly deserve the honor, but I will
be happy to oblige," she told Bernardo Castello. At the reception after the baptism ceremony, Sofonisba scanned the invited
guests and didn't see a single titled person.

Her lot in life had receded a notch, she recognized, not
unhappily, feeling comfortable among the artists and their families. A week later, she again was asked to stand as godmother,
this time for the son of a miniaturist Giovanni Battista. If she
was not to be a mother, she joked to Orazio, at least she could
be the godmother of the local artists' children. Despite her air
of nonchalance, she felt her belly cramp in the church when her
godson wailed at the cold holy water that ran down his forehead. It was like her womb's last desperate cry.

She gifted her godson a painting of the Madonna and Child.

It was some months later when Orazio brought home a special guest. He followed Orazio into their dining room for the
midday meal. "Dear," Orazio said, clearing his throat, "I would
like to present to you my, er, Giulio. Giulio is my boy, my natural
child, as they say." Orazio held out his palm to present the boy

who bowed. He looked to be around fourteen years old, a miniature of the father.

"It is a tremendous honor to meet you, Lady Sofonisba," the boy said.

Sofonisba looked from Giulio to Orazio, the resemblance so striking it was like seeing a Coello copy of her work. "What a surprise," she said, touching her face. "Let's set another place at the table."

Orazio turned from the doorway after seeing Giulio off, eyebrows arched, ready for her questions.

"I must admit my surprise. Why did you not tell me about this earlier?"

"I feared you would be jealous."

"Jealous?" She felt her heart pound faster. "Giulio's mother then?"

"No, that was nothing — and long ago. I thought you might feel jealous that I have a son of my own when we do not — cannot." Orazio smiled, raising his shoulders.

The pounding subsided. "Then, there's not someone else?"

"How could you even think so, Sofi?"

She was touched he took offense at the suggestion. "Still, I am concerned that you have not acknowledged your son, Orazio. My father was not recognized until he was a young man, and I believe the wait scarred him."

"The topic has been on my mind, but I wondered if it would be shameful for you."

"There is no need for shame as far as I am concerned. Why don't you declare Giulio your legal son, *especially* since we have no child of our own?"

Orazio rose, seemingly taller than ever. "Ti amo, cara mia," he said, tears brimming his eyes.

"Giulio, what do you think?" Sofonisba held up her latest. "This is my fifth attempt." She gently lowered the painting to the dining table where her stepson was eating. They had become fast friends. He brought her news from the neighborhood, and she regaled him with stories of court.

Giulio smiled at the miniature. "It's sweet, Mamma Sofi."

She tilted her head. *Sweet.* His innocent compliment stung her. Painstaking work. Such detail. Her fingers were cramping like never before. "You're right, Giulio. It is sweet."

Sofonisba carefully crated all the miniature studies she had been attempting. She was blocked. She needed a new theme — and *invenzione.* She searched the chest they salvaged from the shipwreck in Tuscany, looking for the singular item that reminded her of home and her early struggles, her art kit. She found it resting on the brocade cloth Queen Isabel had bequeathed her, like a bird in a nest. She picked up the art kit and kissed the leather. She envisioned a couple kissing.

She stayed up late sketching studies, discarding then retrieving them from a pile on the floor, attempt after attempt. It had to be just right. Was it inspiration she was looking for or something more? Something to atone her guilt for excluding mother from the family portrait?

The distance of time ate at her. She had been gone so long she couldn't conjure her mother's face in her mind. She decided to use herself and Orazio as models for the piece. She sent up a brief prayer that their marriage be like her mother and father's. She thought of her first husband Fabrizio and shuddered.

The next day, her mother's letter arrived, inviting the newlyweds to Cremona.

"The journey will require a week, at least. What do you say we take a few side excursions — a little holiday for us, love, while I'm taking the time off the ship?"

"You are dear, Orazio, but I can't wait another day to see Mother." Orazio looked disappointed. Sofonisba smiled sweetly. Compromise seemed like the only solution. "How about on the return journey?" Orazio gave her a grateful nod, the corner of his mouth inching into a tiny smile, not a huge joyous smile, but a satisfied one. "Wait." She held her hands up, her fingers framing Orazio's face. She envisioned the countenance of the husband in the double portrait — a look of marital compromise, the ultimate partnership.

Sofonisba's heart raced as their carriage stopped in front of the carved doors to the courtyard of her family home. The doors looked just as Sofonisba remembered, except smaller. The two-story palazzo appeared smaller, too, and less grand. But red geraniums still cascaded off the upper story balcony.

Sofonisba's mother looked out the kitchen window when their carriage pulled into the courtyard. Their eyes met instantly. Sofonisba jumped out of the carriage and dashed into the house and into her mother's arms. Bianca looked barely older than when Sofonisba left — just four deep lines on her forehead as if she earned one for each death: Minerva, Lucia, Europa, and Amilcare. Sofonisba looked over her mother's shoulder as they clung to each other and saw her childhood — *The Chess Game* facing her on the entry parlor wall.

Sofonisba and Bianca held on for a very long embrace and Bianca wept. "If only Amilcare could be here, my dear girl, my dear girl."

Tears of joy streamed down Sofonisba's face. She tried to gulp away the lump in her throat. "I wish he were here, too, Mamma." They dabbed theirs eyes at the same time. "Mother, meet Orazio."

Bianca shook his hand up and down, smiling.

Orazio pulled her toward him. "Mamma Bianca," he said, kissing his new mother-in-law on both cheeks as if he had known her all his life. Sofonisba's love for him exploded.

"He has the same kind eyes as your father, Sofi — almost resembles Amilcare," Bianca said.

"I see it too, Sofi," a pretty and plump young woman said.

"Anna Maria, how you have grown," Sofonisba said, hugging her youngest sister. She pulled away and turned toward Orazio. "May I present my husband, Orazio Lomellini."

"May I present my husband, Giacomo Sommi," Anna Maria said turning to a handsome salt and pepper haired man in a fine brocaded doublet.

Sofonisba curtsied at her new brother-in-law, hiding the jealousy she felt that her sister saw the resemblance between Orazio and Amilcare before she did. Born nearly twenty years apart, Anna Maria and Sofonisba's experiences with their father barely overlapped. Sofonisba had only her distant memory of their father to cling to, and the family portrait. Anna Maria had fresh memories, precious memories.

"You were just a child when I left for Spain and now look at you and all these lovely children." Sofonisba scanned the parlor full of her sister's twelve offspring.

"May I present Niccolo," Anna Maria said indicating the eldest, "and Antonio, Galeazzo, Francesco, Isabetta, Giovanna, Carlo, Lazzaro, Maria, Benedetto, Gregorio and Marsilio." She held her hand out toward the corner of the room, where a young girl of twelve or so shuffled her feet. "Bianca, come be presented to your Aunt. Young Bianca has been the most excited of us all, I think. Sofi, please meet Europa's girl, your niece Bianca."

Bianca looked up shyly at her legendary aunt, her eyes glistening. "I paint too!" she said, blushing when the others chuckled at her exuberance.

"And my dear brother Asdrubale?" Sofonisba asked.

"He's, uh, taking care of some business with Uncle Carlo," Anna Maria said, referring to young Bianca's father.

"He has not forgiven me for disobeying him?"

Orazio looked up at the ceiling like he wanted to escape.

"Sofi, he's sensitive." Her mother paused, tilting her head to the side, "Please understand, Sofi." Sofonisba flinched hearing her mother say her nickname. It made her miss her father all the more. She let the subject drop so as not to spoil the happy occasion.

"This is for you, Mother." She settled onto a side table a canvas no longer than her arm. "Our gift to you — a tribute to you and Father."

In the portrait, a couple gazes out at the viewer, their figures echoing each other. The wife holds forth a piece of plump fruit while the husband's fingers gently rest upon her sleeve. A dark background blends with their dark clothing, encircling the figures, illuminating their faces. They appear as two parts to a whole. A unit. A team. Determined.

Bianca stood close to the painting to inspect. Then she backed away from it to examine it from two paces away. She turned to Sofonisba and touched her daughter's cheek. "I see tenderness yet strength. Two individuals, yet united. It's evident in their eyes. For you, Sofi, the focus is always in the eyes, even when you first sketched as a little girl. Brava, Sofi. Let us have a little toast." Bianca poured little glasses of sweet wine for them from the sideboard and put out a tray of biscotti.

"Mamma, I pray our marriage may be as strong as yours and Father's was. I wanted this painting to reflect the respect you had for each other, the way you acted like partners. I think Orazio and I can be similar. I respect him for what he's accomplished. And he's kind." She smiled at Orazio and he reddened slightly, "Like Father — was." Sofonisba paused and took a breath. "Mamma." She embraced her mother.

The front door burst open, and a haggard looking man let himself in.

"Our illustrious Sofonisba, returned to the family fold." He bowed.

"Ferrante?" Sofonisba barely recognized her cousin. He was around her age but looked like a man of seventy. The cousins embraced and Orazio joined them at the threshold. "Cousin, I present to you my husband, Orazio Lomellini. You may recall him from our voyage to Barcelona in '59," she said, lacing her arm through Orazio's.

Ferrante looked back and forth from Sofonisba to her new husband as if he were trying to remember them together on the long-ago voyage. "Welcome to our little Cremona," he said, bowing to the couple formally, holding a hand on his back hip as he bent, like a much older man.

After supper, Sofonisba approached Ferrante to ask what she could not by letter. "Please, Ferrante, tell me why you were imprisoned. What reason was given?"

"No explanation was offered, Cousin. At first, I was treated harshly," he winced, "but, in time, when no accusation from Spain was forthcoming, they began to lose interest in me. Then, once I thought to bribe the guards, I was treated rather well. Mostly we played cards until the day came when I was released, as mysteriously as I was admitted."

"You do well for yourself now? I pray the contracts you made in Spain were useful to you?"

"Ah, yes, those. I daresay my work is more modest these days."

Sofonisba remembered Ferrante pulling her onto the dance floor at the royal wedding banquet. Her cousin survived his ordeal, a shell of his former self.

When she awoke the next morning, Orazio was out of the bedroom they were sharing, presumably up for many hours as he rose daily before dawn. She glanced up at the birds painted on the rafters of her girlhood room and thought about her father and her deceased sisters Minerva, Lucia and Europa. Had the experience of court been worth missing all these years with her family? Worth leading to Ferrante's incarceration and broken spirit?

Sofonisba went downstairs. Her niece Bianca was waiting in the parlor with Orazio and Mamma Bianca. Her niece no longer looked like the bashful girl she was yesterday. Today, Bianca had a mischievous smile on her face, looking much like her mother Europa in *Chess Game*.

Sofonisba saw her wink at Orazio. "I am taking Aunt Sofi and the captain on a secret mission."

Grandmother Bianca smiled like she already knew where.

Their carriage came to a halt in front of the Church of Saint Agatha, and they entered the church whose walls were half empty when Sofonisba was a child. Now, paintings covered every inch.

"Ah, Bernardino." Sofonisba instantly identified a piece by the hand of her former teacher Bernardino Campi. She turned and noticed the work of her sister Lucia on the next wall, a painting of *Jesus, Mary and the Saints*. She smiled. "You know, our tutor admonished us never to expect our work to be shown publicly. I guess Lucia proved him wrong after all." She hoped she hid her jealousy.

Sofonisba turned toward her niece and noticed that the girl was lost in her own world. She followed her niece's gaze to a painting of the *Stigmata of Saint Francis with a Praying Woman*. The figure of Saint Francis arched up to an illuminated angel, but Sofonisba's attention went directly to the face of the praying woman, recognizable as her own mother. Sofonisba looked at her niece beside her and could tell from the reverence in the girl's eyes that the artist could only have been the girl's deceased mother Europa, Sofonisba's sister. Young Bianca's eyes were fixed on the painting as if she were communing with her mother through it. Two tears rolled down her puffy cheeks.

Sofonisba stepped in front of her little niece and lifted her chin, looking deeply into her large eyes. "Your mother is always with you in spirit." She squeezed her tight. "She is looking down at you right now."

Bianca's tears became a barrage. Sofonisba held tight to the little girl as she looked up at the image of her mother praying. This was the face of the Anguissola circle of women, of her mother, Europa, Lucia, Minerva, Bianca, and Sofonisba herself. All of them.

"Ladies, shall we continue on with our tour? You promised me another stop as I recall," Orazio said smiling at Bianca.

The girl dabbed her nose with her sleeve. "Yes, the Church of San Sigismondo, a location blessed by its relics and its history," the twelve-year old said wagging a finger in the air. Sofonisba saw a hint of her tutor Marco in the gesture.

As soon as Sofonisba entered San Sigismondo, she remembered why she chose to specialize in portraiture. Spiraling, bulging muscles floating in the air, angels so removed they fail to touch anyone. Beauty for the sake of beauty without showing the soul.

And then, the large pleading eyes called out to Sofonisba, the face of Saint Daria, the eyes that set in motion Sofonisba's love for portraiture. Sofonisba had forgotten. Prince Philip's eye-lock with her on her balcony had replaced this face over the years, in Sofonisba's mind, as her inspiration, but no, Saint Daria, this face, this open, inquisitive, contemplative, serene face. This was the face. Impiously, immodestly, Sofonisba couldn't wait to share her thoughts with Bianca next to her.

"Bianca, you see her face?" Sofonisba pointed up to the image of Saint Daria, then looked to see if Bianca understood. "Oh, dear Lord." Sofonisba cupped her mouth. Bianca. Her little niece Bianca was the face of Saint Daria. Like a sign. A sign that it was all meant to be. Sofonisba felt fulfilled.

When their tour was over, the three returned to Sofonisba's childhood home and young Bianca approached her aunt. Sofonisba saw a canvas protruding from behind her back. The girl's shoulders rose as she took a deep breath.

"This may be premature," she blushed, "but it might be my only opportunity, so here." She handed her aunt a *Madonna and Child*.

Sofonisba's gaze went straight to the sad eyes of the Madonna.

"May I?" Sofonisba asked, taking the canvas from the girl to inspect it. "Brava, cara." Sofonisba patted her niece's hand. Bianca stood up straighter at the compliment. "Truly remarkable for a young artist. May I suggest, however, you adjust your shadowing."

They painted together the rest of the day, something like master and pupil, but more like one generation passing down a family recipe to the next.

That night Sofonisba lay down in bed but couldn't sleep. She felt she was being scrutinized — myriad eyes on her — young Bianca's Madonna was staring at her; she and Orazio were watching her from the double portrait; Queen Isabel's Bayonne portrait seemed to float in front of her; young Prince Philip gazed up at her from his horse below the family balcony; the serene eyes of Saint Daria penetrated her.

Missing her father, connecting with her mother, the face of her mother in Elena's Stigmata, the face of Saint Daria, instructing Bianca in painting, the scrutiny of every set of penetrating eyes she ever painted; it all came together for Sofonisba as she lay in the bedroom she occupied as a young girl, Orazio snoring next to her, like a sort of parallel bookend framing the second half of her life. Once upon a time she set a goal to capture the king's image in a quest to validate her father, her family — and she had succeeded. Her fame and work at court elevated the family name.

But what now? Was the best part of her life over? What would sustain her? Was she now useless? In the dark of night, the day's sense of fulfillment vanished.

When she woke in the morning, she imagined a drop of oil on Lucia's shoe. "Panderer." She heard her tutor Marco. "Present your masterpiece to the king." She was sitting with the Friar. "Look to your own goodness to find your worth." Her past taunted her. Her prior accomplishments succeeded; they honored her father and family. What of her own legacy? Her ambitions continued to plague her.

On the morning of Sofonisba and Orazio's departure for Genoa, her brother Asdrubale appeared in the kitchen, holding out a bouquet of flowers for his sister.

"To celebrate your blessed new marriage," he said. Young Bianca smiled widely next to him. Sofonisba never learned what caused Asdrubale's change of heart to accept her and Orazio, but she suspected young Bianca had something to do with it.

"Make room," Orazio bellowed, carrying a large wrapped painting. "We will need to adjust things to fit this in the carriage." Her mother Bianca was following behind with a satisfied smile.

"This is yours now, Sofi. Take it so you feel your family is always with you," Mamma Bianca said. Sofonisba had no doubt the painting was her *Chess Game* — as if her *invenzione* was literally trying to catch up with her.

Many promises for future visits were made all around and then the newlyweds departed for Genoa and Orazio's house. They had taken an extra couple of days to explore the country-side on the journey home. Once home, Orazio began preparations for his next voyage.

"I will think of you day and night and long to return," Orazio promised as they said their farewell in front of *Chess Game*.

"I'll be waiting for you. And when you do return, you will find our nest covered in paintings." They kissed, looking deeply into each other's eyes.

A widow once already, Sofonisba found herself a sea-widow. Resilience. She reminded herself of her father's parting advice. And then she wondered, maybe that was not quite the sentiment. Gratitude. "I'm grateful, profoundly grateful." Sitting under her recently acquired *Chess Game*, Sofonisba set out to envision her next masterpiece.

Chapter 27

Call to Turin: Genoa 1583–1591

In the autumn of 1583, Sofonisba received an order from a magistrate in Sicily. She opened it as Orazio looked on. "They're freezing my pensions until Fabrizio Moncada's estate is resolved," she said without looking up. "No withdrawals will be permitted until the Lady's marriage to Captain Orazio Lomellini is adjudicated," she continued scanning, "deciding whether the Lady's marriage disinherits her from her deceased husband's estate, whether her dowry has been satisfied in kind, and whether her pension withdrawals are permissible, the Lady having departed the island."

Her jaw dropped. "Fabrizio's estate? What did he have? He pawned my jewels. And my dowry and pensions came from the crown. I will go straight to the king."

A letter generally required two weeks to reach Madrid from Genoa, so Sofonisba expected an answer within a month, perhaps two, but months passed while she still waited.

Many more months passed without a reply from King Philip. Was he ignoring her request, siding with her former in-laws? After all, he could not afford to alienate the Moncadas — Aloisa held sway in Sicily, his most strategic Mediterranean post — the strongest buffer between the Turks and Spain.

In July of 1584, when her stepson Giulio was visiting, an elegant messenger delivered a declaration from Madrid.

"Giulio!" Sofonisba called to her stepson as she broke the royal seal. "What we've been waiting for." She smiled as she began to read.

"It's addressed to your father and me," she nodded as she read, "honoring our marriage, awarding us," she sucked in a breath. Her smile faded. "*Dio*, another pension . . . Palermo customs . . . royal instructions, and so on. The king congratulates us on our marriage, but instead of lifting the hold on my accounts, he's bestowed me a new one — another pension to be dispensed through Palermo like the rest. Aloisa will block disbursement of this one along with the others."

She let the document fall to the floor. The parchment stood upright when it hit the ground, looking like an impenetrable castle wall.

Giulio picked up the parchment and read aloud to her. "Recognizing the industry, ingenuity and singular devotion of the noble and sincerely delightful Sofonisba, a former lady to the serene queen Isabel, who served our dear queen most devotedly and honorably, and whose virtues and genius alone warrant this security for her new matrimony to the noble and honorable Orazio Lomellini." He shook his head, palms upward, in awe.

"But, Mamma Sofi, the honor of it!" She smiled, remembering the look on the sisters' faces at the convent in Livorno when she let it slip that she and Orazio married on the ship. A royal proclamation honoring her marriage? Not bad recognition for her first truly independent adult action — not bad acknowledgment for an elopement.

On the eve of Sofonisba's fiftieth birthday, a rap at the door — a messenger in the garb of the Republic of Genoa stood at the threshold presenting a scroll, "from Giulio Pallavicino for the

Very Serene Captain Orazio Lomellini and the Distinguished Lady Sofonisba Anguissola Moncada Lomellini."

Sofonisba recognized the surname of the house her father once served to earn his own family name. How the tables had turned. Now Pallavicino beseeched Sofonisba to honor Genoa with her presence to greet the most serene Duke and Duchess of Savoy at port in Savona as they proceed to court in Turin. Orazio was given the honor of captain of the delegation. Everyone was talking about the marriage arranged between the Duke of Savoy and the Infanta Catalina Micaela, Sofonisba's former charge, the king's second daughter whose sex so troubled Queen Isabel.

Orazio took the scroll from the messenger and studied it. "Please inform Signore Pallavicino that Captain and Signora Lomellini will be most honored."

Orazio prepared his galley with tapestries and velvet cushions for the delegates. The sea was placid and glistening the day they set sail. They arrived at port in Savona in plenty of time to greet the newlywed duke and duchess.

Curtsying before the Duchess of Savoy, Sofonisba could still see the Infanta's childhood face.

"I was told that you would be here, Lady Sofonisba, and I was looking forward to seeing you. I recall how sweet you were to my sister and me after our mother passed." The eighteen-year-old took in a quick breath. "And you gave me my first drawing lessons." She smiled. "May I impose upon you to paint my portrait on this sojourn? Perhaps to offer as a wedding present to the duke? After sitting for Master Coello so often over the years, it would be a pleasure to sit for a woman."

"I would be honored," Sofonisba said, smiling properly but wanting to shout for joy. Five years! It had been too long since the Medici portraits in 1580.

They arranged for a makeshift studio for Sofonisba to begin Catalina Micaela's portrait immediately. Catalina Micaela shared news from court as she posed. The Infanta was six years old when Sofonisba left Madrid, and she remembered that Sofonisba went to marry a Moncada.

"Your Moncada nephew — the young heir whose custody was fought over — he was brought before the Inquisition in Sicily, accused of witchcraft!"

A Moncada brought before the Inquisition?

"The *real* story is that your nephew Francesco pummeled to near death a drunken courtier who did not have funds to pay a gaming debt. The unfortunate victim was an old retired general who fought at Saint Quentin. His name was Pedro de Mendoza. You may recall him from court. His brother was the Cardinal of Burgos."

Sofonisba winced.

"Mendoza took revenge for the beating — used old contacts of the cardinal and had the Moncada boy arrested by the Inquisition."

The absurd coincidence was like a cross-section of Sofonisba's worst nightmares in Spain and Sicily: the Mendoza of Burgos versus the Moncada of Paternò.

"I thought Pedro de Mendoza had been married off — " Sofonisba stopped before finishing her thought — to King Philip's discarded mistress.

"Who knows if that marriage lasted," the duchess said. "Mendoza had quite a reputation. Of course, the accusation was unsubstantiated. Your nephew was fully exonerated, you should be relieved to learn. It is also heard at court that your former in-laws do very well for themselves, indeed. Their estates increased last year from four to thirteen."

And still they held her dowry? Fought her pension withdrawals? She had to seize the opportunity. "I hesitate to impose upon Your Grace with ugly matters, but in fairness to my dear husband Orazio, I feel compelled to say that I remain in constant dispute with my former in-laws — for the return of my dowry, money bequeathed to me by your mother Queen Isabel — and for payment of my pensions, which are mine by order of the crown. I only ask that you might please spare a mention, please inform your father, the king, on my behalf so that he could help me to extract what is mine. He sent a most gracious gift last year to celebrate my marriage to Orazio. I can only hope he regards me as he once did."

The duchess straightened her back.

"Dear Lady Sofonisba, if my father the king sent you a wedding present last year, you should consider yourself most fortunate, given his preoccupations with the wars with the Turks and the Spanish Netherlands and with the empire's finances and such. As loyal as he is to those who serve him, he cannot be available to manage his subject's minutia." A swift nod; the topic was closed.

"Of course, Your Grace."

Sofonisba swallowed a small lump and tried to concentrate on the easel in front of her. She was planning a hand on book position to symbolize the duchess' intelligence, as she had for Francesco de Medici in 1580.

"Please, Your Grace, if you would place your right hand on the edge of the table."

Instead of portraying Catalina Micaela as learned, Sofonisba decided at that moment to show the young duchess as unsteady, holding onto the edge of the table as if she still swayed from her voyage, still needed grounding. She experimented with her brushwork — something she had recently been playing with. The effect lent a certain gravity to the eighteen-year-old. The artist had her revenge, the best way she knew.

The truth was that the second Infanta had little influence with her father. Her older sister Isabella Clara Eugenia took it all. Catalina Micaela earned only token gestures of his attention. She learned early not to squander her influence with him.

Sofonisba and Orazio returned to Genoa after the delegation, and it wasn't long before Orazio was called back out to sea. "I've been awarded a huge contract for the Genoa Merchants' Association, and my rates are up since the delegation. I have you to thank, really. It was your connection to Madrid that won me that job — and that job led to this."

He set off for the voyage on a cloudless September morning. Sofonisba escorted him to the docks to say farewell.

"Until I return, you have my heart in your safekeeping," he said.

"And you have mine."

As he headed up the gangplank to the salutes of his crew, Sofonisba detected an extra charge in his step. Seafaring was his pride and his identity, just as art was hers.

On the fifth day of the voyage, the scout in the bird's nest called down to Orazio at the helm, "Captain, an unidentified galley approaches fast!"

Orazio took out his glass and peered off to the horizon spying a pirate ship. As a commercial vessel, they had no real protection. He ordered the crew to alter course. If Sofonisba had been there, she would have cried tears of joy for her husband's good sense. She'd lost her first husband to pirates. She would not want Orazio to take any risks against pirates now. Orazio was certain.

"Captain, sir," the boy pointed. A storm was gathering.

To escape the pirates, the *Patrona* was forced into a storm. The ship pierced whitecaps as it lurched forward with the waves, rising and falling with each nautical thrust. The crushing weight of nature pounded the ship, tossing it about like a twig atop a rushing river.

Nature did not respect the captain's prudence—nor did the other captains at port.

"I think Orazio's judgment was clouded by that delegation to Savona," one captain nattered at the port. "He thought he could take *La Patrona* into the eye of a storm. The galley took in too much water — the cargo is completely destroyed. Lomellini is fortunate they didn't drown."

"I have been suspended from the official roster of captains," Orazio said, wringing his hands after his hearing before Genoa's shipping commission. "This means that I may no longer captain a ship for other than personal use. My kin intervened. They struck a deal. I can run a Lomellini ship on a limited route. Otherwise, I'm banned." He shuffled his feet. "It went badly before the commissioners but being dependent on my brothers — " He sank into his chair.

She decided not to mention the worsening situation in Sicily. Aloisa's maneuvering now forced a legal response. They would have to hire a lawyer to sue for Sofonisba's pensions or forfeit them.

At least they had each other.

Events of the larger world did not touch Sofonisba the way they did when she was at court, when she felt first-hand the energy around the king's victories and losses.

Sofonisba and Orazio were strolling the port one stifling August evening in 1588 when they heard the news traveling the empire: "Disaster in the North Sea! The Spanish Armada is destroyed! That Protestant whore! Che Vergogna!" The Armada's shame was Genoa's shame too. Theirs was a shipping world, and Genoa had supplied many of the Spanish Armada's ships.

Sofonisba remembered King Philip at the Escorial after the death of Queen Isabel, praying as piously as any person she had witnessed. And then she remembered why she left court, the death toll at Lepanto pushing her away. She wasn't convinced that her king was as righteous as he was pious, but she felt for his personal losses.

Not long after, Sofonisba heard that Catherine de Medici died in France. The gossips never failed to note how she introduced forks to the French table and high heels to their fashion, but her legacy was a mixed one. "They say she conspired with King Philip at Bayonne for the massacre of the French Huguenots," Giulio said.

"Giulio, let me tell you about Catherine de Medici at Bayonne." It had been twenty-three years since Sofonisba met the queen mother at Bayonne, and time had blurred her memory, but Sofonisba recalled the queen mother being a woman who wanted peace and tolerance, and not war.

Between Orazio's clipped wings and the Sicilian magistrate's block on Sofonisba's funds, money was tight. They hired a lawyer named Fabrizio Bargagli to appear on their behalf in Sicily.

"How is it that I have seven, no eight royal pensions, yet we cannot make ends meet?"

"Take heart, we are not the only ones," Orazio said. "The pawn shops near the port are overflowing with furniture and jewelry."

They borrowed from their lawyer—just an advance until the hold was lifted on her pensions and dowry.

Financial constraints forced them to be frugal, but in June of 1591 they received a wedding invitation from her niece Bianca in Cremona that she could not decline. She thought about her niece clinging to her in the Church of St. Agatha, crying before the painting by her dead mother.

"It would break my heart to miss young Bianca's wedding, especially since her mother cannot be there."

Orazio took his wife's fingers into his and raised them to his lips. "I wouldn't hear of it."

They borrowed some more from Bargagli, just enough to cover the expenses to go to Bianca's wedding.

Sofonisba stayed up late calculating what she thought they owed the lawyer and how much of her pensions would cover their debt to him — once the block was lifted. "Ten percent should do it," she announced in the morning. "That's more or less a year of my life at court, but I don't see any alternative but to sign over to Bargagli the right to a tenth of my Palermo pensions."

Bargagli wasted no time responding.

Gentle Sirs,

We are in receipt of your proposal to adjust your accounts owing this firm and accept your method of calculation, with some adjustment to the sum owing. Please see attached addendum and our demand for immediate payment and resolution.

Very truly yours, Fabrizio Bargagli, Esq.,
Fee Statement Attached

She turned to the lawyer's itemization and adjusted total. "Twenty-five percent? Twenty-five percent of my entire pensions for the rest of my life to repay for services to date!" She slumped in her chair.

A formal invitation arrived:

To the Lady Sofonisba Anguissola Moncada Lomellini,
your presence is requested in Turin, at the court of the
Duke and Duchess of Savoy, this September in the year
of our lord Fifteen Hundred and Ninety-One.

Could they afford more travel so soon after Bianca's wedding?
Could she afford not to go? Even though Duchess Catalina
Micaela would not advocate for her to the king, the allure of a
court portrait was impossible to resist.

She took another advance on her pension and hired a carriage for the week-long journey to Turin and extra attendants
because Orazio was at sea. She thought of Amilcare, so proud of
his name, so proud of her. She vowed not to ask the duchess for
help this time. She refused to belittle her name.

Sofonisba was escorted into the palace to a parlor where the
duchess was engaged in a game of chess with a small girl no
more than four years old. The girl wore a velvet dress with golden
flowers embroidered on it. Sofonisba saw the resemblance to
Queen Isabel. This had to be the late queen's granddaughter.
And she was the spitting image of Catalina Micaela at that age.

"Save your queen for when you need her, dear. Don't bring
her out too soon," the Infanta was coaching the girl. The duchess welcomed Sofonisba with a nod. "Lady Sofonisba, how dear
of you to come."

"Your Grace," Sofonisba curtsied, back in the seat of privilege, captivated by the lavish surroundings. "It is my truest happiness to do Your Grace's bidding."

"You are a dear. You were so sweet to my sister and me as
children. Now, I will have you preserve my youth, as only you
can, Lady Sofonisba," the duchess said, still unsmiling. "Let us
begin in the morning. Now, please" — the duchess waved her
hand at the banquet tables set at the side of the hall — "refresh

yourself," she offered, returning to her chess game with her daughter.

Sofonisba was already contemplating the Infanta's portrait. Her porcelain beauty had not diminished in the preceding six years. So young and lovely but never a smile. Large searching eyes that do not seem to look forward. A beautiful court, a lovely daughter, but she longs for something more that is not here. Love? Opportunity? A new identity?

Sofonisba tried to identify in her mind the duchess' elusive quality: Lovely and sad. Lovely sad. The words returned to her over and over again.

As she drifted off to sleep, Sofonisba dwelled on Catalina's sad beauty. She reminded herself how the king favored his first daughter over this one — how Queen Isabel grumbled that a third daughter would be put to death. Catalina Micaela was undoubtedly still looking for the love she missed as a child. Sofonisba thought of her own father, so good to her, always supportive. She pitied the duchess, who had everything the material world could offer, but not the happiness of knowing her father's love. Sofonisba felt compassion for Catalina. She made room in her heart to forgive the duchess for her indifference to Sofonisba's plight in '85.

She would render Catalina Micaela's image softer this time, not echo court sentiments, but rather her tender self.

Instead of a formal gown, Sofonisba posed the duchess in a headscarf wrapped in ermine, as if she were set to travel — ready to go, but waiting for the opportunity. Sofonisba envisioned her Virgin Mary in 1559, also ready for her future. The painter emphasized the duchess' searching eyes; open to possibilities she might never know. The duchess did not look fondly back at Madrid, but neither was she at home in Turin. Sofonisba decided the portrait would have no background.

For the following weeks, the duchess sat for Sofonisba, saying very little, looking very serious, melancholy, and dispirited.

When the painting was nearly completed, the Infanta came to see its progress.

"Lady Sofonisba," the duchess said with a lilt in her voice, "were it not for the ermine, one might think this a portrait of a mere noblewoman rather than a duchess, the Infanta of Spain."

Sofonisba's heart skipped a beat.

"Your Grace —"

Catalina Micaela raised a hand, interrupting her. "I'm not daughter or wife here, but rather Catalina Micaela. No portrait has ever shown me personally as this one does. Thank you, Lady Sofonisba." The duchess put a hand over her heart. "It is as if you have depicted my very truth. Please, accept this gift as a sign of my profound gratitude." Catalina Micaela handed a silk covered box to Sofonisba. "Open it."

Sofonisba opened the box and saw a beautiful ruby set in a gold brooch. "Your Grace is most generous." Sofonisba curtsied to the floor, smiling, satisfied. Even though she knew she would pawn the brooch to cover the expenses of the trip and the materials for the portrait, she felt vindicated by her *al vero* portrait of the Infanta-duchess. For Sofonisba, the *Lady in Ermine* meant forgiveness.

Chapter 28

Road to the Spanish Netherlands 1595–1599

A fellow artist named Luca Cambiaso paid a visit to Sofonisba on his way to Madrid for a royal commission on the endless Escorial project. They spent some time experimenting together with the soft, misty sfumato style of Correggio that Cambiaso had been keen for lately. He wanted her opinion as to how the king might like it.

"Yes, I think the king could use some softness."

Sofonisba began a series of Madonna and Child portrayals, sfumato.

She and Orazio were dining on a hearty root soup on a cold January day when a post arrived from Sicily. "Dio," Sofonisba exhaled as she opened it, dreading the lawyer's bills.

Gentle Sirs:

Please see the attached fides vita assigning a portion of the estate of Fabrizio Moncada, morte intestatum, to the Lady Sofonisba Anguissola Moncada, including the restoration of said lady's dowry in full.

The block on your accounts is lifted. Please note, the royal pension instructions still require a fides vita by you or your representative for withdrawals. This office will gladly file the necessary papers to collect said bequest. Please advise.

> Very truly yours, Fabrizio Bargagli, Esq.
> Palermo, Sicily, 15 January 1595
> Fee statement attached

"Good news at last," she said. "The block on my funds is lifted. Not only have I inherited something from Fabrizio, the Moncadas are returning my dowry. How long has it been? Fifteen? Sixteen years?"

"Better late than not at all," Orazio said. "Why don't we cut Bargagli out now and find someone else to represent us in Sicily?"

"It would be nice to be rid of him — but as expensive as he was, he won. The Moncadas argued for years that I was not entitled to have my dowry returned because they offered the house to me instead. Bargagli defeated that argument. Maybe we still need him. We can't trust Aloisa." She scanned the itemization. "They're even repaying the dowry with interest. We can pay our debt to Bargagli for his fees and advances — have a clean slate."

They turned and hugged each other, holding on until Giulio arrived.

Sofonisba and Orazio enjoyed a spring free of financial stress but did continue to retain Bargagli in Palermo. Someone needed to file for them according to the royal pension instructions. The day after Orazio departed for a Lomellini voyage, Sofonisba received a letter:

> The Duchess of Savoy, Catalina Micaela requests the presence of the Lady Sofonisba Moncada and Lomellini at court in Turin to make the acquaintance of the Lady Margaret of Savoy.

> Court of Turin, 15 June 1595

"Lady Margaret of Savoy," Sofonisba repeated to Giulio, who was visiting with the day's gossip. "She was a little girl when I met her, about four years old or so then. If I paint her, I will have painted three generations of Valois: Isabel, Catalina Micaela, and now the Lady Margaret of Savoy." The theme was irresistible.

Her recent inheritance made the decision to go to Turin an easy one.

As soon as her carriage entered the palazzo courtyard, goose bumps raced up her arms. The opulence contrasted with her simple life in Genoa, transporting her back to Madrid and the energy of court.

The duchess welcomed Sofonisba into a receiving parlor where she sat beneath the *Lady in Ermine*. "Lady Margaret, this is the esteemed painter Lady Sofonisba Moncada Lomellini. We have invited her here to paint you, just as she painted your mother and grandmother before you," the duchess said, tilting her head to Sofonisba.

Sofonisba curtsied, recognizing the girl who played chess four years earlier. A dwarf in a matching gown sat at the girl's feet.

"Lady Sofonisba taught me my letters and painted me as a child, Margaret." The duchess waved toward her likeness. "She did me great honor in this last portrait. I can think of no better painter to capture you, my darling."

"I will be most honored, Your Grace," Sofonisba said. "Perhaps a symbol of your maternal bond across the generations." She instantly regretted divulging her idea before crystalizing it in her own mind.

"Yes," the duchess said, smiling without causing a single line to wrinkle her porcelain skin. It remained as smooth and impassive as it was when Sofonisba painted her years earlier. Sofonisba sent up a little request to her old friend: Dear

Queen Isabel, give me a sign. How can I symbolize your three generations?

She spent time observing Lady Margaret at play, just as she had with Catalina Micaela as a child. The girl pampered her dwarf like a human doll and they wore matching outfits. Lady Margaret whispered secrets to her diminutive companion that she shared with no one else. "I am her mamma. I call her Minna," she told Sofonisba.

Sofonisba's idea came to her that night as she tried to fall asleep. She would pose the girl with her beloved dwarf to symbolize devotion — use the image of a vessel to symbolize the feminine — the maternal link between generations. Minna would be handing the vessel to Lady Margaret — a passage — love from one to another — freely given, one generation to the next. Water as life: posterity.

She worked tirelessly to complete the portrait until — *crack!* went her hip. "One moment, please, Lady Margaret." Sofonisba paused to massage her throbbing hip. At sixty, she did not move quite as quickly as she once had. A pain in her left hip flared up from time to time, reminding her to stop and rest occasionally.

"The water symbolizes life and the jar represents the womb, yes?" the duchess said when Sofonisba unveiled the painting, not waiting for confirmation. She turned to her daughter. "Lady Sofonisba has represented three generations with this one vessel."

Sofonisba was proud of her former charge's grasp of symbolism. She savored her success in Turin, but the attention she paid to the Valois maternal link taunted her. She had to admit, she felt a latent sense of failure, not having children of her own, dear Giulio notwithstanding.

She returned home and transferred her unrequited urges to painting a Madonna and Child for her own collection, employing the soft sfumato she had practiced with Luca Cambiaso on his way along the Spanish road.

Not quite two years later, Giulio reported to his stepmother with news. "Did you hear? The Duchess of Savoy is dead. They say she died in childbirth, her tenth pregnancy. Wouldn't you think she would be expert at it by now?"

"Dear God," Sofonisba whispered, crossing herself as she thought of Catalina Micaela in her ermine collar. "May she rest in peace." Sofonisba had outlived a second generation of Isabel de la paix.

And then, as she was strolling the promenade on a hot September day in 1599, Sofonisba overheard a merchant. "He must have reigned over forty years. Can you believe he was only seventy-one? Seems he could have been a hundred and seventy-one."

"Excuse me, signore," Sofonisba said, feeling a chill. "What news?"

"The king is dead. King Philip has passed."

Sofonisba's knees buckled. She had to find a bench to sit down. King Philip had loomed large in her life ever since the day she saw him as a young prince from her balcony. She owed her success to him, really, to the chance he took having her at court, permitting her to paint while she served the queen. She squelched any lingering resentment toward him for promising limitless protection then abandoning her to financial struggles he could have resolved quickly. Word of his death erased those feelings. She forgave him. *Lady in Ermine.*

The death of King Philip so soon after Catalina Micaela — the death toll in her own family — her father, her sisters, Minerva, Lucia, Europa, and her sister Elena the nun who died at convent in Mantua — long lost Queen Isabel, who had been a sister of sorts to her too.

It all made her evaluate her life, her worth. What was it all for? Did she leave anything behind? Was there really anything to show for her time on earth?

King Philip was succeeded by his son with Anne of Austria, who was to rule as Philip III, King of Spain.

Despite the defeat of the Spanish armada in '88, Spain maintained control over the Spanish Netherlands. Philip II's beloved Isabel Clara Eugenia, Sofonisba's first little charge three decades earlier, inherited them. She was to move north to rule as the Archduchess of the Spanish Netherlands.

Sofonisba received a post soon after.

> The favor of your presence is requested to honor the arrival of the Archduchess Isabella Clara Eugenia to Genoa en route to her archduchy, the Spanish Netherlands.
>
> Madrid, First of June 1599

"They say the king kept her seated next to him for thirty-three years — never let her out of his sight," Giulio said. But Sofonisba told him that was preposterous.

"For one thing, the king, may he rest in peace" — she crossed herself — "did not spend much time in the company of his daughters, no matter how much he spoiled them. I know firsthand that he spent his days mostly in the company of his closest advisors, unless he was in prayer."

"Thirty-three years at her father's court?" — Giulio raised his eyebrows — "and only arranged in marriage when her father was near death?"

Curiosity surrounded the new archduchess. Gossips said that Philip II guarded her jealously until he died. He delayed requesting papal dispensation for her to marry until he was near his deathbed. It was to be his last official act as king. Large crowds gathered to see her parade through Genoa as she was escorted to her temporary residence. Sofonisba was one of the archduchess' first invited guests.

"It is our sincere delight to welcome you to our presence," Isabel Clara Eugenia greeted Sofonisba. "We can trust so few people in our position and it warms our heart to reconnect with one who served us as a child and our mother before us." The archduchess held out her hand for Sofonisba to kiss. "We remember you instructing us to paint to distract us from our loss."

"It was my pleasure to serve you, Your Grace." If Catalina Micaela was porcelain, Isabella Clara Eugenia was marble.

"We have invited you here to execute our official portrait, marking the start of our reign as Sovereign of the Spanish Netherlands," the archduchess said. "It does not escape us that you also painted our sister the Duchess Catalina Micaela for her official portrait in Turin, as well as that of our mother Isabel de Valois for her state portrait for Bayonne."

"It has been my true honor to serve your house," Sofonisba said, curtsying. She almost added that she painted Lady Margaret not long ago too, but decided to be modest.

"Father continued to favor the Italians for his Escorial," the archduchess said, tipping her head slightly to Sofonisba as she began her study of the archduchess. "Recently, he used two of your countrymen, Luca Cambiaso and Federico Zuccaro."

"I have collaborated with both of them," Sofonisba said. "Each stopped by to pay his respects and to discuss the Escorial project."

It felt much like her sitting with Catalina Micaela in 1585 — news of court, references to the king. Sofonisba knew this might be her last touch with the royal circle. Dare she inquire about altering the oppressive pension instructions — still causing her so many headaches and fees simply to collect her money from Palermo? Sofonisba knew her quotidian problems were beneath the archduchess, a woman off to rule a country she inherited, a country steeped in religious turmoil.

At least the exercise gave the artist the image she sought.

Sofonisba decided to render Isabella Clara Eugenia as a serious, mature ruler in a full-length portrait. She positioned her holding onto a chair — the chair of state — her inheritance — her stake. Sofonisba paid painstaking attention to the garments to reflect this woman's power in the world. She made it more sparkling in gold, lavish in detail, and ornate in decoration than any portrait she had done previously. Heavy decoration to show her power and shield the secrets of her marble heart.

And yet, Sofonisba rendered the archduchess as a beautiful woman, just as she promised on the day the archduchess was born.

As the day neared for the archduchess to continue her journey north, she invited Sofonisba into her private chamber. "Please take this as a token of our gratitude for the love and service you have shown to generations of our family." Isabel Clara Eugenia removed a gold chain from around her own neck and placed it around Sofonisba's. The St. Anthony medallion was the same one the archduchess wore for her portrait.

When Sofonisba returned home, she felt a jab of guilt. Would Queen Isabel approve of the severe portrayal of her daughter, even a beautiful one? As a personal gesture to Isabel, she decided to do a second, in miniature, showing a softer Isabella Clara Eugenia, the one who grieves her father's loss, the one who barely knew her mother.

A half year or so after painting the archduchess, Sofonisba received a letter from her brother in Cremona. Their mother passed away just shy of ninety years old. With the distance from Genoa to Cremona, Sofonisba would have to miss her mother's funeral. Instead she painted another sfumato Madonna and

Child, rendering the face of the Madonna as her mother Bianca, and for the Jesus, her brother Asdrubale based on her childhood study for Michelangelo, *Boy Bitten by a Crayfish*.

Chapter 29

The Bargagli Debt: the early seventeenth century

As the sixteenth century became the seventeenth, Sofonisba's inheritance from her first husband's estate was depleted. The troublesome pension instructions in Palermo remained intact. The lawyer Bargagli made withdrawals on their behalf according to protocol. With the lawyer's fees, his advances with interest, his percentage, and the long delays between disbursements, Sofonisba and Orazio found themselves again in debt to the man hired to help them.

"When will we ever be out from under him? It's strangling us." She looked up at her sisters in the *Chess Game* on the wall, wondering again if she could ever part with it, if need be. She pulled her wrap tighter around her.

"Why don't we negotiate with him like we did in '91?" Orazio nodded toward the *Chess Game* and whispered, "Don't even consider it, dear."

They began sorting through the many fides vitae and fee statements they collected over the years from Bargagli. "Ouch," she sucked her forefinger to stop the bleeding from a paper cut.

"This could be symbolic — for one of your paintings — the lawyer bled the artist dry," Orazio said with a chuckle.

"I could title it *The Bloodsucker*."

Orazio handed a draft to Sofonisba. "This should do it. We'll offer another ten percent."

She looked into her husband's eyes and saw love. They were in this together. She knew she had a true partner. The lawyer's response came soon after. She read it aloud to Orazio.

To the Esteemed Lady Sofonisba Anguissola Moncada Lomellini,

Words cannot say how honored I am to be associated with such a distinguished master. May I beg your forgiveness for my previous ignorance.

As God has bestowed upon me many riches, I felt called to visit the Holy City to seek indulgences from his Holiness the year of the great jubilee of 1600. My heart is lighter having made the pilgrimage.

I cannot say how astonished I was to hear the name of my very own client in the most respected circles in Rome. Lady Sofonisba, your virtues are sung throughout the eternal city — recited from the great book of artists by the critic Vasari who praises your own family in Cremona and found all your sisters to be miracles of nature. Yet the most impressive mention was to one piece in particular, a masterpiece called *Chess Game*.

My dear lady, please pardon me for the severity of my tone in business dealings past. Your reputation deserves far greater respect. May I redeem my past with an offer that might alleviate your troubles while doing me the greatest honor? If your family would release the *Chess Game* to me, I would forgive all debts, past and future, in my labors to diligently satisfy the royal instructions for your pension withdrawals.

With this offer, I hope only to make amends for any offense I may have unwittingly imparted. I regret that I cannot accept your recent ten percent calculation for satisfaction.

Very truly yours, your servant,
Fabrizio Bargagli, Esq. January 1601

Sofonisba and Orazio looked at each other. "All our troubles could disappear," she said with a singsong tone.

"You don't mean that."

"How can we refuse, Orazio?"

He touched her wrist. "How about I make Bargagli a counter? He can shove this offer up his ass."

Sofonisba laughed. She looked at her sisters in the *Chess Game.* Lucia, victorious. Europa, mischievous. Minerva, protesting. They seemed to agree.

"Please, Lady Sofonisba, sign here," the notary said, pointing to the document. "And here." He showed her the duplicate. "And finally, here." The calculations page outlined the final figures, guaranteed with a piece of Sofonisba's jewelry, the last piece from her tenure in Spain. "Sorry, one more, if you would please, Lady Sofonisba. Initial next to his annotation in the margin, 'alienable fifty percent — F.B.'"

On August 29, 1608 Sofonisba ceded to her lawyer Fabrizio Bargagli and his heirs, fifty percent of her royal pensions for the rest of her natural life. She handed the document back to the notary. "Good riddance."

Chapter 30

Peter Paul Rubens: Genoa c. 1608

Finally. Free of Bargagli. She could exhale and enjoy a simple life with Orazio, Giulio, and friends.

"Why the frown, Mamma Sofi?"

"I'm stuck. Again."

"It will come to you. You always struggle in between pieces."

Nearing seventy, she couldn't deny she was slowing down — and feeling more pain, especially in her wrists and her left hip. But her mind didn't slow whatsoever. In fact, with age, it taunted her, questioning. She was gripped by the artist's burden — never good enough — only as good as the next piece. What would be her legacy? Was it the ghost of Amilcare's ambition — or her own?

A messenger arrived from the court of Gonzaga in Mantua. She unrolled the thick parchment, anticipating a summons. She recalled the sad De Medici girl she had met in Florence nearly thirty years ago. The girl was twelve then, Sofonisba calculated, so that would make her forty or so. She was married now to the Duke of Mantua. The girl could be a mother by now. Or a grandmother. Would that make the sad girl happy at last?

To the Most Distinguished Portraitist of our Day,

The words of praise that circulate in your honor oblige me to learn from your rare wisdom and talent. Would you deign to receive a novice like myself to educate me in your ways? The courts demand portraiture and I aspire to emulate your success.

I shall await your reply from my position at the Gonzaga court in Mantua, where I remain the undeserved guest of the duke and duchess.

> Your humble servant who prays for your divine
> mentoring, Peter Paul Rubens,
> Mantua, September 1608

Rubens? Sofonisba hadn't heard of him, but his timing was perfect to take her mind off her creative block. As she tapped her quill to draft a response to Mantua, she remembered being rejected at a similar court a half century earlier: "A female painter at our court? You will make us the laughing stocks of all Europe."

This novice obviously had no such obstacle.

When a rosy-cheeked twenty-seven-year-old arrived at her door the following month, Sofonisba had no doubt it was the young artist. What surprised her was the fine quality of his riding clothes, accented with gold trim. A novice?

Dismissing any impropriety, she invited the young man into her studio for a day of collaboration. They set up easels side-by-side and painted together, the master giving advice to the pupil.

"I prefer to paint in the Italian style," Pietro, as he asked to be called, declared in his near-perfect Italian. As his piece took form, he began to conceal it from her view.

"May I peek?" Sofonisba asked, indicating the canvas. He grimaced.

She smiled, recognizing the feeling — the same possessiveness she had when King Philip offered her portrait of Queen Isabel to the pope: the artist protects a piece like a baby. Pietro smiled back, reading her mind; she understood. He turned the canvas around to face the scrutiny of his mentor.

Sofonisba scanned it, nodding. The focus of the piece was the face with soulful inquisitive eyes penetrating the viewer.

They broke at midday for a light meal of bread, cheese, prosciutto, and wine.

"Pietro, you have deceived me," Sofonisba said after they had eaten a bite.

Peter Paul Rubens shook his head in protest.

"Or shall I call you *Master* Rubens," she feigned offense, "as you are hardly the novice you represented yourself to be."

His rosy cheeks reddened. "In your company, madam, I am an ignorant babe."

"I beg to differ, Master Rubens. Your skill is obvious, but your expertise shows more than skill. You have experience. Tell me about your commissions to date."

Rubens confessed to extensive work in Mantua, Rome, Flanders, and the Spanish Netherlands.

"Lady Sofonisba, my current patroness, Eleanora de Medici, the Duchess of Mantua, fondly recalls you from your days in Florence. She tells how you met when she was a young girl after her mother died and her father took up with a mistress. It's plain that your attentions cheered her at a vulnerable time."

She remembered the large eyes of the sad girl she painted in Tuscany. Her mind skipped to her niece Bianca as they viewed her sister's *St. Francis with Praying Woman* together.

" . . . And in the Spanish Netherlands," Pietro was saying, "how the Archduchess Isabella Clara Eugenia sings your praises, my lady. She boasts that you taught her as a child and tells anecdotes about you from her mother's court. You paved the way for me, really, Lady Sofonisba. The archduchess surrounds herself with painters but reminds us all that her first portraitist trained with Master Michelangelo."

"Actually, my father and I corresponded with him —"

"No matter that! Don't you see, my lady? Your life links his era to ours. You are a living legacy connecting the centuries!" He wagged his forefinger heavenward. "I hope to capture the force of the human spirit as the master did, but I also want to focus on showing one's soul through his countenance, as you do, Lady Sofonisba." He tipped his head to her.

A lump formed in her throat. She felt needed — like her life had meaning. Rubens gave to Sofonisba the same boost she gave Michelangelo a half century prior. That her name was circulating from the Spanish Netherlands to the Court of Mantua: a legacy.

On New Year's Eve, 1611, Sofonisba received a letter from Cremona.

> Dear Sister,
>
> Please be advised that our sister Anna Maria, may she rest in peace, has passed from this earth and is in God's hands.
>
> Asdrubale Anguissola, Cremona, 1611

Only Sofonisba and Asdrubale remained of Bianca and Amilcare's seven children. Sofonisba never appreciated her brother's difficulties establishing an independent role in life. As the only son and family heir, he stood to inherit the entire estate, but until his father passed, he had nothing to call his own. Their father, who had done so much to promote Sofonisba's fame, lived a long, productive life. Asdrubale waited to take his inheritance while his sisters were honored, even the nun. Sofonisba's notoriety only made him feel more inferior. Her refusal to obey him — marrying Orazio — insulted his role as head of the family — just like her piece of him as a crying baby seemed to capture his uselessness. After all the deliberate symbolism Sofonisba had painted over the years, she had no idea of the pain her unintended message caused her insecure brother.

But she did wonder about Asdrubale. Why did he not take up a brush or a pen the way she and her sisters had? How did Rubens come to choose art when her brother had not, steeped as he was in Cremona's art world?

She thought of her eye-lock with Prince Philip from the balcony. She thought of the eyes of Saint Daria. Could the smallest outside influence spark a life of passion?

She began a new piece: *Portrait of an Old Woman*. Old age felt like a blessing. Sofonisba was grateful.

Chapter 31

Anthony van Dyck: Sicily 1615–November 1625

In 1615, at eighty years of age, Sofonisba remained in fairly good health, apart from her compromised vision, aching wrists, and painful left hip.

"What's keeping us in Genoa?" Orazio mused as they strolled the port. "Why don't we retire to Tuscany, where we started? That was perhaps our most carefree time."

"Funny, before our marriage was sanctioned by the king," Sofonisba said. "Yet we know no one in Florence these days — a new generation of Medici rule."

"Then what of Sicily? The beautiful air — the smell of sea and citrus."

"Palermo, however — not Paterno`." She waved her hands in front of herself.

"I know just the right neighborhood," Orazio said. "Quartiere Seralcadii, the Genoan quarter."

She rubbed her wrist. "The weather may be kinder to our bones."

Friends of Orazio helped them find a house at a good price. The hardest part was saying goodbye to Giulio, who felt obligated to stay in Genoa to care for his aging mother.

"I don't know what I will do without your encouragement," Sofonisba said, holding Giulio's hands in hers. "Nor your gossip."

She went to her easel and lifted the sheet covering a canvas. "I suppose I should simply title this one, *Self-Portrait as an Old Woman*." They turned together to the painting. She portrayed herself holding a book, green background, highlighted face, simple touches of red and gold as the only color. "My Lombard style." She looked at Giulio. "I would like you to have this. To commemorate the family we are together."

"I'll think of you every day, Mamma Sofi," he said, hugging her. He blinked hard before turning to kiss his father.

Sofonisba and Orazio moved their lives to Sicily. In Palermo, they easily withdrew Sofonisba's pension money—without need of a lawyer. "Good riddance Bargagli!"

"Salute!" Orazio clinked Sofonisba's glass as they toasted on the second story balcony of their little house.

"Why didn't we come here sooner?" Sofonisba smiled, hand on her hip, massaging.

Once she finished decorating their new house, Sofonisba returned to painting. She had no desire to slow down, even though her vision was fading. Ideas came to her often and she experimented with every genre, beginning with seascapes inspired by the voyage down.

In September 1616, when the Sicilian heat drove everyone to the promenade along the port, Sofonisba and Orazio bumped into a widow, recognizable from her cap. "Pardon us, signora," Orazio said.

"Lady Sofonisba," the widow responded. "After all this time, we finally meet again."

Sofonisba instantly recognized Aloisa de Luna y Vega Moncada Aragona.

On this roasting September day, Aloisa rejected the shielded "widow's walk," preferring to stroll the open promenade and take full advantage of the sea-breeze. Sofonisba chuckled seeing

Aloisa's familiar face — and stubborn attitude. She pursed her lips and reminded herself: forgiveness. *Lady in Ermine.* She exhaled and leaned forward to kiss her former nemesis.

"Sister," she said, turning to Orazio. "Husband, may I present to you Aloisa de Luna y Vega Moncada Aragona. My husband, Captain Orazio Lomellini." Sofonisba put a hand on his bicep. His face was reddening. She could feel his arm tensing under her fingers.

"I learned that you had settled here and wondered when I would see you," Aloisa said.

"Are you visiting from Paternò?" Sofonisba asked.

"I relocated to Palermo after the death of my boy." Aloisa nodded as if recollecting. "I no longer wanted to remain in Paternò, the site of so much wrangling over his custody. Please, forgive me for the delay in forwarding your dowry."

A polite way to say it.

"I hope you can understand. I know you were only doing Fabrizio's bidding, but your opposition to my custody of my son stung me for a long time. I'm embarrassed to say that I tortured you as revenge for Fabrizio's ambitions on my son's guardianship. And, of course, it was precisely your connection to the crown that emboldened Fabrizio to seek custody of the estate. I long blamed you for Fabrizio's scheme. Now, I would like to make amends." She reached out and took Sofonisba's fingers into her own.

The passing of Aloisa's beloved son must have made her conciliatory toward her old enemies, Sofonisba being one of many. She could afford to be generous, having increased her estates by 48,000 vassals. Aloisa de Luna y Vega Moncada Aragona was matriarch of this Sicilian dynasty. "I don't want to go to my judgment day regretting the trouble I caused. I have an offer for you."

Sofonisba raised her palm. "That won't be necessary, truly."

Aloisa took Sofonisba's hands back into her own. "Please, Sister, a partnership — in oranges — they are all the rage at the moment. In the north, they pay handsomely for our fruit — one hundred-fold in the Spanish Netherlands. We have contracted with the court of Isabella Clara Eugenia. My man tells me the archduchess recalls you fondly."

Aloisa turned to Orazio. "Captain, you might be interested in this venture, as well. We could use counsel for transporting the oranges north. Please, do pay me a visit when it is convenient, at the Palazzo Butera."

Of all the twists and turns of Sofonisba's life, she never expected to profit from the Sicilian orange trade, providing not just portraiture but fruit to Isabella Clara Eugenia, sovereign of the Spanish Netherlands. But Aloisa was correct: the Moncada's land and labor and Orazio's knowledge were a perfect partnership.

And the enterprise prospered.

Sofonisba was the last one out of the Church of San Giorgio of the Genovese, their Palermo parish, lost in thought about today's sermon: duty and responsibility in men, obedience and modesty in women. She was obedient enough, especially since nobody ordered her around, Orazio being as relaxed as he was. Orders had come mostly from the magistrates in Palermo, sheltering the Moncada all those years. Asdrubale's orders? Irrelevant.

And modesty? Just the week prior, Sofonisba was stuck. Stuck on her next piece. It had to be better than the last — how many paintings had she done? Three a year? Five? It was 1616. She had been actively painting for over sixty years. Sixty times three, one hundred and eighty paintings? Sixty times five, three hundred paintings? Could that be possible? The next piece had to be better than her prior one hundred and eighty to three hundred pieces.

"I've mastered portraiture. I've shown every emotion possible in my sitters. What next?"

"It will come to you, Sofi," Orazio said, patting her hand as she draped it over his arm while they strolled the promenade.

Orazio had predicted correctly. By the next day, her block broke. She began a study of a large-scale Madonna and Child, a mountainous Madonna hovering above a map of Palermo, surrounded by fat guardian angels, smiling, fleshy ones, some springing off the page with their strong, muscular arms.

Sofonisba could only conclude that God had given her some type of indulgence on the modesty obligation.

Four years later, in 1620, the Genoan quarter urged Orazio to run for public office, and he was elected senator. A week after his victory, Sofonisba and he received an invitation. "Aloisa is inviting us to celebrate your victory with a madrigal concert at the Palazzo Butera," Sofonisba said.

When they went to the Palazzo Butera on the intended day, the porter advised them that the concert had been cancelled. "Principessa Aloisa passed at dawn this morning. May she rest in peace."

In July 1624, a dreamy-looking young Dutchman named Anthony van Dyck was taking his grand tour of Europe, studying the Italian masters. "Many stop at Rome or Naples, but I will venture to the Island of Sicily where I shall find the woman who touched Master Michelangelo's hand." He boasted dramatically to the signora who ran the pensione at which he was lodged in Venice. "I intend to be famous myself one day, a court portraitist to kings like my master Peter Paul Rubens!"

"Then the master won't mind paying in advance," the signora said.

The twenty-five-year-old retraced the steps of his mentor Peter Paul Rubens two decades prior: Venice, Mantua, Florence, and Rome. But now that Sofonisba was in Sicily, Anthony van Dyck pressed further south. He arrived at her door, having asked directions around the quarter.

Recognizing a devotee, Orazio admitted the young man with canvases and brushes peeking from his pack. The novice bowed with a flourish when he saw Sofonisba. "Lady Sofonisba, I am honored to stand in your presence, you who have touched the master of all time, the Master Michelangelo. I pray to you, lend my novice heart your divine mastery. The great Giorgio Vasari calls you a marvel. De Branthome says you are full of virtue and knowledge of portraiture au nature. Antonio Campi calls you a painter most famous and rare, a marvel of drawing, of portraiture. *Il Teatro delle Donne Letterate* says of you, 'the most gifted woman of her time at drawing.' And Pietro Paul Ribera lauds, 'in painting she is the most excellent, and surpasses all other painters of her time in portraiture that makes one come alive!' Lady Sofonisba, I submit myself to you." The lanky northerner closed his eyes and put a hand over his heart.

"Dear boy," — Sofonisba smiled and suppressed her urge to laugh — "come, I will show you my portfolio." She took hold of the novice's arm, and he assisted her down the central hallway of her home where she displayed her best pieces.

"Let me tell you a trick of the trade," she said as they padded along. "When you have finished a portrait, be sure to copy one for yourself. That way, you will preserve part of your work. Once you give away your work, you can't control who will own it or what will become of it — or even whether they will remember it was yours. Let me show you what I have saved of my own work."

Sofonisba walked up to the first painting, holding the young man's arm as she leaned close to the canvas and sniffed. "I can smell Isabel de Valois in this one." She moved to the next and leaned forward. "And Alessandro Farnese in this one." She paused. "My vision being what it is, I have to rely on my other senses." She squeezed the young man's forearm. "The greatest honor for a portraitist is to paint the king's portrait, but the greatest task is to reveal the sitter's soul."

The junior artist scribbled in a small notebook. Sofonisba remembered using her little art kit in church as a girl, sketching away as ideas came to her.

"All I can offer in return for your wisdom is to paint you, Master Anguissola," he bowed.

"You flatter me as 'master'."

"It is I who am flattered by you, Master Anguissola."

He began by sketching a study of Sofonisba, posing her seated upright in a chair like a monarch on a throne, a tribute to her mastery and her history. Anthony van Dyck gave the near ninety-year-old wistful, contemplative eyes, as if recounting the events of a full life while envisioning one more concept to execute.

"I will be forever in your debt Master Anguissola for the inspiration you have shown me," the novice said before departing.

"Mamma Sofi," Giulio whispered into the ear of his bedridden stepmother, "they are saying in the piazza that Saint Rosalie appeared in a vision to a farmer and he located her bones — her relics will save Palermo." The patron saint of Palermo had been dead for almost five centuries. Her bones appeared in time to help fend off the plague currently raging through the city.

"Giulio?"

"Mamma Sofi, I'm here now. I've come to live with you and Father." After Giulio's mother passed away in Genoa, he felt free to join his father and Sofonisba in Sicily. He knew it was risky. The plague had taken a quarter of the city of Palermo. But when Orazio wrote him that Sofonisba's age was taking a toll, Giulio knew he had to join them in case it was his last chance to be with her.

"And still you bring me the news," Sofonisba said, putting a hand on his wrist. Her skin was paper-thin. "Dear boy."

By November 1525, the worst of the epidemic subsided. Anthony van Dyck returned to Palermo and the Lomellini household. "I was concerned for you, Lady Sofonisba," van Dyck said, kneeling at her bedside.

"You came to see me?" She barely whispered. "Do you not fear for your own life? Giulio tells me 30,000 have died."

"Please, madam, I am resilient." He patted his chest. "My only concern is to paint you now, as you lie, to record your legacy." She smiled hearing her father's advice in the young man's confidence. He put his face next to hers. "Did Master Michelangelo feel what he portrayed in his *Pietà*? Did Master van der Weyden feel what he portrayed in his *Descent from the Cross*? Permit me to paint you now as I feel compassion for you with my whole heart. Give me this opportunity to experience you as a living and dying legacy, and to capture my own sympathies."

Sofonisba recognized his state of creative reverie, remembering her own bursts of *invenzione*. He stayed with her all that day, taking the details he needed to execute her deathbed portrait. He posed her with a rosary in hand to suggest her last rites, but also as a tribute to her life's triumph, *King Philip II with Rosary*.

When it was time for him to depart, he packed up his kit, walked to her bedside, and gently lifted her hand to his mouth for a very soft kiss, waking her from her slumber.

Sofonisba sensed Anthony standing above her. She flashed back to her young self in Genoa en route to begin her adventures in Spain, seeing the crevices on Andrea Doria's face — confident then that death was far off, just as Anthony must feel now.

Sofonisba heard Orazio ushering the young artist out as her head fell back onto the pillow. She couldn't miss the annoyance in her husband's voice, probably worried the boy had taxed her. She smiled. And slept for the following two days. She woke with the rooster.

"Orazio, please," she called to him, her voice croaking. "Help me write. I've something I must do." He came close to her, quill in hand, ready to write as she dictated. "Send this letter to Bianca in Cremona," she said.

Dear Bianca,

You have been as close to a daughter to me as anyone. I will smile down on you from Heaven if God sees fit to admit me after all my selfishness in life. My dear Orazio pays alms in my name to ease my passage, but I can only await the Lord's grace and forgiveness now.

I wanted you to have the enclosed. I know you have your own, but I would love for you to keep mine close at hand as well. They tend to get misplaced, and you never know what trouble that can lead to.

All my love,
Aunt Sofi, Palermo, Sicily, November 1625

"Please, Orazio." She pointed to her art kit on the table next to her bed. "Send it to her. Send it to Bianca in Cremona."

Orazio picked up the bag and squeezed its supple leather. He opened it and smiled seeing a small rough sketch of a Madonna and Child — something Sofonisba managed on her deathbed.

When he turned back around, her eyes were staring ahead to her next life.

Author's Note

Sofonisba is buried at the Church of San Giorgio dei Genovesi in Palermo, Sicily.

Orazio was elected to local political office in Palermo. In 1632 he dedicated a loving tribute to Sofonisba at her gravesite. Whatever happened to his son Giulio is unknown, but there is evidence that Sofonisba adopted him.

Archduchess Isabella Clara Eugenia ruled the Spanish Netherlands with her husband from 1599 to 1633, maintaining a lively, international court. She was a patron of Peter Paul Rubens and Anthony van Dyck.

For many years at the beginning of the seventeenth century, while Sofonisba was residing in Genoa, Peter Paul Rubens was a guest of the Duchess of Mantua, Eleanora de Medici, whom Sofonisba painted in Florence in 1580 (the sad girl) and as duchess c. 1605–10. Rubens likely sought out the legendary portraitist. In 1603, on Mantua's behalf, Rubens visited Philip III in Madrid and would have seen Sofonisba's court work. In the Spanish Netherlands, Rubens painted Isabella Clara Eugenia multiple times in the seventeenth century and likely saw Sofonisba's work in Isabella's collection.

Anthony van Dyck painted the *Lomellini Family Portrait* after visiting Sofonisba in Sicily and went on to paint King Charles I of England with a face illuminated in the Anguissola style.

After his victory in Lepanto, Don John of Austria served as Governor of the Spanish Netherlands until 1578 when he died at the age of 33. Also known as Don Juan, he was a legendary lover.

Alessandro Farnese replaced Don John in the Spanish Netherlands until his death in 1592. He never returned to Parma where he held the title of duke after the death of his father Ottavio in 1586.

Francisco de Mendoza served as the Bishop of Burgos from 1550 to 1566, the year after the plague of Burgos.

In April 1560, three months after the royal wedding, after twelve years in exile, the amputated veteran servant Martin Guerre returned to the little village in southern France where villagers once taunted his sexuality. Natalie Zemon Davis and Gerard Depardieu recreate his welcome home in the book (Harvard University Press, 1983) and movie *The Return of Martin Guerre*.

Sofonisba's tutor Marco is fiction.

I set out to find a woman whose accomplishments made an impact on history. Sofonisba had an effect on European portraiture, not only because of her innovative art works, but also because her pieces traveled the Habsburg channels, exporting the Lombard style throughout Europe. Sofonisba's personal story and tenacity struck me and seemed right for the medium of fiction.

Lady in Ermine follows the narrative of Sofonisba's life presented in the *Cremona Catalogue*, first published in 1987 and then in 1994: *Sofonisba Anguissola e Le Sue Sorelle* (Cremona: Leonardo Arte, 1994). The *Cremona Catalogue* is an encyclopedic effort that traces every aspect of Sofonisba's life, including the artistic, literary, and legal sources that document her monumental life. Rossana Sacchi, Flavio Caroli, Valerio Guazzoni, Anastasia Gilardi, Maria Kusche, Giovanni Muto, and all of the other contributors to the *Cremona Catalogue* influenced my narrative of Sofonisba's life, in one way or another. I am indebted to all Sofonisba scholars for paving the way for this work of fiction.

This is a work of fiction based on Sofonisba's life and the author's imagination.

I tweak a few historical dates for the sake of flow of the novel:

Most notably, Michelangelo Buonarroti actually died in 1564 and the Anguissolas began corresponding with him earlier than indicated in the novel. Michelangelo's grief over the death of his partner Urbino is documented in his letter to Giorgio Vasari, February 23, 1556. *Il Carteggio di Michelangelo*, Vol. 5 (1983, SPES Editore, Firenze).

Sofonisba visited several northern Italian courts in the 1550s, including the court of Mantua. I collapse those experiences into one visit to the court of Parma for efficiency. (See Cat. 364, Amilcare's letter to the Duchess of Mantua, March 12, 1557, "*Quadretto fatto et depinto per Sophonisba.*")

Queen Anne of Austria actually died in 1580.

I use the term "Inquisition" for the Toledo events in 1560, but "auto de fe" is more accurate. I use "Lombardy" for Sofonisba's region, but in the sixteenth century, it was the "Duchy of Milan."

From my serendipitous meeting of Alfio Nicotra in Catania in 2007, I was introduced to Ferrante Anguissola D'Altoe, Maria Kusche, and Vincenzo Abbate and was honored to be invited to present at *Progetto Sofonisba* in Palermo in 2008. They have been rocks of support and inspiration throughout the development of *Lady in Ermine*. I am especially grateful for the continued friendship of Dr. Anguissola and Dr. Nicotra. We are sad that Dr. Kusche is no longer with us to read the final product.

Sofonisba's work resides across Europe and America but is not entirely public. I want to thank the following for graciously helping me gain access to hidden jewels: Mauro Battocchi, former San Francisco Italian Consul General, and Marco Lattanzi for my visit to the Palazzo Quirinale; Lucy Whitaker for the Royal Collection, Windsor; Leticia Ruiz at the Prado, Madrid; Giovanni Valgussa at the Accademia Carrara in Bergamo; Rhona MacBeth at the Fine Art Museum, Boston; Dr. Gamboni at the Accademia di San Luca, Rome; and the staffs at the Brera, Milan, and the Capodimonte, Naples, for opening their storage to me. To Nicola Massera in Cremona, *Grazie* for letting me inside Sofonisba's childhood home, the thrill of a lifetime.

I am deeply grateful to my thesis committee at San Francisco State University, Jarbel Rodriguez, Richard Hoffman, and Laura Lisy-Wagner and to the readers who helped me shape my manuscript: Eileen Ambre, Roger Guy-Bray, Chiara Calanchini, James S. Galluzzo, Claire Erwin Lee, Deborah Leeds, Jeanine Lewis, Kim Puckett, Raffaella Russo, Anne and Ezio DiGiuseppe, and Rick Matcovich. Thank you to my fellow workshop attendees at the Squaw Valley Community of Writers, especially Michael Garcia and Mark Radoff.

I could not have accomplished this without the support of my family who listened to me talk about the artist over many years. Thank you, Rick, Jeremy, Nolan, and Wesley.

~

De las Casas' disputation is taken with permission from *An Account Much Abbreviated of the Destruction of the Indies with Related Texts*, edited with introduction by Frank W. Knight and translated by Andrew Hurley, Hackett Publishing, Indianapolis, 2003.

Parts of Alba's letter from Cateau-Cambresis, the king's laments at the Escorial, and Isabel's quasi-treason in Toledo are derived with permission from Geoffrey Parker, *Philip II*, 4th ed. Open Court, 2002.

Quotes from the 1573 Ordinance on Pacification are by permission of Jody Schwarz on behalf of the estate of Lewis Hanke, editor of *History of Latin American Civilization Sources and Interpretations Vol. 1, The Colonial Experience* (Boston: Little, Brown, and Company, 1967).

The royal wedding singer's lyrics are my translation of "Deh contentatevi," a cantata by Carissimi, GB-Och ms. 51, 69–73.

The cover image is by license of (c) CSG CIC Glasgow Museums and Libraries Collections/Glasgow. The museum attributes the piece to El Greco.

Further Reading

There are wonderful scholarly sources on Sofonisba in addition to the *Cremona Catalogue*. Sylvia Ferino-Pagden and Maria Kusche have a book in English, *Sofonisba Anguissola: a Renaissance Woman*, and it follows Maria Kusche's work in Spanish, *Retratos y Retratadores, Alonso Sanchez Coello y sus Competidores*, as well as the *Cremona Catalogue*.

Alfio Nicotra has a series of articles exploring recent attributions to Sofonisba in *Incontri la Sicilia e l'altrove* (October-December 2013, April-June 2015, January-March 2018 and April-June 2018). Doctor Nicotra is a true champion of Sofonisba's legacy.

Ilya Sandra Perlingieri has a beautiful volume that covers the span of Sofonisba's life, *Sofonisba Anguissola: the First Great Woman Artist of the Renaissance* (Rizzoli 1992).

Two creative studies in Italian impacted me greatly: Daniela Pizzagalli, *La Signora Della Pittura: Vita di Sofonisba Anguissola, gentildonna e artista nel Rinascimento* (Rizzoli 2003), and Millo Borghini, *Sofonisba. Una Vita per la pittura e la liberta'* (Spirali 2006).

For Sofonisba's time in Sicily: *La Sicilia dei Moncada: Le Corti, l'arte e la cultura nei secoli XVI-XVII, a cura di* Lina Scalisi (Domenico San Filippo Editore, Catania, 2006).

For the letters of Michelangelo to Vasari and Amilcare to Michelangelo I translated from *Il Carteggio di Michelangelo*, edited by Giovanni Poggi. Vol. 5. Firenze: Sansoni, 1965.

For Philip II and Don Carlos, I relied on Geoffrey Parker, *Philip II*, 4th ed. (Open Court, 2002) and Henry Kamen, *Philip of Spain* (Yale University Press, 1997).

For background on Catherine de Medici I used many sources: James Westfall Thompson, *The Wars of Religion in France 1559–1576* (New York: Frederick Ungar Publishing Co., 1957); Irene Mahoney, *Madame Catherine* (New York: Coward, McCann & Geoghegan, 1975); Leonie Frieda, *Catherine de Medici: Renaissance Queen of France* (New York: Harper Perennial 2003); Mark Strage, *Women of Power: The Life and Times of Catherine de Medici* (New York: Harcourt Brace Jovanovich, 1976); De Lamar Jensen, *Catherine de Medici and Her Florentine Friends*, *16th Century Journal*, Vol. 9, No.2, July 1978, 57–74.

For Isabel de Valois: Agustin G. de Amezua y Mayo, *Isabel de Valois Reina de Espana (1546–1568)* 3 Vols. Grafias Ultra, Madrid 1949.

For the Duke of Alba: Henry Kamen, *The Duke of Alba* (New Haven: Yale University Press, 2004) and William S. Malty, *Alba: A Biography of Fernando Alvarez de Toledo, Third Duke of Alba 1507–1582* (Berkeley: University of California Press, 1983).

Francesco de Medici: Caroline P. Murphy, *Murder of a Medici Princess* (Oxford University Press, 2008).

On Renaissance chess: Marilyn Yalom, *Birth of the Chess Queen: A History* (New York: Harper Collins, 2005).

Convent art: Jonathan Nelson, ed. *Suor Plautilla Nelli: The First Woman Painter of Florence: Proceedings of the Symposium Florence-Fiesole (1998)* Fiesole: Cadmo, srl 2000.

Convent culture: K. J. P. Lowe, *Nuns' Chronicles and Convent Culture in Renaissance and Counter-Reformation Italy* (Cambridge University Press, 2003).

Paintings that Influenced 'Lady in Ermine' by Chapter

Chapter 1: Giulio Campi *Virgin in Glory with Saints* (1540) Church of San Sigismondo, Cremona, Italy.

Chapter 2: Sofonisba Anguissola *Dominican Astronomer* (1556) whereabouts unknown (See her upside down signature and date, Cremona Catalogue pp. 20–21) and *Self-Portrait Virgin with Book* (1554) Kunsthistorisches Museum, Vienna, Austria.

Chapter 3: Sofonisba Anguissola or Gervasio Gatti (attribution uncertain) *Portrait of a Soldier* (last half 16th century) Accademia Carrara, Bergamo, Italy.

Sofonisba Anguissola *Self-Portrait with Clavichord* (c. 1556–1557) Museo di Capodimonte, Naples, Italy.

Chapter 4: Sofonisba Anguissola *The Chess Game* (1555) The National Museum, Poznan, Poland, and *Portrait of a Nun* (her sister Elena) (1551) City Art Gallery, Southampton, England.

Chapter 5: Sofonisba Anguissola *Boy Bitten by a Crayfish* (c. 1554) Museo di Capodimonte, Naples, Italy.

Lucia Anguissola *Self-Portrait with Book* (1557) Pinacoteca del Castello Sforzesco, Milan, Italy.

Chapter 6: Sofonisba Anguissola *Portrait of Giulio Clovio* (c. 1556–1557) Collection of Federico Zeri, Mentana, Italy.

Chapter 7: Sofonisba Anguissola *Portrait of Canonico Lateranense Ippolito Chizzola* (1556) Pinacoteca Tosio-Martinengo, Brescia, Italy.

Chapter 8: Sofonisba Anguissola *Portrait of Don Garcia Hurtado de Mendoza* (second half 16th century) Lobkowicz Palace, Prague Castle, Prague, Czech Republic.

Chapter 9: Sofonisba Anguissola *Holy Family* (1559) Accademia Carrara, Bergamo, Italy; *Family Portrait* (c. 1558–1559) Nivaagaards Malerisamling, Niva, Denmark; *Bernardino Campi Painting Sofonisba Anguissola* (1559) Pinacoteca Nazionale, Siena, Italy, and *Pieta'* (c. 1559) Pinacoteca di Brera, Milan, Italy.

Gian Battista Moroni *Portrait of Canonico Gian Grisostomo Zanchi* (1559) Accademia Carrara, Bergamo, Italy and *Portrait of a Gentleman and His Two Children* (c. 1563–1565) National Gallery of Ireland, Dublin, Ireland.

Chapter 10: Leonardo Da Vinci *Portrait of a Musician, Franchino Gaffurio* (1490) Biblioteca Ambrosiana, Milan, Italy, and Gian Battista Moroni *Knight in Black* (c. 1567) Museo Poldi Pezzoli, Milan, Italy.

Chapter 14: Suor Plautilla Nelli *Lamentation with Saints* (mid-16th Century) Museo di San Marco, Florence, Italy.

Chapter 17: Sofonisba Anguissola *Portrait of Isabel de Valois* (1561) given to Pope Pius IV, whereabouts unknown (Sofonisba's letter dated September 16, 1561; Pope Pius letter dated October 15, 1561); variations at Pinacoteca di Brera, Milan, Italy, and post-1580 Kunsthistorisches Museum, Vienna, Austria; *Portrait of Juana of Austria* (1561) Isabella Stewart Gardner Museum, Boston; *Portrait of Alessandro Farnese* (1561) National Museum of Ireland, Dublin, and *Portraits of Don Carlos* see Maria Kusche *Retratos y Retratadores Alonso Sanchez Coello y Sus Competidores Sofonisba Anguissola* 221 & 224.

Chapter 18: Agnolo Bronzino (1551) *Portrait of Francesco de Medici I As a Child* Uffizi Gallery, Florence, Italy.

Sofonisba Anguissola *Self-Portrait "Sofonisba Angosciola-P"* [*Pittrice*] (1564) Accademia Nazionale di San Luca, Rome, Italy.

Chapter 19: Sofonisba Anguissola *Bayonne Portrait of Queen Isabel* (1565) Prado Museum, Madrid, Spain.

Chapter 20: Sofonisba Anguissola, X-rays of *Portrait of Philip II*; for her change of pose from Philip with flowers to Philip in prayer, see Maria Kusche *Retratos y Retratadores Alonso Sanchez Coello Y Sus Competidores Sofonisba Anguissola*, 218 and *Sofonisba Anguissola, A Renaissance Woman, Kusche and Ferino-Pagden*, 68.

Chapter 21: Sofonisba Anguissola *Portrait of Philip II with Rosary* (c. 1568–72) Prado Museum, Madrid, Spain.

Rogier van der Weyden *Descent from the Cross* (c. 1435) Prado Museum, Madrid, Spain.

Chapter 22: Sofonisba Anguissola *Portrait of Anne of Austria* (1573) Prado Museum, Madrid, Spain and *Portrait of Isabella Clara Eugenia* (1573) Sabauda Gallery, Turin, Italy.

Chapter 23: Sofonisba Anguissola *Virgin with Child* (Date Unknown) Palazzo Abatellis, Palermo, Italy.

Chapter 24: Sofonisba Anguissola *Madonna dell'Itria* (1579) Church of the Very Holy Annunciation, Paternò, Italy.

Chapter 25: Sofonisba Anguissola *Portrait of Francesco I de Medici* (1580) Privately owned, whereabouts unknown and *Portrait of Eleonora de Medici* (1580) Lazaro Galdiano Museum, Madrid, Spain.

Chapter 26: Sofonisba Anguissola *Portrait of a Young Man* [Giulio Lomellini] (c. 1580–1590) private collection (Kusche *Retratos* 266), and *Double Portrait of Husband and Wife* (c. 1580) Galleria Doria Pamphilj, Rome, on exhibit at Castel Sant'Angelo, Rome, Italy 2017.

Lucia Anguissola *Jesus and John with Mary and Elizabeth* (c. 1560) and Europa Anguissola *St. Francis Receiving the Stigmata* (c. 1571) Church of Saint Agnes, Cremona, Italy.

Chapter 27: Sofonisba Anguissola *Portrait of Catalina Micaela, Duchess of Savoy* (1585) Prado Museum, Madrid, Spain, and *Lady in Ermine* (1591) Pollok House, Glasgow, Scotland, which attributes the piece to El Greco and gives it a the title, *Lady in a Fur Wrap*.

Chapter 28: Sofonisba Anguissola *Madonna Nursing Child* (1588) Szepmuveszeti Museum, Budapest, Hungary; *Portrait of Margherita of Savoy* (*passing vessel*) (1595) Private Collection Madrid; *Portrait of Isabella Clara Eugenia, Archduchess of Spanish Netherlands* (1599) Spanish Embassy, Paris, France, and *Miniature of Isabella Clara Eugenia* (1599), privately owned, whereabouts unknown.

Chapter 30: Sofonisba Anguissola *Portrait of Eleonora de Medici Duchess of Mantua* (c. 1605–1610) private collection, auctioned Palais Dorotheum, Vienna, Austria (see Alfio Nicotra, *Incontri la Sicilia*, anno III, numero 11, April-June 2015, 31.)

Chapter 31: Anthony van Dyck *Italian Sketchbook* (1624) Prints and Drawings, British Museum, London, England, and *Portrait of Sofonisba Anguissola on her Deathbed* (1625) Sabauda Gallery, Turin, Italy.

Sofonisba enthusiasts hope that her pieces held in private collections will be generously lent to museums so that the world may witness the full artistic influence of Sofonisba Anguissola.

About the Author

Donna DiGiuseppe studied Humanities at UC Berkeley, including a year in Venice at Ca' Foscari, focusing on the northern Italian Renaissance. After a law degree from the University of San Francisco and many years practicing law, she returned to her passion for the Italian Renaissance with a Master's degree in History at San Francisco State University. She lectures frequently on Sofonisba and has traveled the world to view Sofonisba's work. Ms. DiGiuseppe lives with her husband and sons in San Francisco, California, and Abruzzo, Italy.